Praise for Anna [

"Durand's Hot Scots series has been loads of fun to read, and [*Irresistible in a Kilt*] is no exception. [...] The author's action-packed and suspenseful plot keeps the reader on their toes, and the grown-up sizzle never disappoints."
Jack Magnus, Readers' Favorite

"[*Lethal in a Kilt* is] full of hot sex, adventure, and so much laughter. I found myself laughing-out-loud at the antics of the Witches of Ballachulish (Logan's sisters) and the hilarious flirting and sexy banter between Serena and Logan. [...] Recommend highly!"
Sharon Clayton, The Eclectic Review

"[*Insatiable in a Kilt*] smokes from the very first pages... Durand's characters are a delight and seeing how they mix business with their increasing attraction for each other is entertaining indeed. [...] Durand's Hot Scots family saga just keeps on getting better."
Jack Magnus, Readers' Favorite

"I loved the Scottish in Ian and the strength of Rae, but the love of one little girl makes [*Notorious in a Kilt*] something to behold."
Coffee Time Romance

"*Gift-Wrapped in a Kilt* is a marvelous continuation of the author's MacTaggart family saga. Durand's story has an entertaining plot, and her steamy interludes are well-written...a celebration of healthy relationships between loving adults written in a tasteful and compelling manner."
Jack Magnus, Readers' Favorite

"I have enjoyed this whole series, but Emery and Rory [from *Scandalous in a Kilt*] have stolen my heart and are now my favorites!"
The Romance Reviews

"An enthralling story. [...] I highly recommend the writing of Ms. Durand and *Wicked in a Kilt*, but be warned you will find yourself addicted and want your own Hot Scot."
Coffee Time Romance & More

"There's a huge hero's and heroine's journey [in *Dangerous in a Kilt*] that I quite enjoyed, not to mention the hot sex, and again, not to mention the sweet seduction of the Scotsman who pulls out all the stops to get Erica to love him."
Manic Readers

Other Books by Anna Durand

Irresistible
IN A KILT

Hot Scots, Book Eight

ANNA DURAND

JACOBSVILLE BOOKS JB MARIETTA, OHIO

IRRESISTIBLE IN A KILT

Copyright © 2020 by Lisa A. Shiel
All rights reserved.

ISBN: 978-1-949406-25-2 (paperback)
ISBN: 978-1-949406-24-5 (ebook)
ISBN: 978-1-949406-26-9 (audiobook)
Library of Congress Control Number: 2020911888

Manufactured in the United States.

Jacobsville Books
www.JacobsvilleBooks.com

Publisher's Cataloging-in-Publication Data
provided by Five Rainbows Cataloging Services

Names: Durand, Anna.
Title: Irresistible in a kilt / Anna Durand.
Description: Lake Linden, MI : Jacobsville Books, 2020. | Series: Hot Scots, bk. 8.
Identifiers: LCCN 2020911888 (print) | ISBN 978-1-949406-25-2 (paperback) |
    ISBN 978-1-949406-24-5 (ebook) | ISBN 978-1-949406-26-9 (audiobook)
Subjects: LCSH: Man-woman relationships--Fiction. | Scots--Fiction. | British-
    -Fiction. | Highlands (Scotland)--Fiction. | Swindlers and swindling--Fic-
    tion. | Family secrets--Fiction. | Romance fiction. | BISAC: FICTION /
    Romance / Contemporary. | FICTION / Romance / Romantic Comedy. |
    FICTION / Romance / Workplace. | GSAFD: Love stories.
Classification: LCC PS3604.U724 I66 2019 (print) | LCC PS3604.U724 (ebook)
    | DDC 813/.6--dc23.

Prologue

*E*very love story has a beginning, a middle, and an end—but sometimes the cycle repeats, over and over, until the two idiots finally come to their senses. For Alex Thorne and Catriona MacTaggart, the cycle has a little bit of help with those repeats. That help comes from Cat's three brothers, their American wives, her two sisters, and a large cast of meddling cousins. The entire MacTaggart clan wants to see Cat and Alex's love story unfold to a final conclusion, but what will that conclusion be?

Maybe they'll realize they belong together.

Or maybe they'll kill each other.

Either way, the epic tale of their road to that end starts at their second beginning—the day they saw each other again for the first time in more than eleven years. It happened at the castle owned by Rory MacTaggart, Catriona's brother, on a green lawn with the sun shining and every MacTaggart in attendance for the Highland games. Cat's cousin Logan brought Alex here, knowing full well she would blow her top when she saw the man who broke her heart.

After she punched him in the gut, things should have settled down. But Cat is a MacTaggart, and their clan is the most stubborn bunch of Scots in the world. Logan and his wife, Serena, witnessed the argument between Cat and Alex right after their reunion, but only the two idiots themselves know exactly what was said.

Them and you. As you're about to discover.

Dùndubhan Castle, Scotland

Catriona dragged Alex off the green, through the door in the castle wall—slamming it shut, for dramatic effect and to keep her meddling relatives away—and towed him into the center of the garden. A beautiful arbor stood nearby, overflowing with rose vines. The scent of the flowers made no impression on either of them. Neither did the flowering bushes or the stunning blue sky above their heads. No, they were too busy glaring at each other.

Well, *she* was glaring. Alex was affecting an air of amused disinterest, his favorite expression.

"How dare you be here," she said. "In my country. I should call the Home Office and report an ersehole is in the country illegally."

"I'm not here illegally. If you'll calm down and try to behave like a rational adult, I'll explain."

"Rational? How was it *rational* for you to invade my world again?"

"Yes, of course," he said with immense sarcasm, "it's your world. The entirety of Scotland belongs to Catriona MacTaggart. I suppose you've made sure every citizen knows about the dangerous British Bastard. Better lock up all the Scots lasses before I defile and devour them."

He opened his mouth like a ravening beast.

She scowled at him. "I was arrested because of you, Alex. You cannae stop yourself, can ye? Being a lying scunner is your true nature, and I wish I'd realized that before we ever had a poke, much less moved in together." She jabbed a finger into his chest repeatedly, once for every syllable when she said, "You are the worst human being on earth."

"Worse than Hitler? How about Jack the Ripper? Or Charles Manson? Does the Limey Louse outdo all of them?"

Repeating all the nasty names Cat had invented for him over the years, without his knowledge until a few days ago, seemed like the best way to knock sense into her thick Scottish skull. Not that it worked. She was much too stubborn to give in so easily.

Cat bowed her head, pulling in a ragged breath, and looked up at him with tears shimmering in her eyes. "I loved you, Alex. Didn't that matter to you at all? Using me in one of your bloody schemes to— What were you doing, anyway? Why was I arrested for smuggling antiquities?"

"It was a misunderstanding."

"Bollocks. You always know exactly what you're doing."

"The police had the wrong information, that's all. I got you out of jail later that day. The charges were dropped."

"You think that makes everything all right?" She jabbed her finger into his chest again, harder than before. "Stop lying. For once in your life, tell the truth."

"I have told you the truth." He fisted his hands at his sides, fisted them so hard his shoulders bunched. "Why don't you try believing me?"

She threw her head back and growled. "Why in the world should I?"

Deep down, in a part of himself he'd tried very hard to suppress, he wanted to tell her *believe me because you love me*. But he didn't say that. He couldn't. She had no reason to love him anymore, not after all the years they'd been apart and the things that happened to split them in two.

Cat did not love him. He didn't love her anymore either. Absolutely not.

"Not going to answer?" she demanded, sounding wildly sarcastic even while tears rolled down her cheeks. "You are a bastard, Alex Thorne. You might as well be dead because I will never forgive you."

He flung his arms up, then spread them wide as he bent to level their gazes. "Go on and kill me, then. Grab a rock and beat me to death. But you haven't got the nerve for that, have you? Acting like a spoiled child is the best you can manage. Grow up, Catriona. But no, you won't do that because you've got your sainted brothers to do your dirty work for you."

She squeezed her eyes shut but couldn't stop the tears from streaming down her face faster and hotter, their saltiness seeping between her lips to poison her tongue.

"What the fuck do you want from me?" he shouted loud enough that his voice echoed off the walls of the castle compound.

She raised her head and shouted, "Nothing!"

He shoved both hands into his hair, head bowed, shoulders caving in.

Catriona stared at him, but she couldn't see his face, his expression, to know if their argument had affected him in any way other than anger. Had he ever cared about her at all? Or had it been an act, some sort of horrible con? To what end? She didn't know, and Alex would never tell her.

She swiped at her eyes with the hem of her shirt. "I can't ever have anything to do with you again."

He grunted, like he didn't care a whit about what she'd said, but he couldn't quite reassert his disinterested expression.

"Maybe one day," she said, "you'll sort yourself and stop seeing everyone as a pawn in your never-ending games. But you won't, will you? I feel sorry for you, Alex, because you've cursed yourself to be miserable for the rest of your life."

He lifted his head to scowl at her but said nothing.

Tears burned in her eyes anew, and she hurried out of the garden so he wouldn't see her crying anymore. She had to escape him. But could she ever really do that? He'd stayed buried in her heart, deep in a hidden place, for more than eleven years.

Alex stayed in the garden and endured the well-meaning but bloody annoying attempt by Logan and Serena to make him feel better. They'd sneaked in through the garden without Alex or Cat noticing, but then, they'd been rather absorbed in their shouting match. Logan and Serena were terrible at consoling him, but he appreciated their effort. Cat was right about one thing. He was cursed. Damned, actually. Salvation had been too much to hope for, of course. Not that he wanted or needed Cat to forgive him. Not that he still loved her.

No, not that.

On that fateful day at Dùndubhan, Cat and Alex both resolved to forget each other, but of course they can't. They've burrowed too deep under each other's skin. Nine months later, they still can't stop thinking about each other. How will it all end? Maybe they'll never forgive each other. Maybe they're both doomed. Or maybe, just maybe, you'll have to wait a bit longer to find out.

Their journey begins now.

Chapter One

Alex

The truth and I have a different sort of relationship, not best mates, but more like third cousins once removed. Maybe that explains why Catriona MacTaggart storms into my office and whacks me with a book she grabbed off my desk. I've expected to be murdered at any moment, but not by her hand. And not with my own book.

Well, at least it's a paperback.

It's possible I've given her reason to despise me, and despise me she does. Once, long ago, she loved me and wanted to make a future for us together. Whether I'd wanted that or not is irrelevant. Someone like me doesn't get a fairy-tale ending, not that I believe in true love or any of that bollocks. Fate, on the other hand... Let's just say I don't believe it's on my side.

But I should start at the beginning, right before Cat found me in my office.

For me, Monday mornings mean grading papers. Bloody awful ones. How did these children get into college when they can't write coherent sentences? One student composes his essays entirely in capital letters. Another—a girl, naturally—inserts emojis into her opuses. Staring at another depressingly awful essay, I let my mind travel back in time more than a decade, to the one student who had never disappointed me. She hadn't been *my* student. I'd first met her on a bench on the grassy lawn of the campus where I'd been teaching, though we spoke for only a few minutes. But I really met her when I gave a guest lecture in a colleague's classroom later that day.

The lecture hall was cavernous and filled to capacity, though I couldn't see the students in the back as more than blurry shapes. Not that I had vision problems. They were simply too far away.

I remember scanning the crowd, not paying attention to the faces, not really, just taking in the sight of so many people gathered to hear me speak. Archaeology isn't the most popular discipline, after all. But on that day, it seemed like half the campus had turned up. Only one face stood out from the crowd.

The most beautiful face I'd ever seen. The face of the Scots lass who'd told me she loved my accent.

She had creamy skin, with a faint natural blush on her cheeks, and the most captivating blue eyes, as pale as glacial ice but with a warmth behind the cool color. Her sensuous lips seemed ripe for a good, hard kiss. Her cinnamon-brown hair tumbled over her shoulders in loose waves, kissing her cheeks and leading my gaze down to her full breasts, concealed beneath her blouse. She watched me while I watched her, our gazes connected by something I couldn't define or explain. My pulse accelerated, and I licked my lips as I imagined what it might feel like to kiss her beautiful mouth.

Her name was Catriona MacTaggart.

If I'd known then that our affaire de coeur would end in disaster, and that she would curse my name for more than a decade, maybe I wouldn't have spoken to her on that bench or after my lecture. Maybe I would've stayed away from the Scots lass with the fire in her eyes and in her soul.

No, I would've seduced her anyway. The fates be damned.

That's what I'm ruminating on when Cat barges through the door, thrusting it open with such force it slams into the wall and bounces off it.

She stops on the other side of my desk, her eyes wild, breathing hard, and stabs a finger in the air at me. "Alex Thorne, you slimy, conniving bastard. What the bloody hell do you think you're doing?"

I gesture at the essays on my desk. "Grading papers."

"Donnae be cute with me." She peels her lips back, almost hissing at me when she says, "How dare you interfere in my life. I should've known it was one of your games when I was offered a tenure-track position at a university in America. What are you hoping to gain from this?"

Her naked, in my bed, that's what I hope to gain.

But I tell her something a little further from the truth, something more truth adjacent. "You are the cleverest woman I've ever met, and I knew you'd do smashingly here."

Her eyes narrow. She bends over my desk to plant both hands on its surface directly above the papers I'd been grading. "Stop your scheming. I have half a mind to quit right now and go home to Scotland. But I deserve this job, even if I didn't get it on merit, and I will prove I can do it."

The way she's bent over my desk makes her blouse pull away from her skin, revealing her skimpy bra. The breasts I'd dreamed about obsessively for so long nearly spill out of those cups.

"I know you can do the job," I say. "That's why I recommended you."

Yes, I'm sliding a bit further away from the truth, not as adjacent to it as a moment ago.

"No, it's not," she hisses, then slaps both hands on the desk. "Get this through your head, Alex. I will never have sex with you again. Never. If an asteroid were heading straight for Earth, about to annihilate every living thing on the planet, I still wouldn't have sex with you. I will never crawl into whatever dank hole you live in, you...soulless Sassenach."

"I may be British, but I do have a soul." Do I? No idea. That isn't a topic I spend much time examining. Hearing her call me a Sassenach, the Scottish word for an Englishman, I experience a strange sensation of unease. I've been called plenty of insulting names, but Cat's insult... What? Bothers me? No, it must be heartburn.

"Maybe I should have you deported," she announces, lifting her perky little nose.

"You can't. I'm an American citizen."

Cat squints at me, her lips tight. "You gave up being British?"

"No, I'm both British and American. It's called dual citizenship, love. Everyone's doing it these days."

"Cannae see what game you're playing by becoming a citizen, but I'm sure it's something dead rotten." She straightens, lifting her chin this time. "Stay away from me."

"We'll be working in the same department, so that might be rather difficult."

"I don't want to see or speak to you unless it's work related." She leans in again, and her blouse falls away from her breasts again. "No tricks, no schemes, no cons. The only conversations we will ever have will be about work. Nothing else. Understand?"

"Yes, I grasp your subtle meaning."

Her lips pucker. "Donnae be staring at my breasts. You will never see them again."

All right, I am staring at her breasts. I remember how beautiful they look bouncing above my face when she straddles me and—

"Stop that," she says, slapping her hand on my desk. "I know you're thinking about sex. You clearly weren't listening the first time, so I'll say it again." She points that finger at me one more time, the tip of it grazing my nose. "I will never sleep with you. Never. I despise you, Alex Thorne."

"Isn't that what Serena told Logan a few months ago? Now they're married."

"That was different. My cousin is a good man, but you… You're a limey louse."

I chuckle. "Yes, Logan already told me about all the charming little nicknames you've made up for me. It's nice to know you still care enough to despise me. If I were out of your system, you wouldn't bother confronting me this way."

Never mind that every time she calls me one of those names—the British Bastard, the Limey Louse, the Soulless Sassenach—my throat goes thick and acid burns in my gut. It's probably the apple fritter I ate for breakfast. Normally, I eat a decent meal at home, but today I rushed to campus and grabbed a fried breakfast in the cafeteria. Had I been in a hurry because I knew Cat would be on campus today?

Of course not. I have no soul. How can I feel anything?

I sit back in my chair, folding my hands on my lap. "Would you like to punch me again?"

She grabs a paperback book off my desk and smacks me on top of the head with it. Three times. *Whack, whack, whack.*

"For real impact," I say, "try a hardcover."

The lovely lass bares her teeth at me and growls.

"My, but you are beautiful when you're incensed."

She spins around and stomps out of my office.

Well, at least she hit me with my own book, the one I'd written five years ago. I'm awfully proud of that book.

A few months ago, when Logan invited me to a family gathering, I said yes. Why? The entire MacTaggart clan hates me, or so I thought. Now, most of them tolerate me, though Catriona's brothers still glare at me every time I see them. Not as much as her sister Jamie, though. That woman has the most searing glare I've ever seen, not including Logan's. The former spy has intimidation down to an art.

When I'd turned up in Scotland, at the MacTaggart Highland games, Cat's first reaction was to punch me in the gut. That sort of passion doesn't arise without a reason. She must still want me. Maybe she even loves me. Seducing her has become my obsession.

Do I love her? Heaven only knows.

Not that it matters. I'm toxic.

Chapter Two

Catriona

I slam the door to Alex's office and stop. I can't show up at the dean's office for my first day of work like this. My heart pounds, my breathing is unsteady, and I feel like I might vomit any second. Why do I let Alex get to me? I've seen him at several family events since the day Logan brought Alex to the Highland games nine months ago. I'd been furious with Logan for that, but later, I realized he had done it because he cared about me. Maybe I had needed to confront Alex one more time, to get this anger out of my system. If that was the goal, I failed to accomplish it. Just looking at Alex still makes my blood boil.

Anger doesn't suit me. It makes me feel sick. Not because I have residual feelings for Alex, but because I'm not the sort who gets boiling mad, or who shouts at people, or who curses like a sailor. My brothers do all of that. My baby sister, Jamie, learned to curse from Aidan, Lachlan, and Rory, but I always resisted the urge.

Why, then, did I invent obnoxious names for Alex? Why had I kept spouting them every time someone mentioned his name? For twelve years?

I turn to face the door, staring at the words etched on it: "Dr. Alex Thorne, Archaeology and Ancient History." I wrap my arms around myself, suddenly chilled. Because Alex is a lying *bod ceann*, that's why. Arguing with him hasn't made me uneasy for any other reason.

My thoughts rewind to that day nine months ago when I saw him again for the first time. When I spotted him, a storm of emotions had raged inside me, driving me to lash out.

No, that's not entirely true. When I got my first glimpse of him, my heart raced, and my stomach fluttered. A thrill shivered through me, tingling on my skin, raising every hair on my body.

Then the storm had struck.

"You bastard!" I screamed, and barreled toward him, roaring like a wild animal.

While my entire family watched, I slugged Alex. Aye, he had deserved that. When I tried to hit him again, he caught my fist and wouldn't let go. The feel of his hand wrapped around mine affected me in ways I hadn't expected. Why should one touch make my pulse race even faster? Gazing into his eyes, those pools of molten dark caramel, brought back memories I never wanted to relive.

Alex kissing me. Alex smiling at me. His strong arms around me. The look on his face when we made love.

With my fist contained in his, I howled like a banshee.

"Now, now," Alex said in that wryly patient voice, the one that used to make me want him but now infuriated me. "Let's behave like adults, Catriona. Did you honestly expect I'd let you hit me again? One punch, I deserve. Two is a bit much."

That's when I kicked him in the shin.

He winced, but only for a split second. "If I let go, will you promise to end the violence?"

I called him a *bod ceann* right then, though labeling him a dickhead didn't seem to affect him at all. Aye, I remember that about him too. He can conceal his emotions better than anyone. How could I have ever loved him? He's a bloody liar. His scheming had gotten me arrested, and all these years later, I still have no idea why.

But standing here at his door, I can't help reminiscing about the old days with him.

The first time I met Alex, he'd been sitting on a bench under a tree, on the campus of the university where he was a professor and I was a grad student. Coming to America to study had sounded like a great adventure. This was before my brothers, my sister Jamie, and several of my cousins met and married Americans. Iain had lived in the US before, but he never talked about it. So, when I announced I'd been accepted to the PhD program at an American university, no one complained. They were happy for me.

On my eighth day in America, I saw Alex.

He was the most beautiful man I'd ever laid eyes on, with those warm brown eyes and short hair that seemed almost the same color. His face belonged on a Michelangelo statue, so angelic and yet with full lips that seemed made for sin. I'd loved that about him, the juxtaposition of the angelic and the sinful. The first moment I saw him, I wanted him, but I've never been the kind of woman who approaches a strange man.

I'd been about to walk away when he looked up from the open book on his lap and noticed me.

Those lips curled into a sweet, tentative smile, and he waved at me. "Hello there."

A shy smile was all I could manage.

"You must be new here," he said in a British accent, his voice so sexy I'd wanted to kiss him right then and there. "You have that slightly dazed look about you."

I nodded, still unable to speak.

He closed his book and scooted over on the bench, then patted it. "Have a seat. Maybe I can help you with that confusion."

And then he smiled. Really smiled.

My heart stuttered. When Alex smiles, it's like the sun beaming its warmth and light straight into your soul.

I scuffled up to the bench and settled onto it.

He held out his palm, as if for a handshake. "I'm Alex Thorne."

"Catriona MacTaggart," I said, my voice soft and almost breathless as I took his hand. "I just moved here from Scotland. To get my PhD."

"Ah, a grad student." He held onto my hand, his palm warm and his grip firm but not too tight. "What department are you in?"

For a second, I couldn't remember. "Archaeology."

"Me too." He moved his thumb over my skin, eliciting a warm tingle that spread over my whole body. "I'm not your adviser, that I'm sure of. I'd remember being assigned a Scots student."

"No, you're not my adviser. I haven't met her yet."

"Just set foot on campus, have you?"

"Aye."

He smiled again. "I do love the way Scots speak. Your accent is lovely."

"I like yours too." I felt idiotic the second I spoke the words, but I couldn't take them back. He heard what I said, even though I almost whispered it.

"Thank you," he said, tipping his head to the side as if considering me. "I hope we'll see each other again sometime. Even though I'm not your adviser, feel free to stop by my office anytime."

"I appreciate that." Sliding my hand free of his, I stood. "I need to go, or I'll be late for my first meeting with my adviser."

"Good luck, Catriona."

I walked away.

And glanced back at Alex five times before I lost sight of him.

I'd loved the way he said my name. If I'm completely honest with myself, I still love hearing him say it.

The doorknob jiggles, like Alex is about to open the door.

Bod an Donais, I'm still standing here staring at it.

And the thought of him catching me has spurred me to curse in my mind again, thinking my brother Rory's favorite Gaelic curse. *Bod an Donais*, or the devil's penis. It always sounded silly to me, but lately, I find myself muttering it or thinking it often.

I bolt down the hall as Alex opens the door.

Does he see me? Christ, I hope not. That's just what I need, for him to be smugly aware of the fact I've lingered outside his office door. Like I want to see him again. Like speaking to him, simply being in his presence, affects me.

Maybe it does, but he has no need to know about that.

Despite the time it took to confront Alex—a fruitless effort—I still arrive at the dean's office three minutes early. Gus Hooper greets me with a smile and a handshake.

"Welcome to Thensmore University," he says. "We're so pleased to have you here, Dr. MacTaggart."

"I'm pleased to be here," I say, only partially lying. I've looked forward to starting my new job, but not with Alex Thorne here. "I was surprised you chose me for the position, since my resume has been a wee bit slender for the past several years, but I'm honored to have this opportunity."

Hooper waves for me to take a seat and sits down behind his desk. "If Alex Thorne recommends you, I'm sure you'll be exceptional."

Though a chill washes through me, I manage to sit down instead of collapsing onto the chair. Yes, Alex got me this job. I learned that from the woman in human resources who helped me fill out the requisite paperwork. And yes, I fumed while filling out those forms. I fumed and fumed and fumed until I burst into Alex's office. Shouting at him let me expel all that steam.

Well, most of it.

"It was kind of Dr. Thorne to recommend me," I say, and now I am lying outright, like the British Bastard himself. A nasty little part of me wants to mention that Alex had been fired from his job here last year, thanks to his affair with a wealthy donor's ex-wife. The man used his influence to get Alex kicked out. That won't matter anymore. According to Logan, ever since Alex retrieved three stolen Babylonian tablets and returned them to the university, no one cares about his indiscretions.

Except Alex didn't retrieve the tablets. Logan and his wife, Serena, did. I still can't fathom why my cousin let Alex take the credit for it.

"We're so grateful," Gus Hooper says, "that you could fill this position for us on such short notice. Dr. Edwards left so suddenly, it was a huge shock and left a gaping hole in our curriculum."

Three weeks ago, Gus rang me out of the blue to offer me a position here as an assistant professor. I assumed he'd chosen me because no one else would take the job with so little notice. How was I to know Alex had schemed to make it happen? He'd probably kidnapped the professor who quit and forced her to write a resignation letter.

No. More likely, he'd paid her off.

I half listen while Gus Hooper gives me the standard spiel about the university, how wonderful it is, how the faculty are like one big family, et cetera. But my brain keeps torturing me with memories of Alex. The old Alex. The one I'd loved, the one I'd moved in with after knowing him for a month, the one I'd hoped would ask me to marry him. He never had.

Of course not. I'd been nothing but his patsy.

Hooper finishes his spiel, clasping his hands on the desktop. "Now, about your housing situation…"

"What about it?"

"There's been a slight hiccup." He glances down at his hands, then looks at me again. "Faculty housing is all filled up."

"I'm sure I can find something off campus. Or I can stay at the hotel a bit longer."

"Uh…" He looks down at his hands again. "I'm afraid there aren't any rentals available in town either, or in the surrounding area. And we had booked your room at the hotel for one night only. It's no longer available."

"What about another hotel?"

He shakes his head. "We do have another option, but it's a little unorthodox."

Every hair on my body shivers and stands at attention. I have a sinking feeling I know what will come out of Dean Hooper's mouth next.

He sits up straighter. "A member of the faculty has offered to take you in until something else becomes available."

Those hairs, already stiff, now tingle—but not in a pleasant way. "Which faculty member?"

"Alex Thorne."

Bod an Donais. That bleeding ersehole has planned this. Somehow. I don't know what machinations he used to make this happen, but I'm dead certain he did.

"He lives in a great old mansion," Hooper tells me. "Fifteen bedrooms or something like that. I understand you two have met before, so you know he's a nice guy, very personable."

Nice guy? How can anyone call him that after he was fired for sleeping with a donor's ex-wife? But oh, aye, Alex knows how to be very personable.

Hooper eyes me with a guilty expression. "I know this isn't what you were promised. I'm sorry about that, but I hear Alex's house is really something."

"You've never seen it?"

"No, he doesn't do much entertaining at home."

Of course not. Alex probably keeps the mummified bodies of anyone who gets in his way stashed in those fifteen bedrooms.

I groan inwardly, so Gus Hooper can't hear it. No, Alex isn't a murderer. A liar, a cheat, a con—aye, he's all those things. But not a murderer.

The bastard not only conned his way back into the job he'd been fired from, but he also conned his way into my life again.

"So," Hooper says, "are you okay with bunking at Alex's house?"

What else can I say? "Yes, that sounds fine. Thank you."

That old anger swells inside me, but I tamp it down. No more erupting every time I see Alex. He likes that, I'm sure. He enjoys having an effect on me, so I will no longer let him do that. Since I'm forced to share a house with him, I need to stay calm and rational and adult about the whole thing.

No problem.

Who's the bloody liar now, eh?

Chapter Three

Alex

*D*oes Catriona think I didn't see her scurrying down the hall? I'd
watched Cat's backside retreating down the hallway while she sprinted
away from me, enjoying the view of her sweet arse and the way her
pantsuit accentuated those generous cheeks. I've never seen her in a suit of
any kind until today. When I knew her before, she was a grad student who
wore casual clothes. When I saw her again, at the ill-fated Highland games at
her brother Rory's castle, she'd been dressed in a similarly casual way. Today,
on her first day of work at Thensmore, she dresses like a businesswoman.

I might've thought she dressed that way to discourage me from seducing
her, but she didn't know I worked here until she arrived on campus. Lydia, the
fiftyish lady at the human resources office, must have told her. And maybe I
had charmed Lydia into keeping it a secret that I'd been responsible for Cat's
new job and that I'm also a professor here. It's surprisingly easy to sweet-talk a
middle-aged woman who wears Christmas sweaters year-round.

Charming any woman is surprisingly easy for me.

For the rest of the day, I grade papers, plan lessons, and fantasize about
Catriona MacTaggart. Maybe I spend the better part of the day doing the
latter. Maybe I even neglect some of my duties because of that. Can anyone
blame me? Cat in a business suit affects me like...catnip. I laugh softly at
my own joke. Yes, I like that one. Catnip. Maybe that should be her new
nickname. Can't believe I never thought of that one before.

All right, I can admit it. I'm an arrogant, self-important prick.

By four o'clock, I decide I've done enough work. What little of it I managed to do.

Cat's arse looks fantastic in those gray trousers.

I stroll across the campus toward the faculty parking lot, glancing around as I walk, nodding to students and staff I know. When I cross the grassy lawn that separates the sidewalk from the faculty parking lot, I stop.

Catriona is standing beside my car, leaning her lovely arse against the passenger door.

What a sight she is. She has her arms folded under her breasts, pushing them up a touch, enough to make those lush mounds even more enticing. I remember vividly the flavor of her skin when I tasted her nipples, and how it felt to have her breasts in my hands, almost spilling out of my palms.

A breeze tousles her long hair, and she brushes the locks away with one hand.

God, she's beautiful.

Cat notices me and pushes away from my car. She crooks a finger at me.

I stride over to her. "Good afternoon, Catriona."

"You are a right bastard." She pokes my chest with one finger. "I don't know what sort of underhanded scheme you concocted to make this happen, but it won't work."

"Scheme?" I play innocent at least as well as Logan MacTaggart, the former MI6 agent. I'd learned deception in a different way, though, one far less noble.

"You know what I'm talking about," she says. "What did you do? Bribe the dean to claim there's nowhere else for me to stay?"

"Oh, that." I smile. "Come on, Cat. You can admit the truth to me, I won't tell anyone."

She scowls.

I keep smiling. "You want to stay at my house, that's the truth. It'll be easier for you to crawl into my bed overnight if I'm down the hall instead of fifteen miles away."

"Being clever doesn't work with me. I know what a slimy *cacan* you are."

"*Cacan*? I'm assuming that's Gaelic, but I don't remember you using that word before."

"It means you're a wee shit. Though you aren't small. But still, the 'shit' part applies to you." She folds her arms again, pushing those luscious breasts up again. "How did you maneuver me into this corner?"

"You're standing in a parking lot, not a corner."

She fists her hands at her sides. "Do I have to punch you again?"

I consider her for a moment, weighing the options with my mental scale. Option one, tell her the truth. Option two, lie and evade and hope she won't pull out brass knuckles and beat me to death right here in the faculty parking lot. Truth or death, truth or death. The sides of my mental scale stay balanced for a few more seconds, then I decide.

The truth it is.

Not because I feel guilty for what I've done. No, that annoying little itch behind my ribs has nothing to do with it. My conscience likes to, on occasion, pester me to be a good boy. I've been ignoring it for years. Why listen to my conscience now? I'm too old to change—not that I want to. The fact that I've suffered this itch more and more frequently since the day of our reunion at Dùndubhan means nothing.

My hand rises to my chest without my permission, my fingers twitching like they want to scratch that itch.

I shove my hands into the pockets of my trousers. "Maybe I reserved every room at every hotel, motel, and bed-and-breakfast in the area. And maybe I convinced the chap in charge of the maintenance crew that he really needs to redo the plumbing in the two available faculty housing units."

Cat's eyes widen as she clenches her fists tighter. "You did what?"

"That's how I maneuvered you into staying at my house." When was the last time I told anyone the unvarnished truth? I can't remember. It feels odd.

"You bribed the maintenance man?"

"No, I…" My mental scale starts to wiggle. Truth, death. Truth, death. So bloody hard to choose. I rub my neck and sigh. "I might have sneaked into the two housing units and sort of…loosened the pipes. There was an unfortunate amount of flooding in those units, and the maintenance crew needs to clean up the mess."

I might have encouraged those chaps to take their sweet time with the cleanup, but Cat doesn't need to know that.

Her lips pucker, and a breath blusters out her nostrils. "You sneaky, smarmy, conniving jackass."

"Don't you get tired of telling me what an arsehole I am?" I take hold of her upper arms. "Let me make it easy for you. I admit I'm a bastard, a *cacan*, an arse, a *bod ceann*, and anything else your adorable little brain can come up with."

"*Bod ceann*? I called you that once, but I didn't tell you what it means."

"No, but Logan informed me you were calling me a dickhead."

She stares at me for several seconds, hands fisted, shoulders bunched, glowering at me with all the righteous fury of a Valkyrie.

"Anger suits you," I say. "It brings out that fire in your soul, the one you try to hide."

Her hands relax, her fingers hanging loose, and her entire posture slackens too. She gazes at me with a softer expression, though not the sensual one

I've been hoping for. "I suppose I have no choice, do I? You win this time. I'll stay at your mansion."

I won. Hearing her say that doesn't make me feel triumphant. Instead, it triggers that bloody itch again.

This time, I scratch it. Not that my fingers can reach inside to where the itch lives, deep down in the parts of myself I buried a long time ago. Buried but not destroyed. The ghosts of my past live inside me, haunting me every day and every night.

"Where are my suitcases?" she asks. "Lydia Mitchell said I should leave them with her until after my meeting with the dean, since I just flew in this morning. But my things were gone when I went back for them. Lydia was away at lunch, so I couldn't ask her about it. Besides, I had a sneaking suspicion you're the one I should ask."

"Ah, yes." I give her my patented disarming smile and shrug. "Maybe I sweet-talked Lydia into letting me have your bags, since I knew you'd be staying at my house."

Catriona hisses something that sounds like Gaelic, but she says it under her breath, making it hard for me to decipher the words. Probably *bod ceann* or *cacan*. I'm a wee shit and a dickhead? Can't argue with that assessment.

She turns sideways to the car, one hand on the roof. "Are we away now?"

"Yes, we can go." I dig my keys out and click the button on the fob to unlock the car. As I open the passenger door for her, I ask, "Who told you my house is a mansion? It must've been Gus Hooper. He's always pestering me for a tour."

"Aye, it was him." She gets into the car and looks up at me. "Why don't you give him a tour? He'd be thrilled."

"It's my home, not a ruddy museum." Logan and Serena are the only guests ever to set foot in my home—until today. To have Catriona staying with me... I get a strange sensation of static electricity on my skin when I think about it. I am not excited to have her near me. No, I'm excited at the prospect of fucking her.

And the prospect of winning the game. My long con began that day at Dùndubhan, when she slugged me.

Cat raises her brows at me.

I shut the door and climb in on the driver's side. While I navigate the campus streets, heading for the main highway, I try not to look at Cat. Every time I do, that itch starts up again. So I stop looking.

What con am I drawing Cat into? What do I hope to gain?

For the first time in my life, I have no idea.

"Let's talk, Alex."

And shit, her words make me glance at her. The itch pricks at me.

"No talking," I say.

"Considering how you arranged this slumber party, the least you can do is answer a few questions."

"Maybe later."

Never is more like it, but that's a truth she doesn't need to know yet.

"Alex."

I turn on the stereo and crank up the volume, drowning out any potential conversation with Vivaldi's *Four Seasons*. It's playing "Spring," with thunder-like drums rumbling through the car, drowning out any questions Cat wants to ask.

She frowns at me, then turns her gaze to the view outside her window.

Yes, I am a bastard.

Chapter Four

Catriona

We drive down increasingly more deserted roads lined with thicker and thicker forest until Alex steers his Mercedes-Benz onto a narrow gravel track wide enough for one car. I assume it's his driveway, but he still has the music turned up loud enough to make conversation difficult, though not so loud my ears hurt. Maybe I should try Serena's method of dealing with a difficult man and smack Alex's face. I can't do that while he's driving, and neither can I punch him.

Strangely, I don't want to punch him anymore.

For more than a decade, I've convinced myself I hate him. If I'm honest with myself, though, I've always known I don't despise him. I had loved Alex so much back then, back when we were a couple and lived together. He'd been different in those days. Less closed off, less jaded, less evasive. I can't trust him, I know that much. At least, not the way I trusted him before. The old me believed everything he said without question.

Twelve years of life experience taught me to be more circumspect. But it was those last days with Alex that shattered my trust in him or any man.

Alex parks the car in front of a massive mansion.

"Here we are," he says in that breezy tone, the one that implies he has no cares in the world, the one that's total bollocks. "Welcome to my home, also known as the British Bastard's Den of Iniquity."

Does he want me to say something nasty in response? If that's what he expects, I'll give him the opposite.

"Your home is beautiful," I say. "And impressive."

He glances at me sideways, his brows crinkled, but the faint expression of surprise lasts for only a second or two. Then his cheerful facade reasserts itself. "Come, let me show you the inside."

We climb out of the Mercedes, and I get my first good look at the house.

The term mansion hardly describes it. The facade looks Victorian, but something about it gives me the idea it isn't that old. Like a fairy-tale castle, it has round turrets, but that's where the fairy tale ends. The entire structure has an aura of gloom about it, from the dark windows of the large gables to the crimson trim around the variegated gray stone bricks that form the bulk of the walls. Crimson stripes at either side of the massive entrance run from the peak of the roof down to the ground. Ornate black ironwork cages every window, and a set of red brick steps leads up to the entrance, where a pair of massive reddish-brown wood doors hunker.

Glancing over my shoulder, I see that the driveway curves in a semicircle.

The woods surround us, dark and foreboding, the trees taller than the three-story house.

Everything about this place makes me uneasy.

Alex leads me up the steps to the door, swinging them inward as he says, "Welcome to Moirai House."

Moirai. The goddesses of fate in Greek mythology. Why did he name his house after them?

I cross the threshold, turning to look at the doors, and run my hand over the delicately carved, shiny surface of one. "What kind of wood is this? It's beautiful."

And it is. The rich red color has deep undertones of darker shades and a soft satin finish that makes it even more beautiful.

"That's dalbergia from India," Alex tells me, shutting the doors, "also known as East Indian rosewood. It's very expensive and hard to work with, which makes it even more prized."

I turn away from the doors to take in the style of the interior.

Every wall is crimson, with trim fashioned from the same Indian rosewood as the doors. The ceiling is painted a pale silver-gray, and a long crimson-and-cream rug stretches the length of the foyer. Paintings on the walls depict ancient goddesses, including the three Fates or Moirai. Alex guides me across the foyer, but I stop when I reach the painting of the Moirai. It shows three women weaving the fates of mortals, from Clothos spinning the thread of life to Lachesis seated beside her, measuring the length of that thread, and finally to Atropos the Inevitable who decides each mortal's fate by clipping the thread. Something about the gorgeously rendered scene makes my throat tighten and sends a chill down my spine.

The painting tells me something about Alex, I'm sure of it, but I have no idea what message it delivers.

"Why is your home so dark?" I ask. "Crimson walls and red wood? I remember you used to love light and open floor plans, like the loft we used to have. Today, you live in a tomb."

He halts a few meters ahead of me, but now he turns halfway to look at me. Gone is his affable, carefree demeanor. He stares at me with an intensity that makes every hair on my body stiffen, his gaze drilling into me for so long that a tingling chill sweeps through me.

"Maybe it is a tomb," he says, his tone flat.

"Alex, are you all right?"

"Right as rain."

His tone implies the polar opposite of that. He's fisted his hands, and a muscle pulses in his jaw, but I have no idea if he's angry with me for calling his home a tomb or if my statement has unleashed something he'd kept buried deep inside for a long, long time.

The man before me is not the same Alex Thorne I loved all those years ago. Something in him has changed, something fundamental and inexplicable.

Is the man I knew still in there? Or does he fake every smile and every cheerfully annoying thing he says?

Any residual anger left inside me snuffs out in this moment. Confronted with the new Alex, or maybe the one he sublimated when we were together, I know only one thing for certain. To get any measure of closure with him, I need to excavate from the deepest pit of his soul all the secrets he's concealed from me. Once I understand him, will I realize he's better than I thought—or worse than I could ever possibly imagine?

It's long past time I find out.

Serena, Logan's wife, told me once that I needed to confront the ghosts of my past with Alex and lay them to rest for good. She'd been right. Now, here in this crimson tomb, I will exorcise those ghosts once and for all, no matter the consequences. Twelve years of anger and resentment is enough.

I move closer to Alex, laying a hand on his arm, feeling the stiff muscles under his shirt. "Are you sure you're all right? You seem…upset. I didn't mean to offend you by calling this house a tomb. It's just that you used to love natural light and open spaces, and now you live in this dark, enclosed mansion."

"Maybe I've changed." He pulls in a long, deep breath, then exhales it in a rush. All the tension seems to melt out of him, and he smiles, a twinkle in his warm brown eyes. "Let me give you the grand tour."

"Am I getting special treatment? Gus Hooper has been dying to get inside this house, but he says you won't give him a tour."

"This is my home, not a tourist attraction." He grasps my elbow, guiding me down the hall. "You are not the general public, or the nosy dean of the humanities department."

"Is this a genuine Victorian house? Everything seems too new for that unless you gutted the place and started over."

"No, it's not a real Victorian mansion. It's a reproduction. I built it five years ago."

He takes me through a doorway to the base of a massive staircase—fashioned from dalbergia, of course—that curves up toward the second floor and an open hallway that serves as a kind of balcony. I spy another staircase to the left of the main stairs, one that leads up to the top floor. Each end of the balcony-like second-floor hall vanishes into a dark corridor.

Alex flips a switch on the wall, and lights come on down here and up on the second floor. A glow as warm and golden as the morning sun pours through the dark spaces, illuminating every corner.

Suddenly, the house doesn't seem quite so tomblike.

"Better?" he asks.

"Yes." I trace the curving line of the main staircase with my gaze. "Does this house really have fifteen bedrooms?"

"Gus Hooper told you that, didn't he? Yes, there are fifteen bedrooms, so you can choose the one farthest from where I sleep if that will make you more comfortable."

"Why don't you choose one for me?"

His smile evaporates, replaced by that look of faint surprise he had earlier when I told him his home was beautiful. "You want me to pick a room for you?"

"Aye, that's what I said, isn't it?"

Though his mouth opens, he says nothing for several seconds. But of course, he reasserts his air of cheerful indifference before he finally speaks. "What if I choose the room right next to mine? Or perhaps I'll have you sleep in my room."

"You won't."

Earlier today, I told him I will never have sex with him, not even if an asteroid is heading for the Earth. Anger fueled that statement, an anger I've clung to for so long. But seeing his house, seeing his reactions to everything I say about it, all of that has triggered a sudden realization.

Alex isn't the devil. In my mind, I molded him into the embodiment of everything that went wrong in my life, from my lack of gainful employment to the time I'd been arrested because of him. Yes, I can blame him for that. But the rest was not his fault. I haven't been happy with my life, and I can no longer blame him for it.

I also can't deny the truth anymore. I want Alex, and I always will.

While he studies me, I study him right back. He's gotten more muscular over the years, and I have to admit I like that. His tan shirt has golden undertones, much like his caramel eyes, and the fabric accentuates his muscles without sticking to him like cling film. When he'd fisted his hands a moment ago, his biceps bulged, and I couldn't help imagining what his arms look like and how they might feel holding on to me while he drives his cock deep inside my body. I know exactly what that part of him looks like. And feels like. And tastes like. He'd always been—and always will be, I'm fair certain—the best lover I've ever had.

Too bad he's also a bloody liar.

Alex Thorne has always known how to get under my skin and make me do things I never dreamed I would do. He also knows how to make me angrier than I ever dreamed I could be. Punching him? That isn't like me, but ever since the day when Logan and Serena brought Alex to the Highland games, and I saw him again for the first time in ages, anger has become my default state.

Not anymore. Maybe it's time I get under his skin and seduce the seducer. Solving the mystery of the man he's become might give me closure or drag me down into the abyss where he's taken up residence. Either way, I need to unravel the tangled threads of lies, evasions, and half-truths to discover if he's still the man I once loved.

And if he is? What then?

I'll deal with those questions later.

And if all else fails, I can punch him again.

He shepherds me upstairs and watches while I peek inside each bedroom until I find the one I like the best. Standing in the doorway of that room, I announce, "This one."

Alex throws a meaningful glance in the direction of the door at the end of the hallway, right next to the room I've selected. "That door is my room. Are you sure you want to be so close to me?"

"I'm sure, aye."

"Since that's settled, I'll go and get your bags."

"You don't have to do that. I can get them."

He lifts one brow. "What sort of host would I be if I let a lady carry her own suitcases?"

"If you really are a bastard, you wouldn't care."

That brow lifts a touch higher. "Are you implying I might not be a bastard after all?"

"Maybe."

"What happened to hating me and cursing my name?"

He sounds genuinely confused.

"Get my things, Alex. Please."

While he hurries off to do that, I explore the huge room. It's as large as the biggest rooms at Dùndubhan, my brother Rory's castle. That house is so large that my sister Jamie, who had been living in the castle with her husband, decided to move to the cottage in the garden instead. She worried their bairns might fall down the many flights of stairs in Dùndubhan. These days, she and Gavin live in a cottage in the nearby village of Loch Fairbairn.

This room is even more incredible than Rory's castle. The large, four-poster canopy bed occupies the center of the space, pushed up against the wall. Unlike the foyer and the hallways, this room has no crimson walls. Instead, they're a pale, sunny yellow. The bed features a quilt with squares of various flower patterns sewn onto it. I have a lovely armoire and dressing table too, plus a nightstand and an attached bathroom.

Alex returns with my suitcases, setting them down just inside the doorway. "Here you are."

"Thank you."

Standing several meters apart, we stare at each other. His molten caramel eyes seem to glow in the more subdued lighting inside this room, and I can't tear my gaze away from him. That face, like an angel's but with something naughty underneath. Those lips I've kissed so many times. A pang starts behind my ribs, bringing with it a longing so intense it triggers the first burn of tears.

I won't cry. Not in front of Alex.

Sucking in a breath, I struggle to banish the tears before they flow. Once I'd loved him with everything I had. But after the things he's done, can I still love him? Or fall for him again? Yesterday, I would've said no and shouted at anyone who suggested it might happen. Today...

Words tumble out of me of their own volition, climbing up my throat and falling past my lips before I can stop them. "Did you ever love me?"

He doesn't blink, though his gaze stays trained on mine.

For a moment, I think he won't answer or that he'll offer an evasive quip. He doesn't do either of those things.

Alex strides up to me, cradles my face in his hands, and kisses me. He presses his mouth to mine, the pressure both firm and gentle, holding his lips there but not attempting to deepen the kiss.

The breath I've been holding rushes out of me, and I'm helpless to stop myself from moaning softly. So many years have gone by since the last time he kissed me. Countless days and nights without him. Countless hours wasted on convincing myself I hated him. Now, with his warm lips on mine again, I understand one fact.

I could fall for him all over again.

But I can never, never trust him.

He pulls away, taking two steps backward. "You may not believe it, but yes. I loved you, Catriona."

Before I can speak, he hurries out the door and shuts it.

Chapter Five

Alex

Catriona MacTaggart is a witch who's cast a spell over me. I decide that in the middle of the night while I lie tangled in my silk sheets, thanks to tossing and turning for hours while reliving the moment when I kissed the Scots enchantress. Why the bloody hell did I tell her I'd loved her? Yes, I said it past tense. Not that I'm in love with her now. But I didn't mean to say anything of the sort, and I certainly didn't mean to kiss her. But when she looked at me with pain in her eyes and her voice so soft and full of longing, I…lost my mind.

Yes, I went insane. Briefly. For a few seconds. A minute at most.

I do not crumble because a woman looks at me like she might cry. I absolutely do not get a pain in my chest because a woman all but begs me to say I loved her once upon a time. No, I don't do anything of the sort. Not ever.

Until last night.

Maybe I meant it when I answered her question. Maybe it was an honest response. What if it was? That does not mean I still love her.

Well, maybe I do. A little.

Lying in bed with the sheets crumpled in a pile next to me, I rub my eyes and take slow, deep breaths. Catriona is a witch, like her cousins Isla, Kirsty, and Elspeth. Those three, the so-called Witches of Ballachulish, must've woven some sort of insanity-inducing spell over me or taught Cat how to do it herself. It is undoubtedly part of a scheme to drive me barking mad as revenge for what I did to Cat long ago.

Now I believe in magic? Rubbish. I don't subscribe to the barmy notion Logan's three sisters have supernatural powers.

I crawl out of bed and shuffle into the en suite bathroom, cranking up the water temperature in the shower until steam fills the room. A good, hot shower, that's what I need. Burn away all the...whatever it is that seeing Cat again has done to me. Placing my palms on the wall of the shower, I rest my forehead on the tiles and let the hot water sluice over me, scouring away all the nonsense.

Visions of Cat assail me.

That pantsuit she wore yesterday, it clung to her body in all the right places without being unprofessional. She looked every bit the mature, seasoned professor of archaeology and ancient history. The way her jacket molded to her breasts drew my attention inexorably to those full mounds. And Christ, her lips. I wanted to claim her mouth right then, to nibble and suck on those lips until she moaned and opened for me, begging for a deep, all-consuming kiss.

My cock hardens.

Bloody hell. This shower is meant to alleviate my lust and whatever, uh, feelings I might possibly think perhaps I might still suffer from concerning Catriona. Instead, my fantasies have made my dick stiffen until it waves like it's commanding me to act on my desires.

Only one way to deal with this.

I turn down the water temperature until it feels cool on my skin. Then I lean back against the wall, right under the shower head, and take my cock in my hand, pumping it slowly. *Fantasies commence.* Cat in that suit. Me unbuttoning her jacket, sliding it off, unhooking the buttons on her blouse with my teeth. Cat moaning while I remove her blouse, her bra, her trousers, everything. I work myself faster, getting harder, feeling the pressure mounting. Cat spread across the desk in my office, naked, clutching me and writhing beneath me while I thrust into her. Cat's moans growing louder and more desperate, echoing off the walls.

"Fuck!" I half snarl, half shout, while I come so hard my back bows and I can't catch my breath.

Someone bangs on the door to my bedroom.

I pump twice more until I have nothing left to give to the fantasy that torments me.

"Alex!" Catriona shouts, still banging on the door. "Are you all right?"

Several filthy curses, unrepeatable in the presence of women or children, spill out of me while I rinse myself off and get out of the shower. Slinging a towel around my hips, I hold it in place with one hand and jog to the door. When I pull it open, Cat's eyes fly wide.

"What are you on about?" I demand, sounding a bit grumpier than I intended. Getting a leg over with myself isn't as enjoyable as doing it with her.

I really need to get her into my bed. Soon.

The outfit she's wearing doesn't help matters. Her loose-fitting blouse should stem my lust for her breasts, but instead, its billowing fabric makes me crave her tits even more. Something about the way the blouse moves this way and that draws my attention to those lovely mounds even more than a tight-fitting shirt might. The worst part of all is what's covering her lower half. The sky-blue material sheathing those shapely legs hardly qualifies as trousers. The garment clings to her body like a second skin.

And Christ, her shoes. Their heels lift her a few inches higher and give her ankles a seductive curve, and her pink-painted toenails poke out of the sandal-like shoes.

She blinks several times, rapidly at first, then slower as she runs her gaze over me from head to toe. Her cheeks turn a pale shade of pink, the color speckling her skin. Her attention seems to have stalled on my cock, or rather, the bulge under my towel that gives away the fact I'm still semi-aroused. Yes, I relieved the pressure, but I'm not quite back to normal yet. Still somewhat firmer and larger than usual.

Cat licks her lips.

Perfect. Now I know for sure she wants me as much as I want her. No more talk of love and the past. I need her in my bed, not my heart.

If I even have one of those.

Her gaze lifts to mine. "I heard a scream, and I thought you were—I don't know. Having a heart attack or something."

"It's nice to know you'll come to my rescue if I ever do have a heart attack, but no. I'm fine."

"Oh. Good." She glances down at the bulge under my towel again, the pink tip of her tongue poking out between her ripe, luscious lips. After about two seconds of staring at my cock like she wants to devour it, towel and all, she looks at my face again. "Why did you scream?"

"What? I never scream." I had shouted or...something. Rather loudly. Might I have made a louder noise than I realized? Climaxing to visions of Catriona was the most intense release I've experienced in a long time. "You must have imagined it."

Her gaze narrows, and her mouth tightens. "I don't imagine things like that. Besides, I was standing right outside your door when I heard it."

"Right outside my door?" I lean in until I can taste her breaths on my lips. "What were you doing hovering outside my room? If you want to fuck me, walk right in and do it."

If she had joined me in the shower, we both would've come as hard as I did on my own. No, harder. With her willing body milking mine, the release would have been the best I've ever had.

Her breathing has grown labored, hoisting her breasts up with every inhalation.

And my erection is experiencing a rebirth.

"Better make up your mind quickly," I say, lowering my voice to a huskier register on purpose. "Or I'll go back in the shower and rub one off again without you."

She freezes, not even breathing. Her lips slide into a knowing smile, and she laughs softly.

I feel my brows cinch together. "What are you laughing about?"

"You." She clamps her teeth down on her lips, struggling to stave off louder laughter, but it snorts out of her anyway. She touches her fingers to her lips, and her snorts mutate into spluttering. "You masturbated."

"Why is that so amusing?" I grip the towel tighter and snap my spine straight, frowning at her. "Everyone does it."

"Aye, but you did it because of me. I won't let you have a poke at me, so you were forced to get off on your own."

"I still don't see what's funny about it." Her reaction is making me irritable. What the bloody hell? I don't get irritated because a woman laughs at me. Not that any female ever has laughed. When I told her I rubbed one off already, she was meant to be aroused—desperately aroused. Instead, little chuckles keep spluttering out of her.

"Had a dry spell, have you, Alex?" She pulls her fingers away from her mouth, no longer laughing but still smiling at me with an amusement that has me crooking my fingers into my palms. "How long has it been since you've slept with a woman?"

"None of your business."

"That long, eh? No wonder you're so...pent up." She crosses her arms over her chest, pretending to examine me like she's my physician and I'm a patient with an unfortunate disease. "Or do you prefer men these days? I have no problem with that, and it would explain why you keep acting like you want to sleep with me but never actually try to seduce me."

"What the fuck, Cat?" I throw my hands up. "I am not gay. Understand? Not gay. I love to shag women—only women."

"Calm down, Alex." She holds up her hands in a conciliatory gesture. Then her focus swerves to the bottom half of me, now exposed because I've let go of the towel. It lies on the floor. Cat jerks her gaze away from my groin and clears her throat. "Get dressed. I'll meet you downstairs."

She whirls away and sashays toward the stairs.

I groan. Her arse in those leggings, or whatever women call them, the sight of it makes all the blood rush from my brain straight to my cock.

The woman is tormenting me on purpose, and I'm falling for her scheme. Who knew Catriona MacTaggart, the sweet and almost shy girl who'd been embarrassed to sit next to me on a park bench, would become a devious and brazen woman who knows exactly how to get under my skin. I like her this way. Bossy. Sexy. Sarcastic and dismissive.

Shagging her now will be even better than before.

Catriona pauses at the top of the stairs to glance back at me. "Are you sure you're not gay?"

"Yes, Cat, I'm sure." Why did I snarl those words like an enraged dog?

Smirking, she heads down the stairs.

That woman is absolutely going to drive me insane. If Catriona crawls too far under my skin, she might unearth all the dark and twisted secrets I've buried deep inside myself. That will never happen. Unless she keeps acting this way...

Bloody hell.

Chapter Six

Catriona

*A*lex. Naked. Wet. Water dripping from his hair and drizzling down his skin. I've seen him naked before, since we lived together for almost two years, but I haven't seen all of him in a very long time. Most men get less fit and virile as they age, but not Alex. I swear he's developed more muscles instead of less. His thighs are thicker than I remember, thick with powerful sinews, and his biceps have grown too. When he clenched his fists, they bulged. I traced every curving line of muscle on his chest, counted every single one of his six-pack abs, and followed the trail of fine hairs that tapered down to the part of him I'd thought I remembered so well.

I've been wrong. His cock seems larger than I remember too.

That part of him cannot have grown. I assumed if I ever saw his penis again, it would be smaller than I remember. Instead, it's bigger. Thicker. More mouthwatering.

And aye, my mouth watered. I might've licked my lips when I stared at his male member. That singular part of his body mesmerized me and made my body come alive. Aching nipples. Aching breasts. Slick heat between my thighs. And the taut bud of my lust throbbed.

It's humiliating how much I still want him.

Which explains why I said the one thing no straight man ever wants to hear. *Do you prefer men these days?* I know Alex isn't gay. I slept with him for the better part of two years and experienced his very, very heterosexual urges. *Bod a' chac*, the man is an incredible lover. Not gay in the least. I said that to annoy him, to see if he *would* get annoyed. Alex has always been unflappable. My cousin Iain never gets upset either, but he's unflappable in a Zen-like way thanks to years of experience in learning to manage his emotions. Not sublimate them. Just understand and accept them.

My brother Rory used to control his passions for another reason—fear. He didn't want to show his feelings because he was terrified of getting hurt again after his three disastrous marriages. Emery loosened him up, and now Rory doesn't hold back anymore. He will always have that solicitor's levelness, with a hint of menace when necessary.

Alex is not like either of them. He isn't uptight like Rory had been, or as calm as the Buddha-like Iain. He doesn't have Logan's deadly calmness, a residual effect of his years in the military and MI6. No, Alex is cheerfully, playfully cagey. He has dark moments, though they pass quickly. His affable facade conceals layers I need to peel away to find the true core of him.

Maybe I'm getting closer. He had thrown his hands up and growled at me that he isn't gay. I scored a point in this game.

Playing Alex's game? I must be mad to try.

So be it. If I lose my mind, at least I'll have the answers I need.

I go into the kitchen to find something to eat for breakfast. This house is large enough to need a small army of employees—cooks, maids, gardeners, whatever—but Alex seems to have none of those. Serena and Logan mentioned Alex had "servants," as he called them, when they first visited his house. But a few days later, the servants were gone.

That was right after Logan discovered Alex's right-hand man, Reginald, had betrayed him. According to Logan, Alex became "slightly barmy and not like himself" when he found out about Reginald's betrayal. The man had despised Alex, secretly, but I don't know all the details of what happened.

I might've thought Reginald's disloyalty made Alex cagey, but even while we were a couple, he'd possessed that secretive nature around other people. With me, he'd been different. More relaxed. More...human. These days, he never lets his guard down for even one second. He probably sleeps with one eye open and a gun under his pillow.

Logan told me about that too. Alex has a gun.

What is he so afraid of?

I'm rummaging around in the refrigerator when Alex walks into the kitchen. He's put on clothes—gray slacks, a pale-tan dress shirt, and brown socks and shoes. With the top button of his shirt undone, he looks like the sexiest professor ever.

"You don't need to do that," he says, shooing me away from the fridge. "I'll make you breakfast."

"But I don't want to inconvenience you."

"You're staying in my house." He peers into the fridge. "I might be a Limey Louse, but I take care of my guests."

Limey Louse. That's another of my insulting nicknames for him. I never meant for him to hear those names, but Logan told Alex every one of the terms I'd invented to describe him. Well, I can't blame Logan. I'd spouted those epithets whenever anyone mentioned the man I'd once loved in America.

Every time Alex repeats one of those nicknames, I swallow hard to keep the acid boiling in my gut from rising into my throat.

"Wait in the dining room," he says, his gaze still on the contents of the refrigerator. "I'll bring your breakfast to you."

I glance at the large marble island in the center of the kitchen and the stools lined up on the far side of it. "Why don't we eat here? It's cozier."

He jerks his head toward me, his eyes unblinking. "Cozy? You'd better watch it, Cat. I might start to think you like me."

A playful smirk played on his lips when he spoke the last part.

A wee shiver of delight ripples through me. God, how I used to love the way he teased me. Ever since I first saw him again last year, I've hated it when Alex smirks at me that way. Well, maybe I secretly loved it. He seems the most like the man I knew before, the man I worshiped, when he smiles like that.

But ever since that day, I've refused to admit it even to myself.

Time to grow up, Cat, and act like the mature adult you're supposed to be. Don't let him goad you into getting angry.

Right. No more giving him what he wants. To unravel Alex Thorne, I need all my wits about me.

I veer around the island and perch on a stool, my arms folded on the marble surface. "I always liked watching you cook. You're very efficient and expert at it."

He tenses for the briefest moment, but I can't see his expression, with his back turned to me. "Are you complimenting me? I must have misheard you."

Despite the breezy sarcasm in his tone, he hasn't moved one millimeter.

After another few seconds of stone-stillness, he gathers ingredients and sets them on the island. Next, he chooses a frying pan from the pots and pans hanging from hooks above the island.

I watch him crack eggs, beat them, and pour them into the heated pan to make omelets. He moves with precision and grace, spinning around to grab the saltshaker off the counter and dropping cheese and vegetables into the omelet before expertly folding it. He repeats the process to make another omelet, all while toasting bread and laying out silverware on the island.

He sets a plate in front of me. "Your breakfast, milady."

"Thank you." I bend forward a little to sniff the aromas wafting up from my omelet. "It smells heavenly."

Alex retrieves his plate and sits down on the stool beside me.

We eat in silence.

Maybe it should feel awkward, considering the tension between us and the fact we haven't spent any real time together since our reunion at Dùn-dubhan. I'd glare at him every time we were in the same room, and he would smirk and say something rude to me. Now, we sit in his kitchen, in his home, enjoying a delicious breakfast together.

"This is wonderful," I tell him after I've eaten half of my omelet. "You're an even better chef than I remember."

"At least I've improved in one way."

There he goes again, with that breezy sarcasm.

I take a bite of toast and chew it, swallowing before I speak. "You've improved in other ways too."

"Have I?" He slides a forkful of egg, cheese, and vegetables into his mouth.

"Aye." Turning toward him slightly, I study his face, but I can't deduce anything from his bland expression. "You've grown more muscles. It suits you. No wonder all the college lasses drool over you."

He eyes me sideways, his lips curled up at the corners in a slight smirk. "I haven't noticed you drooling."

"I'm not a college lass anymore." I lean in a touch. "But I used to be completely infatuated with you. I would've done anything you wanted."

"The way I remember it, you *did* do anything I wanted. Many times."

"Yes, and I loved every second of it."

Something like a growl rumbles in his throat, resonating through his chest, while he sets down his fork and turns his face to me. "Careful, Catriona. I might take that as an invitation to seduce you."

Every time he says my full name, Catriona, it sends a wicked little thrill through me. The husky tone of his voice. The way he seems to relish speaking my name. The way his lips move when he does say it.

Yes, I still want him. Lust for him. Hunger for his body.

He finishes off his omelet and gets up to clear the dishes.

I should help, but I can't stop staring at him, can't move, paralyzed by the thought that keeps surfacing in my mind over and over.

Maybe I should let him seduce me.

After he places everything in the dishwasher, he faces me again. Leaning back against the sink, he dries his hands with a dish cloth. "So, what's on your agenda today?"

Are we really going to have a normal conversation? It feels odd, but somehow pleasant too.

"I don't officially start work until next Monday," I say, "so I've decided to sit in on some of the classes taught by my new coworkers. The other faculty in the humanities department. I haven't taught adults since I was a graduate teaching assistant. It'll do me good to see how the professionals do it."

And it doesn't help my nerves to know I got this job only because Alex convinced the dean to hire me.

"You'll do fine," Alex says. "Better than fine. You are a bright, capable woman who manages to keep her enormous, testy brothers in line. You can handle college students."

I gawp at him, stunned by his compliment. It sounds like the most honest thing he's said to me since our hostile reunion at Dùndubhan.

Either that or he lies better than anyone in the universe.

"We'd better go," he announces. "Or I'll be late for my first class."

One minute, he's annoying me. The next, he pays me a wonderful compliment. Unraveling the mystery of Alex might take longer than I thought. But I'm in it for the duration. However long it takes, I will ferret out the truth about Alex Thorne.

Chapter Seven

Alex

Catriona and I part ways in the parking lot at Thensmore, where she heads to the administration building to fill out more paperwork and I veer toward the humanities building. After my first class of the day, I sequester myself in my office to grade papers, work on an article for a journal, and fantasize about Cat.

All right, maybe I spend most of the morning doing the latter.

How am I meant to react to having her in my home? Yes, I arranged it that way. I've gone to a bloody lot of trouble to get her in Moirai House, but now I don't know what to do with her. Shag her, of course. What else? What did I hope to gain with my scheming?

Cat asked me that very question on the day she arrived in Montana.

And I still have no answer for it.

What does it matter why? I've done it, she's here, and I plan to take full advantage of that fact. In what way, I've asked myself a thousand times this morning. Take full advantage of her body, naturally. But there might be something else, a secret even I can't unlock.

Or maybe I'm afraid of what the answer might be.

No, that's *not* it. Afraid? Me? Never. As I told Serena and Logan nine months ago, nothing frightens me.

Certainly not Catriona MacTaggart.

Ten minutes before noon, I'm relaxing in my chair, the one I bought and hauled into my office on campus so I could have an actually comfortable piece of furniture on which to rest my arse. It's leather, of course. The butter-soft sort. Expensive, ostentatious, and unnecessary too. Which explains why I had to have it.

I lean my head back and close my eyes, intending to ponder my lecture for this afternoon. I've prepared one about ancient Greek weapons. How bloody boring. Though I considered lecturing on sex in the ancient world, I discarded the idea. The last time I'd done that, four of my fellow faculty members filed complaints about the "noise" and "vulgarity" emanating from my lecture hall.

The lot of them are prudes. Irritating, mentally stunted prudes.

Naturally, thinking about a naughty lecture makes me think of Cat. Her voluptuous body. Those lips I tasted again for the first time in twelve years. How hard I came in the shower while picturing her naked, imagining the sounds she'll make when I finally have her under me. Or over me. Or in any position I can convince her to try, as long as she's naked.

My cock loves the idea. It's grown so hard that it aches from a need I can't satisfy. Not quite yet, at least. I reach down to grasp the button on my trousers, about to unhook it and slide my hand in there to relieve the pressure.

And of course, since the Fates despise me, Cat walks into my office right then.

Yes, I'm the sort of bloke who has a wank in his office with the door wide open.

Maybe I would've closed it before I really got going. Maybe.

Catriona flumps onto the chair across the desk from me. A mischievous little smile tugs at her lips, and her breathtaking blue eyes glint in the sunshine pouring in through the window. The light seems to gild her skin and her hair, transforming her into a golden apparition of Aphrodite.

Oh bloody hell. What, have I turned into a lovestruck idiot? Comparing Catriona to an apparition of the Greek love goddess. *For pity's sake, man, get a grip.*

"It's lovely to see you," I say, maintaining my calm demeanor in spite of my idiotic thoughts. "But why are you here?"

"To see you."

My pulse speeds up.

No, it does not. That thumping in my ears must be air pressure.

"How sweet, Catnip," I say, smiling. "You missed me."

"Catnip?" She wrinkles her nose. "Please donnae ever call me that again."

"Why not? It's a perfect nickname."

She tilts her head to the side, studying me with those luminous eyes. "Why do you keep trying to annoy me?"

"What?"

"Don't pretend you're an eejit. That's how I know when you're lying."

"Maybe I had no intention of annoying you. And in case you're wondering, I'm not irritated in the least that you implied I'm an idiot, in your charming Scots way."

Her gaze sharpens on me, like a well-honed knife driven straight into my forehead and deep into my brain. "Stop doing that."

"What?"

"You're being evasive again."

"Am I?" I rock my chair, hands linked over my lap to hide my erection. "What if I'm unaware of what I'm doing?"

"Bollocks. You always know exactly what you're doing." She rises and approaches my desk, leaning over it, her hands flat on the desktop. "Why do you always couch your responses in 'maybe' and 'what if'? Why cannae ye ever tell the truth?"

"It's never that simple." I sit forward, my face inches away from hers. "Why don't you scurry home to bonnie Scotland? If I'm such an irritating, untruthful bastard, why haven't you left yet?"

Instead of answering, she leans in more, peering into my eyes from a centimeter away.

Her scrutiny makes my skin itch.

"What are you doing?" I ask.

"They say the eyes are the windows to the soul." She tips her head left and right, still boring her gaze into mine. "I'm searching for yours."

"I haven't got one, remember? I'm the Soulless Sassenach."

She straightens, sighing. "I should never have made up all those stupid names for you. I'm sorry."

For the first time in longer than I can remember, I have no flippant response to offer. My brain can't summon any words at all. Catriona apologized. To me.

Her lips tick upward into a charming smile. "A miracle has happened. Alex Thorne is speechless."

"Not speechless." Just because I have no fucking idea what to say to her doesn't mean I'm incapable of speech. I spoke two words, didn't I? There, I'm not speechless. Now that the verbal pump is primed, more syllables flow from me. "You apologized, and I feel rightfully stunned by this turn of events. Wouldn't you rather whack me on the head with a book or punch me in the gut?"

She keeps smiling, like she's discovered a wonderful secret and knows exactly how she wants to use it against me.

I snatch up a book and thrust it at her, realizing too late it's a slender telephone directory. "Here. Beat me with this."

Cat laughs at me. "I love it. You're confused and can't figure out what to say." She bends over my desk again and pats my cheek. "It's adorable, Alex."

Why didn't I grab the unabridged dictionary? Maybe then she would've believed I'm not one bit affected by her.

I toss the phone book onto the desk and make a noise that might be a growl, or possibly a snarl, then I slump back in my chair. No one has ever affected me the way she does—now. When I knew her before, she hadn't done this to me. I'm not at all sure I like it. Being off balance is...disorienting.

At least this bizarre encounter with Cat deflated my cock. I can walk into the lecture hall without being arrested for indecency.

"I have to prepare for a class," I inform her. "You'll need to find another way to amuse yourself."

Her smile broadens into a grin. "I know. I'm sitting in on your lecture."

"My—Why?"

"Because I like this new side of you, the confused and speechless man. He's so much more likable than the evasive, annoying version of you."

I open my mouth but decide against speaking. It seems likely to get me into more trouble. I usually like trouble, but not this kind. She's dangerously close to figuring me out, at least in part, and uncovering the secrets I don't want her to find.

"Go on," I say, waving toward the door. "Get out of my office."

"Yes, Dr. Thorne." She whirls around and marches to the doorway, her hips swaying in a deliberate attempt to tease me with that body. On the threshold, she pauses to look back at me. "I'll see you at two o'clock, Dr. Thorne."

Why the blazes does she keep calling me that? It's rousing my cock again.

"Yes, whatever," I say, pretending to study the papers on my desk.

She leaves, and I sink back in my chair, eyes closed. Cat intends to audit my class. If I want to be vindictive about it, I'll switch to the sex lecture. That will serve her right.

Or get me arrested. Is it illegal to have an iron-hard erection in the middle of a lecture hall?

I'm about to find out, because I've made up my mind.

Oh yes, if Catriona wants to audit my class, she'll get an earful—and an eyeful. What a bloody brilliant idea. First, I need to run home and get a few props. Then...

You're in for it now, Catnip.

Chapter Eight

Catriona

After leaving Alex, I go back to my new office and start organizing it. I don't have files yet, so all I can do is rearrange the pens and pencils someone has left for me and flip through my new desk calendar to mark the days when I have classes to teach. Once I've done that, I lean back in my chair and try to convince myself the past few days haven't been a dream. I'm teaching. Living in America. In Alex's house.

I feel like pinching myself to make sure I'm awake, but I stop short of doing that. Why does everything these days seem unreal?

Because of Alex.

And I can't decide if he fashes me because I despise him, or if it's because I still feel something for him.

The phone on my desk rings, giving me an excuse to stop analyzing my emotions. I'm half sitting on my desk, facing the doorway, and I watch students ambling by outside while I pick up the phone.

Before I can speak, a familiar voice says, "Are you all right, Cat? I heard a rumor Alex Thorne has you locked in his basement. Do I need to fly over there and save you?"

A laugh tries to burst out of me, but I stifle it, resulting in a spluttering noise. "Good morning, Lachlan. It's so nice to hear from my mature older brother who respects me and trusts my judgment."

"Of course I trust you. It's that scunner of a Brit who's up to no good. I've heard he locked you in his basement."

"Who told you that rumor about Alex? He doesn't have a basement." As far as I know, but I won't admit to Lachlan that there's any doubt about that. Overprotective brothers are a damn nuisance.

"Logan suggested it."

I do laugh now, which makes Lachlan huff.

"Why is it funny," Lachlan says, "that Logan told me how depraved Alex Thorne is?"

"Because Logan was having you on." I pause when another bout of laughter takes hold and wait for it to subside. "Logan and Alex are friends. Our cousin has a strange way of bonding with the family, and I'm sure he expected you'd realize he was making a joke."

"I still don't understand Logan. Evan says it was all those years in MI6 that made Logan strange, but I think he's just off his head."

"You like Logan. Admit it, Lachie. We all know it's true."

"What have I told you about calling me that name?" He drops his voice to a lower, harsher tone that's meant to cow me, though it fails. "I said donnae be calling me that ever again."

"Aye, and you've been saying that all my life. Hasn't worked yet, has it?"

"How can you sound happy? You're working in the same building as Alex Thorne."

Lachlan never, never, never says just "Alex". He always says "Alex Thorne." If Lachie knew Alex's middle name, he'd use that too, like Alex is a serial killer. And why do serial killers always have three names, anyway?

"Relax, Lachlan," I say. "I'm fine. Alex is not doing unspeakable things to me in his basement or in a dungeon or in the potting shed."

I have no idea if Alex has a potting shed, but that's not the point.

"You're sure?" my brother asks. "I have a jet, so I can fly over there—"

"No, Lachie, don't you dare. I am an adult, not a bairn. Let me handle Alex in my own way." I might be eleven years younger than Lachlan, but I am not a child.

Movement catches my attention, and I glance at the doorway.

Alex stands there, his expression unreadable, and slides his tongue over his lips like he's staring at the most decadent dessert on earth.

He's looking at me.

"If you're sure," Lachlan says, "then I'll hold off on flying to America. For now."

"Thank you."

Alex stalks up to my desk, plucks the phone from my hand, and smacks it down into its cradle.

"What do you think you're doing?" I ask, flashing him a scowl. "I was talking to my brother."

He throws an arm around my waist and hauls me into him. I don't get a chance to speak. Alex grasps the back of my head, tips it backward, and crushes his mouth to mine. I stay stiff and unresponsive for a few seconds, while he holds his lips to mine with firm pressure, his arm pinning me to his strong body and his hand ensuring I can't jerk my head away.

Not that I want to. I should. But I don't want to, and I can't move.

"Mm," I moan, as a breath rushes out of me. My every muscle softens, my body warms from the top of my head all the way down to my toes, and a silky, liquid heat blossoms between my thighs. I clutch his shirt, pulling myself closer to him, and open my mouth. He plunges his tongue inside, but instead of devouring me like a ravenous beast, he explores my mouth with slow, sensual strokes, like we have all the time in the world to enjoy each other. I moan again and tug him even closer, my fingers clenched in his shirt so tight they start to ache, but I don't care.

The phone rings, though the sound barely penetrates the haze of desire swirling around me, inside me, blocking out everything else. I don't hear the ringing anymore. Whatever it was, it doesn't matter now. Alex wraps his arms around me, widens his stance, and draws me even closer. My legs are between his, and his erection forms a steel bar against my belly. I want him to take me right here, right now, on my desk with the door open. I want it like I've never wanted anything before. I need it. I need him—inside me, thrusting while he consumes my mouth.

A sensation, hot and sweet and intoxicating, shimmers through me.

He moves away, separating our bodies. Breathing hard, he runs a hand over his jaw.

"What was that?" I ask, my voice barely a whisper.

"A kiss." He almost growls the words. "What did you think it was? A bloody handshake?"

I can see how aroused he is, thanks to the bulge in his trousers, and I remember how unquenched lust always used to make him testy. And it still does.

"No," I say, "I didn't think that. I meant why did you kiss me like that? And you made me hang up on my brother, which is not polite. Ye cannae walk into my office and kiss me like that without saying a word."

"Why not? I don't recall hearing you tell me to stop."

His voice still sounds rough and edgy.

Maybe I shouldn't chastise him right now. Besides, I loved that kiss.

Alex lets out a long breath, seeming to shed his edgy mood along with the air in his lungs. He gives me that look of amused indifference. "Well, I've got that out of my system. Cheers, Catriona."

He walks out of the room.

If I were American, I'd probably be offended by the way he said "cheers," since my American sisters-in-law didn't understand that one the first time they'd heard Alex say it. But to a Brit, "cheers" is like saying goodbye. I still don't like that he dismissed me that way, and dismissed that kiss, but I no longer believe his offhanded ways.

Oh no, Alex Thorne, you won't get away with that anymore.

Chapter Nine

Alex

I head to the lecture hall at ten to two since I don't like being late. Early is better. It gives me a chance to observe my students and judge their state of mind before I begin my lecture. I'm not a psychologist, but I can tell from the students' expressions and the way they talk whether they'll behave while I speak.

Gus Hooper has given me the big room, the one that's also used by the drama classes. He knows I draw a crowd. More students sign up for my courses than for any other class in the humanities department. Even the acting seminars don't attract an audience as big as mine.

Yes, I'm bloody proud of that fact.

Though I enter the venue, I'm hiding behind the curtains that block off the rear of the stage. They hide the equipment and backdrops used by the theater classes. I enjoy peering through the small gap between the halves of the curtains, observing my students as they begin to trickle into the hall.

All right, I'm also watching for Catriona.

Five minutes after I arrive, I see her.

Students brush past Cat while she hesitates just inside the double doors that lead into the hall.

This lecture space is enormous, with row after row of seats broken into three sections by two aisles. The floor slopes downward in a gentle grade toward the stage, where a lectern awaits the lecturer—which would be me.

Cat used to love sitting in on my classes. And I loved seeing her face in the crowd. Her smiling, attentive face. It had always made me feel...I don't know. Like I'd discovered a previously unknown civilization and cracked the code of its never-before-seen language.

While the students take seats as close to the stage as possible, swiftly filling in the rows, Cat slinks into the shadowed area behind the last row at the back of the hall. Maybe she hopes I won't notice her. No chance of that. Though she loiters in the shadows, I can still see her silhouette. Knowing she's watching me gives me a strange sensation, like I've gulped down half a bottle of vodka.

Catriona MacTaggart has always intoxicated me.

But not in front of my students.

I step back, so I can't see between the curtains anymore. But I know she's out there. Well, I did change my lecture for today because I wanted her to hear it. And see it. And...hear and see me.

None of that means anything. I like the idea of shocking Cat, that's all. She's doing her best to turn my world upside-down, so I'm responding in kind.

This morning, when she'd come to my bedroom and I'd dropped that towel, her expression and body language had evidenced the truth. She wants me, and I want to have her one more time before I send her back to Scotland. End of story.

When all the students have taken their seats and filled up the hall, my teaching assistant, Todd, trots onto the stage and announces, "Dr. Thorne will be here in a few minutes. He has a special surprise for all of you today."

Do I ever. *Are you ready for this, Cat?* All the dirty things I used to whisper in her ear may pale in comparison to what I'm about to do. I've given a version of this lecture before, but I spent the last hour giving it a little extra spice.

Maybe more than a little.

If I get arrested or fired or both, it will be worth it to see the look on Cat's face.

Todd hurries off the stage.

All the lights go out, and for a moment, everyone—including me—waits in the dark. Then a single spotlight flares on, aimed at the lectern.

Everyone stops talking. The silence seems as deep as an abyssal plain at the bottom of the Atlantic Ocean.

Yes, it's overly dramatic. But I love a bit of drama. So do my students. This is how I keep them engaged while teaching them about history and the science of archaeology. Honestly, that stuff is rather dull on its own.

I push through the curtain and saunter up to the lectern, which has a microphone attached to it to ensure everyone hears me. The spotlight sheds its backwash onto Cat, where she still hides in the dark alcove. Her hand flies to her mouth, a gesture that I'm sure masks a smile.

My students gasp or laugh or simply look stunned.

Well, I am wearing a pink kilt with glitter-coated pink flowers sewn onto it.

Catriona had given me this kilt on the day last year when I'd first seen her again after eleven years apart. Logan and Serena had essentially abducted me, dragging me to Scotland and to the MacTaggart family Highland games, held in a field behind Rory's castle. Anyone who participates in the games has to wear a kilt. Naturally, Rory and his brothers let Cat choose a kilt for me, since I didn't own one. She had, no doubt, hoped I would be embarrassed.

Was I? Of course not. I do not get embarrassed. Not even a pink kilt can accomplish that feat.

Now, I stand at the edge of the stage, lit by that solitary spotlight, wearing the pink kilt—wearing it for Cat. I survey my students, trying to get a final read on their moods. Their shock over my kilt has faded, and most of them seem genuinely interested in whatever I might say.

"Look at that! He's wearing a skirt!"

The first heckler turns out to be a scrawny twat in the third row who wears thick glasses and is illuminated in the ambient glow of the spotlight.

A brawny tosser in the first row half rises from his seat to laugh and say, "Always knew you were a sissy boy. Where's your tiara, princess?"

This isn't the first time I've been harassed by obnoxious children. But I'd hoped for something more creative when the taunts started.

I lay one hand on the lectern, aiming my gaze directly at the tosser who called me "princess." I stare at him for several seconds, doing nothing more threatening than lifting one brow. Still, the boy glances around, his expression anxious, then drops down in his seat.

Yes, it's that easy to silence an irritating buffoon.

"Good afternoon," I say to the crowd. "Would anyone else care to speak up before I begin the lecture?"

Silence. Deep, rapt silence.

I love this part, when the room falls silent and I have their undivided attention.

"Good." I move behind the lectern and place my hands on either side of it, my fingers curled over the edges. "Let's begin. Today's lesson focuses on sexual practices in the ancient world. Or, as I like to call it, The Forbidden History of Shagging and Wanking."

Some students laugh, some gaze at me enraptured, while others look uncomfortable. No one leaves. Even the embarrassed ones want to hear what I might say next.

A solitary hand raises in the front row.

"What is it?" I ask. I smirk when I add, "I haven't gotten to the naughty bits yet."

The lass who raised her hand asks, in a tentative voice, "Will this be on the final exam?"

"Naturally." I wink at her. "Take copious notes, love. I'm sure they'll come in handy outside of school too."

The girl is blushing.

I slant toward the microphone and lower my voice to a deeper register. "Before we begin, a word of warning. If sex and explicit language offend you, please walk out the door. It won't affect your grade."

No one moves. I wait a minute, maybe longer, but every student stays put.

"All right, then," I say. "We need a bit of graphic imagery to excite your... curiosity and stimulate...your minds."

"Oh yes, please!" shouts a female voice.

A girl in the second row fans herself with a sheet of paper, but I have no idea if she's the one who shouted.

I reach under the lectern to pull an item out of the shelf hidden inside it. Raising the item, I ask the class, "Anyone care to guess what this artifact represents?"

"A headless dachshund," a freckle-faced female suggests.

"Sorry, no." I shake the artifact, making the bells attached to it clang. "This is a *fascinum*, a wind chime in the shape of..." I grin like the devil himself because I always love this bit. "A winged penis with three heads and two legs."

The tosser who'd called me a sissy guffaws and slaps his leg. "Damn, you're a real perv, aren't you? Three-headed dicks? I thought this was a history lesson, not show and tell from your toolbox of freaky shit."

He guffaws some more.

Idiots always think they're hilarious.

"The *fascinum*," I say, "was a powerful totem in ancient Rome. This one is a wind chime that people used to hang in their homes to ward off disease and promote fertility." I hold out the *fascinum* as if I'm offering it to the tosser. "Here, you probably need this more than I do. Maybe it will improve your virility. Then again, it may not be powerful enough to accomplish that feat."

Laughter echoes through the hall.

The arrogance floods out of the tosser, who slumps in his seat.

I raise my hand, and the audience settles down, quiet again.

"Romans did more than hang flying penises in their homes," I say, hanging the *fascinum* from the microphone stand. "Sex was an important part of life in the Roman Empire, and they weren't shy about it. They loved erotica." I pull out the remote control for the large screen that was revealed when the curtains parted and click the button to start my slideshow. "Take a good, long look at this one."

"Is that guy killing a goat?" a boy wearing glasses asks.

"No. Look between his legs."

The young man pushes his glasses up and squints at the screen. His mouth twists this way and that while he studies the image. Suddenly, his eyes go wide. He glances around like he's done something wicked, then slowly raises his hand.

"Yes?" I ask.

"That, uh, looks like the hairy-legs guy is, uh...with the goat..." The student pushes up his glasses again, which I decide is a nervous gesture. "He's sort of..."

"Spit it out. There's nothing to be ashamed of." I wait a few seconds before I decide the boy can't make himself speak the words. I lean closer to the microphone. "That's the god Pan getting a leg over with a goat. Or as my Scots friends might say, he's having a poke at it."

Everyone stares at me. Ah well, I am in America—and these are college students. I can't expect them to grasp my meaning without an explicit explanation.

"He's fucking the goat."

"Ew," a female voice says, though I can't see who spoke. "That's, like, so gross."

"The god Pan is half goat himself, so let's give him the benefit of the doubt on this, eh?" I smile and wink at my audience. "Moving on... Something a bit more mainstream, but no less titillating." I tap the button on the remote, changing the slide. "Romans loved a good shag. This lovely lady and two gents are enjoying a three-way."

I glance back at the screen and the image of a bas-relief carving. It depicts a man lying on his back on a chaise longue with a woman on top of him. A third man stands behind the woman. Both blokes have their cocks inside the woman, who seems to be enjoying the attention.

"Look at the ecstasy on her face," I say in my wickedest voice. "This woman is getting it at both ends and loving every second of it, by the looks of things. Not sure if that pose is physically achievable in reality, but if anyone wants to try it and report back to me, I'll give you extra credit."

A pretty redhead waves her hand, grinning at me. "I'll volunteer for that, if you're one of the guys."

Several girls raise their hands and shout, almost at the same instant, "Me too!"

Maybe I should've thought that through before I suggested it. Spur of the moment announcements often get me into trouble.

"That's flattering, but I'm taken." Why I say that, I don't know. I suppose I say it strictly to discourage them from the idea of having a threesome with me. That will definitely get me fired. "Moving on… The Romans didn't invent hot sex. Take this image from Greece, circa fifth century BCE."

I click to the next slide. A wine jug decorated in the typical Greek shades of black and orange depicts a woman bent over at the waist while a man takes her from behind.

"This one is believed to show a prostitute and her client," I say. "Yes, it really is the oldest profession. But my, does that gent look like he's getting his money's worth."

I glance at the alcove, but I can't even see Cat's silhouette anymore. She must have moved back into the deepest shadows. I don't believe for one second that she's left the hall.

"Erotic art has been a part of human society for a very long time," I say. "Even before written language existed, randy men and women found ways to arouse themselves with naughty artwork. Like this piece from the sixth millennium BCE." I switch to another slide. "What do you think that is?"

My students squint at the photo of a sculpture that has two ball-shaped elements side by side and another, longer element protruding from them.

"It's a pair of tits," someone shouts.

"No, that's not it." I pluck the microphone from its stand, walking away from the lectern to point at the elements in the photograph. "These are two testicles, and that's the head of a rather small penis. The model for this might not have been well-endowed, but his cock is immortalized for eternity."

A young woman raises her hand. "Um, was that a decorative thing? Like the wind chime?"

"Possibly." I walk to the edge of the stage, kneeling and looking straight into the eyes of the student who'd spoken. "But for all we know, those ancient ladies used sculptures like this one to pleasure themselves without the aid of a man."

The girl who'd asked the question flutters her lashes at me. "Where can I get one of those?"

Chuckling, I stand and move back behind the lectern. "Maybe the next slide will give you some other ideas." I hit the button on the remote. "This woman is sitting on an upside-down vase, using its conical base for, shall we say, an off-label use. Who wants to take a guess about what this lovely woman is doing?"

"Relieving her constipation?" a male voice suggests.

"Cleaning her vagina!" another male voice offers.

I smile, doing my best to look like a wolf about to devour his prey. Students really are so easy to fool. "You're close, mate. She's not cleaning herself, though, she's enjoying herself."

Everyone seems confused by that statement. Maybe I do love confusing my students more than I should.

I hold the microphone close to my mouth and speak in a low and sensual voice. "Ladies and gentlemen, this woman who lived over two thousand years ago is showing us how randy Egyptian girls pleasured themselves." I give my audience a few seconds to absorb the image and what I've said. Then I announce, "She's masturbating."

Gasps echo throughout the hall.

The tosser who'd called me "princess" pumps his fists in the air and shouts, "Woo-hoo! We get class credit for watching porn!"

"Sit down," I command. "We haven't even gotten to the best part."

The lad sits down.

And I glance at the alcove again, wondering how my performance is affecting Cat. It's making me want to run back there and fuck her like mad. But I have a lecture to finish and young minds to corrupt—ah, inform.

So I continue.

Chapter Ten

Catriona

Alex continues his slideshow of ancient erotica, but I can't focus on what he's saying. His voice, his body language, the look on his face—all these things prove how much he loves teaching. He excites his students even when he's not talking about sex. Once he dives into the topic of excavations and the dating of artifacts, he still keeps his audience enthralled.

I'm enthralled too, like I had been years ago.

When I'd wandered into the lecture hall earlier, a crowd of bright-eyed students had been chattering away as they entered the huge room. They carried various kinds of rucksacks and computer bags, and when they took their seats, they got out their textbooks and notepads. I'm sure none of them had a clue that Alex changed his lecture. I doubt the subjects he's discussed today are in any textbook.

It's been a long time since I set foot on a university campus. Longer still since I was a student. My cousin Iain talked me into teaching a few one-off adult education courses at the University of the Highlands and the Islands, where he's on the faculty. Iain was blacklisted for years thanks to one nasty family that punished him for loving Rae, one of his students. Iain got his job back a couple years ago. Not because a sneaky bastard connived to make it happen for him, but because he deserved it.

Me? I got my new job because of Alex Thorne. My anger over the sneaky bastard's conniving has waned to a low simmer of irritation, but I don't know if I can forgive him for what he's done, now or in the past. I hope once I understand him, his motivations and his desires, I'll be able to lay the ghost of our past relationship to rest once and for all.

And move on with my life. Without Alex interfering.

Without Alex, full stop.

But as I watch him perform for his audience, those old feelings rise up inside me again. Do I want to be rid of him? I lay a hand over my belly as nausea roils in my gut. Why should the thought of getting rid of Alex make me queasy? I suppose I need to understand my own motivations and desires too, before I can cleanse Alex from my life for good.

This lecture hall is enormous. Naturally, Alex needs an enormous room, since he attracts students like flies to honey. He has everything going for him—looks, charisma, intelligence, encyclopedic knowledge of the ancient world, and a talent for turning his lectures into crowd-pleasing events.

I used to love watching him teach.

Maybe I still do.

While the students had swiftly filled in every seat in every row, I had slunk into the shadowed area behind the last row at the back of the hall. Let Alex wonder where I am. Let him think maybe I decided not to come after all. I can't help feeling a wee thrill at the prospect of him not knowing if I'm watching.

But a larger thrill, one that sizzles on my skin, overtook me when I realized that any moment I'd be seeing him in action again for the first time in twelve years. I used to be mesmerized whenever he delivered a lesson. I never took one of his courses, but after we became involved, I would sneak into his classroom just to watch him. After class, I'd beg him to take me to a private place, anyplace as long as it was nearby, and make love to me. Sometimes, we went to not-so-private places. But always, experiencing his lectures drove me wild with lust for him.

That will not happen today. I'm older, more mature, and not enthralled by him anymore.

A memory of this morning flares in my mind. Alex naked and gripping a towel in one hand to keep himself covered. Until he dropped the towel.

Stop thinking about that.

I still can't believe he wore the pink kilt. I made it for my brother Rory as a joke, knowing the Steely Solicitor would never wear such a thing, and Rory passed it on to Gavin, my sister Jamie's American husband. Jamie told me she loves seeing Gavin wear silly things, because his audacity and lack of shame make her "as randy as a wild mare in heat."

Honestly, I didn't need to know that about my sister.

I had reclaimed the pink kilt a few months ago when I arrived at the MacTaggart Highland games to find Alex there. Since he was Logan's guest,

I couldn't tell my brothers to drag Alex off the property and dump him in the nearest rubbish heap. So instead, I took my revenge by asking Rory to get the pink kilt. If Alex insisted on participating in the games, he needed to dress the part. But why should he have a manly kilt created with the Mac-Taggart clan tartan? No, he deserved an embarrassing pink one.

But Alex hadn't been embarrassed. He'd worn the kilt proudly.

Seeing him like that, I'd felt...something. I don't know what it was.

When he lost his grip on his caber, and the tree trunk had crashed down on him, pinning him to the ground...

My throat constricts at the memory of that moment. Aye, in my own thoughts I can admit to the truth. I'd been terrified Alex was seriously injured.

Until he ruined the moment by asking if I would be his physical therapist.

Now, he stands at the edge of the stage, lit by a solitary spotlight, once again proudly wearing the pink, glittery kilt. He holds his chin up, surveying his students with a confident smile, his entire demeanor infused with that indefinable essence of Alex, while he continues his lecture.

I clutch my hands to my belly, though not from nausea this time. My tummy flutters like a thousand tiny butterflies swarm inside me. All the hairs on my arms and at my nape tingle and stiffen. I can't deny it. Alex is magnificent. I want to run onto that stage and kiss him, then rip off that kilt and—

No. Oh God, no. I am not still infatuated with Alex Thorne. He's gorgeous and sexy, and I'm not immune to that aspect of his charms. He's also a liar and the most secretive, conniving person I've ever met. I do not like that part of him.

I will never have sex with him. Solving the mystery of Alex, I can do that. But no sex. None.

My body voices its opinion about my "no sex with Alex" decree when he resumes his slideshow by revealing his favorite image, one I've seen before because he loved to show me this bit of ancient erotica—and he even convinced me to try reenacting the image with him. Aye, that had been an interesting night.

The image shows a temple carving of a couple enjoying a poke. The woman is bent over and grasping her ankles while the man takes her from behind. It isn't the most bizarre of the Kama Sutra statuary, but it's always been Alex's favorite. Seeing the image now, I can't stop my mind from conjuring memories of that night with him, the most erotic and intense night we'd ever shared. We re-created more than one Kama Sutra position before we fell asleep in each other's arms.

I let the memories pour through me like warm, spiced rum, intoxicating me with a mental reenactment of everything Alex did to me that night and the incredible pleasure we gave each other.

Suddenly, I realize the students are filing out of the lecture hall. All but a handful of them have left already.

Alex leaps off the stage and saunters up the aisle toward me, passing a group of students who are having an animated conversation. Everyone else has gone, but that one small group lingers halfway down the aisle.

I move out of the dark spot at the back of the hall, standing at the wall beside the doors.

He stops in front of me, his gaze traveling over my body from head to toe and back again, his lips forming a hungry smirk. "Have I told you how much I love those trousers and that blouse? You look good enough to ravish."

And his tone of voice suggests he wants to do exactly that. Right now.

"Your lecture was very good," I say. "I'm impressed."

His smirk slides into a suggestive smile as he moves closer, standing near enough I can smell his spicy aftershave. "But did it make you randy?"

Aye, it has done that. *He* has done that. He's still doing it.

Why can't I get over this lust for him? I convinced myself I had gotten over it for all those years when I didn't see him. Maybe I've been in denial about how often I made myself come while fantasizing about him. That denial was shattered the first time I laid eyes on him again, at Dùndubhan.

Today, my willpower is strained to the brink of snapping.

Even in a pink kilt, Alex Thorne is the hottest man on earth.

The few students who linger in the hall shuffle past us. One lad, the same boy who heckled Alex about being a princess, pauses to glance at his kilt.

"Whoa, dude," the boy says in a snarky tone, "you've got some cojones wearing a sparkly My Little Pony skirt. My baby sister would love it."

Alex ignores the lad, his gaze still locked on me.

The boy notices me, his focus veering to my breasts. "Who are you? And when can I get it on with you?"

"She is Dr. Catriona MacTaggart," Alex says in a cool tone. "And she doesn't take pity on children who can't get a leg over with the bearded cafeteria woman."

A girl who's standing beside the *bod ceann* tugs on his sleeve. "Cut it out, Darren. Don't harass the hot professor."

Darren rolls his eyes. "All you girls are so totally hypnotized by this dweeb in a skirt. When do the guys get a hot woman professor to drool over?"

Alex tips his head down, staring hard at the *bod ceann*. "You're looking at a hot woman professor right now."

He nods toward me.

Darren grins.

"Not that a twat like you has a chance in hell of seducing a woman like her," Alex says. "Move along, boy."

The laddie and his friends exit the hall, snickering and muttering to each other.

And I'm alone with Alex.

He backs me up to the wall, caging me with his hands at either side of my head. "You never answered my question."

"Why should I? Ye donnae answer any of mine."

"Have it your way." He sets a hand on my hip, sliding his fingers inside the waistband of my trousers. "I'll find out the answer for myself."

I know what he's about. I know, and I don't care. His lecture has gotten me randy, not because of the imagery he offered, but because of him. Alex in his full glory, lecturing to an enthralled class, is the single most arousing thing I've ever seen.

"Did I ever tell you," he says, "about the ancient Egyptian woman who wanted a certain man so badly that she paid a priest to cast a sexual binding spell on him? She wanted him to be so overcome with desire for her that he couldn't stand it. Only one thing could cure his affliction."

He slides his fingers further inside my trousers, and further still until his whole hand rests over my knickers, the heel on my mound.

"To stay sane," he murmurs into my ear, "the man had to copulate with the woman every night. You've cast a spell like that on me, haven't you? Nothing will save my sanity except penetrating the soft, slick flesh inside your body."

His fingers tease me right where my taut nub nestles within the slick folds of my sex.

The breath catches in my throat. My nipples shoot hard.

"Yes," he purrs, our faces millimeters apart, his gaze nailed to mine. "You're wet already, aren't you? Wet and aching, desperate for me to make you come. And it's your fault, because you made me want you this much."

He shifts his hand, sliding it inside my knickers, pushing two fingers between my folds. His thumb finds my clitoris, rubbing gently, while his fingers glide up and down, up and down.

I choke back a whimper, already teetering on the edge. I can't stop myself from moving my hips, thrusting into his touch, starved for more, more, more.

Alex drags me into the dark alcove.

His rigid cock tents his kilt, and intense need tightens his features. He shoves me against the wall, pinning me there with his body, his erection trapped against my belly. "I need to fuck you, Catriona. Can't wait any longer."

"Aye." I can't squeeze out any other words. I want him even more than I had years ago, when I thought I could never want any other man as intensely as I craved him. Today, I crave him more. So much I can't breathe or speak or move a muscle.

Here? In the lecture hall? With the doors open?

Alex yanks my trousers and underwear down to my ankles. From his shirt pocket, he produces a condom packet, tears it open with his teeth, and covers himself.

I fight for every heaving breath, my body alive and sizzling with electric tingles that ripple through me in waves and pulse in my sex. Alex. Inside me. After so long apart. I need his cock buried deep in my body, driving me toward a climax I know will devastate me with its power.

He kicks my feet apart, grasps my hips, and plunges inside me.

My mouth falls open, but my voice has abandoned me, leaving me so speechless that I can't even cry out.

"Try to be quiet," he rasps in my ear while he consumes me with slow, decadent thrusts. "I know you can do it. Remember that day in the library?"

Bod an Donais, I remember—and the memory makes me more aroused, more desperate to hit my release and shatter from the bliss only this man knows how to give me. Once, years ago, we found a dark corner deep in the stacks of the library at the university where he worked and where I was a student. He shagged me in that corner, shagged me like I'd never known anyone could. The need to stay quiet made the whole encounter more erotic, more intense, more...everything.

"Hurry," I whisper to him. "Cannae hold out much longer. Alex. Oh..."

"Catriona..."

My name falling from his lips, it pushes me over the edge. I come like a tidal wave breaking on sheer, vertical cliffs, the spray shooting up and over the top, drenching the landscape. I clutch Alex with my arms and my thighs, my knees bending of their own volition while I squelch my rasping cries against his neck as wild, unstoppable waves break inside me and my body grips him again and again.

He buries his face against my neck, muffling his own hoarse shout while he spends himself inside me.

For a moment, we just stand there. Breathing hard. Wrapped around each other. I feel his shaft softening, but I don't want to give up the sensation of him filling me quite yet. How long has it been? Too long. No one makes me feel the way Alex does. No one understands what I want and need the way he does. When it comes to sex, that is. His secretive nature keeps him from giving me the one thing I've prayed for since the day I met him.

Total honesty.

Alex withdraws, taking three steps backward. "You might want to fix your clothes before you walk out of this room."

He turns and leaves me there, tossing the condom into a rubbish bin alongside the doors.

The bastard fucked me and left.

I pull up my trousers and underwear, attempting to calm my pounding heart and ragged breathing.

He ran away.

And the next time I get him alone, he will tell me why.

Chapter Eleven

Alex

I rush back to my office, exchange the kilt for trousers, and collapse into my chair. I'm breathing hard, from fornicating with Cat and from running away. Why did I do that? Because I'd finished with her, that's why. Not because our encounter disturbed me in ways I prefer not to examine too closely. Catriona will always be the most sensual woman I've ever known, and the most incredible shag on earth. Maybe I loved her once, maybe a part of me still does, but that doesn't matter. I'm meant to be alone, and I will not get entangled in any sort of relationship with her.

My desk phone rings.

Lifting my hand, intending to pick up the receiver, I realize my hand is trembling. I squeeze it into a fist until the tremors subside. Sex doesn't normally have this effect on me, but the suddenness of my lust for Catriona must have shot a massive dose of adrenaline through my body. Adrenaline, yes, that's the problem.

I grab the phone. "Dr. Alex Thorne."

"Why have you been ignoring us?" a familiar female voice asks, her accent mirroring mine. "We're so worried about you, dear."

The tension gushes out of me on a huge sigh. "I'm fine, Imogen, don't worry. Why are you calling my office phone? How did you even get this number?"

"I rang the university switchboard and asked for you."

Of course they would give out my office number. Faculty phone numbers are public so students can call us anytime.

"Well, now that you know I'm alive and kicking," I say, "you can go back to knitting or taxidermy or whatever your hobby is today."

She laughs with deep affection. "You sweet, darling boy. Taxidermy? Don't you know by now that you can't scare us away with that sort of talk? You were much worse about it when we first found you, but we helped get you through the transition. Don't slide backward now, after all these years."

Am I backsliding? Possibly. Does it matter? No.

"I have to go," I say. "It's my office hours, and lots of students need to talk to me."

Few students ever come to my office, mostly females, and all determined to seduce me. Even I'm not a big enough wanker to let them have their way. Those nubile coeds are scrumptious, but I can't muster one iota of desire for any of them. Besides, though I might be a monumental arse, even I don't sleep with students.

What do you know? I have one up on Iain MacTaggart. He'd shagged a student in America and gotten run out of the country for it. He was a resident alien at the time, whereas I'm a citizen, so if I ever should decide to sleep with a student, I can't be run out of the country.

"Goodbye," I say, about to pull the phone away from my ear and hang up.

"Don't you dare hang up on me, Al—"

"Stop that this instant. I can tell by your tone of voice that you're about to say my full name. You know I hate it, especially the last bit. And that part isn't even accurate anymore."

The daft woman will give away everything one day, since she seems incapable of biting her tongue.

Imogen sighs. "We miss you, Alex. Please let us visit you. We've never been to your home, not any of them. No matter how many times you move, you will never escape from your past. It's time to stop running and settle down."

"Maybe I will. Sometime."

Never in a million lifetimes. I can't stay in one place for too long. It isn't in my nature, and a man can't change his essential nature no matter how hard he tries.

Not that I have tried.

The fact I've lived in this place for five years has no bearing on the issue.

"All right," she says. "But ring us more often. Next time, we'll both get on the phone. Henry's at the hardware store right now, getting advice on how to install a dishwasher."

"Dishwasher? And you're letting him do it? The nutter will electrocute himself for sure."

"Unless you want to come and help him…"

"I can't. Sorry. Goodbye."

And I hang up on her. She is the only woman, the only person, who can make me feel guilty about anything.

Catriona walks through the open door into my office, halting at the desk. She raises her brows, her chin lifted.

Well, maybe one other woman can inspire a twinge of guilt in me.

But only a twinge. Hardly one at all, in fact. A tiny pinch is more like it.

"Yes?" I say, leaning back in my chair, elbows on the arms and hands linked. "Did you want something else? I'd thought a good, hard poke would do you for a while, but if you need another one—"

"A poke? You said that during your lecture too."

"Isn't that the Scottish term for it? You say it all the time. Serena thinks the term poke is the 'cutest word on earth' for sex. Interestingly, she started out thinking it was crude and—"

"Shut up, Alex." Catriona bends over to stare at me, resting her palms on the desktop. "I know why you ran away like a flaming ersehole, and why you're trying to distract me by havering about the term 'have a poke.' You're not fooling me."

"Aren't I? Guess I'll need to try harder."

"Nothing you say is what it's bummed up to be, which is why I'm ignoring three-fourths of the words that come out of your mouth." She leans against the desk, her lovely arse perched on its edge. "I know you've never been afraid of much, but I know two things that terrify you—intimacy and honesty. That's why you ran off."

"I honestly wanted to fuck you, and having my cock inside you is as intimate as it gets."

"Bollocks. Intimacy involves more than sex." She slants toward me, planting a hand on the desk. "Honesty terrifies you most of all, but you can't have real intimacy without it."

"Well then, it's a bloody good thing I don't want that."

She shakes her head, clucking her tongue. "Alex Thorne, you naughty laddie. Every word that comes out of your mouth is a con, a half-truth, or an evasion. But sooner or later, you'll have to be honest. Don't wait too long to do it."

"Or what?" Why have I asked? I don't care.

Cat stretches her hand out to touch my lips with one finger. "You know what's at stake."

She hops off the desk, squares her shoulders, and marches out the door.

What the bloody hell?

I grab my mobile phone and ring Logan's number.

"What do you want, Alex?" he demands. "I was seconds away from convincing my wife to have a poke in the backyard."

Ah yes, the lovely Serena. Logan is one lucky bastard.

"Serena having sex outdoors?" I say. "She really has adapted to being married to you."

"Aye. Now what did you want?"

I scratch my neck, just inside the collar of my shirt. "Your cousin has lost the plot. Please retrieve her immediately and rush her to the best psychiatric clinic in Scotland."

"My cousin?" Logan falls silent for a moment, then chuckles. "Catriona's getting to you, isn't she?"

"She will drive me insane if you don't do something about it."

"Afraid Cat's your problem now. You lured her to your corner of America, so you have to figure out how to deal with her."

"Maybe Evan will help."

Logan chuckles again. "No MacTaggart will interfere. If Catriona wants to torment you, better learn how to handle it. A bit of the old hochmagandy ought to do the trick."

"Hochmagandy? Catriona told me no one says that anymore."

"When did she say that?"

I squirm in my seat, though I have no idea why. Possibly because I don't know which MacTaggart to believe. "She told me that at Aidan's birthday party, when you forced me to dress like a Scottish stripper, so I decided to act like one. When I suggested hochmagandy, she informed me nobody uses that term anymore. Then she threatened to slap me and called me a bleeding ersehole."

Logan laughs rather loudly this time. "You really do bring out the beast in her. Cat's normally the sweetest lass you'll ever meet."

Maybe she used to be that way, back when I knew her as a naive grad student who adored me. Today, she's determined to grab me by the balls and strangle me with them.

"She must've suffered a complete personality reversal," I tell Logan. "The woman is a menace."

To my sanity. To my libido. To everything I've worked so hard to conceal.

"Forget I called," I say. "Next time, I'll ring the psychic advice line."

"Oh, you donnae need to spend money on that. Call Kirsty instead."

"Wonderful. I can get advice from one of your barmy sisters. What is it everyone calls them? The Witches of Ballachulish?"

"Aye, that's right. They might be barmy, but they've got woman's intuition on their side." He pauses. "Maybe I should tell Cat to talk to them. She's the one who needs to crack you open and rummage around in there."

"Sounds lovely. Thank you for the pep talk, Logan. Next time, I'll just ring your cousin Rory and invite him to come thrash me with a caber."

"No, if you're wanting a thrashing, call me. I know how to batter you without breaking any bones."

"Yes, I'm sure you do. Goodbye, Logan."

I disconnect the call and slump in my chair.

Catriona walks into my office, again.

Before my brain has time to process what's happening, she races up to me, bends over, and kisses me. Her lips linger on mine for several seconds, then she pulls away. Her blue eyes hover so close I can see the faint lines of darker color in them.

Logan called her "the sweetest lass you'll ever meet," and I remember when she was that way. Her sweet smile. Her shyness. The way she blushed whenever I brushed hair away from her face or told her how beautiful and sexy she is. She's always been strong and known her own mind, but never before has Cat been so hostile.

Which is my fault.

The version of her staring at me from millimeters away doesn't seem likely to blush or smile shyly.

"What are you doing?" I ask.

"You and I had sex, but you still haven't kissed me."

"I did that last night. And this morning."

She shakes her head slowly. "Not kissing me before we have sex is unacceptable."

Maybe I had ravished her body without bothering to kiss her first. Maybe she's right to call me a Limey Louse.

"I'd love to kiss you, Cat. But I'm too knackered."

She straightens and lays a hand on my cheek. "I know the old Alex is in there somewhere, and I'm going to dig him out no matter what it takes."

"You'll only get yourself dirty doing that, and you'll regret it later."

"I'm stronger than you think."

She heads for the door.

An inexplicable impulse seizes me, propelling me to leap out of my chair and hurry to catch her before she walks out the door. I grasp her arms and drag her into me for a kiss of total possession and raw need, spurred by something deep inside me that needs to prove her wrong. I wrap my arms around her waist, delving my tongue deep into her warm, slick mouth, powerless to fight my desire for her any longer. She tastes like everything sweet and good and pure in the world, like things I can never do more than sample for a brief moment.

She holds still at first, stiff and unyielding. Then her body wilts against me, and she responds to every lash of my tongue with a ravenous need that matches my own. We devour each other like we'll starve if we stop kissing, like the entire world might wither away and crumble to dust without our mouths fused.

Her arms come around my neck, and her fingers dive into my hair. She moans softly.

I stop kissing her but can't quite make myself let go of her body. "Was that better?"

"Aye," she says, sounding a bit breathless. "Much better." She gazes into my eyes with a look of wonder, like she's at last discovered my soul in them. "I know you're in there, Alex. It might take a long time to unearth you, but I won't give up until I do."

Catriona hurries out the door, leaving me alone in my office.

Unearth me? I don't like the sound of that. Having her here, in my town and in my home, seemed like a brilliant idea at the time. Now that I've gotten her here, I'm beginning to think I've made a catastrophic mistake. I can't command her to resign from the job I arranged for her, days before she's set to start. She won't do it even if I do command her to. I need to distance myself from her, though, as soon as possible.

If I don't, my past will come crashing down on us both.

Chapter Twelve

Catriona

Alex doesn't speak to me for the rest of the day, or on the drive back to his home. The giant house really does hunker in the woods like a cursed castle haunted by demons and evil spirits. Alex is nothing like that, so I can't understand why he wants to live in this place. I asked him that last night, but he avoided answering. Now I ask him that question again as we're walking through the front doors.

He's just shut the door and pauses with his hand still on the knob. "What?"

"I said why do you live here all alone in this depressingly dark house?"

"Because it suits me."

"No, it doesn't." I remember what Logan and Serena told me and ask, "What happened to your servants?"

"What makes you think I had any?"

I turn toward him, determined to see his face when he tries to not answer another question. "Logan and Serena told me. They also said that a few days later, when they came to your house again, the servants were gone. What happened?"

"Don't you want to tell me the term servants is hopelessly outdated and offensive?"

"Maybe it is, but that's irrelevant. I want to know why you got rid of them. Or did they quit?"

He strides across the foyer while he tells me, "I let them go. They were no longer needed."

I follow him into the main hallway. "Why weren't they needed?"

Alex freezes at the bottom of the staircase but doesn't glance back at me. "That is none of your concern."

"You can't keep sidestepping my questions forever. Eventually, you will have to tell me the truth."

He peeks at me over his shoulder, his lips ticking up at the corners. "You know how I am with the truth. I'm allergic to it."

"Your bum's oot the windae, Alex."

"No, it's quite firmly inside the house." He pats his erse. "See? Still attached and nowhere near a window."

"You know that phrase means you're talking nonsense. I used to say that to you a lot, since you frequently spout nonsense."

"I remember the phrase." He starts to walk up the steps. "Good night, Catriona."

"Aren't you eating dinner?"

"Not hungry."

I shake my head. "Oot the windae again, Alex. Avoiding me won't stop me from wanting answers."

He's halfway up the stairs now, seeming to ignore what I said.

So I try a trick I learned from my sister-in-law Emery and put two fingers in my mouth to whistle. It's so loud and piercing that I wince, and Alex pauses in his flight up the stairs. He doesn't look back, though, not even when he speaks.

"Give it a rest, Cat. You can harangue me more tomorrow."

I decide to do what he asks, this time. I want answers from him. I want the truth from him, about him, but I don't know how to make him cooperate. Maybe in the morning he'll feel more like talking.

Unlikely.

Since there's nothing else I can do tonight, I say, "All right. See you in the morning."

"Make yourself at home and eat whatever you like from the kitchen."

He reaches the second floor and disappears down the hall.

I make myself a light dinner and go to bed, but I can't sleep. I'm lying in Alex's house, in a bed he bought, covered by sheets he chose. Did he make this room for me? The other bedrooms aren't as dark as the rest of the house, but they lack the light and hope conveyed by everything in this room. Maybe I'm ascribing more meaning to the decor than I should. Maybe I want him to have made this room for me, hoping one day we would find each other again.

Aye, maybe I'm a damn eejit. Only an idiot would hope for the man who betrayed her to still love her.

Though I fall asleep sometime after two a.m., I dream of Alex. The old Alex. I remember the good times and the way he used to be, more open and sweet, and the way he used to make me laugh. In my dreams, I don't get arrested because Alex never betrays me.

When I wake up, I'm suffering from a confused tangle of emotions. I need to understand why Alex did what he did back then and why he's acting the way he is now. I need answers. But the feelings I used to have for him resurface more and more the longer I stay in his orbit, especially so close to him in this house. And I still want him. He'll always be the sexiest man I've ever known, and based on that single encounter yesterday in the lecture hall, I already know he's still the best lover I've ever had.

Isn't that sad? The man who got me arrested owns a large piece of me, from my body down to my soul, even twelve years later.

While I get out of bed and dig through my bags to find the right clothes for today, I let my thoughts wander back to that terrible day when everything fell apart.

I woke up that morning feeling wonderful, alive and happy and hopeful for the future, all because Alex had made love to me for hours last night. He whispered the sweetest words while he took my body and brought me to the heights of pleasure. None of the lads back home had a clue about how to give a woman true satisfaction.

None of them could compare to Alex Thorne.

He was lying beside me, asleep, with one arm draped over my hip.

Waking up like this, lying naked on my side facing him and watching him sleep, I experienced a sensation in my chest like I'd sucked in a huge breath and held it. Alex took my breath away, for certain.

I sneaked out of bed without waking him, slipped into a dressing gown, and headed for the kitchen. Our loft had two enormous picture windows that overlooked the town and the campus two blocks away. When I'd come to America, a new and alien place for me, I could never have imagined how things would turn out. I was happy, so happy, thanks to Alex.

While I cooked up a big breakfast for us, I hummed along to the radio and imagined what our wedding might look like. Alex hadn't proposed yet, but I had a feeling he was about to any day.

Catriona Thorne. I liked the sound of it.

A series of swift, powerful knocks reverberated through the front door.

I flinched, wondering who would be so anxious to see us at this time of the morning. Better find out. I abandoned my cooking and rushed to the door.

Alex sprinted out of the bedroom just as I swung the door open.

Two police officers stood there, faces somber.

"Catriona MacTaggart?" one of them asked.

"Aye, that's me." Had I parked in a loading zone by accident yesterday? The signs weren't that clear.

The officer who'd spoken brought out handcuffs. "You're under arrest for suspicion of smuggling antiquities. You have the right to remain silent..."

While he recited the Miranda warning and snapped the cuffs onto my wrists, I stared numbly at the officer and his partner. Arrest? Smuggling? What the bloody hell was going on?

"You've got it wrong," Alex said, coming up beside me. "You don't want to arrest her."

The officer flashed Alex an odd look, something like anger mixed with trepidation. "Stay out of this, Dr. Thorne. We have our orders."

Alex's eyes narrowed, and his lips compressed. "You've got it wrong."

He spoke the words in a deliberate and severe tone, but the officers paid no attention.

"She's coming with us," the officer who'd spoken to Alex said. "You can visit her in county lockup."

"At least let her get dressed," Alex snarled.

"Can't. Got orders." The first officer, the one who'd handcuffed me, aimed a knife-sharp glare at Alex. "Orders from the top."

"You are making a mistake that you will regret."

"Doubt it, pal. You're not as smart as you think."

I had no idea what they were talking about or why Alex seemed to know these two men.

They hauled me out of the apartment in nothing but a dressing gown and shoved me into the back of their car. I sat there, numb to the core and too stunned to think or speak, staring through the cage-like mesh that separated me from the front seat. What had just happened? This made no sense at all.

Suspicion of smuggling antiquities?

I went through the rigmarole of arrest in a dazed state, hardly aware of being fingerprinted and photographed. Nothing broke through the haze until I finally sat down on a bare, uncomfortable bed inside a cell.

Arrested. Me. For smuggling.

What would my family think?

Tears burned down my cheeks, flowing faster and faster until I was sobbing. I pulled my knees up to my chest and hugged them. The sobbing faded away, but the tears kept coming. My eyes grew hot and gritty. My stomach became a churning cesspool, and acid crept up into my throat, souring my mouth.

How many hours did I sit there crying? I had no clock to measure it by.

I dropped my head onto my knees.

A while later, someone banged on the metal bars.

I jumped and looked up at the officer, who still held the baton he'd used to bang on the cell bars. He was the one who'd spoken to Alex in our apartment.

"Your boyfriend's here," he said. "Damn, he's got some cojones, doesn't he? That asshole must have nerves of steel to do what he just did for you."

What had Alex done? I didn't understand anything since the moment I'd opened the door of our apartment. I couldn't summon my voice, so I simply watched the officer unlock the cell door and open it.

"Come on," he said, sounding annoyed. "You're going home."

I shuffled out of the cell, following him down a corridor and through a hefty, locked door into the waiting area.

Alex was standing there. Stoic. Stone-faced. His hands were clenched into fists, the only sign of emotion he gave away.

"Here she is," the officer said, giving me a shove toward Alex. The officer looked at me. "Alex Thorne is seriously bad news. You'd be better off running as fast as you can from him, before he drags you down into the quicksand, for good next time."

"Shut up," Alex hissed. He flung an arm around my shoulders and moved us toward the exit. But he threw a cold glare over his shoulder at the officer. "You'll regret this, the lot of you."

We hurried out of the police station to Alex's car.

He turned to face me, tugged my dressing gown closed more securely, and ran his hands up and down my arms. "Christ, you're barely dressed. You must be freezing."

Gooseflesh had popped up all over my arms, but I didn't notice the chill in the air. That numbness still gripped me, from the inside out.

Alex pulled me into his arms for a quick, firm hug. Then he kissed my forehead and helped me into the car. Once he'd gotten in, he dragged a fleece throw from the backseat and draped it over me.

Neither of us spoke on the ride home.

Back in our apartment, Alex led me into the bedroom and insisted I shower and get dressed. I did it by rote, forgetting every movement as soon as I'd done it, and shuffled out into the living room fifteen minutes later.

Alex was sitting in one of the armchairs by the windows, elbows on his thighs, head down.

I dropped onto the sofa. Though the numbness had dissipated, I still felt disconnected from reality, like I was watching events unfold on a television screen rather than participating in them.

"Bloody hell, Cat," Alex said. He shoved his hands through his hair and threw himself backward into the chair. "I'm sorry. This is all my fault."

"How?" Speaking that solitary word seemed like an enormous effort of will.

Alex studied me for a moment, and in his eyes, I glimpsed a maelstrom of emotions. Fear. Anger. Pain. Other things I couldn't decipher.

Never had I seen him so...distraught.

He did "distraught" in typical Alex fashion, concealing the depths of his distress and letting only the surface emotions show. How could I call his reaction typical? I'd never seen him like this before. Alex was always calm and rational, passionate in bed but otherwise in control, even when he laughed.

And yet I loved him. So much.

"How is it your fault?" I asked.

"It's complicated," he said carefully. "The details aren't important right now. Just know that you are not going to jail. I will not allow that happen. And your arrest record will be expunged."

The clouds in my mind began to clear while I sat there looking at him, at the man I loved and trusted. And I suddenly realized one vital fact. "You know why I was arrested."

"It doesn't matter now." He stood and closed his eyes, holding still for a moment as if he needed to consider his next move carefully. Then he knelt in front of me. "I'm not going to explain any of this. You'll either trust me to take care of things, or you won't."

"That's not good enough, Alex. I deserve the truth. I demand it."

He stared at me, his eyes clear and his demeanor calm. "I can't do that, Catriona."

"Yes, you can." I leaned forward until our noses almost touched and looked straight into his eyes. "Either tell me what is going on, or I will walk out that door and never come back."

Alex kept his gaze on mine, without blinking. "Do what you need to do."

"Dammit, Alex." I slapped my hands on his chest and shoved hard, but he stayed exactly where he was. "Why won't you talk to me? All I want is the truth."

"And that's the one thing I can't give you. Not today. Maybe never."

I gaped at him, searching his eyes and his expression for some sign of the man I knew. It was like he'd mutated into a different form of life that mimicked humanity but was completely alien to me. Whose eyes was I gazing into? Who was this man?

Not Alex. Not anymore.

A chill rattled through me, raising the hairs all over my body and freezing them stiff.

"Then there's only one thing left to say," I told him. "Goodbye, Alex."

He rose and stepped back, giving me room to walk away.

I gathered clothes into a suitcase and carried it to the door. As I laid my hand on the knob, I glanced back at Alex. He stood exactly where he'd been when I rushed into the bedroom to pack.

Though his gaze was aimed at me, I had the strangest feeling that he wasn't really looking at me.

Another chill rattled me.

"I'll come back for the rest of my things," I said, "while you're at work. This is the last time you'll see me, Alex."

Please say something, please beg me not to go and tell me what the hell happened today.

"Goodbye, Catriona."

That was all he said, so I walked out. I flew home the next day, giving up the two years of work I'd completed toward getting my PhD, and started over back in Scotland. Transferring to a new university didn't cost me time in terms of earning my degree. But it cost me so much more in ways that left me scarred on the inside.

I never saw Alex again until that day at Dùndubhan.

Chapter Thirteen

Alex

When I venture downstairs, I find Cat in the kitchen making food. It looks like more than she would eat, so I assume she plans to rope me into sharing breakfast with her. Since I've stopped in the hall, at an angle to the kitchen door where she can't see me, I have two choices. Give in and eat with her. Or flee.

Neither one appeals to me.

So I retreat into my study, taking a seat behind the desk in the leather chair that matches the one in my office on campus. If Catriona wants me to have breakfast with her, she'll need to sit across the desk from me. I glance toward the windows and the bench beneath them. She could sit over there, but that will still keep a distance between us. In fact, it might be better than the chairs on the other side of the desk, since I'll be sideways to her.

I grab a folder from a drawer, choosing one at random, and slide the papers out of it so they lie on my desk in slight disarray. There. Now it looks like I'm busy working on…whatever. I can use that as an excuse to ignore Cat if she insists on invading my study.

My tactic does smell suspiciously like desperation.

No, it's a brilliant plan. Clever. Pragmatic. Not desperate.

The Fates decide to demonstrate their disdain for me yet again by inspiring Cat to sashay into my study thirty seconds after I formulate my brilliant plan.

I focus on my papers, though I have no bloody idea what the pages say. "Busy, Cat. No time to entertain you."

Peripherally, I see her carry a tray of food into the room and set it down on one of the chairs, but I don't pay attention to what's on the tray.

"Go away, Cat."

"But I made you breakfast."

The sultry tone of her voice sends a strange excitement crackling through me. I can smell her too, the feminine scent of her, even through the aromas of the food. Breakfast smells so good my stomach grumbles, but the scent of her makes my cock ache.

"Afraid you'll have to eat alone," I tell her. "As I said, I'm busy."

"Doing what?" She perches on the edge of my desk, plants a hand on it, and leans toward me. She peers down at my papers. "You're too busy to eat because you need to review the instructions for your laser printer?"

Christ, I forgot she can read upside down. I also had no clue what papers I'd dropped on my desk.

"Yes, I need the instructions," I say, trying not to sound annoyed but failing in the attempt. "So I can troubleshoot the printer. It's not working the way I want it to."

If my printer could somehow drive Catriona away, that would be bloody brilliant. It can't do that, though, can it? I'm beginning to think nothing short of alien abduction will drive her away. Maybe I can arrange that. I do know a few college students who are obsessed with UFOs.

Now I stink of desperation.

Cat leans in more. "You have to eat, Alex."

"Not if I'm on a fasting diet, I don't."

"You? Dieting?" She laughs. "The man who once ate ten pancakes in one sitting wants me to believe he's given up food."

"Only for a week or so." However long it will take to get rid of her. "Then I might go on a wheat grass and grapefruit juice diet."

She taps my nose. "You're doing it again, Alex. If this, might that. Why is honesty so difficult for you?"

I drop the pen I hadn't realized I picked up and slump in my chair. "What are the odds I can make you leave me alone?"

"Zero." She smiles. "Might as well eat the food I made for you, since you can't get rid of me."

"Fine. I surrender." I spread my hands to indicate the desktop. "Leave the food here, and I'll eat it while I work."

She shakes her head. "No, *mo luaidh*, we'll have breakfast together. Here or wherever you like, but *together*."

Ah, she's bringing out the big guns—the Gaelic phrases. *Mo luaidh*, which she used to call me ages ago, means my darling or my dear or something like that. Does she think she can charm me with her Scots nonsense? To the point

I'll spill all my secrets to her?

Dimples form at the corners of her smile, and her eyes seem to sparkle more in the sunshine coming through the windows. "Are ye regretting tricking me into staying in your house? Too late to change your mind."

"No, it's not. I could evict you if I wanted." I stand up and move closer, because my body seems to have a large magnet inside it that draws me toward her. Bending down, I bring our faces to within centimeters of each other. "Didn't I tell you to go home?"

"I don't want to."

Gazing into her blue eyes, I lose track of what I'd meant to say to her. Catriona's irises are as pale as pools of glacial meltwater, their color shimmering like ripples on a pond. I could drown in those eyes and never want to escape.

But I will not tell her that.

I lean in to whisper in her ear, lowering my voice to a husky murmur. "If you stay, I can't promise not to corrupt you."

"Go on, then, do it. I dare you."

Christ, I want to do that. Corrupting her sounds like the start of a fantastic night we could spend in my bed, but in reality, it would mean something much different. I've been corrupted for a long, long time, and I can't undo the consequences of the things I've done. It's nothing I want Cat to experience. She's lovely and sweet and kind, all the good things good people should be. Blackening her soul to match mine... I won't do it.

Which is why she needs to leave.

I straighten and step back. "You can have your breakfast in one of those chairs"—I point to them, then to the window seat—"or on the bench there. Your choice. There won't be any conversation, so if that's what you're hoping for, I suggest you ring one of your sisters or cousins."

"Maybe I'll ring Rory. He'd love to hear what you just suggested doing to me."

Feigning complete disinterest, I settle onto my chair again. "Corrupting you isn't worth my time. You're much too...upstanding. It wouldn't be any fun."

She makes a noise that sounds like "hmf," then sets a plate and a glass of milk on my desk.

"Milk?" I say. "Am I a child?"

"It's good for you, Alex, but I gave you tea too." She takes her tray to the window seat and sits down with her legs stretched out across the bench. "Besides, milk goes with what I made you for breakfast."

At least I have tea, so I don't feel like a child, with her as my governess.

But I do like the idea of Cat playing that role the next time I seduce her.

I lift the lid off my plate. It contains waffles. Three of them. Stacked in the center of the plate with a huge mound of melting butter on top and syrup filling the holes in the topmost waffle and dribbling down the sides to pool on the plate.

"You're wanting me to die of a heart attack, then?" I say, glancing sideways at her. "This is enough butter to serve all your brothers, their wives, and their children."

Cat slides a forkful of waffle into her mouth, smiling while she chews and swallows it. "You need to lighten up, *mo luaidh*. Indulge yourself once in a while."

"I made you an omelet yesterday. It overflowed with cheese."

She shakes her head, as if she's sad for me and my lack of indulgence. "That's not decadent enough to count."

"Decadence is my middle name, love."

Catriona laughs. "You're so sweet when you're trying to convince yourself of what a bastard you are. You're not, so it never works. Does it?"

I glare at my stack of waffles, hack off a triple-decker forkful, and shove it into my mouth. At least chewing gives me an excuse to not speak to or look at her. When did Cat become a firebrand? She never used to question me about anything, and she certainly never talked back to me or made fun of me.

Do I have a caber up my arse these days? If so, I must've contracted the disease from Logan or Rory. If I can figure out what Cat is trying to accomplish, I can devise a plan to thwart her. But she keeps surprising me. The cheerily sarcastic woman lounging on my window seat can't be the same girl who adored me in another lifetime.

That's my mistake. I've been treating her like she *is* the same girl. The Catriona of today is a mature woman.

And she must be trying to torture me. Somehow. With waffles.

We finish our meal in silence, but I find myself glancing at her often—too often. As the sun rises higher and higher in the sky, it paints her skin with shades of gold and rose, and the colors make her eyes seem brighter, her skin smoother, her smile more angelic. I can't stop looking at her, even while I stuff food into my mouth. She's beautiful and unattainable.

I had her yesterday, but sex isn't the same as...whatever it is she thinks she wants with me.

Once we're done eating, Catriona collects our plates and cups and sets them on the tray. She comes around behind my desk.

"What now?" I ask.

She rotates my chair toward her, then sits on my lap. "You've got a storm cloud inside you, but when the *fearthainn* ends, the world will be *solasta* again. *Saorsa* will be yours, Alex, if you accept it."

"If I knew what on earth you're talking about, I might have a response to that." Her warm bottom on my lap is making me uneasy even while I enjoy the sensation, and her words are the single most beautiful thing I've ever heard. But I have no idea what she said. "Speak English, please."

She leans in, her hair brushing my cheek and her breaths whispering over my lips. "When the rain ends, the world will be shining again, and freedom can be yours."

"Afraid you're wasting your time, Catnip. I'm a lost cause."

"No, you're not." She touches her lips to mine. "I'm going to work on my lesson plans for next week, so I can make a good first impression. We can talk more later."

She hops off my lap and walks out the door.

My phone rings. I answer with the usual greeting.

"You sound off, mate. Having a bad time with your woman?"

The sound of that Australian accent makes me jerk upright in my chair, gripping the phone tighter. "Reginald Hewitt, how did you get my phone number?"

Since I'd changed the number after my last encounter with him, I want to know how he got the new one. Only a handful of people have it, including Logan and Serena. I haven't even given the number to Catriona.

"I called you on my mobile phone," Reginald says, his voice even more gravelly than I remember.

"How did you get a mobile phone?" I demand. He isn't supposed to be allowed to call me. The warden assured me of that.

Reginald sniggers. "You'd be surprised what I can get from the prison black market. Mobiles are easy. Getting out, that's a lot more difficult."

Getting out? No, he can't have escaped. The warden would've called me. I'd made a sizable donation to the prison library to ensure I would be informed of any changes regarding Reginald Hewitt. Naturally, dear old Reggie has wormed his way into the prison crime syndicate and found a means of escape.

"Going home to Australia, are you?" I ask.

He sniggers again. "No, Your Highness, I'm not going anywhere. Not until I've made you suffer for turning me in."

"You betrayed me first, Reggie."

I'm snarling the words, but I can't seem to calm myself. This man conspired with a student at Thensmore to steal three Babylonian tablets and sell them to a collector on the black market. Since I had sort of borrowed the tablets from the university museum, I could've gone to prison for theft too, even though I'd planned to return them. Reginald and Falk Mullane had hoped to make a fortune selling those artifacts on the black market and send me to prison as a bonus. "Borrowing" artifacts might not be strictly legal, but I meant to put them back before anyone knew they'd gone. Am I as bad as Reginald and Falk?

A chill whispers over my skin, lifting all the fine hairs. Am I that bad? Do I deserve to be punished for my sins?

"You needed to be betrayed," Reginald says, "and brought down a peg or two—or five. You think you're so bloody high and mighty, the king of your self-made castle. I put up with you for three years, just waiting for a chance to make my move. Falk Mullane gave me that chance. Now I'm going to force-feed you a taste of your own medicine."

"What did I ever do to you? Paying you a ridiculously large salary for being my fucking butler?" I snort. "You disgust me, Reggie. Go rot in the Australian outback. With any luck, dingoes will devour your useless carcass." I disconnect the call and dial another number. When Warden Bill Drummond answers, I say, "How did Reginald Hewitt escape from your facility? And why wasn't I informed?"

Drummond groans. "I was going to call you, but Hewitt escaped only this morning. A few hours ago. We've barely had time to search the grounds and contact the state police. Believe me, I was going to let you know."

I rub my hand over my eyes and sink back in my chair. "I'm sorry, Warden. I know you would've told me. It's just that I heard from Reginald a few minutes ago, and he made what could be classified as a threat against me."

"The state guys will talk to you, I'm sure. Other than that, there's not a hell of a lot I can do."

"Yes, I understand."

"Soon as I hear anything, I'll let you know."

"Thank you. Goodbye, Warden."

I hang up and toss my phone onto my desk.

A taste of my own medicine. What on earth did Reginald mean by that? He wants to punish me. I know that much for certain. Maybe I should force Catriona to go home to Scotland, where she'll be out of the line of fire.

But it's too late, isn't it? Reginald mentioned my "woman." How does he know about Catriona? He must, given his statement. I need to convince her to leave, but she won't go along with that—unless I tell her everything. A segment of everything, not the whole puzzle. A jigsaw with missing pieces is all I dare let her see.

If I have to, I'll drug Cat and dump her on a jet to Scotland.

Chapter Fourteen

Catriona

I decide to visit my office on campus today, so I'm changing into work-appropriate clothes. Planning my lectures for next week seems like something I ought to do in my office. That's what I intend to do, but I'm only half dressed when Alex storms into the bedroom.

"Ever hear of knocking?" I ask. Though I have on nothing but a bra and knickers, I don't bother trying to cover myself up with a dressing gown. Alex has seen me naked before, so I don't feel the need to bother.

"No time for knocking," he says, sounding as somber as he looks. "There's a problem I need to make you aware of."

"All right."

He seems to have finally noticed my state of partial dress, skimming his gaze over my body. He scrubs a hand over his mouth, blinks rapidly, and focuses on my face. "A man who used to work for me, Reginald Hewitt, has escaped from prison. He may be coming here."

"I gather it's not a friendly reunion."

Alex huffs. "He wants to punish me. For what, I don't know. Being here with me is not the safest choice for you under these circumstances."

I grab my blouse, shrugging into it, and start to button it up. "Is this the same Reginald that Logan mentioned?"

"Yes."

"What did this man do? Why was he in prison?"

"He conspired to aid and abet the theft of priceless artifacts from the

Thensmore History Museum. He also embezzled from me."

"That doesn't sound like a reason to panic." I pull on the skirt I've decided to wear, tuck my blouse into it, and tug the side zipper closed. "I'm sure the authorities can handle the situation."

Alex stalks closer, hunched over slightly, and his voice drops to a deep, dark register. "Reginald is dangerous, more so than even I realized. He has a grudge against me. He also made a veiled threat against you. Please leave, Catriona. Get away from here as fast as you can."

I stare at him for a moment, studying his expression and his eyes and the tension in his body. On the day I left him twelve years ago, he'd been calm and seemingly unaffected. Today, he behaves like a man on the edge of panic.

"Tell me what's going on," I say. "All of it, Alex, please. Serena and Logan said Reginald secretly despised you."

Alex shambles to the bed and drops onto it. "I met Reginald three years ago, not long after Logan did that spot of work for me. I needed a right-hand man, someone to take care of the household and anything else that might require an extra set of hands. Reginald and I got on from the start. I thought we were mates."

I sit down beside Alex, but I don't try to touch him, unsure if he will want that. "What happened?"

"When Logan found Falk Mullane, the sniveling idiot who stole those Babylonian tablets, Falk claimed he'd paid Reginald to be his mole. Reggie told Falk when I sent Logan after him."

Alex almost spits the name Reggie.

"I thought we were mates," he says again. "What a ruddy moron I am, eh? Thinking I'm cleverer than anyone on earth, that no one can fool me. Yet I had that bastard living in my house for three years and never realized he hates me."

"Everyone makes mistakes. It doesn't mean you're a fool."

He grunts, and one side of his mouth slants into a half sneer. "Not realizing the truth when it's right in front of you is the definition of being a fool. I've made too many mistakes to say this was a one-off, but it isn't my worst mistake."

"What is?"

For a moment, I think he might actually tell me. After all, he's just shared a large dose of the truth with me. I know he's not lying about anything he told me in the last few minutes. The look in his eyes proves it to me. Will he confess his worst mistake?

"Doesn't matter," Alex says, getting up. "You need to go home before Reginald arrives and he—I don't know what he's planning, but I want you far away from here when it happens."

He's worried about me. That's not the behavior of a bastard who cares only about his own wants and needs. He cares about me. My chest constricts, like a huge strap has been cinched tight around it. He cares.

I hop off the bed and lay a hand on his arm. "Thank you for telling the truth, Alex."

He shrugs away from my touch. "I was merely alerting you to the problem. It's nothing I wouldn't do for anyone else."

"Your bum's oot the windae again," I say with a teasing smile. "Donnae ruin the moment by reverting to your ersehole persona."

"Maybe it's not a persona. Maybe it's who I am."

"No, it's not." I move closer and tip my head back to meet his gaze. "I'm not leaving. If you're in trouble, I'm staying here with you."

He stares at me for a long, long moment, his expression so veiled I can't figure out what he's thinking or feeling. This is his usual state. A moment ago, he'd shown me the raw, unveiled truth of his feelings, but now he's slammed that mask down over his face again.

"I'm not leaving," I tell him. "The authorities will be searching for Reginald Hewitt. My concern is for you, Alex, and I will not walk away when you're in trouble."

"You've done it before when the situation was far less serious. Don't be a silly Scots girl, behave like a mature adult. Anyone with half a brain would realize the intelligent thing to do is to leave."

The nasty tone of his voice doesn't fool me one bit, though I can't stop the tears that sting my eyes. Rationally, I know he's saying those things on purpose to chase me away. My heart takes his words as gospel, though, and it hurts.

He will not drive me away this time. I *am* a mature woman now, and I do not let anyone bully me.

Even when they're doing it out of fear and a desperate need to protect me.

"That won't work, Alex," I say as I take his face in my hands. "I will never walk away from you again, not when you need me, not even when you're trying to push me away. I won't make it that easy for you anymore."

"You are a sentimental fool, Catriona."

"No, I'm a woman who knows her own mind. You won't be telling me what to do or think anymore." I press my lips to his, then back away. "Thank you for being honest with me, Alex. But it's time we head to campus. We have jobs to do."

He stalks out of the room.

On the drive into town, we don't speak. He doesn't blare classical music the entire time, but he refuses to acknowledge my existence, never looking at me, much less engaging in conversation. When we reach the faculty parking lot, he jumps out and takes off at a fast walk that verges on a run.

Alex, you poor, frightened man.

I make my way to my new office, which is located a few doors down from Alex's office. He must have arranged it this way, but I have no doubt he regrets his conniving now that he's decided I need to leave. How can I? After twelve years of wondering what happened to us, I finally have the chance to find the answers. I may need to dig them out of Alex by force, but I will get them.

Last night, I got a glimpse of the man I'd loved. I can't forget that. I won't forget it.

An hour later, one of my new colleagues stops by to say hello and welcome me to Thensmore. Virgil Burns is a gray-haired man with kind eyes and an equally kind smile who wears a tweed suit with a bow tie, like he's just stepped out of a Sherlock Holmes novel. Though his accent is American, he talks like a Victorian gentleman, saying things like "nevermore" and "whosoever." I like him immediately.

He asks me to call him Virgil, so I invite him to call me Catriona.

After a few minutes of conversation, he tells me, "I have a class this afternoon, but I have a horrid toothache and need to get that looked at today. Would you mind filling in for me? The topic is the archaeology of Roman England. Since you're from the UK, I thought you might know a bit about that."

I do know about Roman England, though I've never given a lecture on it. I'm also new here and haven't settled in quite yet, but I don't want to turn down a request from a colleague.

"Here's my outline for the lecture," Virgil says, placing the folder he's been holding on my desk. "I can email you the slides I was going to use as visual aids. I know it's last minute, and I understand if you're not comfortable with doing this."

I don't need to think about it. "Of course I'll do it. I haven't lectured in quite some time, so it would be nice to get back to it sooner than expected."

"Wonderful." He shakes my hand vigorously. "You are a lifesaver, Catriona."

Once Virgil leaves, I look over his lecture notes and download the slides to my computer once he sends them to me. Since I'm familiar with the topic, this shouldn't be difficult. I haven't been in front of a class—a real one full of eager students—since my PhD program. Back then, I'd acted as a teaching assistant but hadn't delivered real lectures. I would fill in if the professor couldn't be there. Mostly, I'd handed out tests and monitored the students while they filled in their answers. My cousin Iain had invited me to lecture at the university where he worked, but I'd been a guest who spoke for part of the time, not the sole lecturer.

For the decade before that, I'd spoken in front of schoolchildren, not adults.

Unlike Alex, I don't qualify for the large lecture hall. That's fine with me.

I walk into a regular classroom and take my place at the desk. A projector sits on a metal cart beside it, so I get to work hooking my laptop up to the projector and making sure everything works the way it should. Just as I finish, students begin to shuffle into the room.

Virgil Burns teaches world history, so I'm not required to give a detailed talk about the science of archaeology. This is an introductory lesson, aimed at first-year undergraduates. I'm glad for that. A slow start will get me ready for Monday, when I have my first class full of students who are serious about archaeology and ancient history.

I wind up with twenty students, spread out among thirty desks. Not a bad turnout. The lecture notes are spread out on the desk, so I move behind it to get started.

Movement catches my eye, and I glance toward the back of the room. Alex is hovering just outside the doorway, half hidden by the jamb, like he's trying to secretly watch me.

I pretend not to notice. After our emotional talk this morning, I don't want to embarrass him. If he wants to hide and watch me, I'll act as if I haven't seen him. But the idea that he wants to observe my class gives me an odd warmth in my chest.

"Good morning," I say to the students. "So, Roman Britain. Does anyone know how much of Great Britain the Romans conquered?"

A lad raises his hand and says, "All of it?"

"Not quite. Anyone else want to guess?"

This time a lass answers. "Not Scotland."

"Good," I say, "but still not entirely accurate. Rome did gain control of a part of southern Scotland, though not for long. We'll get into the details a bit later. Let's start at the beginning, shall we? Anyone care to hazard a guess about which emperor set the wheels of conquest in motion?"

The lad who'd responded earlier says, "Hadrian?"

I shake my head.

Another lad calls out, "Nero."

One girl seated in back raises her hand.

"Go on," I tell her.

She hunches her shoulders. "Claudius?"

"You are correct," I tell her, "Claudius was the first to conquer Britain. But there's a bit more to the story than that. Claudius initiated the first successful invasion, but it was Julius Caesar who first invaded Britain. Those pesky Gauls over in France kept him so busy that he lost his hold on the British territory. After the death of Caligula, Claudius became emperor and mounted the first all-out invasion and conquest of Britain."

My students are paying attention. Looking interested. I've engaged my audience with the first try. Maybe I'm not as out of place here as I thought. Maybe I really do deserve this job.

And I have the man hiding in the doorway to thank for that.

Chapter Fifteen

Alex

*O*bserving Catriona's lecture leaves me awestruck. I've always known she has the brains and determination to do whatever she wants. But I never had the chance to see her giving a lecture. Cat has enthusiasm for the subject matter, but more importantly, she is an expert on it. When she talks about the archaeological evidence of the Roman invasion, I'm spellbound by her excitement and the easy, natural charisma she evinces.

I want to fuck her again. Immediately.

That's a bad idea, though. After spilling my ruddy guts to her this morning, I'm much too raw to risk even kissing, much less having sex with, Cat. I need her to leave. My brilliant idea to lure her into my domain and trick her into staying in my house has begun to seem like the worst bollocks I've ever invented. She won't give up. I already know the new Cat is not shy or unassuming. She's a firebrand, and my house of cards is highly flammable.

Yes, I'm mixing metaphors. Christ, that woman is turning me into a nutter. Maybe I need to get myself away to…anywhere she isn't.

Running away? From a woman? I'm worse than a nutter. I've become a bloody coward.

Moirai House is enormous. I can hide from her quite well without leaving home.

Catriona is just wrapping up her lecture, so I sneak away before she catches me spying on her. I don't know why I felt the need to see her, to listen to her voice, and I'm not going to do any navel-gazing to figure out the answer. When I bumped into Virgil Burns in the hallway, he told me Cat would be handling his lecture for him. The thought of watching Cat teach a class made me bizarrely excited. I've never seen her teach before. Curiosity, that's all it was. I needed to watch, I've done it, and now I no longer need her in any way, shape, or form.

But her shape still entices me. Her lovely, sexy shape.

I've run away to my office, sitting in my chair with my eyes closed, thinking about how to keep Catriona MacTaggart away from me, when a throat-clearing makes me glance at the doorway.

A student whose name I can't remember stands there. She smiles and flutters her lashes at me. "May I have a minute of your time, Dr. Thorne?"

"Yes, fine. Have a seat."

I don't want to talk to anyone, but it's part of my job to have conferences with students. The only ones who want to confer with me are boys who want me to give them an A without requiring them to do any work, because they're athletes and deserve it, and also girls who want to bat their eyelashes at me.

Christ, I'd kill for an intelligent, hard-working student who wants a genuine student-teacher conference.

The girl sits down in one of the chairs opposite my desk. "I'm Candy, remember? I asked the questions about Greek sports last week."

Oh yes, I remember her now. She'd raised her hand in class and asked if the Greek athletes got sunburn because they engaged in sports in the nude. She had also asked me whether the Greeks invented aloe body lotion to treat their sunburns.

"What can I do for you, Candy?" I ask.

"I'm really confused. Can you help me understand?"

"Help you with what?"

She catches her lip between her teeth and flutters her lashes again. "Today, you talked about those cuneiform tablets and how that's the earliest known written language."

"Yes." I'm starting to feel a headache coming on and want this child to get to the point, but I can't be rude. I've been chastised for that before, when I told a muddle-brained boy that I didn't have time to indulge his obsession with conspiracy theories.

Candy licks her lips, slowly, and her voice turns sultry—or at least, the college student version of it. "I don't understand why that's a language. It's scratch marks on clay. Can you please explain it to me? Show me those pictures of the tablets again? I didn't get a good look at the slides in class."

"There are similar images in your textbook."

"Please, Dr. Thorne, I just need a little help."

It's my job to teach these children, but I know what she's angling for—and I will get fired if anyone sees her coming on to me, even if I shove her away.

"All right," I say, pulling up the slide on my computer. "I'll show you."

Before I can turn the monitor toward her, she jumps up and hurries around the desk to stand beside my chair. Leaning in, she manages to place her cleavage a few centimeters away from my face. I slide my chair sideways, creating a space between us, and point at the image on the screen. "This is a Babylonian cuneiform tablet. Those scratch marks are—"

Candy lunges at me, aiming her puckered lips toward my mouth.

I whirl my chair away from her and leap up.

The chair spins into the wall with a thump.

Candy pouts. "Come on, Dr. Thorne, everybody knows you like young girls. Don't you think I'm hot?"

"No, I do not. I'm sorry you've gotten the wrong impression of me, but I do not kiss students or have sex with them." I point toward the door. "Please leave."

She sighs. "You're no fun."

I'd much rather be no fun than fired for defiling a student—and blacklisted for the rest of my life. Working at a fast-food restaurant does not appeal to me.

Candy turns toward the doorway, pouting again. Her eyes widen.

I glance in that direction.

And of course, Catriona is leaning against the doorjamb, arms crossed over her chest, watching Candy with a mildly amused expression. She glances at me. "My, Alex, you do have a powerful effect on silly young girls."

"I'm not silly," Candy says, then she stomps out of my office, brushing past Cat.

Thank goodness that little tart is gone.

Cat ambles up to my desk. "You've been a busy boy, haven't you? Crushing the hopes and dreams of a college student."

Growling under my breath, I shove my chair back where it belongs and drop onto it. "She wanted to molest me. And I don't particularly want to be fired today."

"Did you want to do it?"

"No, I most certainly did not." I slouch in my chair, frowning at her. "Do you honestly think I'd shag a student?"

"You slept with me when I was a grad student."

"That was different." I gesture toward the doorway through which Candy disappeared. "That girl is a freshman. You were a grown woman."

Catriona crosses behind my desk and leans her bottom against it. She's so close to me that I could lay a hand on her thigh, but I don't.

She bends toward my chair, her gaze trained on me. "I want the truth, Alex. One way or another, I'll get the answers I need, but I'd rather you tell me of your own free will."

"What if I don't tell you? Are you going to torture me for those answers you think you want to hear?"

"Aye, I'll torture you." She slants in even more, which makes her blouse fall away from her body, granting me a view of her lacy bra and those delectable breasts. "But I don't need to strap you down on a table and drag razors across your skin to make you talk. I can torture you with the one thing you've never been able to resist."

"What do you believe that one thing is?"

She smiles. "Sex."

This woman knows me too well. After all these years, she ought to be wrong about me in at least a few ways. She's not. She understands me far better than I'd anticipated, and that realization sends excitement rushing through me. Catriona wants to seduce me. I've never been seduced by a woman. College freshman don't count as women. Adult females try to lure me into giving them what they want, but I remain in control of the situation no matter what.

Except with Cat. She's right about that. I've never been in control with her, never held back when we made love, never resisted her in any way—sexually. Maybe I'd believed I held back when we had sex, but that's a lie I told myself. Yet for the entire time we lived together, I'd withheld many, many things from her. For her own good. It had nothing to do with fear. Nothing at all.

No, that's not me trying to convince myself. Absolutely not.

I run a hand over my eyes. *You're an idiot, aren't you?*

Cat's face is close enough to mine that her breaths tickle my skin. I want to lunge forward and kiss her, but that would be what she wants. My only option is to pretend I don't lust for her and refuse to kiss her, touch her, or shove my head under her skirt.

No sex. Whatever she does, I will not give in.

"You can't fuck the truth out of me, Cat."

She smiles again, this time with a lustful slant to her lips. "Of course I can. We had sex in the lecture hall yesterday, which is all the more proof that you have no willpower with me. What makes you think you can say no if I beg you to make love to me?"

Begging sounds...good. The idea makes my cock wake up. But making love sounds much too intimate. Not that I'm afraid she really can dig my secrets out of me, in or out of bed.

Why, then, do I invent a reason to get away from her?

Because I'm an idiot.

I push my chair back and stand. "I need to get to the museum. There's paperwork to take care of."

The fact that the office where I go to do bollocks like that is in a private area protected by doors that require a passcode to enter has nothing whatever to do with my announcement.

She laughs, and it's the most enchanting sound I've ever heard. "Paperwork? I expect better lies from you than that. Desperate to avoid me, aren't you?"

"No, I am not. I need to—" I grab my mobile phone and stalk toward the door. "Goodbye, Catriona."

And she laughs.

Chapter Sixteen

Catriona

What am I going to do with Alex? He insists on clinging to his secrets, even after admitting he worries for my safety with his former right-hand man on the loose again. Alex's anxiety about that had been real, and it might be the most honest thing he's done in years. Now he feels embarrassed about it and thinks he can hide from me. *Not likely, Dr. Thorne*. I have a plan. Nothing will stop me from enacting it.

I'm going to crawl under his skin so deep he'll never get me out of his system. And aye, sex is the keystone of my plan.

The fact I will enjoy seducing him has no bearing on my scheme. It's a bonus, not the reason for my tactic. *Bod an Donais*, I want that man.

Alex stays at the museum for the rest of the afternoon. I know this because I go to the museum three times to make sure he's there. The security guard on duty tells me so.

"Dr. Thorne is holed up in the office," the guard says, "and he said not to let anyone in, not even nosy little Scots." The man winces. "His words, not mine. I'm sorry, Dr. MacTaggart."

"Call me Catriona, please. And I know it's not your fault Alex is an erse."

"He's really a nice guy."

Yes, Alex can charm the trousers off anyone. With women, he charms the knickers off them even when he doesn't mean to or want to do it. That bonnie little freshman is a prime example. Alex could have taken what she offered, had his fun, and never thought about her again. He didn't. And I believe him when he says he's never slept with a student.

However much he havers about being a bastard, I know the truth. Deep down, underneath all those layers of subterfuge and evasion, lies a good man.

After work, I wait by his car in the faculty parking lot.

The impossible man walks up to me, punches the button on his key fob to unlock the car, and says, "I'll be playing Bach today, at the loudest possible volume. You'll want earplugs."

He hands me an unopened package of foam earplugs.

I hold up my hand to tell him I don't want them. "I'll be fine. I can handle loud noises." I lay my hand on his chest. "I like *making* loud noises too. But you know all about that, don't you?"

He grunts and climbs into the driver's side.

On the trip home, he doesn't blast classical music. He keeps the radio off, leaving us in silence for the entire ride. I decide not to say anything and give him this time to get used to the idea I won't give up. I want the truth, once and for all, and I will do whatever it takes to get it.

The second we get inside Alex's house, he announces, "Good night, Catriona. I'll see you in the morning."

He turns to walk away.

I grab his arm. "It's seven o'clock, Alex. You're not going to bed, so where are you planning to hide this evening?"

He smirks a wee bit. "If I tell you, it won't be hiding."

"Wherever you go, I'll find you."

A strange expression flickers over his face, something reminiscent of… regret.

"Good night," he says again, and he heads upstairs.

"You have to eat, Alex."

He waves a hand in a dismissive manner without glancing back at me.

I want to growl and snarl at him, but I don't. He wants to annoy, confuse, and hurt me so I might go away and let him wallow in whatever he's trying to wallow in. Guilt? Fear? Self-loathing? Maybe it's all three, and more.

Making dinner for both of us distracts me for a while, though my mind keeps working on the Alex problem in the background of my thoughts. I've made a meal for two. Alex is going to eat, even if I have to stand there holding a *sgian-dubh* to his throat to make him do it. Only a dagger might make an impression on him.

Half an hour after he dismissed me, I knock on his bedroom door.

No response.

I try the knob. It's unlocked, so I swing the door open.

The room is empty. I check the attached bathroom, but he's not there either. I hurry down the hall, checking every bedroom including mine, but I can't find Alex. Downstairs, I search room by room, beginning with his study. No Alex in the study. Or in the living room. Or in the room that looks sort of like a solarium. It has many large windows that must let the sun pour in during the day, but right now it's dark.

When I reach the door at the end of the long hallway, I twist the knob. It's locked.

Eureka. The Sassenach has been found.

I knock lightly. "Alex? Are you in there?"

Silence follows.

"Come on, Alex, I made you dinner. You need to eat, or you'll never have the energy to keep running away from me."

Footsteps. Coming closer.

The door pivots inward.

Alex stands there, his clothes in disarray and his hair mussed. It looks like he's been shoving his fingers into that hair and whisking them around like, well, a whisk. His shirt is untucked and rumpled as well as half unbuttoned. He's also gripping the doorknob tightly.

"What do you want?" he asks, his voice rough.

"To feed you." I grasp his hand, prying it away from the knob. "Donnae be an ogre about it. I've made you a good meal. Please come and eat it."

He stares down at our hands.

I rub my thumb in circles on his skin.

Alex swallows visibly, then lets out a sigh that deflates his shoulders.

He nods once.

I lead him into the kitchen, and I let him get away with sitting on the opposite side of the island from me. He looks exhausted. After we eat, he'll feel better. I hope. Interrogating him when he's in a weakened condition won't help anything.

"Sorry there's no dessert," I say when we're both done eating. "Didnae want to spend time making something when I knew you were somewhere starving."

"Not starving." He pushes his empty plate toward the island's center. "I was resting."

"You do look tired, more than when we first got home."

"Home?" He squints at me. "Why are you referring to my house as 'home'? You are a guest."

Alex is right. I called this gloomy house "home." Why did I do that? I could dismiss it as a common way of referring to a house, but deep down, I know there's more to it. So I tell Alex the truth.

"I called it home," I say, "because being with you feels like it did when we used to live together. It feels comfortable and…right."

He stares at me without expression, for so long that my pulse accelerates while I wonder if I've said too much. Will he run away again? Will he get angry and toss me out the door?

Alex does neither of those. He bows his head, resting his arms on the island. "You think you want the truth, but trust me, you don't. If you leave tonight, at least you can hold on to your fantasy that I'm a decent man somewhere deep inside. If you stay, if you keep trying to get the truth out of me, you will regret it."

The words don't strike me as a threat. Given his fear this morning, I think he's terrified I won't like what I see when he finally shows me everything.

I stretch my arms out to close my hands around his. "Don't worry, Alex. I won't leave you."

He studies my hands, where they lie atop his. His brows draw together, and he swallows again, so hard I can see it.

Then he gets up and walks out the door.

I'll give him tonight to get used to the idea I'm not leaving him and he can't get rid of me. But tomorrow…

Get ready, Alex, I'm coming for you.

Chapter Seventeen

Alex

I hide in my bedroom. Yes, I'm hiding from a woman. Catriona wants to fuck me until I lose my mind and spill my guts again like I did this morning, but this time she'll get every last bit of them. If she tries to seduce me, I know she'll succeed. My guts will be all over the Persian rug that surrounds my bed.

No, I have willpower. She's not so sexy that I can't say no to her. Cat isn't the sort who will go to any lengths to have her way.

The old Cat wasn't. The new Cat... Christ, I might be in trouble.

I've just finished undressing when someone knocks on the door. Someone? I know bloody well who it is and what she's after—my intestines, all over the rug. Either she'll murder me, or I'll tell her everything. I'm still debating which of those options is the least dangerous when I open the door.

Catriona stands there wearing nothing but her underwear. Her knickers are made of lace, which lets her skin and pubic hair show through the flimsy fabric. Her bra is lace too, and her stiff nipples push against the cups. That bra is also strapless, giving me a fantastic view of her creamy shoulders.

"What do you want?" I ask, trying to snarl but managing only to sound like I have a scratchy throat.

She sweeps her gaze over me from head to toe. "Do you still sleep in the nude?"

"Yes." That should be obvious since I'm naked. "Now that I've answered your question, leave me alone."

I move to shut the door, but she thrusts out a hand to stop me. "Not yet. I need your help."

The tone of her voice, sultry and soft, awakens the hungry beast in me. She really has no idea what effect she has on me when she talks that way. If she knew, she wouldn't tempt me like this.

"Help with what?" I ask.

She turns around, looking at me over her shoulder while she bends an arm behind her to point at her bra. "I cannae get this unhooked. Would you mind?"

Catriona wants me to remove her bra.

Do I seem stupid enough to fall for this ploy? She seems to think I am, or maybe she knows full well I realize what she's about when she asks me to unhook those tiny clasps for her. Either way, I'm in no condition to play these games. I still don't feel quite like myself again after this morning's ridiculous confessions.

I sprint into the bathroom and grab a pair of hair-trimming shears. When I return to her, I offer up the scissors. "Cut your way out of it, darling. I'm sure you can manage that on your own."

The condescension dripping from my words has no effect on her.

Cat smiles at me over her shoulder. "You wouldn't want me to hurt myself, would you? I can barely reach back there."

Dammit, she's right. She really could injure herself trying to cut the bra off. I also realize she knows how to unhook her own bra. I've seen how she does it when she's having trouble with the task.

"If you don't want the scissors," I say, "then slide the bra around until you can unhook it in front."

There. That should end the discussion.

Until she speaks again, in that sexy voice. "Tried that already. It won't slide. Please, Alex, I need you."

I'm not sure whether to believe a word she's saying, but the only way to get rid of her is to do what she wants. I don't have to do it the way she clearly wants me to do it, though. With my fingers. On her skin.

"Have it your way," I tell her.

Then I slip the scissors under her bra and cut it free.

Before I can congratulate myself on sidestepping the problem, she raises her arms, letting the bra fall to the floor. Cat turns around to face me, now naked except for her flimsy lace knickers.

The blasted woman shimmies out of those too.

We're both naked. In my bedroom. Close enough to the bed that I could toss her onto it.

I've seen her nude body before, but this time feels different. I can't stop myself from admiring every inch of her, from those perfect lips to her flat stomach and the curly hairs between her thighs that I know will be silky if I run my fingers through them. Her breasts may not be quite as perky as they were a decade ago, but they still make my mouth water. I want to consume her in every way imaginable. No other woman has ever stoked my lust the way Catriona does, or made me feel the uncomfortable things she always forces me to experience.

Right now, all I can think about is tossing her onto the bed and making love to her until we're both too weak to do it anymore.

She comes closer and splays her palms on my chest. "Why are you fighting this, Alex? You want me, and I want you. The only reason I can see for you to keep saying no is because you're afraid you might show me the real you again."

"No one sees the real me."

"I do." She skates her palms up to my throat. "You don't scare me. I want to know all of you, every little thing you think you need to hide. Show it all to me, Alex. I'm ready."

She has no idea what she's asking me to do. The truth about me will either send her scurrying back to Scotland on the next flight out or corrupt her in ways she can't even imagine.

My cock is ready to give her what she wants, but my brain knows what I have to do.

I pick her up, carry her to the bedroom where she's taken up residence, and dump her on the bed. "Good night, Catriona."

On my way out, I slam the door. Both doors. The one to her room and the one to mine. The bangs echo through the house.

Nighttime is not my friend. I can't sleep and wind up doing the most clichéd thing in the world—tossing and turning, so much that I get the sheets tangled around my legs. When I finally fall asleep, I dream of Cat. Naked. Purring that she wants me.

When I wake in the morning, it takes me five minutes to untangle myself from the sheets. I need another ten minutes to relieve my lust in the shower. Maybe I should just shag Cat again and get it over with, instead of torturing myself this way.

But that's what she wants. The woman has a plan, and though I don't know what it is, I'm sure it's more nefarious than any plot I've ever devised. I had no idea how devious she can be until she moved into my house. Yes, I'd brought this on myself, hadn't I?

You think you're so bloody clever, don't you? Catriona is laughing at you now.

No, she wouldn't laugh at me. She might smile and tease and torment me with her body, but she won't ridicule me. I wish she would. Her derision might make it easier for me to get rid of her.

Why haven't I done that already? I can kick her out of my house any-time. Change the locks. Hide inside until she gives up.

Bloody hell. What kind of spineless moron have I become?

If I could punch myself, I would. Only a violent shock seems likely to snap me out of this bizarre condition Cat has inflicted on me.

When I head downstairs, I don't see her anywhere. Maybe she's still in her room. I sigh with relief, literally, and decide I'll eat breakfast on campus. That will show Catriona how much I don't want to live with her.

I walk out of the kitchen.

And Catriona stumbles into me.

"Oh!" she gasps. "Alex, you gave me a fright."

"If you move out of my house, I won't be able to frighten you ever again."

Her body is millimeters away from mine, and she smells so good I want to inhale a deep breath of that scent. I don't, because that would be ridiculous.

"No, you don't want me to go," she says with a teasing smile. "You wanted me here, and now you have me. I'm not leaving until I get what I want."

"I won't have sex with you again."

"That's not what I want the most." She presses her soft, warm body against me. "The truth will set you free."

My chuckle has a dark edge to it. "That's bollocks. The truth locks you up even more securely. Steel bars, no windows, no hope of escape." I catch her wrists and pin them behind her back. "Would you want to live with me then? Inside a dark, impenetrable cell?"

"You won't know unless you trust me and tell the truth."

I hold on to her wrists with one hand, lifting the other to grasp her face. "Careful what you wish for. Hasn't anyone told you it might backfire?"

"You're trying to scare me, but it won't work." She turns her face into my hand and licks my palm with slow, sensuous strokes of her hot tongue. "Ahmno a naive lass anymore. Ahm stronger than ye think, and more stubborn too."

"My dark side is much blacker than you think."

"Not scaring me off, Alex." She draws my thumb into her mouth and sucks on it. "There's only one way I can make you crack, and I plan to ex-ploit that method until I get what I want."

I have no capacity to think, not with every iota of blood flooding into my groin. Suddenly, I'm having trouble breathing, like there's a massive weight strapped to my chest.

"Just to be clear," she says, suckling my thumb again, "the way I'll break you is with sex."

She knows my weaknesses. She understands me more than anyone else on earth, but she has no idea what darkness lurks deep inside me. I can't let her do this. If I crumble for her, if she digs out every last one of my secrets, it will destroy us both.

But I want her. With Cat's body plastered to mine, with the heat of her penetrating me and the scent of her desire tormenting me, I have no willpower at all.

I shove my hand into her hair and drag her closer, taking her mouth in a brutal kiss. I consume her like she's the only sustenance in the entire world, the only thing that can save me from starvation. Every time I plow my tongue into her mouth, she responds with the same raw hunger, consuming me the way I'm doing to her, not at all like the sweet, innocent girl I'd known years ago. The Catriona of today rubs her body against mine in a blatant expression of lust and throws her arms around my neck, plunging her fingers into my hair and refusing to let me pull away. I don't want to pull away. She tastes like sin and heaven, sex and innocence, like everything I've ever wanted but that I can never have.

She severs the kiss, though she keeps her body crushed to mine. With a wicked little smile, she slides her tongue across her kiss-swollen lips. "Mm, you taste better than ever today."

I try to speak, but nothing comes out of my mouth.

Catriona wriggles free of me, turns away, and sashays down the hall toward the main doors. Over her shoulder, she calls, "Are you coming? I want to have breakfast at a restaurant today."

"Sorry," I say. Though I've finally regained my voice, my brain hasn't caught up to it yet. "Can't do that. I have, ah…things to do. Alone."

Cat wags a finger at me. "No, Alex, that won't work. I'm driving, which means you have no choice in the matter."

"You are not driving my car."

She reaches into the pocket of her trousers and produces a set of keys, jingling them at me.

My keys. The woman stole them? Cat doesn't do things like that.

"You're commandeering my car?" I ask. "Do you even know how to drive on the right side of the road?"

Her laughter tickles my senses. "Of course I do. I have American sisters-in-law and an American brother-in-law." She skips up to me—I swear she actually skips—and dangles the keys in front of my face. "Besides, I lived in America before. Have you forgotten?"

Not likely. How could I forget living with her for almost two years? I have no idea why I suggested she doesn't know how to drive the American way.

Catriona MacTaggart turns my brain to jelly.

I try to grab the keys, but she snatches them away.

"You sneaked into my room," I say, "and nicked my keys. That's not a very Catriona-like thing to do."

"When will you get it through your head that I'm not an innocent grad student anymore?"

Before I can respond, she whirls around and breezes out of the house.

Since I seem to have no choice, I follow her.

Cat is already behind the wheel when I get into the car.

I fasten my seatbelt and glance at her sideways. "You've become a cat burglar. It seems appropriate, doesn't it?"

She laughs, starts up the engine, and roars down the driveway.

Chapter Eighteen

Catriona

Alex got flustered. Who knew that could happen? I'd never seen him that way before, and I have to admit I like it. Anything that knocks him off his axis has to be a good thing. I get bloody sick of his "maybe" this and "what if" that. I want him to tell me one true thing, without equivocation, before this day ends.

He wants to have breakfast at a fast-food restaurant via the drive-through. I nix that idea the instant he suggests it. Of course, he tries to change my mind. First, he uses his considerable charm in an attempt to sweet-talk me into agreeing to his idea. I pat his cheek and call him "an adorable lad," which makes him grimace. He switches to explaining that we can both get to work faster if we use the drive-through and eat in the car. I tell him that won't work for me, since I plan to order something decadent that drips with syrup and butter, and those sorts of foods require both hands and silverware.

Alex clenches his teeth.

His last-ditch attempt proves to be the hardest to resist. He slides a hand along my inner thigh, brushing the heel against my groin, and speaks in the deepest, sexiest voice imaginable. The devil himself couldn't sound hotter than Alex Thorne does when he tells me, "If we avail ourselves of the drive-through, I'll feed you every luscious bite of whatever you order. By the time I'm done, you'll beg me to fuck you in this car. While you're driving."

"Ye cannae fuck me while I'm driving. It's physically impossible."

I sound breathless and lustful, which doesn't help me resist him. Oh, he knows every little way to tease me and tempt me and make me give in to his demands. This time, I won't do it. I'm on a mission, and giving him what he wants does not suit my plans.

"Come on," he purrs in that silky, sexy, panty-melting voice, which only sounds better and more enticing because he's British. "You want it as much as I do."

Bod an Donais. I've never thought the British accent was arousing—never except with Alex. American women apparently love any Brit's voice, but I love only his.

He knows that. And he's using it against me, the bastard.

I have only one option to stop myself from giving in. I veer into the parking lot of an IHOP and shut off the engine. "We're eating here, Alex. At a restaurant. With other people all around us."

"But that's not what you really want."

"You expect me to deny that." I shove the door open and swing my feet down onto the asphalt. "Of course I want you. But that doesn't mean I'll give in every time you speak to me in your silky sex voice."

"My what?" He chuckles. "I have a sex voice, do I? You never mentioned that before. And it's a silky one too." He smirks. "Have you just shown me your Achilles heel? You know I'll have to exploit it at every opportunity." He leans toward me. "And I'll do it with my silky sex voice."

He speaks those words in that very voice.

I want to smack him, but I know that will only make him smugger, so I stick my tongue out at him instead.

And he chuckles.

"Breakfast, Alex. We will eat breakfast and go to work." I jump up, almost hitting my head on the car's roof, and duck down to aim a hard stare at him. "No matter how sexy your voice and your body are, I am not having a poke with you until I decide it's time."

I slam the door.

We have our breakfast, and he watches me with an amused expression while I consume the French toast, crepes, waffles, and pancakes I ordered. Not to mention the bacon and sausage. And the large glass of milk. Two large glasses, since I need a refill to finish off my breakfast. I don't actually eat all the food, so I get the rest of it to go.

Alex has no right to feel so smugly entertained by my eating habits. He ordered an enormous omelet with pancakes on the side, and after he finished that, he ordered buttermilk biscuits and gravy. I think he wound up eating more than I did, since he didn't have any leftovers to take home.

I let him drive the rest of the way to the campus, despite the way he'd chuckled when I dribbled syrup on my blouse. He'd laughed even more when I'd daubed water onto the fabric and sucked on it to get the syrup out.

As soon as he pulls into his assigned parking spot in the faculty lot, I jump out of the car and hurry away.

I swear I hear Alex chuckling again.

Oh aye, he knows every way to drive me insane—with lust, with annoyance, with complete frustration. I need a little time away from him to gather my wits and come up with a plan to drive him insane, so he'll finally confess his secrets to me.

After two hours of devising lesson plans, I've had enough. I walk to Alex's office, but his TA tells me Alex is at the museum. Aye, the man is hiding behind locked doors in a secure area he knows I don't have access to, that's how afraid he is of me. I take that as a good sign and do my job for the rest of the day.

I do occasionally call his office to check if he's there. He isn't. The man is still hiding. He even told his TA to handle the one class he has scheduled this afternoon, claiming he has urgent business to handle at the museum. *Your bum's oot the windae again, Alex.*

He also sends a car for me, to take me home. Alex Thorne, the best liar in the world who never flinches from a confrontation, is so frightened of me that he hired a car and a driver to take me back to Moirai House.

When I get there, his car is already parked in the driveway. I give my driver a tip and then hurry into the house to search for Alex. I don't see him, but I know where he's hiding this time. The door to his study is closed, and light creeps out underneath it.

I skulk up to the door, gently resting my ear on it. I hear nothing except the ticking of the clock that hangs on the wall in there.

"Alex," I say, knocking on the door, "I'm home. I'll make dinner, and I expect you to join me. Avoiding your roommate is rude, and it won't stop me. I'll hound you until your dying day, so you might as well come out and eat something."

The only response I receive is the ticking of the clock.

I get down on my hands and knees to peer under the door.

Ah-ha. I can see his feet under the desk.

Now that I have proof he's in there, I clamber to my feet and knock again. "Ye cannae hide forever, Alex. If you don't open this door in the next thirty seconds, I will come in there anyway."

A noise that might be a grunt is all the response I get.

"You are acting like a bairn, Alex."

The distinctive sound of papers rustling tells me he's doing something. Will he open the door? Or is he trying to distract himself by pretending to read papers on his desk? I count the seconds in my head.

When I've reached thirty, Alex still hasn't emerged.

"Have it your way," I say. "Donnae say I didn't warn you."

I rush upstairs to get my tools and change clothes.

Chapter Nineteen

Alex

*C*at's footsteps recede, suggesting she's given up on convincing me
to come out of my study. Do I believe she's given up? Not entirely. The
woman is relentless in her determination to make me expose all my secrets to her, but that will never happen. I can stay in here as long as it takes
for her to get tired of waiting for me to open the door.

I turn my chair sideways to the desk, facing the tall windows. The sunlight wanes as I stare at the green vines and the pale-pink flowers on the
bushes. I relax into my chair, closing my eyes. Maybe this is a sort of medita-
tion, but no one taught it to me, and I've never thought of it that way. I'm
collecting my thoughts, sorting through them, and finding peace in the process. This has been my way for a long time, not just since Catriona decided
to torment me.

She failed. I'm in here, and she's out there. Somewhere.

Doing what?

No more thinking about her. I take in a long breath, letting it out little by
little, feeling the tension melt away.

Strange noises originate from the door. Ticking. Scratching. A click.

I will not open my eyes. It's probably a mouse. So I resume my relax-
ation routine, letting my mind drift into a state free of thoughts and worries
and—

The door opens. I hear the click as the knob turns and feel the rush of
cooler air from the hallway.

"Your stronghold has been breached," Cat says cheerfully.

What the bloody hell is she doing? How can she be cheerful about invading my private sanctum?

I sit there trying to ignore her, my eyes still closed, but one thought flares in my mind. How did she get in here? Since I know she wants me to look at her, I refuse to do it. With my eyes closed, I say in a disinterested tone, "How did you get through the door? I locked it."

Maybe that doesn't sound as disinterested as I'd hoped. Bollocks.

"Open your eyes and I'll tell you," she says, humor in her voice, like she can't wait to show me and have a jolly good laugh about how stupid I am.

"I can live without knowing the answer." I tip my chair back a touch, locking my hands over my belly. "Good night, Catriona."

Despite the fact I can't hear her moving, I sense she's coming closer. But that's ludicrous. I can't sense her. Logan's sisters might claim to have psychic powers, but I do not believe in that nonsense. I can smell Cat, though. The scent of cocoa butter wafts over me. Christ, she still uses the same body lotion after all these years? I remember the scent, and it makes every hair on my body stiffen and my cock start to harden too. She always used to slather that lotion all over herself when we got into bed, and I loved watching her smooth it over her legs.

On more than one occasion, I'd massaged that lotion into her flesh as foreplay. She loved that, and I loved taking her body afterward.

"If you don't look at me, Alex, you'll never know how I got inside your study."

"Doesn't matter." I want to know, want to look at her, and need it so badly that I'm squeezing my eyes shut to keep from opening them. I won't tell her that. So instead I say, "Go eat something or...whatever."

"No."

Christ, she won't go away until I look at her and listen to her explanation of how she so cleverly breached my study. I will pretend to be impressed, solely to get rid of her.

I open my eyes.

And almost choke on my own saliva.

She stands an arm's length away dressed in a black lace teddy. It's almost transparent, giving me a glimpse of her taut nipples and the hairs between her thighs. The teddy's slender straps leave her shoulders and most of her chest exposed.

She's virtually naked.

I rest my hands on the chair's arms, rocking gently like I don't give a toss about how sexy she looks or how good she smells. "Go on, tell me. How did you get inside this room?"

Cat grins. "I picked the lock."

For a moment, all I can do is stare at her. Catriona MacTaggart, the straitlaced lass who never exceeded the speed limit, knows how to pick a lock? She must be lying. She got into the room some other way.

"You're having me on," I say. "You don't know how to pick locks."

"My brother Aidan taught me how to do it. He used to lock himself out of his car so often that he asked Uncle Angus to teach him lock picking."

"Angus?"

"My cousin Iain's father. Angus used to be a petty criminal, though he only broke into the homes of rich scunners and only stole what he needed to keep his family fed."

"Well, if he did it for noble reasons..." I tip my head to the side, studying her with a new appreciation. "You actually picked the lock?"

"Aye."

"I thought the MacTaggarts were a bunch of puritanical prigs. Now it turns out you're a larcenous lot."

"Angus stopped being a thief years ago. He's reformed."

"Hmm." I rock the chair more vigorously, fascinated by this turn of events. Cat broke into my study. She knows how to pick locks. It makes me want her even more. "What's your plan now that you've done your cat burgling for the evening?"

"I haven't stolen anything." She smiles. "Yet."

"You stole my keys this morning. What will you take from me this evening?" The woman has already robbed me of my sanity. I probably shouldn't have asked the question.

"Nothing." She opens her hand to reveal a small, soft case that I'm sure holds her lock-picking tools. Setting that on the desk, she kneels in front of me. "I'm not taking anything. I'm giving you a chance to be honest with me, and I'll do whatever it takes to convince you to do that."

"Afraid I don't have time to play with you, Cat. I have work to do."

"You were asleep when I came in."

"No, I was thinking."

She pushes between my legs, forcing me to spread them, and lays her hands on my wrists where they rest on the chair's arms. "In a few minutes, ye willnae be thinking at all."

With her body so close to my cock, I can't disagree with her statement.

Keeping one hand on my left wrist, she reaches behind her and brings out a pair of—

"Handcuffs?" I say. "That's not the Cat I know."

"Maybe you don't know me as well as you thought." She slips the cuffs, which have fluffy pink padding, around my right wrist and closes them snugly without making them too tight. Then she secures the other cuff to the chair's arm. "Cannae have ye running away again."

I seem to have lost all control over my body, because I sit there like a statue while I watch in mute fascination as she pulls out another pair of pink handcuffs and secures my left wrist to the chair.

"Where did you get handcuffs?" I ask.

"There's an adult novelty store one block from the campus." She wriggles even closer, pushing my thighs further apart. "We drove by it this morning, but I guess you were too busy complaining about my driving and my choice of restaurant to notice."

I've lived in this area for several years, but I never noticed an adult store. How had I missed that?

"To be fair, though," she says, "the store doesn't look like much from the outside. It's called The Cave, which doesn't sound erotic."

Well, at least I'm not a blind moron. I do vaguely recall a place called The Cave, but I never went inside the store.

She snakes an arm behind her back again and brings out a clear plastic packet of what looks like some sort of multi-colored granules. I can't read the label on the packet.

"Have you got an arsenal in your knickers?" I ask.

"This is the last thing I hid back there. It was tucked inside my waistband, just like the handcuffs were."

I lean forward to peer down at the packet. "What is that? If you're going to drug me so I'll talk—"

"No, I wouldn't do that. Your confession needs to be your choice." She sets the packet on the desktop. "My method will be erotic, not coercive."

Her method. That sounds...like exactly the sort of thing I'd love under normal circumstances. But I can't have her breaking my will. My gut-spilling was an aberration, one that I will never repeat.

She plants a hand on the chair between my legs and pushes down so it's not tilting backward anymore. Then she sneaks a hand under the seat to lock it in place.

"I can roll my chair backward to get away from you," I say. "And what if you're not the only one who knows how to pick locks?"

Cat is the only one of us who can, but she doesn't know that.

She slides her hands up and down my thighs. "Try picking the locks with both your hands bound to the chair. You won't escape from these cuffs." She scoots backward a little and turns my chair so it's facing away from the desk, then pushes it backward until it meets the obstacle. "I've got you right where I want you."

"This is lunacy, Cat. You resorting to sexual torture? Not convincing at all. What's your real plan?"

"Maybe I will torture you. Sexually."

She picks up the packet and tears it open with her teeth.

Now I can see the front of it and read the words emblazoned on the packaging: oral sex candy. What the...

Holding the packet between her teeth, she unhooks my belt and the button on my trousers. The intensity with which she focuses on the task turns me on even more. But when she drags my zipper down millimeter by millimeter, I get so hard I wonder if my cock could explode from the pressure.

"Stop this nonsense," I command her, though she pays no attention to what I've said. "You won't torture me with sex."

Her long, delicate fingers close around my cock and liberate it from my trousers.

"This is absurd, Cat."

With her head still bowed, she looks up at me through her lashes.

My cock throbs. Moisture beads on the crown, and I know I will explode any second if she doesn't stop what she's doing. But I can't speak to tell her to stop. I'm breathing so hard and so fast my head feels light. I have never gotten so sexually excited that I can't speak or breathe or think. It's nonsense.

But it feels incredible. The mystery of what she might do to me excites me more than anything or anyone ever has.

She keeps one hand on my cock while she plucks the packet from her teeth and pours some of the crystals into her tongue. Keeping her mouth open, she smiles.

A breath erupts out of me with such force it flutters her hair.

I try to roll my chair sideways, but her body blocks me from doing that. I am her prisoner.

She firms up her hold on the base of my cock and slides her mouth over the tip.

Tiny shocks explode on my flesh.

What is oral sex candy? It feels like a filthy version of those candies children like to eat, the ones that burst on their tongues.

She takes more of me into her mouth, setting off more tiny fireworks.

Fuck, it feels...so bloody good. I squirm in my chair, gasp at every little explosion, and stop breathing again from the sensation of her hot, slick mouth sliding along my flesh, detonating the candy with every centimeter more of me she consumes.

When the candy stops bursting, she stops moving. Her mouth encloses me, but she just waits there like that.

I still can't catch my breath. Can't move. Can't convince my vocal cords to function. I try not to look at her, but my eyes have other ideas. They force me to gaze down at the woman who has my dick in her mouth. She's looking at me too. When she flutters her lashes and smiles, the pressure inside me builds into a painful sort of pleasure.

She moans and begins to glide her mouth up and down my length, up and down, up and down. Every time she withdraws her mouth, the air cools the moisture left behind, and I shudder from the arousing sensation. Her fingers grip the base of my erection, and when she wiggles them, they torment my balls.

"Cat," I growl, my voice so harsh and strangled I barely recognize it.

The faint suction of her mouth sends a jolt of pain and pleasure through me. I throw my head back and shout something that's not quite a word, and I know I'll come any second. She begins to suck gently while she works me, her cheeks caving in and her eyes half closed, like she loves doing this to me. More than loves it. She seems lost to the ecstasy of it all.

"Catriona," I gasp, and then I'm lost too. My back arches, my head slams backward into the chair as I come inside her hot, greedy mouth, and I swear I see stars exploding in front of my eyes, or maybe behind my lids. I don't know if my eyes are open or closed. I come so powerfully that even after I'm done, I stay frozen in that position—frozen and speechless, breathless too.

When I realize my eyes are closed, I pry them open by sheer force of will.

She removes her mouth and her hand from my dick, sitting back on her heels. "How was that?"

"Fucking incredible." I take a moment to regain my ability to breathe without gasping. Then I regard her anew, struck once again by these revelations she keeps throwing at me. "You clearly don't understand the concept of sexual torture."

"I don't want to torture you. I said maybe I would, which is Alex-speak." She crawls onto my lap and loops her arms around my neck. "Thought it was about time I used your own tricks against you. 'Maybe' and 'what if' are your favorite diversionary tactics."

"How does giving me intense pleasure get you what you want?"

Yes, I'm blatantly ignoring her statement about my tricks and diversionary tactics. She's spot on, of course, but I refuse to give her the satisfaction of hearing me admit to that.

I would love to give her satisfaction in other ways.

"Now you're relaxed," she says in a sweetly seductive voice. "The only time you ever let your guard down is during or right after sex. That's how I get what I want."

"When I'm weakened by a mind-altering climax? Dirty tricks, Cat."

"Aye, but you leave me no choice." She strokes my cheek with her palm, her fingers trailing down my skin. "You can't chase me away, Alex."

She touches her lips to mine in a feather-light kiss. Gazing into my eyes, she smiles like she...

No, I won't finish that thought. She can't feel that way anymore, and I don't want to know even if she does.

"I'll ask you only one question tonight," she says.

Her mouth finds mine again, pressing more firmly, and the softness and warmth of her lips affects me in the strangest way. My muscles relax, but my heart thumps faster. When she pulls away, I experience something like regret or longing.

I shut my eyes and mutter a curse under my breath. "What's your question?"

"Why was I arrested for antiquities smuggling?"

Chapter Twenty

Catriona

I've wanted to know the answer to that question for over a decade. Needed to know. But Alex wouldn't tell me at the time, and I'd had no choice but to walk away from him. Tonight, when I'm about to get that answer, I wonder if I really want to know. My gut churns, pushing acid up into my throat and my mouth.

Why am I afraid to hear the answer?

Maybe I'm still in love with him. That might explain my anxiety at this moment, but I don't want to think about that right now.

"It's complicated," he says, avoiding my gaze despite the fact I'm on his lap with my face so close to his I can feel his breaths tickling my lips.

"No more excuses, Alex. You said you'd answer my question."

He tries to lift his wrist but can't, so he sighs and leans his head back.

I reach for the lock-picking kit, unzip it, and take out the small key I'd hidden inside the kit earlier. Alex is going to share the truth with me, I believe that, so I take pity on him. I unlock the handcuffs and toss them onto the desk. I toss the lock-picking kit and the key there too.

He eyes me with a mixture of curiosity and anxiety.

Why does that make me want to hug him?

I settle for kissing his cheek.

His brows crinkle. "What was that for?"

"Call it encouragement. Why was I arrest—"

"Because of me." He turns his head to the side, away from me. "The chief of police had you arrested as a means of coercing me to do what he wanted."

"Which was what?"

Alex shifts in his seat like he can't get comfortable, and he still grips the chair's arms even though I've removed the handcuffs. "He ordered me to nick something for him. I refused, so he invented a charge against you and told his men to arrest you."

"Nick something? Why would the police chief blackmail you into stealing for him? You're an archaeologist, not a thief."

"I'm the British Bastard, remember? I can't be trusted, and I have no morals whatsoever."

"No morals? I've never said that."

"But it's true." He swivels his head toward me, his lips kinked into a nasty smirk, devoid of humor or sly seduction. "I'm the devil, Catriona. Don't sell your soul to me, or I will corrupt you—even if I don't mean to do it."

"Not selling you anything. I'm trying to understand why a police chief would blackmail you."

"He was bent. The law was a means to an end for him, not a sacred duty."

"Aye, but I still don't understand." I study his face, but I can't see anything in his expression. He's hiding behind a mask of hard indifference, like he doesn't care about me or anything. His act doesn't fool me, though. "Have you ever stolen anything? Logan said you 'borrowed' those Babylonian tablets, but you intended to return them to the museum. Is that true?"

"What happened to one question only?"

"These are follow-on questions, which means they count as part of the original one question."

His smirk turns playful, and he slips his arms around my waist, clasping his hands at the small of my back. "I've always known you're clever, but now I see you're devious too. A lock-picking, key stealing, devious little siren. It's incredibly arousing."

Maybe his comment should fash me, but I take it as a positive sign. He's relaxed again, and I hope ready to tell me more.

Before I can repeat my question, he answers it.

"Have I stolen anything," he says with a sigh, "that's your question. I'm afraid the answer to that is not at all simple, and I'd rather not discuss it tonight. I will tell you this. In all my adult life, I have never stolen anything outright. I occasionally borrow items that don't strictly belong to me, but I always return them."

"How did you deal with the police chief, then?"

"What do you think?" He tugs me closer, and his lips curve into a devilishly sexy smile. "I tricked the wanker. When I said I would 'take care of the matter,' he assumed I meant to steal the diamond necklace he was lusting after. It belonged to the wife of a trustee at the university. Instead of stealing it, I sent a videotape to that trustee, one that showed the police chief shagging his wife."

"How did that stop the police chief?"

"The trustee had influential friends who were very loyal to him." Alex's smile turns smugly satisfied. "Let's just say that getting a leg over with that man's wife was not good for the police chief's career."

I plant a quick, firm kiss on his lips. "You're the clever one, Alex. I knew you wouldn't steal anything."

No, I didn't miss the part of his explanation where he said he'd never stolen anything in all his "adult life." I want to interrogate him about that, but I don't want to spoil the trust he's shown me tonight by sharing the whole story of that awful day so long ago.

I kiss him again, taking my time, loving the way his lips soften and yield to mine and his mouth opens just enough to let my tongue slip inside. He slips his tongue inside my mouth too, and soon we're engaged in a steamy dance that makes me randy all over again. What I'd done to him earlier got me aroused, but this kiss affects me even more. He tastes like... Mm, I delve deeper to get a better taste of him, moaning and thrusting my fingers into his hair.

He groans into my mouth.

Oh, that flavor. It's familiar and intoxicating, but every time I try to identify it, he slides his tongue around mine and I forget what I was thinking. His hands glide up to my breasts, palming them.

I give up his lips, though I don't want to, and gaze into his hooded eyes. "Alex..."

"Hush, love. Don't ruin the moment."

"All right." I lick my lips, and suddenly I remember where I've tasted this flavor before. "Have you been drinking Ben Nevis whisky?"

"Maybe I have."

I seal two fingers over his lips. "No more 'maybe' and 'what if.' Forthright answers, or I'll pick the lock on your desk drawer next time."

"Have it your way. Yes, I sometimes drink Ben Nevis."

"Why? It's from Scotland."

"Logan introduced me to it. Before that, I enjoyed Talisker."

I lean back, considering him for a moment. "That's my brother Lachlan's favorite whisky."

Alex shrugs.

"When we lived together," I say, "I told you about Talisker. You ordered a bottle from Scotland and gave it to me for my birthday. But you claimed you didn't like it. Why would you be drinking Talisker years later?"

"Does it matter? A drink is a drink."

I know that's nonsense, but he won't tell me anything more tonight. And I promised to leave him be after he answered the question about my arrest. Why did I promise that?

"*Mhac na galla*," I mutter under my breath.

"Son of a bitch?" Alex says, seeming much too pleased with himself for knowing what the Gaelic phrase means. "Are you cursing me for drinking your favorite whisky?"

"Drink what you like, it makes no difference to me." I hop off his lap and straighten my clothes, which aren't exactly clothes. The fabric is almost transparent everywhere except where the lace pattern obscures it. "I'll make dinner."

Alex stares at me, seeming dumbfounded, while I walk out of his study. He meets me in the kitchen a while later and helps me finish making our meal. We talk while we eat. It's more like I talk, and he occasionally inserts a sarcastic comment softened by his usual practiced cheerfulness. I tell him about all the barmy things my brothers and sisters and cousins have done over the years, but despite his smile, he doesn't laugh. For Alex not to even chuckle is unusual. He stops smiling too, especially when I mention my cousin Logan.

"I know all about Logan," Alex says while scrutinizing the food that's left on his plate and poking it with his fork. "You know I'm acquainted with Logan and his wife, Serena, not to mention her son. I've heard enough about your family for one night."

"Then tell me about yours."

"My what?"

"Your family, Alex."

He stabs his fork into a tiny piece of meat, pulls the tines free, and stabs it again. "You never asked me about that before."

"When we were together the first time, I was too infatuated with you to ask questions. It's different this time." I move his plate away and pluck the fork from his fingers, dropping it onto the island. "Do you have brothers or sisters? Are your parents still alive?"

He pushes off his stool but still refuses to look at me. "I'll wash the dishes. You can go...do whatever it is you do in my house in the evening."

"Why did that police chief think he could blackmail you? It implies he had something on you."

"Everyone has secrets, some of us more than others."

He carries our plates to the sink and turns on the faucet.

"I should help you with the dishes," I say.

"That won't be necessary." He glances at me, though he keeps his head down. "I prefer to be alone tonight."

Maybe I should give him that time. I forced him into a confession he hadn't wanted to make, because I needed to know the truth. Alex does not like to open up about anything.

So I leave him in the kitchen and head upstairs to ring my sister Jamie. She's pregnant with her third child, and I feel odd about not being there for that. She's not due for another four months, but still... I miss my family. Jamie's not the only MacTaggart woman who's up the duff these days. I want to be there, but I need to be here. Alex has more to tell me, whether he knows it or not.

Jamie answers on the first ring. "Are you chained to the wall in Alex Thorne's dungeon?"

"No, I am not."

I'm lying on the four-poster bed in the room next to Alex's, wearing only a dressing gown. I've slept in the nude ever since I moved into Alex's house. It feels...appropriate. And aye, maybe I hope one night he'll sneak into my room and wake me up with his mouth on my body. I don't care if it's on my lips, my breast, or my clitoris. I've given up denying I want him, so I embrace the fantasies without any hesitation.

Except at this moment, I can't fantasize. My sister is talking again.

"Where are you staying?" Jamie asks. "Logan and Serena think you're in Alex's house, but I couldnae believe it. You? In the British Bastard's house? It's not possible."

I squirm a little, knowing she won't like my answer. "Aye, I'm in Alex's house. It has fifteen bedrooms, you know."

"Which one are you in?"

The tone of her voice assures me she thinks, or hopes, I'll tell her I'm in the room farthest from where Alex sleeps. I have to disappoint her.

"I'm in the room next to his," I tell Jamie. "And before you start havering about what an eejit I am, let me explain. Alex is not the devil incarnate, and he's not a sex fiend either." Well, I don't think he is. I'm not sure whether I'll care if I turn out to be wrong. "He and I have unfinished business. That's all."

"Would that be unfinished shagging? Please tell me that's all it is. Not sure I can take hearing how you want to reform him."

"Alex is not a criminal." As far as I know. I can't believe he would break the law, despite the fact he has a habit of "borrowing" artifacts. He always returns them.

"What is he, then?" Jamie asks. "I searched Google to find out what Alex is up to lately, and it came up with a video of his lecture this week. The one where he showed off a..." She clears her throat and speaks in a hushed tone.

"A giant, dangling *slat*."

I can't stop the laughter that bursts out of me. "Giant, dangling penis? It was a *fascinum* wind chime, which was a good luck charm in ancient Rome."

Jamie snorts. "It looked like a *slat* to me."

"That's what a *fascinum* is."

"I knew it. That man is a sexual deviant."

Alex might be intensely sexual and fond of making filthy jokes, but he's not a deviant. I don't bother trying to explain that to Jamie. She's already made up her mind.

"Tell me what our brothers are doing lately," I say.

Jamie starts talking, her tone excited while she explains what's happened since I left Scotland barely a week ago.

The door to my bedroom pivots inward.

I stop listening to Jamie, suddenly warm and relaxed and oblivious to my sister's blethering.

Alex saunters over to the foot of the bed and crawls up it toward me. He's wearing nothing but a pair of pajama bottoms. The expression on his face, carnal and determined, makes my body rouse and tingle, every hair shivering and stiffening.

I set the phone on the mattress a few feet away from me. While Jamie keeps talking, I whisper to Alex, "What are you doing?"

"I owe you one," he murmurs, still crawling closer and closer. When his head hovers over my hips, he slants one side of his mouth into a naughty smile. With his fingers, he pushes the dressing gown away from my thighs and whispers, "Hang up the phone."

"No," I mouth.

"Have it your way," he murmurs.

Jamie's voice continues to broadcast from my phone. "So then Emery told Rory he should—"

I'm not listening. My focus is locked on Alex, as he eases my legs apart and kisses my inner thigh, laving his tongue over my skin. I shiver, though not from cold. I know what he's about, and I don't care. How can that be? Alex entices me to do things I would never have done with anyone else, like having sex in a lecture hall with the doors wide open. Tonight, he wants to give me pleasure with his mouth while my sister is talking to me on the phone.

And I want him to do it.

Why haven't I hung up on Jamie? I should. It's the sensible thing to do. But the idea of having his mouth on me while I'm on the phone with my sister, it makes me so turned on I can hardly breathe.

Maybe I've had enough of being sensible.

Alex dives his head between my thighs and begins to lick, nibble, and suckle on my flesh. When he seals his mouth over my hard nub, I gasp.

"What's wrong?" Jamie asks. "Are you all right, Cat?"

"Fine, aye."

Hang up, my brain tells me. But Alex is suckling my clitoris, and when he slips his hands under my bottom and hoists it up, my head falls back against the wall.

"Oh, Alex."

Did I say that out loud? Donnae care if I did.

"What is Alex Thorne doing to you?" Jamie demands. "Do I need to send Rory to America to check on you?"

"No." My neck arches as Alex licks faster, tugs harder on my clit, and makes grunting sounds like he can't get enough of me. "Goodbye, Jamie."

I mash my finger to the phone to disconnect the call.

Then I abandon myself to the pleasure of Alex's mouth on me, his hands holding my erse off the bed and tilting my hips, giving him full access to my body. I gasp and fist my hands in the sheets.

He watches me, his mouth hidden in my folds but his eyes locked onto mine.

"I'm still here," Jamie shouts. "Disconnect the bloody call, Cat. I donnae want to hear you having sex."

"Sorry," I say, but it comes out on another gasp.

This time, I grab the phone and make sure I end the call. Then I toss the mobile, not caring where it lands.

And I come. A tidal wave of pleasure crashes through me, and my body bows inward. I clutch at Alex's head, crying out, my eyes squeezed shut until the climax subsides. Breathing hard, I slump against the wall.

He sits up, licking his lips. "Mm, I've missed the taste of you."

I can't speak. Or move. Or get my brain to function.

Alex slides his tongue over his lips again, groaning like he's sampled the best food on earth. He pats my leg and jumps off the bed.

"Now we're even," he says, and he walks out of the room, shutting the door.

Even? The man is off his head.

If he thinks sex will make us even, he's in for a nasty surprise. We won't be on a level playing field until he explains everything to me. I have questions. He will answer them.

No matter what I have to do to make that happen.

Chapter Twenty-One

Alex

The next morning, I wake up to the sound of Cat picking the lock on my bedroom door. She swings it open, picks up a tray she'd set on the floor, and carries it to my bed. Since I haven't bothered to get out of bed yet, she sets the tray over my lap with its legs on either side of my hips. A half-dome lid covers the large plate, but I see an oversize mug of steaming coffee, plus silverware.

"Good morning," she says, smiling. "I've made you breakfast. You can eat it in bed."

I push up into a sitting position. "Aren't you eating?"

"Aye." She lifts the lid off the plate. "We're sharing."

"What if I don't want to share? You might infect me with your Scottish germs."

"Since when are you a germophobe?"

"I'm not. But I prefer to eat my own food without any help."

She laughs and pinches my cheek. "You are so adorable when you're full of shit. I remember how you used to love sharing a meal with me. I would feed you, and you would feed me, and you said it was your favorite way of eating."

"Did I? Maybe I was lying. Or I'd been taken over by an alien parasite."

She climbs over me to get onto the bed, snuggling up beside me. "I'll start."

Catriona picks up a fork, slides scrambles eggs onto it, and stabs a hunk of sausage with the tines. She holds the loaded fork to my lips. "Open up."

What's the point in arguing? I open my mouth and take the huge bite of food she's prepared for me. It tastes delicious, but I'd rather she wasn't sitting next to me wearing nothing but that dressing gown she'd worn last night. When she bends her knee, the gown falls away from her leg.

She reaches for the coffee mug.

"I can do that myself," I say, snatching up the mug before she can grab it. "I'm not an invalid."

"No, but you are grumpy this morning." She slides a hand along my thigh, leaning in so her lips are a breath away from mine. "We can have a poke if you like. All you have to do is answer another question for me."

"Yes, I remember how that went last night. One question turned into a multitude of follow-on harassment."

"Not a multitude, and not harassment." She laughs again, and her breaths flutter on my skin. "Stop being so uptight about this. I won't tell anyone the things you tell me. It's just between us."

"I should trust you?" I glance at her sideways. "You picked the lock on my bedroom door."

"That's right. Why did you bother locking it? You knew I could pick it."

"Maybe I still can't accept that you're a naughty little lock-picking Scot."

"Or maybe you hoped I'd break in. Maybe you like it." She glides her hand up my bare chest and dances her fingers up my throat. "It's exciting, isn't it? Not knowing what I might do next."

I can't deny the idea does appeal to me. Her larcenous side intrigues me much more than I want to admit to her. I know she's trying to use sex as leverage to pry all my secrets out of me, but I can't let her succeed.

So I turn my face toward her, moving in like I intend to kiss her. She parts her lips, and I glimpse her tongue.

Then I grab a piece of sausage and shove it into her mouth. "There. I fed you. Now you can scamper back to your room."

Cat chews the sausage with such deliberate slowness, transforming the simple act of chewing into an erotic display, that I know she means to torture me this morning. She swallows the food and licks her lips. "That was delicious, but you taste better."

And she licks her lips again.

No, I will not fall for her tricks today.

I gulp down the coffee—too quickly—and start coughing and spluttering.

She slaps my back several times. "Take it easy, Alex. You're not meant to inhale coffee."

"Thank you for the helpful tip."

Cat leans back against the wall. "What should we do today? I was thinking a walk might be nice."

"I don't do the outdoors."

"But you live in the forest."

"Only as a means of keeping other people away."

She clucks her tongue. "No more lies, Alex. Tell me the real reason you live in the forest, all alone, in a huge, depressing mansion."

"What's depressing about it?"

"The walls. Dark wood and crimson." She shakes her head. "*A Dhia*, it's no wonder you're so crabby when you live in a house Edgar Allan Poe would've loved to write about."

I grunt. It's not the most eloquent response, but I have no bloody clue what to say to her. Or how to make her go away. She picks locks, which means I'll have to flee to a place farther away than my study to escape her.

Having her here unsettles me. But it also…makes me feel more alive than I have in ages.

"Let's stay in," I say, "and shag all day. That's better exercise than walking."

She sighs, rolling her eyes at me. "Oh Alex, what am I going to do with you? You're so obstinate."

"Yes, I'm an infuriating bastard. Better go home to Scotland."

"No," she says with a laugh. "That won't work either. I'm staying. Now, you can either go outside with me willingly, or I can get the handcuffs and make sure you can't get away."

"Those are my only choices?"

"Yes."

I shove a forkful of eggs and sausage into my mouth and devour it, then I slump backward and stare up at the ceiling. "Have it your way. I will go outside with you."

She claps and cheers.

"For heaven's sake, Cat, it's not like I promised to bare my soul to you. It's a walk, nothing more."

"It's a start."

After breakfast, we dress—in our separate rooms—and head downstairs. I try to distract her from this silly walk idea by suggesting we ought to clean up the dishes first. She politely commands me to abandon the dirty dishes in the sink, saying, "We can take care of that later." When I realize she's digging her heels in like a sodding mule, determined to drag me outdoors, I surrender.

Once we've exited the house through the back door, Catriona clasps my hand and guides me into the woods.

I have never walked in the woods. Not these woods, for certain. I'm ninety-nine percent positive I have never trekked through any sort of forest before. Why should I want to? It's not interesting at all. Trees. Grass. Birds making irritating noises. I'd lived in cities until I moved to Montana and built a house in the middle of the type of geography I'd never wanted to experience.

Cat tows me down a narrow path which she informs me is a deer trail.

"Why should I want to follow deer?" I ask. "Seeing animals in the wild appeals to me even less than consuming haggis, which Logan tried to convince me to eat."

She pulls us to a halt inside a small clearing. "What do you have against the forest? It's nature. And it's a fair sight more pleasant than that gloomy house you live in."

Will she never give up insulting my home? "It's not gloomy. It's atmospheric."

"No, Alex, it's a beautifully decorated tomb." She leans against a tree, waving at our surroundings. "Stop being so uptight. Relax and enjoy the wildflowers, the bird songs, the scent of pine and grass, and the sunshine." She tips her head to the side. "You do remember what sunshine is, don't you?"

"Maybe I'm a vampire and sunlight will burn me to ashes."

She shakes her head. "I willnae give up, so ye might as well give in."

"I have. I'm here in the forest, aren't I?"

"You are, but you can do better." She wanders into a patch of wildflowers and lies down, sighing with contentment. "Join me, Alex. Unclench your erse and take a moment to enjoy nature."

I open my mouth to inform her I do not have my arse clenched but decide against it. She'll only make another silly comment about my gloomy house or my supposed uptight attitude.

Since I seem to have no choice, I lie down among the flowers with Catriona.

The sun warms my face, a not-unpleasant sensation. I close my eyes, letting myself feel the grass under me, tickling my arms and hands. I hadn't realized grass could feel so soft.

"Listen to the birds," Cat says. "And the breeze rustling the leaves in the trees."

"Are you trying to hypnotize me? I'm immune to that."

"It wouldn't kill you to loosen up."

She begins to hum, though I don't recognize the tune. Her voice is hushed and soothing. The breeze makes the leaves shiver, the sound almost like the sizzling of food on a grill. Which makes me hungry. But her voice lulls me into a trance-like state, and all my thoughts drift away on the wind.

I'm not hypnotized. I'm…relaxed. That's what she wanted me to do, I've done it, and I can go back into the house.

My muscles refuse to move.

"Alex," she murmurs, her voice still soothing and hushed, "why do you punish yourself?"

I make a noise but can't summon any words. Her voice, the feel of the grass, the scent of the flowers, it all keeps me drifting on that cloud of nothingness. I don't think I've ever been this at ease before. It feels strange and yet pleasant.

"Wake up," she says, her voice much closer now.

"Sorry, I can't. You must've drugged me."

"Maybe you're in the right mood after all."

"The right mood for what?"

She lays a hand on my chest. "Why do you punish yourself, Alex? Living in a huge, gloomy house. Not having friends, until Logan adopted you."

"I don't play well with others."

"Why?"

The scent of her surrounds me, something like vanilla and cinnamon and woman. God, she smells wonderful.

"Why?" she asks again. "Why don't you have friends?"

My breathing has become slower, my pulse too. I feel like I'm floating in space, but with the sun toasting my skin. Maybe that explains why I answer her question. "I never learned how to make friends. All my parents ever taught me was how to lie and how to protect myself."

"From what?"

My body feels like it's dissolved into a pool of warmth and comfort and peace, leaving me incapable of moving or speaking.

"What did you need to protect yourself from?" she asks. "And why did your parents want you to lie?"

"Had to. It's the lifestyle—" My eyelids spring open, and my heart thuds. I had almost told her. What in the world is wrong with me? Lying here in the grass with Catriona has actually mesmerized me. "Forget it. You don't want to know those answers, believe me. I wish I didn't know."

"Why are you so afraid to share your past with me?"

"I'm protecting you." From more than she can possibly imagine.

"Alex, please. Don't keep shutting me out. I can handle whatever it is you think you've done."

"No, you really can't." My phone chimes, letting me know I have a new text. "We're done here."

She slaps both hands down on my chest. "Not yet. I want to know one more thing. It has nothing to do with your secrets that you won't tell me."

"Go on."

"Do you remember the time we went swimming naked?"

What on earth is she doing now? "Of course I remember."

"I was embarrassed to take my clothes off, even though there was nobody else at the lake."

"Yes, I was there. I know what happened."

She lowers her body half onto mine, with our faces close together. "Close your eyes and remember when we were in the water."

"This is ridiculous."

"Please, Alex. As a favor to me."

I grumble but close my eyes, picturing that day—the sun, the wispy clouds scudding across the blue sky, the smile on Cat's face when she stripped off her clothes and jumped into the water. I'd already been in the water, naked, trying to talk her into joining me. When she did, she jumped in feet first and shrieked with joy. I can almost feel the water spraying up around me.

And I heard her laughter, bright and exuberant.

"Remember how you kissed me," she purrs into my ear.

Though I shouldn't want to, I can't stop my mind from conjuring an image of Cat in my arms, drenched and naked, water drizzling off her hair and onto me. I'd wrapped my arms around her body and kissed her like I'd drown without her breaths feeding me oxygen and her tongue twining with mine. She'd tasted like sunshine and woman and all the beautiful things I had never allowed myself to have until I met her. It had been more than a kiss. That moment changed everything.

"Remember what you said to me after," she whispers.

Memories and reality converge in my mind, and I repeat the words I'd spoken to her years earlier, in a different time and a different place, in a different lifetime.

"Never leave me, Cat."

"I won't, Alex. Not ever."

The bird songs and the rustling leaves rouse me from the memories. When I open my eyes, she's watching me with her lips curled into a sweet, almost loving smile.

"You tricked me," I say. "That's not a very nice thing to do."

"I have no choice. Trickery is the only way I can make you talk to me." She touches her lips to mine, only for a fraction of a second, then sits up. "I meant it. I won't leave you."

Never leave me, Cat. I'd said that out loud. Why? Not a clue.

"Do what you want. I obviously can't stop you." I get to my feet, wiping grass off my trousers. "But I have nothing more to say to you."

While I walk away from her, I dig my mobile out of my pocket and check the new text. It says, "You will pay - RH."

Reginald Hewitt. Of course. The blighter hasn't had his fill of harassing me yet.

Another good reason to push Cat away. I may need to kidnap the woman and drop her off at the airport to make sure she gets the idea that she can't stay here anymore. No, that won't work. She'll hike all the way from the airport to my home just to torture me more with her presence.

I intend to make a dramatic exit by stalking off down the trail, but I trip on a root. Cursing, I try again.

As I head down the narrow trail, Cat calls out to me, "Ye cannae outrun the past, Alex. It will catch up to you."

If only she knew how true that statement is.

Chapter Twenty-Two

Catriona

I follow Alex back to the house, but we split off once we're inside. He veers off to go into his office—to hide from me, I'm sure—and I let him. After the way he'd opened up to me a few minutes ago, I decide he needs a wee bit of time to himself to process what happened. The fact that I had to trick him into sharing something, anything, with me makes me uncomfortable. He left me no choice. Trickery is the only way I can crack his shell and peek inside.

Still, I need a wee break from him too. So I grab a bottle of water from the kitchen and rush upstairs to my room. Once I'm there, the only thing I can do is think. About Alex. About what he'd accidentally let slip while we lay in the grass together. *I never learned how to make friends*, he said. *All my parents ever taught me was how to lie and how to protect myself.*

What sort of people had Alex's parents been? I can't imagine my mother or father teaching me to lie. If he had no friends, Alex must've been a very lonely boy. I can't imagine that either. Besides having friends, I had my brothers and sisters, and cousins too. Evan had always been the most reserved of my cousins, the one who kept to himself most of the time, but Iain changed that. He and his wife, Rae, refused to let Evan go on being a recluse, inviting him to dinner and eventually to a shinty match at Iain and Rae's home near Loch Fairbairn. Their efforts paid off. Today, Evan has a wonderful wife and daughter, and they love spending time with the rest of the family too.

Then there's Logan. He had been standoffish until recently, until Evan decided to become Logan's friend whether Logan liked it or not. Now Logan and Serena attend every family event.

Can I ever convince Alex to stop hiding? The rest of the family will like him if he gives them a chance to, I know it. But how do I help him get there? Every crack in his armor gives me hope I can do it, but I don't know how.

MacTaggarts never give up, but we also know when to ask for help.

I grab my mobile phone, scrolling through my list of contacts until I find the one I need. Only one MacTaggart has firsthand experience with taming a stubborn man who keeps secrets. I tap the screen to dial her number.

"Cat, sweetie, what's up?" Emery says, sounding as cheerful as ever.

As the leader of the American Wives Club, and the wife of my stubbornest brother, Emery is the only one who might be able to help me.

"I need advice," I tell her. "It's about Alex."

"Oh, you mean the British Bastard." She doesn't sound disgusted or angry. No, Emery is always upbeat, and she gives everyone the benefit of the doubt. "Not that I'm judging. You know I never do that."

"Which is why I rang you. Rory won't like what I'm about to tell you, but I know you'll break it to him gently."

"The best way to deliver bad news to my honey is while we're naked."

"I didn't need to know that."

She laughs. "Yeah, I guess that was over-sharing. Don't worry, I can handle your brother."

Aye, Emery is the only person on earth who can do that with any measure of success. Rory, aka the Steely Solicitor, always listens to his wife.

"So," Emery says, "tell me what's up."

"I've been trying to get through to Alex, to make him open up to me so I can understand why he is the way he is. I want—no, I need to see the real Alex, not just the smiling, what-the-fuck-do-I-care persona he puts on for everyone else."

"What do you need from me?"

"You've met Alex several times. You're the most perceptive person I know, so, um…what do you think of him?"

She hums for a moment, like she's thinking about how to respond. "I haven't had any long conversations with Alex, but I've always liked him. Rory gave up trying to drag me over to the We Hate Alex camp, but he thinks I'm 'off my head' for being friendly with the British Bastard."

"Would you mind not calling him that? I apologized to Alex for making up those stupid nicknames for him."

She falls silent for a few seconds, then her voice takes on a knowing tone. "Ohhhh, I get it. You're falling for him all over again, aren't you?"

"I don't know. That's why I need your help."

"You know I'm here for whatever you need." She hesitates, and when she speaks again, she sounds much more serious. "I hope you're prepared for what you'll have to go through to get this done. If you're determined to break through Alex's shell, get ready for an emotional beating. He'll fight you every step of the way, and he might say things that will hurt—a lot. I went through this with Rory, but I get the feeling Alex will be much harder to crack. You need patience, tenderness, and a thick skin. Are you ready for that?"

"Yes, I'm ready."

"Remember, you have a secret weapon at your disposal."

"What is it?"

She laughs again. "Sex, of course."

"Donnae think that works on Alex. We had a poke already, and he still won't tell me everything."

"You already slept with him? Well, I'm sure you can think of other sexy ways to break his willpower. But the most important weapon in your arsenal is the most deceptively simple and the most devastatingly effective."

"Can you not be so cryptic?"

"Sure. I'm talking about love, Cat. You can't save a man from himself unless your heart is invested in the mission."

Am I in love with Alex? I don't know. He won't let me figure that out because he won't show me his true self. Armed with Emery's advice, maybe I have a chance. I owe it to myself and to Alex to try.

"Thank you, Em," I say. "You're my favorite sister-in-law."

"I won't tell Erica and Calli you said that." She pauses, then adds, "You can call me anytime, if you need more advice or just emotional support. I'm here for you."

"You're an angel, Emery."

"No, I've learned from hard experience, that's all. Before you get too deeply into this thing with Alex, you need to answer one question. Is he worth it?"

"I believe he is."

"Then good luck, Cat. You'll need it."

We say goodbye, and I resolve to begin my mission. I am invested. Every iota of strength, determination, and love in my soul will guide me and empower me. I know Alex is worth the pain and the struggle. No one else knew him before he became the closed-off, impenetrable version of himself. I didn't simply know him back then. I loved him. No one on earth had ever made me feel the way he did, like I could jump off a cliff and he would always be there to catch me. He still has that effect on me.

I've caught glimpses of the old Alex. Now, I need to excavate his soul and wash off the dirt.

But I can't do that in my bedroom.

So I trot downstairs to his study. He's left the door open, but I don't see him in there. Has he left the house? I walk into the study and glance around, still not seeing him.

Wait. I see something…

Edging around the desk, I realize what I'm seeing. Alex's feet stick out from behind his big leather chair. I move closer, and the rest of him comes into view.

Alex is lying on the floor on his back, eyes closed, hands clasped over his belly.

I kneel beside him. "Alex, are you asleep?"

"Obviously not, or I wouldn't be able to answer your question."

"Good, I'm glad you're awake." I pry one of his hands away from his body. "We're going into town for lunch and to have fun."

He groans, twisting his mouth into an annoyed expression. "I am not in the mood, Catriona. You go on, though. When you get home, you can tell me all about how much fun you had in that boring little town."

"No, Alex. We are going together." I tug on his hand while I rise to a half-standing position. "Get up, or I'll make you do it."

He chuckles and opens one eye. "Your determination is charming, but I'm much bigger and heavier than you. No woman can make me move unless I want to."

I wag a finger at him, clucking my tongue. "Donnae underestimate a MacTaggart woman."

"Ah yes, you MacTaggarts are a bloody stubborn lot." He opens his other eye, aiming both of them at me. "Go on, then. Move me."

He's daring me to do it, but I know he's right about one thing. I can't pull him up off the floor without his cooperation. How else can I force him to move?

An idea occurs to me, and I smile.

Then I race into the kitchen, get what I need, and race back to Alex. He's still lying there on the floor, but his arrogantly certain expression dissolves when he sees what I'm holding. His brows knit together.

I dump a pail of cold water onto him. Ice cubes tumble out along with the water.

He shouts and splutters.

And then he jumps to his feet.

Shaking himself, he scowls at me. "That was cheating."

"Never said I'd make you move by physical force."

He studies me like this is the first time he's really seen me. "How did I never realize your soul is full of wicked trickery and larceny?"

"I'm not the infatuated girl you used to know." I drop the pail on the floor. "Now, will you come with me willingly? Or do I need to bring my secret weapon?"

"Since I'm not sure I'll survive your secret weapon…" He raises his hands, palms out. "I surrender to you, Catriona MacTaggart. Do with me what you will."

"You surrender? Hmm, that has interesting possibilities." I seize his shirt and haul him closer. "I own you, Alex Thorne."

"I believe you just might." He bends his head to whisper in my ear, "This means I will be corrupting you."

Excitement sizzles through me, awakening my skin and every fine hair on my body. "Cannae wait for that."

Chapter Twenty-Three

Alex

Why did I agree to this? The things most people think are fun seem annoying and dull to me—like amusement parks, which I've never understood. Wait in a queue for hours so you can have the privilege of being flung around for a few minutes? That sounds like torture to me. But then, I've never visited an amusement park. Maybe it's more enjoyable than it sounds.

Cat feigns shock when I tell her I've never been to an amusement park. "Alex Thorne, the daredevil who loves to shag me in public places, has never ridden on a roller coaster?"

"Make fun of me all you want. It doesn't bother me."

"I know that." She uses my hand, which she insists on holding while we stroll down the streets of this town, as leverage to pull me closer to her. Then she bumps her shoulder into me and smiles with saccharine charm. "It's telling the truth that scares you."

For a second or two, I consider reminding her that I'm not afraid of anything. Why waste oxygen on that? The bloody woman won't believe me no matter how many times I say it.

"Where are you abducting me to, anyway?" I ask. "This town doesn't have anything that even remotely resembles amusement."

"Of course it does." She points at a shop we've almost reached. "There. Let's look for gifts to send to our families."

The sneaky woman. She thinks she can trick me into revealing my history to her by suggesting "we" buy gifts for "our" families.

"Nice try," I tell her. "But I'm not that easy to manipulate."

"You were back in the wood this morning."

"Say 'woods,' Cat. Americans might think you're talking about something very different if you refer to the forest as the wood."

"Will they?" She glances at my groin. "Donnae worry. No one will think I mean your *slat* is hard when I talk about the wood. It's flat as a burst balloon."

"It is not—" I stop myself from defending the state of my cock and grumble instead as we stop at the door to the shop she wants to visit. "Oh lord, please tell me you're not serious."

"Of course I am. It's a gift shop, Alex, and we agreed to buy gifts for our families."

"No, you said we should. I ignored your comment."

"Which is tacit agreement." She moves toward the door, tugging on my hand, and lays her free hand on the knob. "What's wrong with this shop? It's adorable."

"That's the problem. It's full of adorable little knickknacks and adorable novelty shirts and sickeningly adorable hats." I squint, peering through the window. "Bloody hell. Are those slippers made to look like furry rabbits?"

"Aye." While she pulls the door open, making a bell jingle, she smiles at me. "I'll be sure to buy you a pair."

"No thank you. I already have a pair of kitten-shaped slippers."

"Good, then the bunny ones will fit right in."

For reasons I can't fathom, I let her haul me into the shop. For twenty minutes, we browse all the nauseatingly cheerful items arranged on shelves and in wooden boxes. Cat selects silly gifts for her brothers, sisters, in-laws, and cousins—so many items that I wind up carrying two shopping baskets while she carries another one. When we reach a shelf of wooden boxes filled with various kinds of rocks, she digs through one full of polished pink stones, finally excavating a single specimen the size of a quarter.

"Here," she says, offering me the stone. "I'm buying this for you. No one needs rose quartz as much as you do."

I take the stone, turning it between my fingers. "Why do I need this? It's a rock."

"Rose quartz is said to have magical effects. Maybe its spell will penetrate that iron skin of yours and make you more receptive."

"And what exactly are you trying to make me receptive to?"

She touches the stone with the tip of one finger. "Rose quartz represents love and passion."

I stare down at the stone, a coldness rushing through me. Rocks don't have supernatural powers, but Catriona seems to have the unerring ability to crawl under my skin and reawaken parts of me I'd laid to rest long ago. I had good reasons for doing that. Reasons I will never tell Cat.

"Love and passion," she repeats, leaning closer, her voice hushed and filled with emotions I don't care to decipher.

I toss the stone back into the bin. "No thank you."

She pulls back, but only a little. "Fine, forget the stone. But we are going to buy gifts for our families."

"Repeatedly using the word family won't make me tell you about mine."

Her eyes light up, and her brows rise a touch. "So, you do have a family. That's a start."

"Everyone has a family. I wasn't born from Zeus's skull."

"I know that," she says, looking at me like I'm a clueless child. "But you admitted you have family, which means one day you will tell me about them."

Though I frown at her, she just smiles and takes my hand again, leading me toward a display of—

"Ruddy novelty shirts?" I say, stopping dead like a stubborn mule. "No, Cat, I am not trying on any ridiculous clothing."

"No need to try it on." She releases my hand so she can flip through the shirts on hangers. When she finds the one she wants, at the back of the rack, she pulls it out and grins. "This is perfect. Let's see if it fits."

She holds the shirt, still on its hanger, up to my chest. Turning her head side to side, she nods. "Aye, it's the right size."

I glance down at the garment she's holding to my chest. The tie-dyed shirt features bright colors and the saying "Don't hate me because I'm pretty."

"That's very funny," I say, "but no. I will not wear this."

"Embarrassed?" she asks. "All right. Maybe I'll send this to Rory. He won't be ashamed to be seen in it."

"Ashamed? Me?" I set down the two baskets I've been carrying, tear the shirt off its hanger, and whip off the one I'm wearing. While she smirks, I tug the new shirt on over my head. The price tag dangles from the armpit. "See? Not the slightest bit embarrassed."

Cat's lips flatten, the corners ticking up, and she makes a soft snorting noise. "Thought it would be much harder to get under your skin. Turns out it's not as thick and ironclad as I thought."

My shoulders sag. Oh bloody fucking hell, she's done it. The woman has driven me completely insane.

"Uh, you have to pay for that," calls out a young man behind the sales counter. "Dude, we don't give those away for free, ya know."

"Yes, I'll pay for it." I suppose I have to, now that I've worn the blasted thing. Growling under my breath, I pick up the shopping baskets and look at Cat. "Now that you've made your point, can we please leave this ridiculous shop?"

"After we pay for everything."

"*I* will pay for everything. Consider it my donation to the MacTaggart family lunatic asylum. The lot of you are barmy to the core."

"Thank you." She pats my cheek. "For the gifts and for the compliment. Being barmy is much more fun than hiding out in a gloomy mansion."

After we pay for the treasure trove of outlandish gifts she's bought, we have to go back to the car to stash all of it in the trunk. I want to go home. She insists we visit one more shop and then have lunch at the "wee cafe" she found by asking the clerk in the gift shop for advice on the best place to eat. The cafe in question is, according to the young man in the shop, "totally dope and sick to the extreme."

Yes, doesn't that sound lovely.

Cat makes me cover my eyes while she leads me down the sidewalk to the next shop she wants to visit. Only after we've walked inside does she let me see where she's taken me.

I glance around, trying hard not to grimace. She really does seem intent on driving me to drink. If I had a full bottle of Ben Nevis in my hand, I'd pour the entire contents down my throat.

The wily Scot leans into me and whispers, "Welcome to The Cave. I think you're familiar with their line of bondage gear."

"So this is where you found fuzzy pink handcuffs."

"It is. But they have a lot more than handcuffs." She claims my hand again. "Come on, Alex, be adventurous."

I sigh, resigned to my fate. "If we must."

"Aye, we must." She leads me down an aisle. "You used to be so open and free. Now you're a walking automaton."

"That's what you think?" I grab her wrist and pull her snug against me, her breasts crushed against my chest. "Then who was it who fucked you in the lecture hall?"

"I wish you'd be like that all the time. Instead, you're uptight."

"You have me confused with someone else. Or have you forgotten that I crawled onto your bed and devoured you while you were talking to your sister on the phone?"

"But you've done that sort of thing only twice. If you're still as naughty as ever"—she grinds her hips into me, rubbing herself against my cock—"prove it. Right here, right now."

She wants me to ravish her in the middle of a sex shop, with a display of dildos on one side of the aisle and an assortment of nipple clamps on the other side. Catriona MacTaggart wants me to do it. She's daring me to.

My cock is getting hard, which is exactly what she intended.

I want to do it. Feeling her warm, supple body pressed against mine is dissolving all my willpower. I need to shove her trousers and knickers down to her ankles, back her up to that display of dildos, and drive into her wet heat.

"Hey guys, no hanky-panky in the store."

"Sorry," I call out to the tattooed woman behind the counter, at the front of the shop. "We'll behave."

Cat peels her body away from mine. "I guess you're not the naughty man I used to know after all."

"Later, I'll show you just how naughty I am."

"Is that a promise?"

"Yes."

She looks far too pleased with herself while she saunters down the aisle admiring the merchandise.

I see an item I recognize and hold it up. "Remember these?"

Cat grins. "Oral sex candy. I remember how much you liked that."

"They should label it as a health hazard. I think I had a mild heart attack when you used this candy on me." I wave the packet at her. "Maybe I should buy some of this, so I can give you a taste of your own medicine."

"No need. I still have some at home."

Christ, I wish she would stop calling my house "home." It makes my skin itch.

She goes back to browsing the offerings.

I peer down at small cardboard boxes hanging on a rod. "Edible knickers? What's the point of that?"

"For fun. It tastes good. Maybe we should try it."

"But then I wouldn't have the joy of ripping your knickers off. I love the way you gasp when I do that."

Head down, studying a rack of temporary tattoos, she glances at me. "It's been years since you tore my underwear off. I miss your passionate enthusiasm for...everything."

I ignore her statement, pretending to be obsessed with the assortment of edible underwear.

"Look at this," she says. "You can get a custom temporary tattoo of your name."

"How fascinating."

She throws me a sly, sideways look. "I wonder if your name would fit on my arm. What is your full name?"

"Alexander the Great."

She gives me a look that implies I'm being a stubborn arse.

Which I am, of course.

"Your name isn't a state secret," she says.

"I don't know your full name, so we're even."

She straightens and lifts her chin. "I'm Catriona Sorcha MacTaggart. Now it's your turn."

I walked right into that one, didn't I? "Alex Thorne. That is the only name you need to know."

"But is it your real name? The one you were born with?"

For decades, I've tried not to think about the name I was born with or who my parents were. I won't do it today either. Not think it. Not speak it. Not let that part of my past worm its way into my present.

"I've had enough shopping," I say. "Let's have lunch and go home."

Chapter Twenty-Four

Catriona

Despite the grumpy way he said we should eat and go home, Alex relaxes during lunch. He becomes more like the open and carefree man I knew all those years ago, the man I'd fallen in love with. He seems more at ease and alive, not bound by secrets he thinks he shouldn't tell me. When I tease him, he teases me back.

Progress? I try not to read too much into his behavior.

On the drive home, his good mood wanes the closer we get to his house. Does he not like it? If not, then I wonder why he built it. I wonder that every day, actually, and decide it's about time I got an answer.

Assuming Alex will tell me.

I wait until we walk inside the house, since I don't want us to have a car accident because he's so determined not to open up to me. He's done it more than once already. Why not again? I have to approach this the right way, though, or he'll never answer my question.

He disappears into his study, and I go upstairs to call Emery for more advice. She's not home. Rory asks if he can help, but there's absolutely no way I am going to discuss my relationship with Alex Thorne with my disapproving brother. When Rory suggests he "might need to borrow Lachlan's jet, or maybe Iain's" to fly across the pond and "deal with the problem," I order him to do no such thing. Will he listen? He'd better, or I will teach him a lesson about interfering in my life.

My family doesn't understand why I want to be here with Alex. They don't understand him, full stop. I can't blame them, but I don't need meddling MacTaggarts to deal with my problems for me.

I draft a lesson plan for this coming week as well as a trivia game we can play in class to encourage my students to become fully engaged in topics that can be rather dry. I'm also giving Alex time to recover from our conversation earlier. When evening arrives, I change into something more likely to put him in a good mood for talking. The only thing I know for sure will do that is sex, so I walk into his study wearing only a bra and knickers—both made from sapphire-blue lace.

Alex is sitting behind his desk, his arms resting on it while he stares down at the big calendar that takes up a large part of the surface. He doesn't even glance up when I stroll into the room.

"Not in the mood for an inquisition," he says. "Find another way to entertain yourself."

Disappointment makes me want to blow out a gusty breath and droop my head, but I refuse to let him have that effect on me. It's what he wants. This time I'll get what I want, one way or another.

I stroll around the desk to him and lean over his shoulder, doing my best to infuse my voice with an irresistible sensuality. "I want to talk to you, Alex."

He stiffens a wee bit.

"This will be more fun than staring at your desk calendar." I brush my lips over the shell of his ear. "I promise."

"Are you teasing me, or do you want me to fuck you on my desk?"

"We can do that after we talk."

He groans. "No thank you."

I swivel his chair toward me, surprised when he doesn't try to stop me. This has to be progress. I perch on his lap with my legs draped across it.

Alex keeps his arms on the chair and remains stiff.

"Relax," I say. "I'm not here to demand you tell me your full name."

"What do you want, then?"

I snuggle up to him, my head under his chin. "An answer to one simple question."

"Your questions are never simple."

"They should be. You make everything so complicated." I stroke his cheek with my fingertips. "Just this once, answer my question honestly without complaining or getting angry."

"I'll try. That's the best I can offer."

"Good enough." I lay my hand on his chest, over his heart. "Why did you build this house?"

"I needed a place to live."

"You could've lived in faculty housing or an apartment or—"

"No, I couldn't. I need privacy."

I slide my hand up to his shoulder. "Moving to the middle of nowhere, surrounded by nothing but trees, is an extreme version of privacy."

"My needs are extreme."

"Why?"

"Because."

I raise my head to look at him. "Don't act like a bairn, Alex. Answering a question shouldn't be like having a limb amputated."

"Maybe it is for me."

Time for a different approach. "All right, if you won't answer that question, answer this one. You're obviously rich, based on what I've seen in this house, but you didn't seem wealthy when we first met. How did you get to have so much money?"

"I stole it."

He must be lying. Alex wants to make me angry, so I'll leave him alone. He wouldn't steal anything. Would he? Well, he has borrowed artifacts, like those Babylonian tablets.

No, he's not a thief.

"Who did you steal from?" I ask.

"Maybe I broke into the Smithsonian and nicked the Hope Diamond, then replaced it with a replica."

"No, you wouldn't do that. You value artifacts as historical treasures, which is why you sometimes borrow them but never pinch anything."

"Most people would say borrowing without permission is theft."

"Those people don't know you. I do."

He harrumphs.

I think about everything I've seen in this house and the things Logan told me. Alex had servants the first time Logan and Serena visited him here. A few days later, the servants had gone and so had Reginald, his friend and employee. I know from Logan that Reginald had betrayed Alex, but I still have no idea why Alex let his servants go. When I asked him about it several days ago, he said, "They were no longer needed."

But I don't believe that's the whole story.

I cuddle up to him again, with my head on his shoulder this time. "Why did you get rid of all your household employees? I know why you fired Reginald, but the others…"

"Does it matter? I no longer wanted their services. End of story."

"But it's not the end. I'm starting to think it's only the beginning."

He growls, like a cornered beast. "I suppose if I want to shag you, I'll be required to answer your questions."

"No, I'll have sex with you either way." And it's true. I will. The one time he told me the truth was after the oral sex candy incident. But I won't sleep with him to get answers. Not only for that reason, at least. I want him, and I need to feel close to him.

If that makes me an eejit, I can live with it.

"You're giving up your leverage?" he says. "That's not the way to seduce me into giving you answers."

"But it's the way to show you I'm here because I want to be, not for the sole purpose of wheedling answers out of you."

He says nothing, but he slides a hand into my hair and combs it with his fingers, over and over, the movements gentle and soothing.

I let my body go soft, and my eyes drift shut. This feels so good, to be close to him, to have this intimacy again, like we used to have years ago.

"The servants are gone," he says, "because I couldn't trust them anymore, after Reginald Hewitt turned on me. But I hired those people only as temporary servants, anyway, so Logan and Serena wouldn't realize the truth."

"And what is the truth?"

"I can't let anyone get too close to me. It's dangerous."

My eyes pop open, but I can't move to lift my head. Though the honesty of his words surprises me, I still feel relaxed. "Dangerous for them or for you?"

He lowers his face into my hair, fluttering it with his breaths. "Both."

"I don't understand."

"And I hope you never do. That's all I'm going to say about it."

The more he tells me, the less I understand about him. I want to ask him why he's so afraid, but he won't answer tonight. I know that, so I move on to a subject that seems less painful. "You built this enormous house and furnished it with lavish things like East Indian rosewood. Why? It must've cost a fortune."

He lifts his head away from mine and goes back to brushing his hand through my hair. "I sank the bulk of my disposable income into this house, to make it ostentatious. I held on to enough to keep me afloat in case things go wrong and I find myself in need of cash."

"Logan said you have family money."

"I do. In a way." He moves his arms around my waist, linking his hands at my hip. "I'd rather not discuss that tonight. It's a long and not very pleasant story."

"Why did you spend so much on this house that you don't even like?"

"Because I—You can't understand unless you know everything, and I have no intention of revealing my life history to you."

I lift my head again. "One day, you will tell me. I believe that."

"Believe whatever you like. I can't give you what you want or what you deserve." When I open my mouth to ask another question, he shakes his head. "That's enough, Cat. No more plumbing the depths of my soul tonight."

"All right."

He has told me more than he's ever told me before, so I let it go. Tomorrow, maybe he'll share even more. I'll hold fast to that hope because it's all I have.

I straddle his lap. "Do you want me on the desk? Or here in the chair?"

"Neither." He stands up, forcing me to dismount his lap. "I'm knackered, Cat. Afraid you'll have to wait until another time to seduce me."

He shuffles to the doorway and stops.

"What is it?" I ask.

Alex doesn't glance back when he says, "I forgot to tell you. The faculty housing units have been repaired. You should pack your things and move there."

"I don't want to."

"Go, Cat. You'll be better off away from me."

Though I can see his profile, I can't decipher his expression. "Stop telling me that, Alex. I am not leaving you."

He doesn't really want me to, I'm sure of it. Out in that little meadow in the forest, when I'd talked about the day we went swimming naked, he had repeated the words he said to me so long ago. *Never leave me, Cat.* I know he meant it. I heard the truth of it in his voice, and he will never convince me that he genuinely wants me gone.

"If you don't go," he says, "I will."

"No, you won't. And I will not walk away from you again. Twice I've promised I'll never leave you, and I meant it. I let my fear drive me away from you once. I'm stronger now, and I won't give up on you."

"You stupid little girl," he snarls, "get the fuck out of my house."

"I cannae do that."

He clenches his fists so hard his shoulders bunch up.

Then he storms out of the room and upstairs. I hear his footfalls pounding on the steps, the sound echoing through the hall.

Have I pushed him too far? Or not quite far enough?

Fear fuels his anger. I know this, and I cannot let him get to me.

Emery's advice replays in my mind. *Get ready for an emotional beating,* she said. *He'll fight you every step of the way.* I told Emery that Alex is worth the pain. His anger a moment ago stemmed from fear, and I know he will never hurt me physically. But he will try to break my heart. Rory did that to

Emery, but she stuck with him anyway. They have one of the best marriages I've ever seen, and they're very happy in their life with their twin bairns.

Her last bit of advice reverberates in my mind. *You need patience, tenderness, and a thick skin.*

I can do this. I have to do this. MacTaggarts never give up on anyone they love. We charge through the fire and keep going even when we get burned, because love is stronger than pain. I've learned that lesson from my brothers, from my sister Jamie, and from Logan and Evan and Iain.

Strangely, remembering their mistakes makes me feel better, stronger, more ready for the battle ahead. If they could find their happy endings despite the struggles and the pain, so can I.

But maybe I should give Alex the rest of tonight to recover from the revelations he shared with me. Patience is the key.

I go to the kitchen to have a piece, sitting alone at the island while I eat my sandwich and potato crisps. Aye, I'm eating ham and cheese while wearing nothing but my lingerie. So what? Alex and I are the only ones in this dreary, lonely house.

When I finish my meal, I slog upstairs and halt at the landing.

The door to Alex's room is open. He stands on the threshold, hands fisted, his expression blank.

"Good night, Alex," I say. "I'm going to bed."

I walk to my door, turning around to look at him again.

Before I can speak, he rushes toward me, slapping his palms on either side of the jamb, penning me between his body and the door. "Why are you still here?"

There's no anger in his voice, only anguish and confusion.

"I told you, Alex, I'm not leaving."

"But I keep telling you to go. I snarl at you, and still you refuse to walk out the door." He shakes his head, his features contorting. "Why the fuck won't you go away?"

Since I want honesty from him, I realize I must give him the same thing. Until this moment, I haven't allowed myself to acknowledge what I suddenly know is true. I have no idea how he'll react when I speak the words, but the time has come to tell him. "Because I love you."

His jaw quivers, and the starkness in his gaze stabs pain into my heart. "You can't."

"I do." Laying my palm on his cheek, I say it again with even more conviction. "I love you, Alex."

Though his mouth opens, he can't seem to find any words. He drops his head onto my shoulder.

I stroke his hair, whispering into his ear. "I will never leave you."

He makes a sound, something like a sob but not really that. The noise conveys a depth of emotion I've never known from him, but I don't dare ask him what he's feeling. Not yet.

Maybe tomorrow.

Alex lifts his head, his face a stoic mask. "You're a fool, Catriona."

He stalks into his room and slams the door.

If I am a fool, so be it. Patience, tenderness, and a thick skin are the tools I need to break through Alex's shell and free the man trapped inside it.

I glance at his door, then go into my room. I won't sleep tonight.

Chapter Twenty-Five

Alex

For all of Sunday, Cat leaves me alone. Her only explanation for this stay of execution is that she thinks I need "time to adjust." I don't ask what I need to adjust to, since I'm certain I don't want to know. She seems to be drafting lesson plans and having video chats with her army of relatives. I spend the day trying to figure out what to do—about Cat, about Reginald, about all the things I've deliberately ignored for too long.

Monday morning, I wake up feeling like I've slept inside a filthy trash bin and fed on the leftovers rotting in its depths. Why do I keep letting Cat trick me into confessing things to her? Not only do I have no desire whatsoever to share my past with her, but the more she knows the more danger she might be in. Dear old Reggie seems to have broken out of prison for the sole purpose of driving me barking mad with idiotic phone calls and text messages. *You will pay*, he said Saturday in his text. That wanker has no idea how much I've paid already, or to what lengths I'll go to keep him as far away from Cat as possible.

Maybe I should ring one of her brothers and suggest the lot of them shanghai her back to Scotland. Rory and Lachlan own a private jet. They could come and get her.

But I can't make myself pick up the phone.

I avoid the Scots siren by getting up before she does—I peek inside her room to make sure she's still asleep—and arrange for a taxi to take me to campus. It costs a ruddy fortune to get a taxi service to send a driver all the way out here, but I need to escape from the woman in the blue lingerie who seems determined to wreck me in every way imaginable. I might enjoy the way she'll wreck me, but it will lead to disaster. I'm toxic, after all. Everything I touch will be poisoned, eventually.

Never let that happen to Cat. It's my new mantra.

Like a coward, I slip a note under her bedroom door and sneak out of the house. The ride to campus gives me too much time to think. Last night Catriona said she loves me. Twice. How am I meant to react to that? She shouldn't feel that way, not after what I did to her twelve years ago. But women always think they can save a man, even when the bloke growls and declares he does not need or want to be saved.

I love you, Alex.

Cat's voice echoes in my mind. The look on her face... She meant those words, though I wish to hell she didn't.

The campus is deserted this early in the morning. It's half seven when I step out of the taxi and trudge to the humanities building. The janitorial staff unlock the doors at seven o'clock, so I have no trouble getting inside the building. The lights are on in the halls, but the rooms remain dark, though the doors are open.

I feel like I'm walking into the Minotaur's labyrinth to be sacrificed, unless I can find my way out of the impossible maze I've built around myself. I have no bloody clue how to escape or if I deserve to be set free. I haven't considered that idea in years, because pretending I don't give a fuck about anything has become my best survival strategy.

As I sit down at my desk, a single thought torments me. Do I want to go on surviving? *Only* surviving?

Fate doesn't give me more than a moment to think about the answer. My desk phone rings, and I see it's the extension for Gus Hooper's office. I'm surprised he's on campus this early, but then, I have no idea when he normally shows up to work.

"Good morning," I say when I pick up the call.

"Alex, we need to talk."

I slump in my chair, because his tone assures me he's not about to award me the medal for most loved professor. "When?"

"My office. Ten o'clock."

"Fine. I'll see you then."

I hang up the phone, knowing full well what Gus will say to me when I see him in a few hours. This was inevitable.

Though I'd planned to craft my lectures for the week, I give up on that idea. It will be pointless. I have a class to teach this afternoon, but I know my TA will be taking over for me.

Since I have nothing else to do, I play solitaire on my computer until nine o'clock, then I sneak down the hall to the room where Catriona is lecturing to her class. I ease the door open only enough to grant me a view of her and make sure she doesn't notice me hovering outside the door.

Cat is gesturing while she explains about the Viking invasion of Scotland. Her eyes sparkle, not only from the sunshine streaming through the windows but also from her excitement and passion for the subject.

For half an hour, I watch her. My appointment with Gus Hooper is coming up soon, but I can't make myself walk away from this door. Cat is glorious. Breathtaking. Electrifying. I want to drag her home and make love to her for hours, to show her everything I've never told her about what she means to me.

But I can't do that. So I make my way up to the second floor and Gus Hooper's office. He wastes no time once I sit down on the other side of the desk from him.

"You won't be getting tenure, Alex," he says. "I have to let you go."

"I'm fired, that's what you mean."

He winces. "Yeah. I'm sorry. I was only able to give you back your job last year because you recovered the Babylonian tablets. This time, I don't have any leverage to convince the trustees to forgive you. That lecture you gave last week..." He shuts his eyes, shakes his head, and aims a regretful look at me. "You talked about things the trustees deem to be inappropriate for an educational setting."

"What you mean is that the arsehole whose ex-wife I shagged last year has found yet another excuse to sack me."

Gus winces again. "Yes. I really am sorry."

I shrug one shoulder, once again pretending I don't give a fuck about anything. "Doesn't matter to me. This job was a distraction, not my life's passion."

Which is total bollocks. I love my job, I love teaching, and I've had enough of prudish pricks taking that away from me.

"You'll get severance pay," Gus says, then he winces yet again. "But I'm afraid I can't give you a letter of recommendation. If anyone calls to check your credentials, I've been ordered to tell them you violated the university's code of ethics."

Christ, why don't they just castrate me and have done with it? No one will hire a twice-disgraced professor who violated the ethics code. Everyone will assume I slept with a student, if I'm lucky. These days, too many people will decide "ethics violation" means I forced myself on an innocent girl who refused to press charges.

My career is over.

But I maintain my who-gives-a-toss demeanor. "Thank you for helping me get my job back last time. I understand you can't do anything about it this go-round. I appreciate your candor." I rise and shake Gus's hand. "It was a pleasure working with you."

"I really am sorry, Alex. You're our most popular teacher, and I hate to see you go."

"No worries. I always land on my feet."

"Good luck."

I leave his office and hurry downstairs to my office, intending to gather my personal things and leave. Once I'm in my office, I shut the door and sag against it. I'm fired. *Fuck*. What had I expected? Maybe I shouldn't have made a spectacle of myself last week, strictly to impress Cat. Give the sex lecture. What a fantastic idea. Maybe a small part of me, buried deep down, had wanted to lose this job.

"Goddammit," I hiss and stalk up to my desk, smacking my palms down on the surface. Why do I keep doing this to myself? Find a position at a university, find a way to cock it up, and move on to the next job. I'm out of places to run to, and this time I can't buy my way into a new position. I really am toxic now. And I'm cornered—by Cat, by my own hubris, and by Reginald sodding Hewitt.

As if on cue, my mobile chimes. I have a new text.

Groaning, I pull out my phone and read the message: *We're coming for you - RH.*

We? I hope to hell Reggie hasn't liberated Falk Mullane from prison too. A pair of maggots hunting me down so they can have their pathetic revenge is the last thing I need today. Knowing those two, they'll come up with a bumbling plan.

I'd love to get pissed, but no amount of whisky will fix the mess I've made of my life.

Though I'm not afraid of Reginald Hewitt, when I think about Cat and about Reggie's threat to make me pay, my throat thickens. My chest hurts, and my jaw clenches too. He will not hurt her. I won't allow it.

Suddenly, I need to see her.

The idea is ludicrous, but I can't stop myself from rushing to her office.

Chapter Twenty-Six

Catriona

I do not want to make out with you," I say to the undergraduate standing in front of me, the one who has cornered me outside the door to my office. A moment ago, he asked if I wanted to "do the bump and grind" with him. I said no, so he suggested making out would be a good start to "warm me up" to the idea of shagging him.

"Come on," he says, "I know you're a dirty girl. You screwed Alex Thorne in the lecture hall. Everybody knows about that."

Everyone knows? I have no idea whether to believe his claim, but the thought of it doesn't disturb me as much as it might have a few months ago. I'd loved it when Alex backed me into the dark alcove and ravished me.

"How many times do I have to say no?" I tell the scunner. With exaggerated lip movements and deliberate overemphasis, I add, "I will never, never, never have sex with you."

The lad moves closer, forcing me to press my back against the doorjamb. He sets a hand on the jamb, bending his arm to bring his face closer to mine.

"Stop playing games," he says in a low voice. "I know you want me. I have a sixth sense about things like that. I mean, if you'll bang Alex Thorne, you'll bang anybody. Right?"

"Move away."

"Playing hard to get can be hot, but I'm getting tired of it."

"Back away or I will ram my knee into your miserable wee balls."

He lunges his head down, aiming for my mouth.

Before I can knee him in the groin, he's yanked away from me.

Alex is gripping the back of the scunner's shirt in his fist. Everything about him conveys menace and a darkness I've never witnessed in him before, from his slitted gaze to his flaring nostrils, and from the way his lips have compressed into a slash to the tension in his every muscle.

His voice conveys the same dark tension when he hisses, "Get your ruddy hands off her. When a woman says no, it means no."

"Jeez, man, back off. This is a private conversation." The scunner manages to look snotty and self-satisfied while he's virtually dangling from Alex's fist. "A perv like you shouldn't talk about how to treat women. You did this chick in the lecture hall."

Alex tows the laddie away from me and shoves him against the wall. With his teeth gritted, he peels his lips back and says, "Stay away from Catriona MacTaggart."

"What if I don't?"

"You have no idea what I'm capable of. This won't be the first time I've left a tosser lying in a pool of his own blood and spitting out his own teeth."

A shiver rattles through me. Is Alex lying to convince the lad to behave? I get the impression he isn't. He means what he says, and I believe he might have beaten someone bloody.

But I can't believe he would do something like that without severe provocation.

The *cacan* seems to have realized Alex is not bluffing. He wilts, like a dying flower, and swallows hard enough that his Adam's apple jumps. "Okay, okay, don't go postal or anything. I'll leave, but um...you kind of have to let go of me first."

Alex's nostrils flare again, and he gives the *cacan* a ferocious shake. "Never harass another woman ever again."

The boy raises his hands in surrender. "I won't, I swear it."

I settle a hand on Alex's arm. "Let him go. It's all right."

Alex keeps his searing gaze locked on the boy, but he releases the *bod ceann*.

The boy scurries away.

I move closer to Alex. "Everything is all right. You can relax."

He turns his face to me, his chest still heaving—from the adrenaline spike brought on by his confrontation with the student, no doubt. He stays silent, though his gaze drills into me.

"Calm down, Alex," I say, giving his arm a light squeeze. "It's over."

"I hate bastards who take advantage of people they think are weaker."

Anger transforms the tone of his voice into something dark and rough but tinged with pain. Did someone treat him the way he described? Is that why he reacted so fiercely to the student's aggression? I want to ask him that, but I can see he's still teetering on a knife's edge. Questions can wait until later.

"Alex, please," I say, "take a deep breath and get hold of yourself. No one hurt me, and no one is going to hurt you."

He stares at me, not blinking, not moving.

I cradle his face in my hands. "Everything is all right."

The starkness in his gaze makes my heart and soul ache for him. Whatever he experienced in the past, it must have been awful.

He shuts his eyes, pulls in a deep breath, and exhales it little by little. His shoulders sag. His hands unclench. Every muscle in his body slackens, and his expression softens too, though he keeps his eyes closed for several more seconds before he looks at me.

"I apologize," he says in a hushed tone. "That was uncalled for."

He'd told me that all his parents ever taught him was how to lie and how to protect himself. When I asked why they would do that, he said it was because of "the lifestyle." I still don't know what that means, but I remember his response when I asked why he wouldn't confide in me about his past. "I'm protecting you," he told me.

"Don't apologize," I say. "You were protecting me, weren't you?"

He's watching me again, like he worries he might blurt out the truth without meaning to do it.

"Thank you, Alex, for protecting me."

"But I... You can't be happy that I'm a rampaging beast."

"You don't rampage." I place a gentle kiss on his lips. "You have pain deep inside you. I can see that now. If you'll let me, maybe I can help you deal with the past and move on from it. I want to be here for you, in any way you need me."

I fold my arms around his neck and hold him close, nestling my face against his throat, breathing in the scent of him. He tenses up again, but only for a moment. Then he slips his arms around me and splays his palms over my lower back, dipping his head to bury his face in my hair.

"Catriona," he murmurs. "Sweet, barmy Catriona."

Though his words seem like sarcasm, his voice conveys nothing like it. He speaks in a soft, tender voice. Maybe he thinks I am barmy, but he must like that about me. I might be crazy for staying with Alex, for wanting to dive into the darkness with him in the hopes of pulling him out the other side and into the sunshine.

He nuzzles my ear and my cheek. "You should have left me already."

"I will never leave you."

"That's your worst mistake." He lifts his head and backs away from me. "I will ruin you. Maybe I already have."

"What are you talking about?"

"I've been sacked, Catriona." His lips warp into a nasty smirk. "And thanks to a vengeful bastard, I'm a walking ethics violation. That means I will never get another position at any university in this country, perhaps not anywhere on this planet."

"Things cannae be that bad."

"You are so charmingly blind."

He pivots on his heels and stalks away from me.

Mercurial doesn't even begin to describe Alex Thorne.

Chapter Twenty-Seven

Alex

When I leave Cat standing there in the hall, I leg it to my car. Luckily, she left it parked in my reserved slot. The faculty parking lot is full today, and the crowd of vehicles affords me a measure of privacy while I sit here and brood. What am I meant to do now? I'm unemployed. Most likely blacklisted. Labeled a sexual predator, for sure.

And Cat wants to save me.

"Fuck," I mutter, thumping my forehead on the steering wheel.

When I saw that slimy arsehole manhandling Catriona, I'd lost all my good sense—not that I've ever suffered from much of it. Blind rage had seized me. Stop the little fucker, that was all I'd thought about in that moment. Well, that and "beat the little fucker to death." Violence has never been my strong suit, but the thought of anyone harming Cat turned me into an animal.

I needed to protect her. Sending her away seemed like the best option, but she refused to leave. She's gone insane. She must have done. Why else would she insist on staying with me?

Despite my every effort to stop it from happening, our conversation replays in my mind.

Why the fuck won't you go away?

Because I love you.

I thump my fist on the steering wheel and grit my teeth. Goddammit, I do not want this. A woman who loves me? That will only complicate my life even more than I've already managed to do on my own. I need to get away from Cat.

So why haven't I done that yet?

Now that I'm unemployed, I can take off to a remote corner of the world where she will never find me.

Instead of doing the intelligent thing, the pragmatic thing, I drive home and sequester myself in my study with a bottle of Talisker single malt Scotch. Why am I drinking the whisky favored by Cat's extremely large and annoying brothers? It hardly matters. Getting pissed requires alcohol, not self-analysis.

But I don't get drunk. I stare at the whisky bottle for ten minutes, then I put it back in the drinks cupboard.

Since I've clearly gone insane, I give in to the madness. I ring a car rental agency and arrange for them to deliver a Mercedes to the faculty parking lot, then I send Cat a text informing her that I've hired a car so she can drive herself to and from campus. Hiring a car for her implies I want her to stay here with me.

I do *not* want that.

But the thought of not having her here makes me...uneasy.

Since I have nothing else to do, I ring Logan. Serena tells me her husband has gone to a client's home for a consultation. Logan works for his cousin Evan, the billionaire CEO of a company that makes security and surveillance devices. I know Logan does these consultations to teach Evan's clients about the old-fashioned kinds of security that don't involve computer chips.

Since I've turned into a foolish, desperate moron, I try to engage Serena in conversation. She informs me she's home sick—the flu, nothing serious—and she needs to rest. We say goodbye.

I have no other friends, which leaves me with nothing to do.

Observing the birds outside my study window doesn't appeal to me at all. What do I do, then? Naturally, I opt for the worst thing I can do in this moment. I pick up my mobile and dial the first number on my list of contacts.

"Alex, I'm so happy to hear your voice," Imogen says.

"Yes, it's a thrill for me too." Do I sound grumpy? Cat accused me of behaving that way, but to me it sounds like I'm speaking normally. I am being a bit sarcastic, though.

"Henry will want to talk to you today."

"I take it he survived installing the dishwasher?"

"No," she says, sounding rather disappointed, "he had to set that aside while he cleans out the gutters and power washes the siding."

Power wash? I have no idea what that means, but it sounds suspiciously like something a seventy-four-year-old man should not be doing. Cleaning gutters is definitely not for a man his age.

"Is Henry up on a ladder?" I ask. "You shouldn't let him do that."

"You know how he gets. Henry's as stubborn as you are, which has always made me wonder if children can absorb their adopted parents' psychological traits."

"The other way round," I say. "Henry must have absorbed it from me. I was a stubborn little prick before I ever met you two."

"You are not a prick." She makes a clicking noise with her tongue, the way she always does when she's plotting something. "Can we do a video call? Henry would love that, and so would I. You don't send pictures anymore."

"I don't do selfies, Mum." The realization of what I called her hits me, and I freeze. When had I last called her Mum? I'd stopped doing that ages ago, so I must have genuinely lost my mind today. Which explains why I tell her, "All right. We'll do a video call."

For the next hour, I sit at my desk with a webcam aimed at myself while the screen shows me the faces of the two people who know me better than almost anyone in the world does. Anyone except Catriona MacTaggart. I think she might qualify for the number one position. She seems to understand me with a disturbing accuracy.

I don't know why, but the video call makes me feel better.

By the time Cat arrives home, I've cooked us a veritable feast. We eat it in the dining room, on the ridiculously expensive dalbergia table, and she tells me all about her day. I laugh when she relates a story about a misinformed student who thought Cat was talking about dead bodies of Celtic warriors when she discussed the celts on display in museums. A celt is a stone tool, something like an axe. Cat makes a hacking motion, as if she's holding a celt in her hands, as a visual aid.

She can be so...endearing.

After dinner, we enjoy a dram of Talisker.

That's when the inquisition begins again.

"I wish you would tell me about your parents," she says.

"No."

"Just no?" She rests her elbows on the table, slanting toward me, though I'm on the opposite side of the table. "That's not good enough, Alex. Not anymore. I won't judge you, no matter what you've done."

"That's a mistake."

"Please tell me."

"My answer is still no." I jump up from my chair, sending it tumbling over backward. "I'll wash the dishes."

"Let me. You've had a rough day." She pushes her chair back and stands, smiling tenderly at me. "You should have a shower. It might make you feel better."

Why is she being so sweet? I've refused to tell her what she wants to know. She ought to shout at me.

But instead, she comes around the table to me, raises onto her tiptoes, and kisses me. "Have a shower, Alex. I'll take care of everything."

I assume she means the dishes, but with this woman, I never can tell for sure.

Half an hour later, I step out of the steaming shower, dry off, and sling a towel around my hips. After a quick shave, I walk out into the bedroom.

And I freeze.

What I see makes my pulse accelerate and sends all the blood rushing into my cock.

Cat lies on my bed, naked, with the covers pulled back as if she's waiting for me to join her. She skims her hand over the sheet, and her lips slide into a seductive smile.

"What are you doing?" I ask.

"I want you, Alex."

"Maybe I don't want you."

She laughs, the sound light and affectionate. "We both know that's not true. Donnae ruin the moment by lying or getting grumpy. Come over here and make love to me."

I want to do that, desperately, but my hunger for her seems to short-circuit my brain. Whenever she acts this way, I do and say things I never want to do or say. She is dangerously close to uncovering all my secrets. I can't allow that to happen. This woman is beautiful, sensual, kind, compassionate, clever, determined—all the things that will doom her if she stays with me.

Tell her to go to hell and shout the words if you have to. But I can't form the syllables. I can't speak at all while she's lying there naked, waiting for me to crawl into bed with her.

What do I say? The most idiotic thing imaginable, of course. "Sorry, I'm not in the mood tonight."

She glances at my hardening cock, then shakes her finger at me. "Donnae lie. Didn't I tell you that already? Anyone can see you are in the mood."

My cock might be, but I know if I walk over there, I'll say and do things that will give her the wrong impression about my feelings for her. Not that I have a single sodding idea about what I feel.

She's so beautiful, so enticing with her lithe body spread out on the bed. I trace the lines of that body with my gaze, from her full breasts, down her flat belly to her hips and the hairs between her thighs. Looking at her, seeing her sweetly seductive smile, it triggers a pain in my chest.

I shuffle over to the bed and set my arse down on its edge, facing away from her. "I don't understand why you're still here."

Why do I sound completely baffled?

Because I am.

She glides a hand up my back, the warmth of her skin a tantalizing sensation. "How many times do I need to tell you? I'm here because I want to be. Because I love you."

My mouth opens, and I intend to tell her I don't love her, but the words die on my tongue.

"For one night," she says, "forget about everything else. Forget your secrets and your fears. Just come to bed and make love to me."

I glance at her over my shoulder, letting my gaze wander over her creamy skin and the waves of cinnamon-colored hair that cascade over her shoulders. Everything else seems to fade away. All I see is her. All I feel is an inexplicable need to be as close to her as humanly possible.

For one night, she says. One night and then...

I'll worry about that later.

Getting up, I strip off the towel.

Her eyes flutter half closed, and she clasps her hands above her head on the pillow.

I crawl onto the bed, straddling her body. "We might both regret this later, but I can't say no to you any longer. You are so lovely, so luscious, so... impossible to resist."

She arches her back, spreads her thighs, and licks her lips. "For one night, nothing else matters."

My throat's gone dry, my mouth too. Nothing else tonight. Just our bodies.

Even when we'd lived together, I couldn't erase the rest of the world. Maybe I came close to that, and maybe I didn't hold back in terms of sex, but I never quite broke free of everything else. Tonight, I want to.

I lower myself onto her, held up by my elbows braced at either side of her. The scent of her desire teases my senses, and I close my eyes for a moment to inhale the heady aroma. God, why do I feel drunk from the scent of her? It's mad, but I don't care. I skate my lips over hers, relishing the way she sucks in a breath and arches her neck, then I claim her mouth. The flavor of her overpowers my senses while I slip my tongue between her lips, flicking and lunging it to explore every last millimeter of her mouth. She moans and opens more for me, licking and gliding her tongue around mine, nipping at my lips, infusing my tongue with the flavor of her breaths. As the kiss intensifies, our teeth bump into each other, and suddenly I can't breathe anymore.

Cat moans again, long and low, the sound vibrating through her mouth into mine.

Though I want to keep kissing her forever, I pull my head back to catch my breath and appreciate her expression. Desire has turned her cheeks a rosy shade of pink, and the color speckles her throat and chest too. Her mouth falls open as she slides her tongue around the rim of her lips, her eyes hooded and hungry.

I've never seen anything so beautiful in my life.

"Alex," she murmurs, her voice sultry.

"Catriona, I…" Have no fucking idea what to say. So I give up on speaking.

I slither down her body, feathering kisses over her skin while I move, tasting and smelling her flesh, getting drunker with every bit of her I experience. When I reach her breasts, I pull one nipple into my mouth and lick and suckle it until she gasps, then I inch further down her body, loving her with my mouth and my hands, caressing her skin like I'm worshiping her. Maybe I am. Maybe? No, in this moment I can at least speak the truth in my own mind. I am worshiping her. And I'll keep doing this until neither of us has the energy to move.

As I travel ever lower down her delicious body, my cock gets stiffer, and I'm positive I have no blood left in my brain because it's all down there. Who needs a brain? I have Cat underneath me, wriggling and moaning and gasping my name. I pause with my face above her hips and the silky hairs below them, closing my eyes while I inhale the intoxicating scent of her. I've become obsessed with the way she smells, from her mouth to her breasts to the part of her I want to devour. Fuck, I love the way she smells, like musk and honey. I sneak my mouth between those luscious folds, latch onto her taut nub, and swirl my tongue around it over and over until she's clenching the sheets and bowing her back up so high that her shoulders almost lift off the bed too. I feast on that hard little button like her body and her pleasure are the only food that can satisfy my hunger.

"Alex!" she cries out, every muscle in her body going rigid, and she comes with her eyes squeezed shut and her scream strangled by the power of her climax.

Once I've coaxed every bit of pleasure out of her, I position myself over her body, my knees between her legs and my hands on the bed at either side of her, my arms straight. For a few seconds, all I can do is gaze down at her, at those lovely parted lips and the way her breasts heave with each breath. *So fucking perfect.* I push inside her and groan deeply, the feel of her slick heat around me such a bloody wonderful sensation. I rock my hips, diving in and pulling out in a measured, luxurious rhythm while I revel in how snugly her body molds to my cock and the way her hairs tease my skin. Every sensation seems heightened, so much better than any of the countless other times when I've made love to her. How can this feel so different tonight?

I can't waste any energy on figuring that out. The need to come deep inside her body escalates with every thrust and every ravenous noise she makes. I drop onto my elbows, crushing her with my weight though she doesn't seem to care. She slides her hands up my arms to grasp the back of my neck, and her breaths gust over my face. I know I can't last much longer, but I need to get her there with me.

"Catriona," I gasp, and I reach down to separate her folds so I'm pressing into her clit with every thrust.

"Aye, more, please," she begs, her voice strained from the rising pressure inside her.

I can see the strain on her face, the desperate need to let go and tumble off that cliff. I pump my hips faster and harder, grazing her clit with every stroke, and within seconds I feel her sheath tighten around me and her body stiffen while her mouth falls open on a sound that's barely a gasp. Her release rolls through her, not as powerfully as the first time but with a languor that's even more beautiful. I watch her face for a second or two until the pressure inside my cock tells me I'm about to follow her over the edge. I let my chin fall onto her shoulder, burrowing my face into her silky hair.

And I come.

I can't speak or breathe, the intensity of it making my body jerk while I let out a choked shout that's muffled by her skin and her hair—and the pillow, which I'm now smashing my face into while I plow into her one last time. I go limp on top of her, so spent I can't even lift my face off the pillow. I blow out breath after breath, sucking in a bit of the pillow every time I inhale.

Cat caresses the back of my neck with her fingers.

A moment or two—possibly three or four or ten—ticks by before I summon the energy to roll off her body. Sprawled on my back, I stare up at the ceiling, dazed and exhausted in the most pleasurable way. I've never felt like this after sex. Not even with Cat. Everything between us is different now, and I'm not sure if that's safe.

She turns onto her side, her hands tucked under her cheek. "Donnae worry. I willnae ask ye any questions tonight. But I'd like to sleep with you, if that's all right."

I cast a sidelong glance at her. "The last time I shared my bed with a woman all night was the last night you and I were together."

"The same for me. I haven't actually slept with a man since you."

Cat must've had sex with other men, though I can't bring myself to ask how many blokes have enjoyed the bliss of her body. I don't want to know. Why should it bother me? I have no right to be jealous. But if she tells me she's had dozens of lovers over the past twelve years, I think I might develop an ulcer.

So I raise an arm as an invitation for her to cuddle that sensual body against me, and when she does, I hold her close. Tonight, she's mine.

Tomorrow... That depends on what she asks me next.

Chapter Twenty-Eight

Catriona

I throw my head back and let out a throaty cry, riding Alex through the last waves of my climax while he comes apart inside me. His shouts echo in the clearing. I stay seated on top of him, my hands on his chest, breathing hard. Wildflowers surround us, their bright shades standing out against the green grass, but a blanket beneath us shields our bodies from the earth. The silken texture of the microfiber blanket feels like heaven against my skin.

"My God, Cat," Alex says, his grin slightly crooked. "I had no idea you're such an insatiable lass. Waking me up with your mouth on me. Insisting I have you in the shower, on the staircase, on my desk in the study. Then you drag me out here so you can abuse my body in the outdoors."

"Abuse?" I say with a laugh. "I didn't hear any complaints from you when I told you to get on your back on the blanket. In fact, you dared me to see if I could make you come so hard you'd go blind."

"Which I'm positive you did, for a moment." He grasps my hips and smiles with wolfish hunger. "Maybe I had my eyes closed, though. We'd better do that again so I can make sure you accomplished that feat."

"Aye, please. Let's do that again."

I've never had this much sex in one day. Alex no longer has a job, but I do. I should be teaching a class right now, yet here I am sitting on top of him with his cock still inside me instead of educating young minds. I rang Gus Hooper to tell him I'm sick, and he seemed to believe me. Never have I ever pretended to be ill so I could take a day off, but I don't want to lose this intimacy Alex and I have developed since last night. Soon I'll have to give it up and go back to work. For today, I have nothing else to do but be with Alex.

"You are such a naughty girl," he says in a teasing tone. "Blowing off work to shag me all day long? That's not the Cat I used to know."

"I keep telling you, I'm not the naive lass you knew. I'm a mature woman who knows what she wants, and right now"—I lean in to take his bottom lip between my teeth, releasing it slowly—"what I want is you."

"Again? At least feed me lunch before you start in again." He grasps my head when I start to pull away, holding it close to his. "You, love, are draining me like a succubus."

"Does that mean you want me to stop?"

"No, it means it's my turn to drain you." He flips over, taking me with him, pinning me to the blanket with his body. "I have plans for you, Catriona."

I wriggle my hips and smile when he hisses in a breath.

Then he holds my wrists above my head and kisses me.

A phone rings.

"Bloody hell," he groans. "That's mine, isn't it?"

"Aye. This morning I changed my ringtone to bagpipes so we can tell whose mobile is ringing."

"Wonderful. You know how I love bagpipes." Alex rolls his eyes, then moves off me to sit on the blanket and grab his mobile. He glances at the screen and winces. "I have to take this."

"Go on. I don't mind."

He eyes me with a strange expression, almost like embarrassment. "I'll go over there to take this call."

"Over where?"

Without answering my question, he jumps up and walks to the opposite side of the clearing, where he leans against a tree facing away from me. And he's still naked.

I can hear him talking, but I can't understand the words. He's too far away and speaking too softly. So I ignore his conversation and admire the view of his backside, with those taut erse muscles and his strong thighs. I enjoy it until his shoulders bunch up and he smacks his palm on the tree.

"Dammit," he says. "Why did you let him do that?"

Sitting up, I find my clothes and wriggle on the blanket to get them on. Whoever he's talking to and whatever they're saying, it's clear he will be upset afterward. I'm dressed and have my shoes on by the time he ends his call and stalks back to me.

Alex scans me up and down, his frown deepening. Without a word, he snatches his clothes off the ground and pulls them on, along with his shoes.

"What's wrong?" I ask.

"It's my—Never mind."

"Talk to me. Please."

Alex stares at me without expression for several seconds, then he exhales a long breath and slumps his shoulders. "Not here."

He grabs my hand and tows me down the deer trail toward the house. I manage to snag the blanket off the ground before we start our forced march toward home. He doesn't speak again until we're inside the house, in his study.

"You'll want to sit down for this," he tells me, while he goes to the windows and leans against the frame, gazing out at the shadowy forest.

I move past him to sit on the window bench an arm's length away.

He flicks his gaze to me but quickly veers it back to the window. "Are you sure you want to know the truth about me?"

Is he going to tell me everything? My heart beats faster at the possibility, and a shiver of excitement courses through me.

"Yes," I tell him, "I'm sure."

He scrubs a hand over his face and shuts his eyes. "I have to go to Nevada. Today."

"Because of the call you got earlier."

"Yes." He covers his face with both hands, like he doesn't want me to see his expression when he tells me more. "My... Well, they're essentially my parents. They live in Nevada. Imogen and Henry Bennett raised me from the time I was eight years old."

"What happened to your real parents?"

He drops his hand, his eyes squinted, his whole expression harder and darker. "Henry and Imogen are my parents. They adopted me. The why of the story will have to wait a few minutes. I need to go to Nevada because Henry, the bloody fool, tried to clean the gutters on their house by himself using a very tall and not terribly sturdy ladder. He fell and broke his leg."

"Oh no. Will he be all right?"

"Yes, he's fine. But Imogen can't manage on her own right now. She panics at every little thing, especially when one of us gets sick or injured. I need to be there for a few days until she settles down."

"I'll go with you."

His eyes widen, though only for a second. "You had better hear the rest of the story before you decide to get embroiled in my life."

"Alex, I'm already embroiled. It's too late to chase me off. Not that you have a chance in hell of doing that."

"It hasn't worked for me so far." He looks out the windows again. "I suppose it's time I told you everything."

"Whenever you're ready."

He scratches his head, contorting his mouth into a pained expression. Then he sighs and slumps against the window frame. "My parents—or rather, the man and woman who brought me into the world and raised me for eight years—were not upstanding citizens. They lied, cheated, schemed, connived, and generally did everything they could to avoid making an honest living."

"Were they homeless?"

"No," he says with a hefty dose of sarcasm, throwing me an equally sarcastic look. "Mummy and Daddy are grifters."

My mouth opens, but I need a few seconds before I can speak. Even then, I can make myself say only one word. "Grifters?"

"It means they're criminals." He leans toward me, his face and voice evidencing an anger he's kept buried deep inside himself. "They conned and swindled their way into quite a lot of money. For years, no one caught on to them. We lived in a posh neighborhood in London, in a posh house with posh servants. I had a live-in tutor to teach me the usual things, but my parents taught me everything I needed to know to become as masterful a grifter as they are."

I can't think of anything to say in response. At least this explains his tendency to sidestep the truth. He'd told me the other day that his parents taught him to lie and protect himself, that it was their lifestyle, but I still can't believe what I'm hearing. Alex might have a roguish side, and he often avoids answering questions, but he has never lied to me outright. How could he have lived that way? No wonder he has so much pain inside him.

Alex straightens and glares out the window. "You can go now. I'm sure one of your relatives will lend you a jet to get you home."

He assumes I'll want out because he confessed his secret to me. The daft man really doesn't understand how invested I am in making our relationship work.

I approach him, holding his face in my hands so I can rotate his head toward me. Once I have him looking at me, I explain what he refuses to understand. "I love you, Alex. That means I am not leaving, not for any reason, and certainly not because you had a terrible childhood. The fact that you turned out so well despite your past makes me love you even more."

His brows draw together over his nose.

"Aye, that's right," I say, answering the question he hasn't asked. I see the question in his eyes. "I'm not disgusted with you. I do not hate you. Nothing you say will make me want to run away."

"You might change your mind," he says, "once I tell you the rest."

"Go on. I can handle it."

He screws up his mouth, then flattens it out into a hard line. "I've been a grifter all my life. I still am one."

"No, you are not."

"Stop forgiving me. It's not the intelligent thing to do."

"Maybe not, but it is the compassionate thing."

He groans, shutting his eyes for a moment. "If I'm going to explain all of it, I need a drink first."

Chapter Twenty-Nine

Alex

I pour myself two fingers of Talisker and wander back to my chair, dropping onto it with a thump, like my body suddenly weighs a metric ton. The weight of guilt, I suppose. After years of hiding my past from everyone, except for Henry and Imogen, I find myself wanting to confess all of it to Catriona.

Will telling her lift any of this weight off me?

Only one way to find out.

Cat walks over to my desk and rests her shapely arse on it while she watches me.

I shift around in my chair, uncomfortable for reasons that have nothing to do with how much padding the seat has.

She tips her head to the side, examining me with those glacial-blue eyes that have fire behind them. "You said you didn't have friends when you were a lad. That must've been lonely."

"Maybe it was." I take a sip of my whisky, but the burn of it barely makes an impression on me. My mind is traveling back to those days and everything that had gone on. "You see, my parents believed the way to keep me under their collective thumb was to make sure I never had any friends and that I was afraid of the authorities. They drummed that into me until I believed that so much as looking at a policeman would lead to disaster."

"Oh, Alex—"

"Stop that. I do not want to hear pity in your voice or see it on your face." I swallow the rest of my drink and smack the glass down on the desk. "I won't have any of it. You want to know everything? Then keep your emotions to yourself."

"All right, have it your way. For now." She shimmies backward until she's sitting on the desk with her legs hanging off it, then folds her hands on her lap. "Go on."

I've always loved being in front of an audience, entertaining my students while I educate them. But an auditorium full of undergraduates is different than an audience of one determined Scotswoman who has decided to love me no matter what I have done or ever will do. It makes me want to pour an entire bottle of Scotch down my throat.

But I don't do that. Instead, I grip the arms of my chair and stumble on.

"My parents had never been arrested. They had a few close calls, but bribery and blackmail always did the trick." That old itch starts up again, and I'm fighting the urge to scratch my entire body like a bear rubbing against a tree. "They groomed me to become their cohort. By the time I was six, I could put on a good show of being a starving street urchin and earn a hundred quid in an afternoon."

Cat starts to speak, a hint of pity in her eyes, but she stops before one syllable escapes her lips.

God, I need more Scotch.

She puckers her lips, clearly wanting to say something. But she must think better of it because she grabs my empty glass and marches straight to the drinks cabinet where she pours two glasses of Talisker, bringing them both back to the desk. She perches on it again, handing me a glass.

Can she read my mind? Maybe she just understands me far too well. I can't decide which option is the most disturbing.

I take the glass and knock it back in one swallow. As I set the glass down, I continue. "By the time I was eight, I'd become a masterful pickpocket. I could also nick small items from shops without getting caught. I hated what they made me do, but I thought that was my lot in life. I didn't know anything else. Things might have gone on that way, and maybe I would be a confirmed grifter today, if my parents hadn't gotten greedy."

She angles her head again, biting down on her lip like she wants to ask a question.

"Yes, I know what you're thinking. How did it all go wrong?" I tap my finger on my empty glass, resigned to finishing the story. "My parents decided to go after a very big fish, who turned out to be a sweet, elderly woman who had no family. Her name was Honoria Parker. She planned to leave her fortune to charity, so Mummy and Daddy thought she sounded like the perfect mark."

"How were they caught?"

"They sent me in to do my pathetic urchin routine." I stared down at my shoes, counting the stitches in the leather to collect myself. It's always worked before. Count the stitches on my shoes, count the tiles in a ceiling, count anything. It calms me, but not today. "No one had ever been as kind to me as that woman. She offered me tea and cakes, and she insisted on buying me new clothes. I was dressed in rags, naturally, to play the part. But I couldn't do it. I couldn't let my parents swindle this sweet woman who had no one in her life."

"What did you do?"

"I walked into the nearest police station and told everything to a detective inspector. And I do mean *everything.*"

Cat gasps so softly I almost don't hear it. "And they were arrested?"

I nod with all the gravity these memories deserve. "More than that, they were convicted and sent to prison. I was taken into care, with a social worker at first—until two barmy people decided to straighten me out."

"Henry and Imogen. They adopted you?"

"Eventually. First, they became my foster parents. It took a long legal battle to have my parents' rights stripped, but eventually, we won. Henry and Imogen became my mother and father, in every way that matters." My lips twitch, wanting to form a smile, but they can't quite get there. "Not that they ever managed to straighten me out all the way. I've stayed somewhat bent."

Cat is studying me again, and I can almost see her mind working behind those lustrous eyes. She's too clever, too stubborn, too…irresistible. She wants to save me, and I don't know if I have the willpower to stop her.

"If their last name is Bennett," she says, "why is yours Thorne? Is that your birth parents' last name?"

"No." I want another glass of whisky, want it so much my mouth waters thinking about it, but I refuse to give in to the impulse to drown my memories in alcohol. "Does it really matter what name I was born with?"

"Aye, it does." Cat slides off the desk and sets her lovely bum on my lap. "I want to know you, Alex. All of you, not the parts you feel comfortable sharing with me. Everything. You've told me a lot, but I need to know more. Starting with what your real name is."

Had I really thought she'd give up? Of course she won't.

"Get it over with," she says. Then she uses her fingertips to move my lips as if I were speaking. "Come on, you can do it."

"Bloody hell." I swing my gaze up to the ceiling, shaking my head. "My name was Alexis Lucian Charnley-Ainsworth."

Her lips twitch, a definite sign she's trying hard not to smile.

Naturally, my discomfort amuses her. Why wouldn't it? I am a fucking moron, after all.

"What's wrong with that name?" she asks. "It sounds very British to me."

"That's the problem. It's too British. My parents made it up and started using that ridiculous hyphenated name to impress people. They thought it made them seem more upper-class." I cover my face with both hands and groan. "I was given their ludicrous invented name at birth. They started out as Nigel and Julia Sewell."

"Oh, I see." She leans against me, her face too close to mine. "Why are you Alex Thorne instead of Alex Charnley-Ainsworth?"

"Because I don't want to be. Why should I want the name of the two people who ruined me? I don't want anything of Nigel and Julia in me."

"You aren't ruined." She hesitates, and I swear I can hear her brain clicking away while she tries to figure me out. "I still don't understand. Why aren't you Alex Bennett? That's the name of your adopted parents."

"I was a Bennett for a long time." I drop my head back against the chair, staring up at the ceiling. "Eventually, I decided to rename myself, legally, to make it harder for anyone who knew me before to find me after I moved to America."

"But you kept your first name," Cat says. "Why didn't you change it too?"

I squirm. Me. Squirming. It's ridiculous. And that seems to have become my favorite word lately, that and ludicrous. Maybe I'm the one who's ridiculous and barmy and ludicrous.

Cat angles in closer, our noses almost touching. "Why didn't you change—"

"Because Henry and Imogen insisted I keep my first name." I resist the urge for about five seconds, then I slip my arms around her waist. "They said I should keep something of myself because I can't erase the past. I was an adult when I changed my name, but I did what they suggested. I stayed Alex."

"Why did you choose Thorne?"

"It's a reference to a thorn bush, which seemed appropriate at the time. Outwardly pleasant, but sharp and painful to the touch. That was my life."

She touches her lips to mine, keeping her eyes open.

I gaze into those eyes, and for the first time I wonder if maybe I might possibly be able to… No, I can't. After the things I've done, I don't get a second chance. Besides, I've had one of those already, thanks to Imogen and Henry. I don't get a third go at not bollocksing up my life.

"There's more," she says. "Isn't there?"

"Yes, but I'd rather not talk about it now. I need to get to Nevada to take care of Imogen and Henry." I frown as I realize the problem with that statement. "What are the odds I can get a flight this afternoon? Zero, I imagine."

Cat smiles and taps my nose. "I can get you a private jet that will take you anywhere you want. It can be here to pick us up in less than two hours."

"How—Oh no, I am not borrowing your cousin Evan's jet."

"Why not? I'm sure he'll be happy to lend it to you."

"To *you*, not me." What she said a moment ago suddenly reaches my brain, and I squint at her. "Why did you say pick 'us' up? I'm going alone."

"We are going to Nevada together. You need support."

"Is this your devious way of arranging to meet my parents? Henry and Imogen, I mean. You wouldn't want to meet Nigel and Julia."

She kisses me again, holding her lips to mine for a long moment, her eyes closed. Mine ease shut little by little, and every muscle in my body decides to soften, as if her lips have injected a sedative into me.

"Please take me with you," she murmurs, her breath whispering over my lips.

"Don't you still have a job?"

"Yes, but I'll call Gus Hooper and tell him I'm still sick and can't go back to work until Monday."

"Why would you risk losing your job?"

"For you." She flicks her tongue out to tease my lips. "I love you, Alex. When will you get that through your head? The people I love are more important than any job."

I swallow, my throat suddenly tight. "Have it your way. Come along if it will make you stop harassing me."

She tickles my mouth with her fingers. "Ye cannae fool me, Alexis. You're glad I'm going with you."

"Please don't ever call me that name again." The way she said it made my cock throb, but that's irrelevant. I hate that name.

Cat reaches behind her to pick up the telephone and dial a number. She holds the receiver to her ear, watching me while she waits for her cousin to answer. "Hello, Evan, it's Catriona. I need a favor. It's urgent."

I listen while she explains the situation, leaving out the details she knows I won't want her family to know. Her consideration makes me feel...something. I can't describe it because I've never experienced this sensation before. It can't be what it seems like. She can't be making me feel safe and accepted and...that other word I will not even use in my head. The one that starts with L.

When she says goodbye and hangs up the phone, she gives me a quick kiss. "It's settled. Evan is arranging it as we speak, and the jet will pick us up at the airport in one hour and twenty minutes."

Having a billionaire as a cousin certainly has its perks. One call to Evan MacTaggart and we're off.

"Better pack," she says, hopping off my lap. "How long will we be staying in Nevada?"

"Not sure. A few days, at least."

She pats my cheek and trots out of the room.

I stare at the doorway long after she's left. Catriona MacTaggart confuses the fuck out of me. But strangely, after sharing a large chunk of my past with her, I feel more relaxed. The whisky might have something to do with it, but I know most of the reason for my improved mood stems from a single source.

Catriona.

And I'm about to introduce her to the only two people I've ever really thought of as my parents. Christ, no one has ever met them. I might have let Cat believe I'm allowing her to tag along against my will, but the truth is far more disturbing.

I want her to meet my parents.

Chapter Thirty

Catriona

We stand on the porch of a modest-size ranch house in the town of Fernley, Nevada, with Alex holding my hand. He seems to need the contact, though he won't admit to it, because he's the one who clasped my hand while we walked up the concrete path from the street. The house doesn't look like much from the outside, though it's well-kept and clean. The yard has been mowed, and the bushes have been trimmed.

Sweat dribbles down the back of my neck. Aye, it's hot here.

Alex presses the doorbell button.

I glance at him, offering an encouraging smile.

He makes a face that's like a frown and a sarcastic smile are vying for control of his features.

No, I don't expect he'll admit he's glad I'm here with him. Not yet.

The door opens.

A plump, gray-haired woman rushes at Alex, flinging her arms around him. "Oh, I'm so happy you're here. We've missed you so much."

She speaks with a British accent. This must be his mother.

The woman kisses Alex's cheek, which makes him smile just enough to create wrinkles around his eyes. When she notices me, her smile broadens. "And you've brought a girl with you. Oh Alex, this is wonderful. You've never brought a girl home."

He opens his mouth but doesn't get a chance to speak.

She hugs him again. "I can't believe it's really you."

"Yes, Mum, it's me," he says, looking slightly exasperated, though he smiles. "And yes, I've brought a woman. This is Catriona MacTaggart. Cat, this is my mother, Imogen Bennett."

Before I can say hello, Imogen drags me into a fierce hug. She kisses my cheek and backs away a wee bit, though she holds onto my hands. "Please come inside, Catriona. Henry will want to meet you, and he's not up to walking yet."

Imogen leads us into the house, which isn't posh but has all the charm of a real home, a place where people live, a place that's been cared for with love. When we reach the living room, I see a slender, bald man relaxing in a recliner with his feet on the attached footrest. His left ankle is bandaged, and he has a single crutch propped against the wall beside his chair.

"Alex," he says with a grin. He tries to get up, but Imogen rushes over to stop him. Sitting back down, he looks at me. "Who have you brought with you?"

"Henry, this is Catriona MacTaggart," Imogen tells her husband. "I think she's Alex's girlfriend, but he hasn't said anything about her yet, other than her name."

"Our boy likes his secrets," Henry says.

Alex approaches Henry's chair, and since he's still holding my hand, I get dragged along with him. Alex squints at Henry's bandaged ankle, then aims his suspicious gaze at his father. "I thought you had a broken leg."

"Broken? Is that what Imogen told you?" Henry chuckles. "You know how Mum gets when anything happens. If I stub my toe, she'll call for an ambulance."

"I will not," Imogen says, though she doesn't sound offended. "But you were screaming like a banshee about how much your leg hurt. I assumed you'd broken it. How was I to know you only sprained it?"

Alex eyes his mother with affectionate suspicion. "Are you sure this wasn't a scheme to get me to visit?"

"No, I honestly thought Henry had broken his leg." Imogen pinches Alex's cheek. "But I'm glad for the confusion, since it got you here."

"Are you Alex's girlfriend?" Henry asks me.

I don't know whether Alex will agree that I'm his girlfriend, so I don't know how to answer the question. To say no would be a lie.

"Yes," Alex says. "Cat and I are a couple."

The shock of his statement hits me like a bucket of water thrown in my face, but then it gives way to a sweet warmth that blossoms in my chest and spreads outward. He admits we're a couple. He's told his parents that.

Alex puts his arm around me.

I glance at his face, and I can't help smiling.

"How long have you two known each other?" Imogen asks, waving for us to sit down on the sofa.

We sit, with Alex's arm still around me.

I lean into him while that warmth keeps simmering inside me. I haven't felt this contented in years.

"We met fourteen years ago," Alex says. "That's when I was teaching at the college in New Mexico. Catriona was a student there. We started seeing each other and, well…things progressed from there."

"Progressed?" Henry says. "What does that mean?"

"Cat and I, ah, lived together for almost two years."

Both his parents stare at him blankly.

Alex hugs me closer to him.

"Two years?" Imogen says. "But you never mentioned having a girl."

"I—It seemed like—" Alex darts his gaze left, right, up, down, like his mother's question has him in a near panic. But he gets hold of himself after a few seconds and tells her, "Things ended badly, but we've reconciled."

Henry looks puzzled. "Why did you never mention living with a woman?"

"Alex is very private," I say, then I feel like an eejit for saying it. They know him better than I do. Or do they? I'll have to ask Alex about that later. "You know how he is with secrets."

"Oh yes," Imogen says, nodding. "Alex has always needed to keep certain things to himself. But he's a good boy, and we love him dearly."

I swear Alex blushes.

He aims his attention at the floor, clearing his throat. "Since Henry is all right, I suppose Cat and I should head home."

"Please stay," his mother says. "We would love to get to know your sweetheart. Please, Alex, stay for a few days."

"Fine, yes. We'll stay."

Since it's almost dinnertime, Imogen announces she will make us a "good, hearty meal" because she knows "Alex likes to live on restaurant food, which isn't healthy." I offer to help her with the cooking, and we go into the kitchen while Alex moves into the armchair beside Henry's recliner so the two of them can talk.

Alex's parents are the sweetest people I've ever met.

While Imogen and I make dinner, she tells me stories about when Alex was a laddie. We laugh at his childhood antics, and I tell her some of what Alex and I did together when we knew each other the first time, along with a few things from more recently. She loves the story of how Alex showed up at my brother Rory's castle and wore the pink kilt I gave him as a joke. I leave out the bit where Alex almost got crushed under a caber. I do share the times he has attended MacTaggart family gatherings and the humorous moments that came out of those encounters with my overprotective brothers and cousins.

Imogen beams when I tell her Alex and my cousin Logan have become good friends. "I'm so glad my boy has a friend. He never wanted to get close to anyone when he was in school. His past made it difficult for him to trust anyone."

"Aye, Alex told me all about Nigel and Julia."

She stares at me, her surprise evident on her face. "Alex told you about them? He never talks about Nigel and Julia. He must really love you."

My heart skips a beat when she says that. Does Alex love me? He hasn't said it, but then, he might not even if he felt that way. Like Imogen said, his past makes it hard for him to trust anyone. Maybe he worries I'll leave him again, the way I did twelve years ago. Everything is different now, and I need to show him I won't run away this time.

I hear laughter coming from the living room, and I can't resist peeking out there to see what Alex and Henry are doing.

Alex is leaning over the arm of his chair to get closer to Henry. They both grin and laugh again, I assume because Alex told a joke. He slaps his father's arm and smiles even more broadly.

I've never seen him so happy, except for those days when we lived together. He loves his parents, and they love him. Tears sting my eyes. My throat constricts. I love him. So much. I want to see him happy, but I never thought I would. Yet here he is laughing with his father, looking so much like the man I used to know.

After dinner and cognac, which I learn is Henry's favorite evening cocktail, Alex and I retreat into his old bedroom. He tells me he bought this house for his parents not long after they all moved to America, but he'd lived in Fernley with them only for a few months, until he'd gotten a job in New Mexico. He used to sleep in this room when he came for visits, but I know from Imogen that Alex hasn't been here in two years. I ask Alex about that after we undress for bed. Aye, we're sleeping naked together, but we're both too exhausted to do anything more than talk and go to sleep.

"Why haven't you seen your parents in two years?" I ask while I nestle under his arm on the bed.

"I don't know. Every time they asked me to come here, or suggested they might go to Montana, I told them no." He trails his fingers up and down my arm, seeming lost in the memories. "They would want me to tell them what I've been doing, and I suppose that's why I've stayed away."

"But why don't you tell them? It's not like you're a criminal."

"Aren't I? Borrowing items from museums isn't an above-board way of doing things."

"You always return the things you borrow."

He wriggles like he can't get comfortable. "I've also slept with more women than I'd want my parents to know. Every time I see them, they ask if I'm dating anyone. All I can say is no. Shagging women just for the hell of it doesn't count as dating."

"My family doesn't know about all the men I've shagged either."

"Please don't tell me how many men you've been with." He gives me a quick squeeze. "I can't promise not to get insanely jealous of every bloke who's had the pleasure of enjoying your body."

"We won't talk about our past lovers."

"Agreed."

We fall asleep in each other's arms and don't wake up until nearly ten o'clock the next morning. Alex and Imogen make breakfast, giving me time to get to know Henry. He has an impish sense of humor and a deep vein of kindness running through his soul. I met Alex's parents yesterday, and already I adore them.

After breakfast, Alex goes into the garage to get some tools so he can fix the leaky sink in the bathroom. He comes back from the garage looking exasperated.

Imogen and I are sitting on the sofa while Henry lounges in his recliner.

"What happened to the car?" Alex asks Henry. "The rear bumper is crumpled."

"Oh that," Henry says with a dismissive wave of his hand. "Some blighter backed into our car in the parking lot of the grocery store."

"Why haven't you gotten it repaired? The other person's insurance should pay for it."

"Ah…" Henry grimaces. "We don't know who did it. The accident happened while we were in the store."

"But why haven't you fixed the damage?"

"Too expensive. It still runs fine."

Alex throws his head back and groans. "Dad, you don't need to worry about that. How many times have I offered to buy you a new car? You should've told me about this."

Henry shrugs, seeming embarrassed. "I don't like to ask you for help every time something goes wrong."

"For heaven's sake, Dad." Alex shakes his head at Henry. "We are going to buy you a new car *today*."

And we do. Alex tries to talk his father out of going along on our car-shopping trip, but Henry insists his ankle is much better today. They compromise—Alex agreeing to let Henry come along, and Henry agreeing to use his crutch. The four of us pile into the car Alex had hired at the airport when we arrived in Nevada. It's not a luxury model, but then, we'd been forced to take whatever the agency had left. Last-minute travel doesn't come with all the perks. At the dealership, Henry and Imogen wander among the vehicles hunting for one they like, while Alex and I straggle after them.

When Alex notices his parents admiring a used car, he calls out to them, "New cars only, please."

"Used ones are just as good," Henry announces, "but they're cheaper."

"Forget the bloody price tag. Pick a new car."

They give each other mulish looks, then Henry relents and shepherds his wife back into the area designated for new models. They're looking at compact cars when Alex rushes over to herd them toward the luxury models.

"You need a comfortable car," he tells Henry. "You lot aren't twenty anymore. Your arthritis won't like a hard seat, and you'll have a bloody awful time squeezing into a compact car."

"It's too expensive," Imogen says.

"For the hundredth time, ignore the price tag. Choose a car you like, not one you think is affordable."

Henry and Imogen finally agree to look for a higher-end vehicle and start exploring the options.

Alex and I follow at a slower pace, holding hands, so we can talk. When we stop so his parents can explore the interior of a model they like, I rest my chin on Alex's shoulder.

"I'm confused," I say. "You said you invested almost all of your money in building your house. How can you afford a luxury car for your parents?"

"The bulk of my disposable income went into the house," he says, "but I never said I was destitute. I told you I kept some."

"But you led me to believe you don't have much money."

"Is it my fault you assumed that?" He sighs, lifting our joined hands to wrap his free hand around them. "Honoria Parker, the big fish my parents wanted me to reel in for them, left half of her estate to me when she died. I hadn't seen her in more than a decade, but in her will she said that I deserved the money for sparing her from being swindled and because I was brave enough to turn my parents in to the police." He makes a pained face. "Not sure she was right about that. I used most of the money to buy things for Henry and Imogen, but I also have investments which have paid significant dividends in the five years since I built the house."

"So you're still rich."

"Didn't Logan tell you how much I paid him for that job he did for me?"

"Of course not. Logan is discreet, which is why you hired him."

"That's true."

Henry waves his arms in the air to get our attention and shouts, "We found one!"

Alex goes off with his father to buy the car, leaving me with questions I want answered. Later, I'll ask him. Finally, after all these years, I'm getting to know him, all of him. And it makes me love him even more.

Chapter Thirty-One

Alex

I still can't believe I've introduced Catriona to my parents. What I can believe is that they've fallen in love with her right away and welcomed her like they've known her for years. Cat treats them the same way. I suppose that's a MacTaggart clan trait, treating strangers like family. Her relatives haven't made me feel as welcome as my parents have done with her, but I never expected they would. After the way I hurt Cat the first time we were together, I don't deserve to be greeted with open arms.

Serena and Keely always hug me, but they married into the MacTaggart clan. That's not the same as being in the Scots cult from birth.

Henry insists on driving the new car home, though both Imogen and I try to discourage him. The stubborn man won't concede. So my parents drive home in their vehicle while Cat and I ride in our hired car. Cat refuses to let me drive, though, claiming I must be exhausted. I'm not, but I've learned the futility of arguing with a determined MacTaggart woman.

Even Gavin Douglas, an ex-Marine who served in a war zone, doesn't argue too strenuously with his wife. Jamie is just as bloody-minded as Cat. The first time I'd met Jamie, she slapped me in the face—rather hard. Oh yes, she shares her sister's fiery temperament.

Cat and I cook lunch for my parents, and I discover I enjoy cooking with her. We trade stories about our families and make each other laugh, though I have nowhere near as many humorous stories as Cat does. Her brothers, sisters, and cousins are a gang of nutters. This means she makes me laugh a lot more than I make her laugh, but that's all right. I might have possibly, just a touch, missed times like this with her. We used to make each other laugh all the time. Feeling this way again, with her, makes me want to stay here at my parents' cozy little house forever.

But we can't. Her brothers get in the way, again.

We've just finished washing up the dishes when Cat's mobile phone rings. She manages to say hello, but then the person on the other end of the call starts speaking so loudly I can hear it, though I can't make out the words.

Cat rolls her eyes at whatever's been said. "Of course nobody's answering the door, Rory. We're not there."

Why would she say that? *We're not there.*

Oh no. I groan as I finally understand what's happening. Her brothers have turned up on my doorstep in Montana only to find out Cat and I aren't there. Rory and who-knows-who-else have descended on my home. Uninvited. Without notice.

"Don't you dare," Cat says. "I forbid you to have Logan break into the house. You can stay at a hotel, or better yet, go home to Scotland."

I have no doubt Logan would enjoy breaking into my home and snooping in every nook and cranny. He and Serena had made a halfhearted attempt at that the first time they visited me.

But Catriona looks ready to shove her fist through the phone and strangle her brother via the cell network. I doubt a virtual throttling will have any effect on him.

"Give me that," I say, snatching the phone from her. "Rory, how nice to hear from you."

"Where have ye taken my sister, ye *bod ceann*?"

"You're calling me a dickhead? Whatever happened to the MacTaggart charm? I thought you lot were more open-minded."

"Tell me where you are, or I'll have Emery trace this call."

I can't help chuckling. Cat's brothers are so easily vexed. "You dragged your wife to America? Are the twins there too? Maybe Logan will teach them how to pick the locks."

"My wife and bairns are at home. Now, where is my sister?"

"Standing right next to me. In my parents' house."

Rory stays silent for a few seconds, and he sounds genuinely baffled when he says, "You have parents?"

"Did you think I was created by the angels?" I give him a long-suffering sigh, but I suspect the sarcasm of it will fly right past him. "Cat and I are coming home right away. Your cousin Evan lent us his jet. So why don't you and your Scots mafia mates go into town for lunch and meet us back at the house in two hours."

"Aye, we'll do that. But if you don't produce Catriona in two hours—"

"Produce her?" I say with a laugh. "Sorry, that sounded like you think I can make her appear by magic. I'm afraid only Logan's sisters might pull that off."

"Be here in two hours. With Cat. Or else—"

"Yes, yes, I know. You will beat me bloody, tear me limb from limb, pummel me into the dirt, and whatever other clichés you can think of." I glance at Cat, whose eyes are large. I wink. "We'll see you in two hours. Cheers."

I end the call and hand the phone back to Cat.

"Cannae believe you did that," she says.

"Did you think I'd roll over and beg for a belly rub from Rory?"

"No, but—" She shuts her eyes for a moment, but then her lips slide into a faint smile. "You really are fearless, aren't you?"

"I think I've demonstrated that I'm not. Took me well over a decade to finally tell you the truth."

"But you told Logan and Serena nothing frightens you."

"Honestly, Cat, you have a disarming but dangerous need to believe everything I say." Leaning in, I spear her gaze with mine. "I lied. It's what liars like me do."

"You're not a liar. You...throw up a smoke screen with your words."

"It seems your memory is selective." I slant in even closer, lowering my voice to a near-whisper. "The day you walked into my office last week, you called me a slimy, conniving bastard and said you despise me. You declared you would never have sex with me, not even if an asteroid were heading straight for Earth, and that you would never crawl into the dank hole I live in."

"I was angry. You hurt me, Alex, badly. But that was a long time ago, and I've gotten over it."

"And yet you forgave me. One of us is a fool, but I can't decide if it's me or you."

She bumps her shoulder into my arm. "I like it when you're confused. It's sweet."

I give up on trying to convince her I'm a lying bastard. Not that long ago, she cursed my name and portrayed me as the devil incarnate. Now she refuses to believe I've done anything bad.

Cat smiles and laughs with more enthusiasm.

"What's so bloody entertaining?" I ask.

"I was imagining what will happen when my brothers see you."

"Well, if I get beaten to a pulp, it's your responsibility to tend to my wounds."

"I promise this time I'll be your physical therapist."

Of course she remembers when I asked if she'd be my physical therapist back at Dùndubhan, right after I'd dropped a caber on myself. At the time, Cat responded by saying, "You're still a bastard, and I still despise you." I can't decide whether to feel triumphant or terrified by the fact she now wants to take care of me after her brothers assault me like a pack of wolves taking down a moose.

"I'm not entirely fearless, you know," I tell her. "But your brothers don't frighten me."

"Someone does. Who is it?"

"What makes you think there's a specific someone?"

She lifts one shoulder. "You were terrified the other day when you tried to convince me to go away. It's Reginald Hewitt, isn't it? You're afraid of what he might do now that he's escaped from prison."

"No, I—" Am about to lie through my teeth, but not for underhanded reasons. It's a simple matter of pride, the kind that often gets men into trouble. "I was trying to protect you, but that's not in my skill set. I'm an expert pickpocket and grifter, but I have no fucking idea how to stop my former butler from coming after you to get to me."

"It's a good thing Logan is waiting for us at home, then. Isn't it?"

"Oh yes, I love that I need to ask your cousin for help." I shove my hands through my hair and groan, knowing I need to tell her I've heard from my best mate Reggie since the day I begged her to leave. "Reginald has texted me. Twice. First, he said 'you will pay.' The second time he told me 'we're coming for you.' I have no idea who else he's convinced to take part in his moronic revenge scheme, but I'm praying it's not Falk Mullane. The last thing I need right now is to see that whingeing little wanker again."

Cat lays her hands on my chest, leaning her body into mine. "Whatever they're planning, we will deal with it together."

I can't imagine why, but she means it. And that makes me feel better.

"Let's pack," I announce, "and say goodbye to my parents."

We can't leave her brothers waiting.

Chapter Thirty-Two

Catriona

I wait until we're on the jet and in the air before I decide to push Alex for more information. I still have questions he hasn't answered, not completely. So I start with the one I've wondered about for the longest. We're sitting on the sofa by the windows, snuggled up with his arm around my shoulders and my legs tucked under me.

"How much did you pay Logan?" I ask.

Alex glances at me sideways. "What?"

"You heard me. How much did you pay Logan for the two times when he helped you with your problems?"

"Does it matter?"

"Please, Alex, tell me."

He lets his head fall back against the sofa, exhaling a long breath. "The first time, I paid him fifteen thousand dollars. The second time, it was twenty thousand."

For a moment, I'm convinced I've hallucinated what he said. But I haven't. It's true.

I turn my whole body toward him. "Why would you pay him so much?"

"Because the missions turned out to be more complicated than they seemed, and because Logan did a fine job."

"What about your parents? Nigel and Julia. They must've gotten out of prison sometime."

"They were each sentenced to four years but served only two." He shuts his eyes, his expression pinched. "They tried to reclaim me, but Henry and Imogen fought to keep me. Eventually, they won. Nigel and Julia didn't want to give up, though. They tried to kidnap me twice, but both times I managed to get away from them."

I want to touch him, to say something, but I know he needs to tell me the story in his own time.

"Henry and Imogen took me to Cornwall when I was sixteen," he says. "They thought it would be safer for me there and harder for my charming parents to track us down. It worked for a long time, but I found out later that's because Nigel and Julia had gotten arrested again and sent back to prison."

Imogen and Henry seem like sweet, loving people, but they clearly possess a strength and determination hidden under the surface. The way they fought for Alex proves how much they love him, and I can tell he loves them just as much. He might not have a large family like I do, but he has parents who will sacrifice anything for him.

"Nigel and Julia were in and out of prison for years," Alex says. "They seemed to have given up on taking me back, and I let myself get comfortable in my new life. I had just received my PhD when they were given early release and decided to come for me a third time. They wanted my help in executing a dangerous con. When I refused, they threatened Henry and Imogen."

"What did you do?"

"I pretended I was going to cooperate when I was actually working with the police. Nigel and Julia went back to prison." He sits up, rubbing his forehead, but won't look at me. "I'd had enough of worrying when they might come back to try something worse, so I took a job in America, far away from my darling parents. Henry and Imogen came with me, and we've been here ever since."

"Did you change your last name before or after you moved here?"

"Before. I wanted a clean break from my past. I tried to talk Henry and Imogen into changing their last name, but they wouldn't do it."

"I know I've asked a lot of you lately, but there's one more question I'd like to know the answer to."

"Go on."

"What did that police chief in New Mexico have on you? Why would he think he could blackmail you into stealing a necklace for him?"

It's the reason I walked out on Alex twelve years ago, and I need to understand why it happened.

"He found out who I really am," Alex says. "He had a friend in the UK who worked at Scotland Yard, so he asked that bloke to search for Alex

Thorne in their databases. Since I'd changed my name legally, there was a paper trail. He found out my original parents and I had been grifters."

"But you didn't let him use that against you. You exposed his affair with a university trustee's wife."

Alex smiles in his sexy-smug way. "Yes, and he got what he deserved." His smile fades. "But I lost you in the process."

"You have me now. I'm not going anywhere."

"I know, and it doesn't disturb me as much as it used to. I hope that's all your questions because I'm ready for a lie-down."

What can I say? What should I say? He's told me everything now, I'm sure of it, and I want to let him know how much it means to me that he trusted me with his secrets. But it might make him uncomfortable, so I'll wait until another time, when he's gotten used to this new, deeper intimacy between us.

"Tell me something," he says. "Why did you take a job in America? You knew I lived here. Logan told you as much."

"If you'd asked me that a few weeks ago, I would've said you tricked me and that's the only reason I took the job."

"What do you say today?"

I study his face for a moment, noting his tense expression and the wariness in his eyes. Though I'm not sure if he'll like my answer, I tell him the truth. "I think deep down I was hoping I'd see you again. That maybe, somehow, you would be here waiting for me."

"And since you know I'm a conniving shit, you knew there was a better-than-average chance I'd arranged the sudden job offer."

"Maybe."

He finally looks at me. "Did you hope I had?"

"Aye. But I never would have admitted to that."

"Naturally." He raises a hand to touch my lips with his fingertips. "What have you been doing all these years?"

"Teaching children about history. The work was sporadic, but I enjoyed it. I never could get a job at a university—until recently, after Iain became a professor at the University of the Highlands and the Islands. He asked me to give guest lectures in his classes now and then."

"What else have you done without me?"

"Living with my parents and living my life. A few years ago, my sister Fiona and I moved into our own house. I was Rory's legal secretary for a while, then I worked at Aidan's construction company until he married Calli. And I dated, off and on, but nothing ever came of it." I lay a hand on his cheek. "I was still in love with you. No one else can compare to Alex Thorne."

"You're massaging my ego, aren't you? I don't need the reassurance."

"I'm telling you the truth, that's all."

He considers me for a moment, his gaze flitting around like he's examining every part of me. "Family is the cornerstone of your life, isn't it? You must want children."

"I haven't thought about it."

Alex runs a hand over his mouth. "I can't give you a family. My genetic pool is rancid. The thought of bringing another Nigel or Julia into the world is unacceptable."

"But you are a good man, Alex. In spite of what they did to you."

He gets up and ambles to the other side of the cabin, then glances around like he has no idea how he got there. Frowning, he comes back to me and sits on the table in front of the sofa. With his head down, he wrings his hands. "You shouldn't stay with me, Cat. It will be your undoing."

"Rubbish. You are not evil." I clasp his hands, halting his nervous wringing. "Do you have any other family? Aunts or uncles? Cousins? What about your grandparents?"

"I have no bloody idea." He smiles with an acidic edge. "If I have any relatives, I'm sure they're in prison."

"You should find out. Maybe you have family who aren't criminals. They might be decent people who would love to meet you."

He bows his head again, concentrating on our joined hands. "Henry and Imogen have harassed me occasionally about looking into my family tree. I, ah, worry about what I'll find if I do look."

"Donnae worry, Alex. You won't be doing it alone. I'll be here with you, always."

Lifting his head, he gazes at me like he's never seen me before.

I kiss him, the barest touch of my lips on his. "You can think about it and let me know. But I do believe it could be good for you to find your family."

The pilot announces over the intercom that we're about to land. Neither of us moves, and I keep holding his hands until the jet touches down on the runway and the engines wind down. Then he leads me down the stairs to the tarmac.

We're about to confront my brothers.

And I will punch any of them who tries to hurt Alex.

Chapter Thirty-Three

Alex

When we pull up in front of the house, four burly Scots are waiting at the door. Three of them have their arms crossed over their chests and aim severe looks at me as I get out and come around to the passenger side to open Cat's door for her. I offer her my hand to help her up. All the while, her brothers glare at me.

The fourth Scot, Logan, leans against the house beside the door looking relaxed and faintly amused.

Catriona and I walk up the steps hand in hand.

Rory's eyes narrow to slits.

Lachlan grits his teeth hard enough to make a muscle pulse in his jaw.

Aidan continues glaring at me, but not as hard as his brothers do.

Cat and I stop at the top of the steps.

I raise my brows at them. "Is this the entire delegation? Or should I expect more surly Scots to arrive and glower at me?"

"That depends," Rory says, "on whether you give us our sister back."

Cat stiffens beside me, and even her hand tenses. "Give me back? Ahm-no a car Alex borrowed from you."

"If he did borrow my car," Lachlan says, "he wouldn't give it back, would he? We've all heard about Alex Thorne's definition of borrowing."

"Have you?" I say. "I suppose it's not unlike your definition of overkill. You're misinformed, anyway. I return the things I borrow."

I don't ask permission first, but that's nothing Lachlan needs to know.

That muscle pulses in his jaw again. "What are you havering about?"

Cat nudges me with her elbow but doesn't let go of my hand. "He means you've gone too far, Lachie, but you won't admit it."

"Too far?" Lachlan takes a single step toward us. "I haven't gone far enough if my sister is living with the British Bastard."

"I prefer Limey Louse," I tell him. "But this is all an assortment of moot points. Catriona is a grown woman who makes up her own mind."

"Aye," she says, "and I've made up my mind to be with Alex."

Logan steps forward and announces, in a calm voice that implies he doesn't give a toss about any of this, "Let's go inside to continue this conversation. I'd hate to have to clean up the mess when you three push Alex down the steps and he breaks every bone in his body. It's hell washing blood off my hands."

Oh yes, I'm well acquainted with Logan's bizarre sense of humor. Most of the MacTaggart men share his unusual sensibility, but none do it as expertly or with as much inherent menace as Logan.

Cat and I follow her brothers and Logan into the house, but they stop us in the main hall, just past the foyer. Her brothers take up a large amount of the space in the wide hall. Logan leans against the wall, like he had outside, while his cousins round on me in unison.

And Cat is still holding my hand.

Waiting for Reginald Hewitt to make his move has been a new kind of torture. I won't wait for the Three Macs, aka Cat's brothers, to lunge at me.

"You want to beat me," I say, spreading my arms wide. "So go on and do it."

Logan arches a single brow, but his bland expression doesn't change.

Rory looks at Lachlan, who shrugs and looks at Aidan. The youngest of the Three Macs holds up his hands.

"Donnae ask me," Aidan says. "This was your idea, Rory. You and Lachlan dragged me into this. Maybe Alex isn't the worst human being on the planet after all."

"What?" Rory snaps, almost shouting the word. "Ye cannae be serious. He's a con man, Aidan. Who knows what he's doing to Catriona."

Cat rushes up to Rory and stabs a finger into his chest. "You have no idea who Alex is or what he's done. I know everything. That means I'm the only one here who's qualified to judge his character." She stabs her finger into Rory even harder, making him wince the slightest bit. "Alex Thorne is a good man, and I love him."

Her brothers freeze, not blinking, their expressions going blank.

Logan smiles in the subtle way I've come to know as Logan the Ex-Spy enjoying the show. He seems to like it when his cousins turn into barbarians bent on destroying me, but he really gets cheerful when their own sister shocks them into silence. I know this because his smile slowly broadens into a devious grin.

Rory aims his blank stare at Catriona. "You what?"

"I love Alex," she says, enunciating each word with exaggerated precision. "I will not leave him because you three are determined to smother me with your overprotective nonsense."

"But he—That man is—" Rory shakes his head, his face the picture of pure confusion, and flaps a hand toward me. "He's the British Bastard."

Cat takes half a step backward and scans her gaze over all of her brothers. Shoulders back, chin held high, she tells them, "None of you will ever again call Alex the British Bastard or the Limey Louse or any of those other names I made up for him. It's over. I'm staying with Alex, and you had better get used to the idea."

Lachlan opens his mouth.

She holds up a hand. "Haud yer wheesht, Lachie."

He closes his mouth.

I can't stop myself from smiling. I might actually be grinning. Catriona has silenced her much larger, very annoyed brothers. Rory, the Steely Solicitor, is speechless. Lachlan is afraid to speak after being chastised by his sister. Aidan... Well, he's gone back to his usual demeanor, bright-eyed and entertained by the proceedings.

Logan winks at me.

What does that mean? I have no idea, but I'm sure he's expressing solidarity in some strange, Logan-like way.

Cat looks at me over her shoulder. "Is it all right if I fill them in on the problem we're having?"

For a second, I have no clue what she means. Then it dawns on me, and I nod. "Why not? Since they came all this way to wage war against someone, might as well redirect that energy toward a genuine threat."

She moves to stand by me again, her hand slipping into mine.

I listen while Cat explains the Reginald situation to her brothers and Logan. He already knows what Reginald did last year, but he gets that deadly calm look on his face as he hears what's happened lately.

When Cat finishes reading them in on the situation, it's after ten o'clock. We've already gotten sandwiches from the kitchen and eaten them in my study while discussing the Reginald problem. Logan, of course, has ideas that involve him belly-crawling through the woods and waylaying Reggie if he tries to sneak onto the premises. I wish I'd been there to see how Logan dealt with Falk Mullane. It would have been fantastic entertainment.

Everyone agrees we need to sleep on it. We'll have fresh ideas in the morning, after a good night's rest.

I'm sitting in the chair behind my desk, watching the Three Macs and Logan walk out the door and head upstairs.

Cat, who had been sitting on the window ledge, sashays over to me and settles her lovely bottom on my lap. She slouches down so she can rest her head on my shoulder, looping her arms around me. "Everything will work out. You'll see. My brothers are willing to help you, which means they've accepted you, at least provisionally."

"How comforting. I can sleep soundly knowing they won't murder me tonight, but maybe they'll do it tomorrow."

"No, they won't. Not unless they want to be murdered next."

"You would kill your brothers to avenge my death?"

"Aye." She smiles sweetly, which seems incongruous with our conversation. But then, we're only joking. She nuzzles my cheek. "You are a good man, Alex. They'll see that, eventually."

Pressure bears down on my chest, but it's not a bad feeling. A sort of excitement rushes through me, and I can't hold back anymore. I've wondered what's come over me since Cat announced she loves me, but tonight I know the answer.

I cup her cheek and murmur, "I love you, Cat."

She smiles again, with so much sweetness and affection that it seems to light her up from the inside out. "I love you too."

Our lips meet, and I'm not sure if I kiss her or she kisses me. Does it matter? Her mouth is warm and soft and welcoming, and so is her body. I want to make love to her, but I'm too knackered for that.

"Let's go to bed," I say, standing up and holding her in my arms. "In the morning, we'll all come up with a plan. Somehow. Preferably one that doesn't get us killed."

She kisses my cheek. "For once in your life, look on the bright side. You're not alone anymore. Not only do you have me, but you've got my brothers and cousins too."

"Cousins plural? I knew it. More of your family are on the way."

"Not yet. They'll come if we need them."

I carry her up to my bedroom, and we both undress in silence. Once we've crawled under the covers, she snuggles up to me the way she often does lately. I like it. Which is bizarre. I've never cared for physical intimacy—except for sex, and then only while we're shagging. But with Catriona, I've always enjoyed this kind of closeness. I'd forgotten how much I liked it until she showed me.

"Good night," I whisper to her, "my beautiful, sweet, fiery Cat."

She stretches an arm over my chest to hug me. "Good night, Alex."

For the first time in longer than I can remember, I fall asleep right away.

And I dream of Cat.

Chapter Thirty-Four

Catriona

istant shouting rouses me from a deep sleep, but my foggy brain can't interpret what I'm hearing. Is that Rory? Or Lachlan? I rub my eyes and take a deep breath to wake myself up, but the smell of smoke fills my nostrils. Alex doesn't smoke cigarettes. I push up, straightening my arms, blinking furiously while I struggle to sort out the signals my brain is receiving.

A fist pounds on the bedroom door. "Catriona! Alex! Wake up, the house is on fire!"

"What?" I say in a groggy voice.

The sleepiness lasts only a split second more, then reality wallops me in the face.

Smoke seeps under the door into the room as a faint wisp, but the smell of it surrounds me.

My pulse pounds in my ears. My breaths shorten. I punch Alex's arm and shout, "Wake up! Alex, wake up!"

He rouses as slowly as I had, but catches on much faster, hurling the covers off us and leaping off the bed.

I leap off it too, but suddenly realize we're both naked.

Alex is thinking faster than I am, though. He grabs two dressing gowns and tosses one at me while he yanks on the other one. I've just gotten mine on when he seizes my hand and tows me out the door.

Into an oppressive cloud of smoke.

My eyes burn and water, but Alex drags me in the direction of the staircase. Flames crackle and snap. Sparks float on the air, carried along on a wind created by the fire. When we reach the landing, Logan appears out of the smoke like an apparition—one who's wearing a face mask fashioned from a pillowcase he's tied around his head. He thrusts two pillowcases at us. Alex and I struggle to get ours on even while Logan leads us down the staircase to the first floor, where the smoke is less dense.

The lights are off, but Logan has a flashlight. He leads us toward the foyer.

My brothers are waiting there, each wearing a different kind of makeshift face mask.

We rush out of the house, through the already open double doors, and stop on the other side of the driveway. My eyes still burn, triggering tears that stream down my cheeks. Alex still grips my hand, not quite hard enough to hurt. For several minutes, the six of us stand there staring up at the flames engulfing the house. The smoke snakes upward, visible in the light of a full moon.

The night is warm, but a shiver rattles my entire body.

Alex hugs me to his side, rubbing my arm.

Sirens wail from further down the long driveway. The noise grows louder with every passing second, and soon red lights coruscate around us as the first responders arrive. A fire truck pulls up first, then an ambulance, and finally a sheriff's department car. We move further away from the house to give the firefighters more room to work. I haven't processed what's already happened, but now the firefighters are aiming a hose at the house, its powerful jet shooting up to the second floor.

I suddenly realize it's the second floor that's burning the brightest and hottest. Smoke pours out of the ground floor, but I can't see flames there.

The whole scene unfolds in a blur. I feel like I can't focus on anything, like my mind can't sort out what I'm seeing and hearing and smelling and feeling. Eventually, we all climb into our two cars—my brothers in the one they hired at the airport, and Logan in the car with me and Alex. I stay trapped in a mental haze until we reach a hotel and get into the adjoining rooms we've rented. Aidan lends Alex some of his clothes since Alex is wearing only a dressing gown. I wear Aidan's clothes too, though I need the belt from my dressing gown to hold up the trousers that are much too big for me.

I sit on the end of the bed in the room Alex and I share. "What happened?"

He crouches in front of me, taking my hands in his. "Someone burnt the house down."

"The house is gone?"

"No, I imagine there will be some part of it left." He brushes his fingers over my cheek. "But I think it will be gutted. I'm essentially homeless."

"We're homeless."

"Yes, *we* are." He tries for a smile. "Guess I'll have to move in with Mum and Dad. Their unemployed son comes home to sponge off them."

I know he's joking, since he apparently has a small fortune in the bank—or maybe it's a large fortune, I don't know—but his smile falters and his voice cracks. He's lost his home, the house he built and has lived in for years. He would've lost his possessions too. I've lost only what I brought with me from Scotland, and that was mostly clothes and shoes. The rest of my belongings were to be shipped here later, once I got settled in.

"Alex," I say, holding his face in my hands, "I'm so sorry. You've lost everything."

"No, I haven't done." He turns his face into my hand, kissing the palm. "I have you."

Someone knocks on the door that connects our room to the one where my brothers are. Logan paid for his own room on the other side of mine and Alex's.

"Come in," I call out.

Alex and I both stand.

Lachlan opens the door and hovers on the threshold, as if he's not sure whether he'll be welcome in our room. "We've been talking. You should join us and hear what we think you two should do now."

Alex doesn't even complain about my brother announcing that he and the other MacTaggart men have decided for us what we should do. He's still in shock, I assume. I know I am.

We tramp into the other room, where my brothers and Logan wait for us. Logan sits in a chair by the window while Rory, Lachlan, and Aidan all sit on the same bed. Lachlan gestures for me and Alex to take the other bed. My brothers turn to face us once we've sat down.

Alex slips an arm around my shoulders.

Logan speaks first. "I spoke to the sheriff. He told me the fire in your home seems to have started upstairs. He won't know for sure until there's been an investigation, but there's evidence of arson. They found a scorched metal container that most likely held petrol."

"Someone emptied a can of gasoline in my house?" Alex says.

"Then they lit a match, or something like that."

Alex bows his head, staying silent for several seconds, then he looks at Logan. "It was Reginald Hewitt. It has to be. He said I would pay."

"Aye, that does make sense." Logan shifts in his chair, grimacing like he can't get comfortable. "You still think he's brought Falk Mullane with him."

"Don't you? I can't imagine who else would team up with that bastard."

"Maybe." Logan glances at Lachlan. "Why don't you tell them our plan?"

Lachlan nods and turns to me and Alex. "We want you two to come back to Scotland with us. Let the authorities sort out what happened here. You'll be safe at Dùndubhan. It is a fortress, after all, and very difficult to breach—not to mention difficult to burn down."

A solid stone fortress. It does sound like the safest place. Evan and Keely had taken shelter there when Ron Tulloch came after them, so maybe it is the best place for me and Alex. Will he balk at the idea of staying in Rory's castle? My brother doesn't live there anymore, but he still owns it. Jamie and Gavin don't live there anymore either, though they run the museum at Dùndubhan, and I'm sure they won't mind letting Alex on the grounds under the circumstances.

They'd better get used to him, full stop.

"Henry and Imogen should come too," Logan says, "to be safe. We can pick them up on the way."

"My parents?" Alex says, his brows rising. "How do you know about them? I never told you."

Logan smiles in that way he does whenever he knows a secret the other person thought he could never uncover. "I was a spy, Alex. Did you really think I wouldn't know?"

"I suppose I should've guessed you'd find out."

Alex's mobile rings. He answers with a gruff hello, then his forehead crinkles while he listens to the caller. "Thank you for letting me know, Gus. And yes, you need to tell the police about it even though nothing was taken. My house was burnt down early this morning, so I'm sure the break-in is connected. I'm glad no one was hurt." He nods at whatever Gus Hooper says. "I will. Goodbye."

"What was that about?" I ask.

"Someone broke into my former office on campus an hour ago." He scrapes a hand through his hair. "They set the trash bin on fire, but luckily it wasn't large enough to swallow up the whole room. Someone spotted the smoke and put out the fire."

"Whoever set these fires," Logan says, "has no idea you've lost your job. Sounds like Reginald is out to destroy you."

"Yes, it does seem that way."

"This changes the plan. We need to be away immediately."

Alex's parents. We need to get to them before Reginald and whoever he's working with find them—if they find them. We can't take the chance. Logan already knows that.

"You can wash off the smoke on the jet," Logan says, rising and stretching. "It's equipped with a shower. Let's go."

My brothers have left their bags in their hired car. Alex and I have no luggage. I can get fresh clothes from my house once we arrive in Scotland, but Alex has nothing.

While we walk out to the car, I tell him, "I'm so sorry, Alex. You don't have any clothes but the borrowed ones you're wearing."

"Not your fault." He opens the car door for me. "Besides, this isn't the first time I've started over from scratch."

My heart aches for him. For the laddie who'd been forced to turn his parents in to the police and go live with strangers. For the boy who'd constantly worried about what his parents might do when they got out of prison. For the young man who had moved his new parents to another country to escape his past. And now, for the mature man who has lost his job and his home.

But he has everything that matters. He has me, Henry, and Imogen.

And soon, he'll have the entire MacTaggart clan behind him.

Chapter Thirty-Five

Alex

Since Cat is wearing Aidan's clothes, which are far too big for her, we make a quick stop at a discount clothing store on the way to the airport. It's the only place open at eight o'clock in the morning. She buys a pair of skintight trousers that she calls leggings. They look more like tights to me, but she insists they're real clothes suitable for public viewing. The oversize T-shirt she picks out hangs below her hips. I suspect she chose that shirt because I complained about her choice of so-called trousers.

We all shower on the jet, on our short trip to Nevada to pick up Henry and Imogen.

They're thrilled to see us, even though we tell them about the Reginald problem and the fires at my house and my old office. My parents love the idea of spending more time with me and Cat, but they know we're exhausted from the morning's events. They watch the on-board telly, using headsets to hear it so they won't disturb the rest of us.

We fall asleep on various pieces of furniture. Logan collapses on the sofa. Lachlan sits sideways on a chair, with his legs draped over the adjacent chair. Soon, he's snoring. Rory sits in a chair the proper way, but his head lolls to the side when he falls asleep. Aidan decides to lie on the floor.

Cat and I take the bedroom.

I wake up when the jet begins its descent toward landing, but I let Cat sleep until we've touched down.

A limousine is waiting for us on the tarmac.

Rory had made the call to arrange for a car while we were still in the air. He'd also warned the other MacTaggarts I was coming. Those Scots might dislike me, but I know they won't assault me given what's happened. They aren't bastards like me.

I'm in Scotland again. I've never spent more than four consecutive days in the country, and that had been on my first visit when Logan and Serena insisted I stay to celebrate their engagement with them. Their wedding had taken place in America.

Cat holds my hand as we exit the plane. She keeps holding it while we get into the limousine and during the entire trip to Rory's castle. When the car stops inside the castle walls, in the gravel drive, Cat lets go of my hand only long enough to get out of the car, then she reclaims it. I...don't mind. If I'm completely honest, which I admit is a rare thing for me, I would've wanted to hold her hand even if she hadn't initiated the contact.

My house is gone. Up in smoke, literally.

I still can't decide how to feel about that.

Henry and Imogen have been to Scotland before. They even honeymooned here, which I hadn't known.

"Why did you never mention that before?" I ask while we walk across the courtyard toward the house—the castle—where we'll all be staying. Though it's late according to UK time, the sun is still shining from low on the horizon.

"I don't know," my mother says. "It just never came up in conversation."

"But I introduced you to Cat, who is from Scotland."

"We were so happy to see you again that we didn't think about silly things like our honeymoon in Edinburgh."

Apparently, I still have a lot to learn about my parents.

Cat's brother Aidan comes up beside me. "If you need more clothes, you can always wear a kilt. It's very comfortable and lets everything swing free."

He makes a swinging motion in front of his groin.

"Thank you for the advice," I say, "but I'm afraid the pink kilt Cat gave me was destroyed in the fire."

"Oh, we've got plenty more." He winks. "Or maybe Cat will make you a lavender one this time."

I can tell he's trying to cheer me up, and that fact surprises me. One of Catriona's brothers wants to make me feel better. I glance up at the sky, sure the sun must have split in two. For any of her brothers to be nice to me seems like a sign of an impending apocalypse. I haven't tried very hard, or at all, to make peace with her brothers, so maybe Aidan's attempt to cheer me up has nothing to do with doomsday.

Cat squeezes my hand, making me look at her, and she smiles with genuine affection.

She's smiled at me that way a lot lately. It makes my chest feel like there's a large weight pressing down on it, but the sensation isn't bad. It ought to feel awful, but instead it makes me smile the same way at her.

Jamie and Gavin greet us at the door to the castle that masquerades as a house and a museum. Cat's youngest sister slapped me soundly the first time we met, but today she pulls me into a brief but firm hug. Once she lets me go, her husband shakes my hand and claps me on the shoulder. Fiona, Cat's older sister, also hugs me.

I suppose they feel sorry for me because my house burnt to the ground along with all my possessions. No need to play the pathetic, homeless urchin today. I've become a genuine one.

Catriona wants to show me around Dùndubhan and tell me about its history, but all I want to do is sleep. Since Cat yawns while she's suggesting the tour, I realize we both need a good night's rest. We fall asleep on a large canopy bed in a room inside a medieval castle.

When I wake up the next morning, I lie there staring up at the canopy while I consider the motives of Reginald Hewitt. He despises me, that much I know. But why has he gone on a vendetta to destroy me? He thinks I'm an irritating arse, but that hardly justifies his behavior.

Cat sighs the way she always does when she wakes up, the sound as delicate as a summer breeze. Maybe I haven't slept with her much since our reunion, but I remember every little thing she used to do when we lived together. She'll keep her eyes closed for a few minutes, though she's awake, and then she'll wriggle closer to me and drape half her body over mine. Since I'm lying on my back, that's what she'll do. If I were on my side, she would drape her leg over mine and cozy up to my chest. Once, I'd woken up on my stomach. Cat had laid her entire body on top of me that time.

Maybe I should roll over onto my stomach this morning.

Cat wriggles closer and drapes one arm and one leg over me, placing her head on my chest. Her hair tickles my skin, and I lift my head to push my nose into those silky locks and inhale the scent of them.

"Good morning, love," I say. "Care for a shag before breakfast?"

"I'd love to make love with you, Alex." She raises her head, aiming those beautiful blue eyes at me. "But we have too much to do. Better eat breakfast and get started."

"On what? We have no bloody idea where Reginald is." I clasp my hands at the small of her back, and though I shouldn't feel happy right now, I love the sensation of her breasts mounded against my chest and the warmth of her supple body pressed to mine. "We're to let the authorities handle the manhunt. Remember?"

"You don't want to lie around in bed while your arch-nemesis is out there."

"What would you suggest I do? I'm a grifter, not a bounty hunter."

She seals two fingers over my lips. "Donnae ever call yourself a grifter again. You're not like that anymore, not since you got away from your birth parents. You are a good man."

"Fine. I'm a sodding good man. Let's have a party to celebrate my law-abiding lifestyle." I sigh, but it sounds more like grumbling. "None of that helps us with our problem."

She smiles, her eyes twinkling. "You keep saying 'us' and 'we' and 'our.' You know what that means, don't you? We're a team."

My mouth hangs open, like I'm inviting every insect in Scotland to fly in there. Did I say those words? Us. Our. We. Yes, I did say that. I told my parents we're a couple, but I haven't included anyone else in my decisions for so long that I can't remember when I last did that.

"Yes, we are a team," I say. "For better or worse."

The second I speak those words, I realize I've recited part of the standard wedding vows. That is not what I meant. Not at all.

But the idea of marrying Cat doesn't disturb me.

"We need help," Cat says while drawing invisible, abstract patterns on my chest with her finger. "Luckily, the MacTaggarts can give us that help. We have every sort of expert you might possibly want or need. Logan is a covert operative, Evan designs surveillance and security devices, Rory is a solicitor, Aidan owns a construction company—"

"If we need your brother's construction expertise, then we're in worse trouble than I thought. Is he going to build us an underground bunker?"

She rolls her eyes at me but continues listing the skill set of every MacTaggart in creation. "Lachlan used to be a financial adviser, but he also has connections in government. So does Rory. And Gavin is an ex-Marine."

"But he's not a MacTaggart. You said your family can offer all the skills we need."

"Aye, and Gavin is my brother-in-law. That makes him a MacTaggart." She taps her finger on my chest. "May I go on? Or are you going to interrupt with another sarcastic comment?"

"Go on. But I reserve the right to heckle you."

She sits up, then swings one leg over me to straddle my hips and lays both hands on my chest. "Then there's Iain, who's an archaeologist like me. His wife, Rae, had a sheep ranch in Texas and now she and Iain have one at their home near Loch Fairbairn. She knows all about sheep, llamas, and horses. Oh, and they have chickens now too."

"Wonderful. We can hurl chickens at Reggie when he storms this castle. Or maybe we could have the sheep trample him while Iain excavates ancient bones that we can use to pummel Reginald."

"Rae went undercover to get Iain out of jail. And Keely stabbed the scunner who went after Evan."

"Hmm, yes. I'd almost forgotten about you MacTaggart women and your tendency toward violence. Even the Americans who are MacTaggarts by marriage have fiery tempers, but only you have that smoldering fire in your soul."

She kisses me. "Thank you, Alex. I'm glad you've gotten back to being your old self."

"I can't go back to the way I was. This is the new me, the bastard you like to punch."

"Only did that once. But you are becoming the old you again. Don't fight it, Alex, let it happen."

Should I do that? Not sure I can, but for her, I'll try. The old me had been a grifter too. It's something I can never cleanse from my nature because it's tattooed on my soul.

"Tell me more about the amazing MacTaggarts," I say. "I'm sure you have several thousand more cousins I haven't met."

"Not thousands." She slaps her palms on my chest, leaning into them. "My cousin Arran is an estate agent, which means he knows a lot of people since he's sold a lot of real estate. Then there's my cousin Callum, who's a fireman."

"Finally, someone who has a useful skill."

She seems to ignore my comment, tapping her chin while gazing at the headboard. "But I think my cousin Jack could be the most helpful to you. I'd rather not say why yet. You won't want to do it at first, but I'm sure Jack and I together can convince you to give it a go."

"Give what a go?"

She looks at me, her smile secretive and a touch smug. "You'll find out."

Cat slides off my body to hop off the bed.

"Where are you going?" I ask, pushing up on my elbows. "And where's the bloody toilet?"

"Down the hall," she says, tugging on the clothes she'd bought yesterday, the large T-shirt and skintight pseudo-trousers. "Follow me. We can have a shower first."

"Together?"

"Maybe."

"Only maybe?" I leap off the bed, rush to Cat, and sweep her up in my arms. "No, love. 'Definitely' is the correct answer."

She laughs while I carry her off to the bathroom.

Logan opens his bedroom door just as we pass by it. He smirks and covers his eyes with his hands. "Donnae need to see your erse first thing in the morning, Alex. Donnae ever need to see it, actually."

I carry Catriona into the bathroom and kick the door shut.

Chapter Thirty-Six

Catriona

I love taking a shower with Alex, but we have problems to deal with that won't wait. Alex thought it was a joke, but I was serious about enlisting members of my family to help us. Jack in particular has a special set of skills that Alex needs badly, though he'll never agree to letting Jack help him unless I maneuver him into it. Why shouldn't I? He maneuvered me into moving to America and living in his house. My conniving is for a good cause, and it's done with love. Alex needs a sort of help he would never admit to needing.

Which means it's up to me to secure that assistance for him.

According to Jamie and the American Wives Club, wives often need to trick their husbands into accepting a hand—from anyone, not just from strangers. Alex is even more stubborn than Rory and Lachlan combined. But if Erica and Emery could straighten them out, I can do the same with Alex.

Before I talk to Jack, I need to speak to someone else.

So I corner Rory in his office. Well, it used to be his office when he lived here.

He's sitting behind the desk with his head resting on his raised hand, his reading glasses perched on his nose. Though he's staring down at the desktop, I don't see any papers there. He's staring at the shiny wood.

This isn't his office anymore, but I know he's come here to think. A lot has happened recently, so I don't blame him for needing time alone.

"Are you all right?" I ask, sitting down on one of the chairs in front of the desk.

Rory startles like he hadn't noticed me walking into the room. "I'm fine, Cat."

"Good. I need your help." I sit up straighter, clearing my throat. "With Alex."

"Logan is talking to his contacts to find out more about Reginald Hewitt's escape and the status of the arson investigation. In the meantime, there isn't much we can do."

"That's rubbish. We can do plenty for Alex."

"Such as?" He winces as soon as he's asked the question, probably because he realizes he's just offered to help Alex.

Well, he sort of offered.

Have I maneuvered him into doing that? I hadn't meant to, but I like that I'd been able to do it.

"Alex needs our support," I tell Rory. "While we wait for answers, we should do something to make him feel better, to take his mind off things. I also think Jack could be helpful."

"Our cousin Jack?"

"That's right."

Rory sinks back in his leather chair. "I may not know Alex well, but I'm fair certain he will never agree to Jack's methods."

"You mean because you would never do it." I shake my head. "Why are all the men in the MacTaggart clan so bloody stubborn? It took a free-spirited, determined woman like Emery to set you straight. Otherwise, you'd stilwl be the Ogre of Loch Fairbairn, wouldn't you?"

He studies me for a moment, his lips working and his flinty gaze narrowed on me.

"Come off it, Rory," I say. "You know that look doesn't scare me. I'm even more stubborn than you are, so you might as well agree to my plan."

"What plan? All you've said is we need to make Alex feel better." He squirms in his chair, his expression pinched. "Ahmno hugging Alex, if that's your plan."

I can't help laughing. "That won't be necessary. I was thinking we could use your favorite tactic for getting bloody-minded men to see the light. It worked with Gavin, Evan, and Logan." I smile sweetly at my brother. "It certainly worked for you, Rory."

He squints at me, but this time I know he's thinking, not trying to intimidate me. Honestly, he knows he can't intimidate me, so he's wasting energy every time he tries it. At last, he rolls his chair closer to the desk and folds his arms on it.

"All right," he says. "I'll arrange it."

"Thank you, Rory." I spring out of my chair and bend over his desk to kiss his cheek. "You're my favorite brother."

"Yes, I'm sure I am. Until you ask Lachlan to do something for you and have to wheedle him into agreeing." Rory gives me a halfhearted scowl. "But you get to ring Jack and talk him into his part of your plot."

"Agreed."

"I doubt Alex will appreciate what you're doing for him."

"Not at first, but eventually he'll see it for what it is. An act of love."

Rory purses his lips. "You do love him, don't you?"

"Isn't that what I've said several times? Yes, I love Alex. Stop being grumpy about it, Rory, and try being happy for me."

"That might take considerable time."

"Fine, but at least stop glowering at him." I rest my erse on the desk. "May I borrow your office for a while?"

"Yes."

"And may Alex borrow it too? He's used to hiding in his study, but he doesn't have a house anymore, much less a study."

Rory purses his lips again, but after a few seconds his mouth relaxes. "All right. You can both use my office today."

"And make sure everyone stays away from the sitting room this morning."

"I'll do that too. Any other orders?"

"No, nothing else. Thank you." I kiss the top of his head. "You really are a sweetie-pie, just like your wife says."

He grunts, then gets up and walks out of the office.

I take the big leather chair behind his desk and pick up the phone to ring Jack. When he answers, I say, "It's Catriona. I have a problem that requires your professional expertise."

"You've never wanted my kind of help before, but I'm happy to—"

"No, Jack, it's not for me. My boyfriend needs your help."

"Boyfriend?" Jack is quiet for a moment before he says, "Is this the British Bastard we're talking about? I heard you've been living with him in America."

"No, I'm not talking about any British Bastard. This is for Alex Thorne, the man I love."

"Sorry, I didn't mean to offend you. That's what everyone's calling him. But I did hear about the fire that destroyed his home. I imagine he does need a neutral party to talk to." He hums notes that aren't really a tune, the way he often does when he's thinking. "I'll clear my calendar and come right over."

"Thank you, Jack. You're my favorite cousin."

He chuckles. "That's sweet, but you don't need to butter me up. I'm happy to help."

"There's one more thing." I chew on my fingernail but catch myself doing it and stop. "Alex doesn't know you're coming, and he has no idea what you do for a living."

"A sneak attack? Sounds like fun. I've been left out of the adventures so far, though I was there when you and Alex met again for the first time in...how long?"

"Eleven years."

"That's a long time. No wonder Alex needs help adjusting."

I tell Jack where to meet me and Alex, and we say goodbye. When I join everyone in the dining room for breakfast, Alex is already there, sitting next to Emery. Rory has taken the seat at the head of the table. An empty chair waits for me beside Alex.

Mrs. Brody, the housekeeper at Dùndubhan, has made a large breakfast for us full of all the Scots foods we love. I accidentally call her Mrs. Darroch, which was her name before she married the gardener, Tavish Brody. Sometimes I forget that. She doesn't mind, though. No one talks much during the meal, but afterward, I convince Alex to come with me to the sitting room.

Jack is waiting for us. He stands by the fireplace with his hand on the mantle, gazing out the tall windows at the mist-shrouded morning.

When we enter the room, Jack steps away from the fireplace and smiles at us. "Good morning, Cat. And you must be Alex Thorne."

Alex casts me an annoyed glance. "What have you done now?"

"I found someone who can help you." I gesture toward Jack. "And here he is. This is my cousin, Jack MacTaggart. And Jack, this is Alex Thorne, my boyfriend."

Alex's brows lift, and his gaze swerves to me.

Probably because I called him my boyfriend. What would he rather I call him? He doesn't like the British Bastard.

Jack approaches Alex and offers his hand. "Glad to meet you."

Alex eyes Jack's hand with suspicion but then clasps it. "Glad to meet you too. If you're here to batter sense into me, there's no need. Her brothers will take care of that."

"No, I'm not here for that," Jack says with a hint of laughter in his voice. "I'm here to shrink your head."

"What?"

"Didn't Cat tell you?" Jack crosses his arms over his chest. "I'm a psychologist."

Chapter Thirty-Seven

Alex

Bloody hell, Cat," I say while her cousin stands there looking rather pleased with himself. Shouldn't a psychologist evince empathy and sensitivity? Jack MacTaggart seems like he can't wait to crack open my skull and dig around inside my brain.

"Donnae say 'bloody hell,' Alex," Cat tells me, "before you give it a go. Jack is very good at his job, and he has no agenda."

"I'm meant to spill my ruddy guts to a MacTaggart? Your entire family hates me."

"Not Logan or Evan. Not even Rory…anymore."

"Anymore?" I laugh, but there's no humor in it. I feel like a condemned man who just got delivered to the executioner. Is that a guillotine I see outside the window? "Even if your brother doesn't want to murder me anymore, I'm sure that's a temporary situation."

Jack tips his head to the side, analyzing me with his gaze. "Interesting. Why do you assume Rory won't tolerate you for long?"

Cat backs up toward the door. "I'll let you and Jack talk in private."

I squint at her. "You're not leaving me alone with your psychotic cousin."

"The term is psychologist," Jack says, "not psychotic."

Cat, who's now halfway out the door, blows me a kiss. Then she hurries out and shuts the door.

Oh, that woman is underhanded. Tricking me into enduring a therapy session with her cousin? She'd better have barred the door from the outside, otherwise I will leave the second Jack asks me how I feel about whatever thing from my past he thinks I need to examine with a microscope.

"Cat warned me you'd be extremely resistant," Jack says, "maybe even hostile, to the idea of therapy. Don't worry, I've dealt with much more stubborn men than you."

"I doubt that."

He gestures for me to sit in one of two high-backed chairs positioned by the windows. "Have a seat, Alex. Get comfortable."

Yes, I'll feel very relaxed and completely comfortable while being coerced into sharing my feelings with a total stranger. Well, lying is my forte. I don't have to tell this man the truth about anything. If I weave a fantastic web of lies around Jack, it will serve Cat right for pushing me into this.

Therapy is rubbish.

Jack settles onto a chair, bracing his ankle on the other knee.

I approach the second chair, turn it slightly toward the windows, then sit down and prop my feet on the windowsill, ankles crossed. "Do you have a PhD?"

"This therapy session is about you, not me."

"Ah, that means no. You're a con man pretending to be a psychologist."

"That won't work, Alex. I can sit here for hours listening to you insult me and dodge answering my questions."

"Can you? Let's test that theory." I link my hands behind my head and slouch a little in my chair, like I'm as comfortable as any human can be. It's rubbish, but rubbish and bollocks and bullshit are my best tools. "If you don't have a PhD, you really shouldn't advertise yourself as a psychologist. What sort of therapy do you specialize in, anyway? Brainwashing the men who date the sisters of the Three Macs?"

"I have a PhD, so you can rest easy knowing I am qualified to listen to every crumb of pig's wallow you want to throw at me." He tips his head to the side again, and I'm beginning to hate that little action. "I specialize in couples therapy."

"Couples?" I laugh like he's told me the barmiest thing ever. Which he has. "Then why am I in this room alone with you? I'm sure you're a decent bloke, but I'm not interested in dating you."

"But you are involved with Catriona. How do you feel about that?"

"Let's revisit your qualifications to advise me on my relationship with Catriona. Do you have a wife or girlfriend?"

Jack watches me for a moment before he answers. "I'm divorced. No girlfriend at the moment."

"Why on earth should I listen to a man who couldn't make his own marriage work?"

"Sometimes it's easier to see other people's relationships clearly. You have more distance from it." He steeples his fingers, tapping the tips of them. "So tell me, how do you feel about reconciling with Cat? How's the sex?"

I fly out of my chair. "This session is over."

"Calm down, Alex. Let's talk about why the idea of discussing your relationship with Cat makes you want to run and hide."

"My feelings are none of your business."

He watches me with a bland expression while I stand there fuming, my fists clenched.

Finally, Jack asks, "You do love Cat, don't you?"

I look at the door, wanting to leave, but my feet won't move.

"You can go," Jack says. "But you know Cat will be disappointed if you don't at least try talking to me. Think of it as a conversation, not therapy."

"Bugger it all," I mutter, then I drop onto the chair. "Of course I love Cat."

"Do you want to marry her?"

"How is that any of your concern?"

Jack shrugs. "It's not, but I'm wondering if the rebirth of your relationship with Cat is making you doubt everything. What are you most afraid of?"

I turn my chair fully toward the windows, and the rug under it gets crumpled up. I half rise from the chair to lift one of its legs and fix the rug.

"Why can't you face me while we're talking?" Jack asks. "What are you afraid of?"

"You already asked that question."

"Answer it, then."

I scowl, glancing at him. "You're a bloody annoying wanker, do you know that? Repeating questions over and over won't make me more inclined to answer."

"Maybe not, but I'm fair certain it'll be fun for me, watching you squirm. Have you ever seen someone plunge an electrified rod into the ground to make the worms come out? You remind me of those wriggling little beasties."

"Oh, thank you so much," I say with enough sarcasm to prove to him what a bastard I am. That ought to convince him how much I don't want to bare my soul to him. What does he expect? The arse just compared me to wriggling earthworms. "If you're planning to use electric shock therapy on me, may I at least have a glass of Scotch first?"

"You're sidestepping again. Try answering one question, honestly, with no verbal tap dancing."

"Now I'm a tap-dancing earthworm?"

"One question," Jack says, leaning forward to rest his elbows on his thighs. "Answer one question for me."

Grumbling, I gaze out the window at the grey sky. "Go on. Ask."

"Don't think about your answer, just say it. What are you most afraid of?"

"Losing Cat again."

Why am I playing this game? It's ridiculous, and I hadn't meant to say that. Jack MacTaggart is driving me insane with his irritating calmness and his caring voice that makes me want to bludgeon him with my shoe.

"Why would you lose her?" Jack asks. "She loves you, and you've told her everything she wanted to know. Haven't you?"

"Yes, but—" I shake my head. "It doesn't matter."

"People say that about things that matter the most." He pauses, but I refuse to glance at him and find out why. "I was there, you know. On the day you and Cat were reunited here at Dùndubhan. As I recall, she hit you."

"Catriona punched me in the gut."

He chuckles. "Aye, she's a feisty one. Did you deserve it?"

"What if I did?"

"I saw the argument you two had in the garden that day."

"How? The only ones there besides me and Cat were Logan and Serena."

Jack taps his steepled fingers like he had a few minutes ago. "I'd gone into the garden to relieve myself behind a large bush. When you two started arguing, I thought it was best to wait it out and not disturb you."

"You're an eavesdropper? So much for client confidentiality."

"Neither of you was my client then, but I've never told anyone what I saw and heard."

I grumble, because I can't think of a thing to say. Snarling at him doesn't work. He's like Logan in that way, though Jack's annoying calmness is far more annoying than Logan's.

"On to another topic," Jack says. "Tell me about your parents, Henry and Imogen. You're adopted, aren't you?"

I jerk my head to glare at him. "How do you know that? Henry and Imogen wouldn't tell you."

"We had breakfast together this morning, but they didn't tell me. You just called them by their given names, and you don't resemble them."

"Not all children resemble their parents."

"I also asked them what you were like as a toddler. They changed the subject, but they're not as good at deflection as you are."

No, of course they're not. They're honest people.

"Yes, all right," I say. "Henry and Imogen became my foster parents when I was taken into care at eight years old. Eventually, they adopted me."

"What happened to your birth parents?"

"They're still alive, somewhere."

Jack is silent for long enough that the urge to look at him becomes irresistible. When I do look, he's wearing a serene smile—a serenely smug smile.

"Aren't you meant to be sympathetic?" I ask. "You look like you're terribly proud of yourself for getting me to confess."

"You haven't confessed, not yet." He walks to the window and sits on the wide sill facing me. "What do you need to confess, Alex?"

I doubt I'm getting out of this room until I've told this man something. What the hell. It's not like I've committed a crime, not since I was a child, at any rate. "Everyone I love is in danger because of me. Because one sodding moron decided I've wronged him by being a pompous arse."

"So it's not because of you. It's because of him. I assume we're talking about Reginald Hewitt." He holds up a hand when I open my mouth to speak. "Logan told me all about that."

I suppose I can't be angry with Logan. Everyone knows about it by now, since Cat's brothers witnessed the fire that destroyed my home. And I told them about Reginald.

Jack leans back against the window frame. "Let's talk about why you feel the need to blame yourself for what Reginald Hewitt did."

I drop my head into my palm and mutter an oath. "Therapy sessions last for an hour, don't they?"

"Oh, donnae worry." Jack bends toward me, smiling. "I've got the whole morning set aside for you."

Sinking lower in my chair, I groan.

Chapter Thirty-Eight

Catriona

I wait in the main hallway while Alex and Jack have their meeting, though I really want to be hovering outside the door to the sitting room with my ear to the wood, listening in. That would be wrong, though. Alex needs someone to talk to who's not me, and he needs to know whatever they talk about is private. Jack is one of the kindest people I've ever known, but he's also not fazed by recalcitrant clients.

Maybe he can get through to Alex.

Why does Alex insist he's a criminal? Whatever his parents forced him to do when he was a child has nothing to do with his true nature. He's a good man, and I pray Jack can convince him of that.

Oh, but Alex is also a stubborn goat. He'll kick and bite to keep anyone from asking uncomfortable questions.

Jack can handle it. I know that.

So why am I pacing in the long hallway, wringing my hands and checking the time on the wall clock? Alex and Jack have been sequestered in the sitting room for over an hour.

I want to run down the hall, through the dining room, and down the guest wing hall to the sitting room door. I want to burst into the room, to check on Alex. But I won't do any of that. Alex will come out when he's ready. I have to wait.

"*Mhac na galla,*" I mutter.

Laughter echoes down the hall from the direction of the dining room.

Spinning around, I trot toward the sound.

Jack and Alex walk out of the dining room, smiling and laughing.

I stop, my attention locked on them. Alex is laughing. He's happy. After a therapy session. I expected he would resign himself to the idea and become somewhat cooperative, but I hadn't expected him to come out of it laughing.

Jack slaps a hand on Alex's shoulder. "See? Therapy isn't a torture session."

Alex twists one side of his mouth into a half smile. "I have a feeling your version of therapy isn't standard."

"There's no single method that works for everyone." Jack pats Alex's shoulder. "Especially for someone like you."

Both men notice me, where I'm frozen in place a few meters from them.

"Catriona, you can have Alex back now. I've shrunk his head to just the right size and polished him up for you." Jack walks past me, pausing to whisper in my ear, "You and Alex are good for each other."

Then he ambles into the vestibule. The door to the outside clicks open and shut.

Alex jams his hands into his trouser pockets. "I suppose talking to your psychologist cousin wasn't a rubbish idea after all."

"Did you just admit you liked therapy?"

"I like Jack. That's all." He approaches me, settling his hands on my arms, skating them up and down my skin. "I love you, Cat, and I'll do whatever I have to do to make this work. Honestly, I might cock it up, but I'm trying not to."

"You won't cock it up. Now that you've told me everything, we don't have a wall of secrets between us anymore."

"True." He draws me closer, not quite close enough to kiss me. "Jack suggested I look into my family. Logan has said the same thing. There seems to be a consensus among the people who don't hate me that I should explore the possibility I might have relatives who aren't criminals."

"You should." I move closer, wrapping my arms around his midsection. "I'll be with you every step of the way. You're not alone anymore."

"I know." He brushes a kiss over my forehead. "You want children, and I need to make sure I don't have a rancid gene pool."

"Let's go talk to Rory. He knows investigators who I'm sure can help you trace your family."

"That will need to wait a bit. Jack informed me that my presence is required on the green." He grimaces. "I have a feeling your brothers and cousins have devised a series of Highland games to make me feel more...masculine."

"You participated last time they held the games."

"And it worked out brilliantly, didn't it? I nearly killed myself."

I raise onto my toes to level our gazes. "Maybe they think you need to prove to yourself you can do it."

"Please tell me you're not suggesting I toss a caber again."

"The decision is up to you. But remember, my brothers and cousins want to help you. This is their way of showing it."

He rolls his eyes toward the ceiling, groans, and looks at me again. "Yes, yes, I'll do my bit. This time when I'm crushed under a caber, if I ask you to be my physical therapist, say yes."

"Of course I will. I told you that before." I rub myself against his body, grinding my hips into his groin. "I know all the best kinds of physical therapy."

I take his hand and lead him outside and into the garden, heading for the door hidden behind a flowering bush. The last time we were in this garden together, Alex and I had been arguing. That was the day I'd seen him again for the first time in years. So much has changed in the nine months since that day. I've gone from cursing his name to telling Alex I love him, and now I've brought him home with me—and my entire family has welcomed him.

Alex pulls the old door open, but he has to tug on it so hard it opens with a loud popping noise.

"Why doesn't anyone fix this door?" he asks. "It's bloody hard to open."

"That door is hundreds of years old. It's historic."

"Not all very old things are worth saving." He gives the door a light kick with his foot. "And this is one of the things that isn't."

"But you're one of the things that is."

He lifts his brows. "You're calling me old? Careful, you might ruin all the progress I made in therapy if you keep insulting me."

"You are older than I am, but I meant because we knew each other years ago. You're an old boyfriend."

I glance out the door and see a small crowd out there—my brothers, several of my cousins, and two of their wives. The children have stayed home. I notice Emery and Rae standing beside their husbands while Rory and Iain are having a discussion. My sisters, Fiona and Jamie, loiter just behind the others, while Gavin is rolling the cabers into position. Evan isn't here, of course. He still doesn't like to leave Keely and baby Joy.

As soon as Alex and I walk out the garden door, Lachlan and Aidan approach us.

Lachlan offers Alex a package wrapped in brown paper. "We got you a new kilt."

"Do I dare open this?" Alex asks me. "You might have made me a lavender kilt with glitter-soaked images of ponies on it this time."

"I didn't have time to make you a kilt. Whatever that is, my brothers came up with it."

"Yes, that eases my mind so much." Alex unwraps the package, revealing a kilt fashioned from the MacTaggart clan tartan of blue, green, and orange. He stares at the kilt for several seconds without blinking, then shifts his surprised gaze to Lachlan. "Ah, thank you. This is... Thank you, Lachlan, and all of you."

My brothers have given him an official MacTaggart clan kilt. The simple, tacit act of acceptance makes me want to cry, but I don't. My brothers are always embarrassed when any of their sisters gets emotional with them.

Instead, I hug Lachlan and kiss his cheek, then do the same to Aidan. "Thank you for this, thank you, thank you, thank you."

When I smile at Alex, he still looks stunned.

Clasping his hand, I lead him out onto the green where everything needed for a good round of Highland games is already set up. The crisp, refreshing scent of newly mowed grass envelops us. They've laid out a chalk line to indicate where contestants should stand.

Alex unzips his trousers and puts on his kilt over them, then he gets rid of his trousers. I know for a fact he doesn't have any underwear on. If a breeze kicks up, his kilt might fly up and show everyone just how much of a man he is.

I'm not sure I want Emery and Rae to see Alex's dangly bits. They're mine.

Rory shakes Alex's hand. "Welcome to a special edition of the MacTaggart Highland games. This time there are only two contestants." He points at himself and then Alex. "Are ye ready for it, Sassenach?"

Alex glances at the two cabers lying on the grass several meters away. "Yes, I'm ready."

Rory smiles in his devilish way, the expression that makes most men cringe.

Alex doesn't.

My brother gestures toward the chalk line with one arm. "Sassenachs first."

"We're starting with the caber toss, then?" Alex asks.

"I'm letting you start easy, with the stone put. We'll work up to the cabers."

Once Alex approaches the combat zone, Iain carries a large, smooth stone over to him. Alex accepts it, hefting the stone in his hand like he's adjusting to its weight. Once he's ready, he spins around twice and hurls the rock. It thumps down ten meters away, by my estimate. Iain rushes out to measure the distance, declaring it to be twelve point two meters. Rory throws his stone next, landing it a few centimeters past Alex's. They have another go, but this time Alex beats Rory. A third round breaks the tie—and Alex wins.

I wonder if Rory threw the match, but I decide he wouldn't do that. Rory knows Alex needs to win the right way.

They do weight for height next, each man grasping a heavy stone by its metal handle and flinging it over a crossbar. Rory wins this time, though not by much. Alex wins the next game, the hammer throw, and then it's time for the caber toss.

During the last Highland games, Alex had tripped and nearly gotten crushed by his caber. While I watch him walk his hands up the caber to get it upright, I strap my arms around myself and chew on my lip. A memory of a caber slamming down on him barrels through my mind. I squeeze my eyes shut for a second before I force myself to watch. When Alex defeats Rory, I want to see it.

Alex gets his caber upright, and with a shout, launches it end over end.

I cheer and clap, hopping up and down. "Go, Alex!"

Rory lands his caber less than a meter past Alex's.

Alex wins the second round, and it's time for the final throw. Rory goes first, hurling his caber even farther than the first two times. Alex gets ready, taking a moment to prepare while he holds the caber upright with its end on the ground. Rory bars his arms over his chest and aims his famous steely expression at Alex.

I want to run over there and smack Rory. If he distracts Alex and makes him drop the caber, I will murder my brother.

But Alex doesn't get distracted. He doesn't even flinch. Instead, he flashes Rory a smirk and heaves his caber.

And it whumps down well past Rory's throw.

I scream and clap, jumping up and down, then I race across the green to Alex and throw myself at him. He catches me, so my feet are dangling above the ground. I lock my arms around his neck and kiss him.

The crowd cheers.

Which means my brothers are cheering too, since I hear more than the three voices of Iain, Logan, and Jack.

By the time I stop kissing Alex and he lowers me onto the ground, everyone has gathered around us.

Rory offers Alex his hand. "Congratulations. You won the MacTaggart family Highland games. For the first time in history, a Sassenach beat a MacTaggart."

Alex shakes Rory's hand.

The other men come over to congratulate him with a handshake too. But Rae, Emery, and Fiona kiss his cheek.

I almost pass out from shock when Jamie hugs and kisses Alex. She's hated him more than anyone since the day he first turned up at Dùndubhan. Now she's kissing his cheek and smiling at him. I'm so stunned, in fact, that I blurt out the question that's echoing in my mind.

"Jamie, why are you kissing Alex? You hate him."

She rolls her eyes. "Donnae hate him. Not anymore. You love him, and Jack says he's not the devil, so that's good enough for me."

"Only pregnancy hormones could make you so forgiving."

She huffs.

Rory interrupts us, speaking to Alex. "I think you and I should talk. Alone."

Alex glances at me like he wants my permission. Or maybe he wants me to insist on going with him to talk to my brother.

I decide he doesn't want that, so I tell him, "Go on. It's all right."

Jamie hooks her arm under mine. "You can find her in the dining room when you and Rory are done. Lunch will be served in thirty minutes."

Rory and Alex stride through the garden gate and disappear from sight.

Should I worry about why my brother wants to see Alex alone?

No, that's barmy. I don't need to worry.

"Come on," Jamie says. "Let's go make sandwiches for our men."

"Don't the women get to eat?"

She rolls her eyes again. "Being with Alex has made you a fair sight more sarcastic than you used to be."

I take that as a compliment.

Chapter Thirty-Nine

Alex

I've barely sat down in the chair across the desk from Rory, inside the office here at Dùndubhan, when he starts in on me. He leans back in his chair, affecting a posture that's relaxed and vaguely threatening. Not that I feel threatened by him. But he's trying to intimidate me, for sure.

Rory rests a hand on the desk. "Are you using my sister?"

"Using her?" I consider reverting to my air of casual disinterest, but I realize he won't appreciate that. Honesty is not my strong suit, but for Cat, I'm trying my best. "I would never use Cat in any way. I love her."

He stares at me for a long, long moment. My skin starts to itch, and I can't stop myself from scratching my neck. At last, he sits forward, bracing his elbows on the desktop.

"Good," he says. "Cat thinks you need to find out if you have any family, other than your birth parents."

"Yes, Jack shares that opinion." I rub my neck, averting my attention to the floor. But I look straight at Rory when I say, "I want to find out the answer. If I have any relatives who aren't bent, it would be...reassuring, I suppose."

Rory nods. "All right, then. I know an investigator who has helped me find missing heirs before, so I know he's good at tracing family. With your permission, I'll contact him."

"Go ahead."

He retrieves a pad of paper from a drawer, places it on the desktop, and picks up a pen. "I'll need to know more about your birth parents."

I give him all the information he asks for, which isn't as trying as I thought it would be. I'd already told the MacTaggarts about Nigel and Julia, since Cat insisted I share everything so her brothers and cousins who are helping me will have all the information they might need. Well, I gave them the abridged version. I don't see how Nigel and Julia could have any connection to Reginald Hewitt and his idiotic vendetta, but I trust Cat's judgment on that.

Now I'm telling Rory, Cat's most hostile brother, all about my darling parents. The unabridged version. Somehow, I know he won't leak the information to anyone else except his investigator.

Once we're done, I leave Rory in the office and make my way to the dining room. Everyone is already there, seated around the table. Another table, longer and narrower, sits against the wall and holds a buffet feast.

Cat saved a seat for me beside her.

Erica and Calli, Lachlan and Aidan's wives, carry in the last of the buffet items. They must have arrived while I was telling Rory all about my original parents.

Lachlan seems surprised to see his wife. "Where are the bairns?"

She sits down beside him. "Relax, honey. The kids are in the cottage with the Brodys."

Calli sits down beside her husband. They kiss with more passion than I would've expected considering the crowd around them.

I lean toward Cat. "Who are these Brodys everyone keeps mentioning?"

"Tavish and Evelyn Brody. She used to be Mrs. Darroch, but Evelyn married Tavish last year. She started out as Rory's housekeeper when he lived here at Dùndubhan, but now she works here and at Rory and Emery's house in North Ballachulish. Tavish is the groundskeeper at Dùndubhan."

"I see." When I notice Aidan and Calli have stopped snogging, I lean toward Cat more. Nodding toward her brother and his wife, I murmur, "Should we show them what a public spectacle really is?"

"Maybe later. I'm fair starved."

"Yes, I am too." Caber tossing burns more calories than I'd realized. I feel like eating every last bit of food on that buffet table. "Are we all waiting for something? Or can we start eating?"

"Let's eat."

Once Cat and I start for the buffet, everyone else lines up behind us. Though the MacTaggarts seem to have accepted me, I'm still surprised when they all begin to tell me humorous stories from Cat's life, from childhood to just before she moved to America for the second time. Cat tells them stories about the two of us when we first knew each other, leaving out the naughty parts and the fact that she was arrested and then she left me.

After lunch, her brothers and cousins try to teach me how to play shinty. It's sort of like lacrosse, but not quite. I've never liked sports, which is an attitude Evan and I share, but Logan convinces me to try it. Rory encourages me to do it too.

He can't possibly like me. Maybe he hopes to trounce me on the field. I've heard the MacTaggart version of shinty has few rules and plenty of dirty plays. I don't do too badly, but I'm not the star player either. I manage to score one goal, but I wind up flat on the ground, my face in the dirt, when I pull off that feat. At the end of the game, I have a few scrapes. Cat assures me I've done well by not getting bruises or a black eye.

After the game, Cat and I use cleaning ourselves up as an excuse for a long, hot shower in the ground-floor bathroom. We make enough noise that I feel sure at least a few of the other MacTaggarts in residence here must've heard us. Not that I care. I wonder if Cat does, but when I ask her, she just smiles.

I take that as a no.

Have I corrupted her, like I said I might? If I have, I can't regret it. This naughty side of her makes me so fucking randy that I want to shag her twenty-four hours a day.

Instead, I let her give me the grand tour of Dùndubhan like she'd wanted to do when we first arrived. After that, Catriona and I head back to the office, where Rory and Jack are waiting for us.

"We have your answers," Rory says, gesturing for us to sit down in the chairs opposite the desk.

Jack is standing near the tall windows, leaning against the frame.

"Already?" I say. "It's only been a few hours."

"My investigator is that good," Rory says. "And it wasn't too difficult for him to find the records. Knowing your birth name sped up the process, since you changed your name when you moved to America."

I shift in my chair, suddenly feeling like I'm sitting on a bed of hot coals that have needles sticking out of them.

Cat grasps my hand, giving it a reassuring squeeze.

And I ask the inevitable question. "What did you find?"

Rory focuses on the papers on his desk. He traces a finger along the lines he seems to be reading. "Your mother, Julia Charnley-Ainsworth, separated from your father, Nigel, shortly after Henry and Imogen took you to Cornwall for safe keeping."

"I'm heartbroken that their marriage fell apart."

"That's not the whole story." He looks up at me. "While they were separated, Julia had an affair with a man called Selwyn Dixon. She fleeced him out of a good deal of money and then she ran away. Nine months later, Julia sent him a gift."

"My mother is a slag as well as a grifter. I'm shocked and horrified. But what does any of this have to do with me?"

Rory holds up a hand, silently asking me to wait. "I'm not done yet. The gift Julia sent to Selwyn was a bairn. A six-week-old baby boy."

Everything inside me goes as cold as the Arctic Ocean. I can't move, can't think, can't speak except to say, "What?"

"Julia didn't want the baby. How could she? Nigel would've known the bairn wasn't his since he hadn't seen his wife in fifteen months." Rory flips to another page in his dossier or whatever he calls his file. "By all accounts, Selwyn Dixon was a good man. He raised the lad by himself and saved up enough money to send him to university. Unfortunately, Selwyn died of a heart attack before the boy graduated."

What the fuck am I meant to say to all this? Rory is telling me I have... No, it can't be true.

Cat squeezes my hand again.

Rory clears his throat. "Alex, you have a half-brother."

I open my mouth several seconds before I can produce any words. "Are you sure?"

"Yes." Rory hands me a sheet of paper. "This is a copy of his birth certificate."

When I accept the paper, it shivers in my hand, just a touch. My throat has turned as dry and tight as a desiccated mummy. I read the words on the birth certificate but can't understand them.

"Your brother is twenty-six years old," Rory says. "His name is Grey Dixon."

Catriona clasps my hand in both of hers. "Did you hear that, Alex? You have family. Good family."

"Aye," Rory says. "Grey attended Bournemouth University and graduated with high marks. He's currently employed as a freelance business intelligence analyst in London." Rory sighs, shaking his head. "I have no bloody idea what a business intelligence analyst does."

Neither do I, but I don't have the extra brainpower to figure that out. All my cognitive energy is taken up by trying to comprehend what Rory has told me. I have a brother. A clever one, apparently.

"Has this Grey person ever been arrested?" I ask.

"No, he's an upstanding citizen," Rory says.

"Are you sure he's not secretly a criminal? In cahoots with Julia and Nigel?"

Maybe I sound desperate. Can anyone blame me? The only blood relatives I've ever known were my original parents.

"No, Alex," Rory says, "Grey Dixon is a good person. He volunteers at a church and a food bank. He puts flowers on his father's grave every Sunday. Those aren't the actions of a heartless criminal."

I lose the power of speech again, thoughts reeling through my mind. A brother. His name is Grey. We share our mother's genes. But he's...not a grifter. I am.

"There's more," Rory says. "You have cousins too. Their names are Chance, Dane, and Reese Dixon. All three are married, and Chance's wife is pregnant. So you'll have another cousin soon enough."

"Is—" I swallow, but the constriction in my throat won't let up. "Is my brother married?"

"No. He lives in London, alone, though he often visits America. Apparently, he has a girl there, but it's unclear whether they're a couple or just friends."

I move my lips as if I were speaking, but I'm not.

"There's more you need to know," Rory says. "I understand you've already had a shock, but this bit is important."

"Go on," I mumble.

"Logan heard from his contact at Homeland Security in America." Rory clasps his hands on the desktop. "A man matching Reginald Hewitt's description was seen boarding a cargo plane headed for the UK."

"What? How did an escaped felon get out of the country?"

"Hewitt bribed a member of the crew to help him sneak on board. The FBI had Hewitt's picture shown on television and asked everyone to watch for him. An ordinary citizen called in the tip about Reginald sneaking onto a cargo plane in Salt Lake City. Unfortunately, the plane was over international waters by the time the FBI was notified."

"Where did Reginald go?"

"It's unclear." Rory scratches his jaw, as if he doesn't want to tell me the rest. "The, ah, cargo plane made a stop in the Azores, but Reginald Hewitt was no longer on board when authorities arrived to search the plane. There had been a chartered flight that took off ten minutes earlier. We suspect Hewitt was on it."

"And...where did he go?" I don't want to hear the answer, but I need to hear it. The sinking sensation in my stomach tells me I already know.

"Heathrow."

"England? I would've thought he'd come straight to Scotland. He must know I've come here, or else why bother flying halfway around the world?"

Rory shrugs. "Only Reginald Hewitt knows the answer to that."

Someone knocks on the door.

"We're busy," Rory calls out.

"It's Logan. I have urgent news."

"Come in."

Logan shoves the door open and marches straight to the desk, angling sideways to Rory as well as me and Cat. "Late this morning, Reginald Hewitt was seen buying petrol in Carlisle for the car he stole in London. My contact at MI6 did some digging and found out Reginald abandoned that car not long after he crossed the border into Scotland. He's got a new one by now, I'm sure, and I think we all can guess where he's going."

"Here?" Cat says.

"That's right." Logan looks straight at me. "This man has one bloody strong vendetta against you."

"I never did a sodding thing to that bastard."

"But in his twisted mind, you have wronged him. Stay inside the castle until further notice."

Stay here? A prisoner in a medieval castle? I still have no idea what I did to make Reginald Hewitt despise me with such intensity. I'd treated him as a friend, trusted him, gave him a job in my home. For three years.

"Alex needs time to process this," Catriona says. "Let me take him for a walk. We'll stay close to the house."

Logan nods. "But be careful. And donnae take too long."

Jack steps away from the windows. "If you need me, I'll be staying here at Dùndubhan tonight, in the tower bedroom."

"Thank you," Cat says.

I drag my body out of the chair, though it seems to weigh fifty stone more than it did ten minutes ago.

Logan slaps a hand on my shoulder, pressing down so firmly I think he's about to tie me to the chair to stop me from going outdoors. "You'll never be too far away for me to find you."

That statement sounds almost reassuring, but with a hint of a threat in it too. Logan does have an odd sense of humor. I should've guessed he would have an odd way of being supportive too. Or maybe that statement means something else.

Cat ushers me out of the office and out of the house, through the garden, out onto the green. She suggests we should stroll back and forth here, but I can't stop moving. What in the name of heaven is Reginald plotting now? And why? Burning down my home wasn't enough for him? My mind spins like the wheels of an out-of-control bicycle, and I have to keep moving, get away, silence the questions by exhausting my body and brain.

"Alex! Wait!"

I hear Cat's voice, but my feet keep moving. My mind keeps moving. Is this the sins of my past come back to haunt me? Is Reginald bloody Hewitt my reckoning?

Catriona catches up to me, tugging my arm, forcing me to pause in my flight to who-knows-where. "Stop, Alex. I know you've gotten two big shocks today, but ye cannae outrun your fears."

"I can try."

We've wound up on a well-worn trail through the forest. It looks like a game trail, like the sort deer might use, but I know nothing about the wildlife in Scotland. Thoughts ricochet in my mind, like bullets fired into my psyche that bounce right off the steel walls of my brain. I have…a brother. And cousins.

Blimey.

Cat moves to stand in front of me. "Let's go back to the house and have sex. Lots and lots of it. Loud, hot, frenetic sex."

Yes, that idea appeals to me. My cock certainly wants that. I know she's trying to distract me, desperately trying, but I don't care.

I haul her into my body and ravage her with a rough kiss.

Something whacks into the back of my head.

My arms fall away from Cat, and the world begins to gyrate. Darkness infiltrates my vision, closing in faster and faster.

And I pass out.

Chapter Forty

Catriona

The only light inside this huge room comes from the big windows high up on the metal walls. The fixtures hanging from the ceiling aren't on, but I think that's because this place has no electricity. It seems abandoned. Rusting pieces of equipment squat on the floor here and there, and even the chairs Alex and I are bound to show plenty of rust, as do the pipes and other metal scraps strewn around the floor. The old warehouse clearly hasn't been used in a long time.

I glance at Alex. His chair sits an arm's length from mine, lined up side by side so we both face toward the human-size door of the warehouse, which stands shut. The other set of doors, both enormous and undoubtedly used for offloading equipment and supplies, are also closed.

Alex slumps in his chair, head bowed, eyes closed.

He still hasn't woken up since that man cracked him on the head with a rock. Is he injured? Or dead? I stare at his chest, watching for the faint rising and falling of each breath. It's there. He's alive, but he might still be seriously injured. He needs a doctor.

But we're stuck here. Our two captors, a man and a woman who look old enough to be grandparents, secured our hands behind our chairs with handcuffs. They also tied our ankles to our chairs with rope. Back at Dùn-dubhan, these two had threatened to hurt Alex if I didn't go along with them. Of course I came. Logan will find us, I'm sure, but there was no way on earth I would've let them touch Alex—or let them take him without me. They blindfolded us both for the long ride, in what I'm sure is a stolen car, that brought us to this place. Then our captors hauled us into this abandoned warehouse.

It stinks of fish in here. Dead, rotting fish.

Alex moans, winces, and opens his eyes. He lifts his head to look around, blinking rapidly, until his gaze lands on me. "Cat? What's going on?"

"We've been kidnapped."

He comes fully awake with a start, his gaze now clear and zeroed in on me. "What happened?"

I tell him the story.

When I'm done, he asks, "What did these two older people look like?"

"The man has gray hair, but the woman's is blonde. He's average height, a bit pudgy, and has dark eyes. She's a little taller than he is, slender, and her eyes are hazel."

He gazes past me, into a distance beyond the real world. When he focuses on me again, he grinds out words through his clenched teeth. "Those sodding arseholes have done it this time, after all their failed attempts. They've kidnapped me."

"You know who they are?"

"I have a suspicion. It's like I've stuck my finger into a socket and the electricity is crackling through my veins. I always get this feeling whenever my parents are in the vicinity."

"Your parents? Do you mean Nigel and Julia?"

He nods, his mouth flattening.

I stare at him, struggling to understand. "But I thought Reginald was the one after you."

"So did I."

Alex glares at nothing in particular, grinding his teeth.

None of this makes sense. How did Nigel and Julia find Alex? He changed his last name when he moved to America, and he hasn't gone back to England since he left sixteen years ago. He flew to Scotland on Evan's private jet, so no one could've known about it. Only someone who knew about me and Alex, and that I'm from Scotland, could've found us. Even then, they would need to find out where my family lives and when Alex might leave America to come home with me.

"I don't understand," I tell Alex. "How could your parents have found you, here in Scotland?"

"They're criminals. They have criminal connections."

"But how could they know you're in Scotland? And what does our kidnapping have to do with Reginald Hewitt?"

"Do I look like bloody Sherlock Holmes? I have no idea."

"We need to get out of these handcuffs."

"How do you suggest we do that?"

I scan the area with my gaze, searching for something we might use to get free, but I don't see anything useful. When I try to shift my chair, it scrapes across the floor with a loud metal shriek that echoes through the warehouse.

Alex gives me an exasperated look. "Why don't you scream and have done with it? Your chair just made enough noise to deafen half of Scotland, so I'm sure Mummy and Daddy will be in here any second."

"I need a small piece of metal, like a pin."

"For what?"

This time I give him an exasperated look. "To pick the lock on the handcuffs."

"Oh. Sorry, I don't have any pins on me."

"I have one in my hair."

He squints at my head. "Unless you're a contortionist, I don't see how you'll reach it." He stretches his neck out, leaning toward me. "Maybe if you bend this way, I can reach that hairpin and pull it out."

"Good. You can get out of your cuffs and then do mine."

"Uh...no, I can't."

"Of course you can."

He grimaces. "I can't pick a lock. Pick a pocket, yes. But not handcuffs."

I should've guessed as much when he'd told me "maybe" I wasn't the only one who had lock-picking skills. Evasion, as usual.

"Well, I can do it," I say. "You get the hairpin and pass it to me."

"I suppose it can't hurt to try."

He leans toward me again, craning his neck, while I slant toward him doing the same thing. His lips wriggle in my hair while he tries to grasp the hairpin. The tickling sensation makes me want to squirm and, strangely, sneeze. I clamp my teeth shut and fight the sneeze reflex as best I can.

"Would ye hurry?" I say.

Alex mumbles something I can't understand since he has his mouth in my hair. Finally, he gets hold of the pin and tugs it free. Holding it between his teeth, he mumbles, "Your turn."

I twist sideways, as much as I can while bound to a chair, and cup my hands like a small bowl. "Toss it into my hands."

His brows knit together, and he looks like he wants to complain about my plan but can't, considering he has a hairpin in his mouth.

"Just try," I tell him by way of encouragement. "You can do it."

Alex groans, then stretches his neck out even more, the effort making sweat break out on his forehead. He pushes the hairpin almost all the way out of his mouth, holding on to the tip with his teeth.

He takes a deep breath, exhales it, and tosses the pin.

It lands in my hands.

Alex's mouth falls open. "That actually worked."

"Of course it did. Scots ingenuity never fails."

"I'll never doubt a plan of yours ever again."

With my hands cuffed behind my chair, I know picking the lock won't be easy. First, I need to unfold the prong-like pin. That might take more dexterity than I have.

"Don't doubt yourself now," Alex says. "You're the cleverest woman I've never known. If anyone can pick a lock with their hands bound behind their back, it's you, Catriona Sorcha MacTaggart."

Despite the situation, I smile. "That's the sweetest thing you've ever said to me."

The human-size door swings open.

Our two kidnappers stalk across the warehouse to us with a third man following behind. I can't see the man's face until they stop in front of us and he steps out from behind the other two.

The new man sneers at Alex and says, in an Australian accent, "Good on ya, making our job so easy. Ya served yourself up on the barbie for us, and your sweet little girl along with ya. This is going to be fun."

Chapter Forty-One

Alex

Hello, Reggie," I say, all but snarling the words. The sight of that bastard makes me want to throw myself at him, still attached to the chair, and head-butt him. "I've missed you terribly. There's been no snake in my house to hiss at me behind my back and plot asinine ways to take revenge on me for... What was it again? I can't remember. All your whingeing sounded like flies buzzing around me."

Reginald Hewitt sneers at me again.

Honestly, he'll have to come up with something much more menacing if he wants to intimidate me.

I don't want to glance at Cat, since that might draw the attention of our three kidnappers, and they might notice she's unbending the hairpin. I can just see that in my peripheral vision. Her job is lock-picking. Mine is to distract these three. I might have no skills when it comes to picking locks, but I excel at distraction.

Nigel and Julia stay slightly behind and to the side of Reginald.

Until this moment, I'd been focused on Reginald. Now, I can't help looking at the two people who created me—biologically and criminally. They look so...old. I know they must be in their late sixties, but they seem even older than that. Two codgers with sour looks on their faces. My parents.

No, not my parents. They spawned me, but they're not the ones who raised me, not really. The eight years I spent with them taught me nothing except how to con and evade the law. Henry and Imogen are my parents. They're the ones who loved me, believed in me, and never gave up even when I fought back against their kindness. They've stuck with me through everything.

The two people currently staring at me like I'm radioactive mean nothing to me.

I relax my posture, affecting my favorite air of indifference, the old "I don't give a flying fuck what you do or say" attitude.

"Well, Reggie, what will you do now?" I ask. "Beat me? Electrocute me? Maybe first you should tell me what it is you want. Villains always have demands. And don't they always need to brag about how clever they are?"

"Don't worry, mate. I'll tell you everything, when I feel like it."

I sigh like being abducted is the most boring thing that's ever happened to me. "Go on, *mate*. I'm in the mood for more whingeing."

Reginald moves closer, bending over to sneer at me yet again.

"Come on," I say. "At least come up with a new facial expression. That one's getting tiresome."

"Still arrogant, aren't you?" He sniggers, his sneer mutating into a nasty grin. "Alex Thorne, the man who always has the upper hand and never gets taken in by a con. That's rot, mate. I fooled you for nearly three years, and you didn't even notice when I cleaned out the household account. For ten days, it was empty. But you were too busy blackmailing a student into stealing artifacts for you to notice what I was doing."

He might as well have backhanded me. His statement of fact hits me like a blow to the face. The cretin is right. No one had ever conned me until Reginald Hewitt came into my life, and I'd been blind to his treachery until the very end. I hadn't guessed Falk Mullane would blackmail me either. Maybe I've lost my touch. Maybe I'm not the grifter I used to be.

But here, in this warehouse, I will be the best bloody grifter in the room. I have to be. Catriona is counting on it. Counting on me.

I fake an Aussie accent as best I can, strictly to annoy the arse who's towering over me. "Good on ya, Reggie. Ya conned me good."

He jabs a finger in my face, right between my eyes. "Don't make fun of me, ya mongrel."

"Piss off, Reggie." I peer around him to see Nigel and Julia, but I focus on her. "Hello, Mummy darling. How did a sweet woman like you ever get tangled up with this plonker? Reggie doesn't seem like your type, but then, you never were particularly...particular, were you?"

Nigel clenches his fists. "Don't speak to your mother that way."

I laugh, and though the sound is bitter, it's not feigned. "When did you start to care about how anyone speaks to your wife? She's your whore for hire."

Reginald smacks me.

And yes, it smarts a little. But it also means I'm getting to the lot of them. *Who's the cleverest now, eh, Reggie?*

I lean sideways to get a better view of Julia. "Mum, would you mind terribly kissing away the pain? That's what mothers are for, after all. Oh wait. You're not a mother, you're a grifter with a heart of rusted steel."

"Shut up," Reginald snarls. "You won't be so up yourself once you hear what we want."

"How did you find those two, anyway? I'm sure you'll want to brag about that before you make your demands."

Peripherally, I see Cat has unbent the hairpin and is starting to pick the lock on her handcuffs. How long will that take? I have no idea, so I'd better keep tormenting these three morons.

"How did I find them?" Reginald says. He straightens, puffing up like a peacock. "I broke into your desk, into the drawer you always kept locked. And I found the papers that said you legally changed your name to Alex Thorne and that showed what your old name was. I can't blame you for changing it. Alexis Lucian Charnley-Ainsworth is a bloody stupid name. Once I knew that, it wasn't hard to get a mate of mine to track down your parents."

Why had I made the name change legal? I should've just started using a different name and not bothered with the formal paperwork. A true grifter would never go through legal channels to change his identity. Why had I?

The truth is obvious, and not as disturbing as I would've thought. I did it because I'm not a grifter anymore. I'm a law-abiding citizen. Well, mostly law-abiding. Borrowing artifacts without permission doesn't count. I always give them back.

"Now for what we want," Reginald says.

"About bloody time." I peer around him again to see Nigel and Julia. "You two used to be the ones running every con. But you're hiding behind this bastard. That's quite a comedown, isn't it? I guess you're just too old these days to handle a simple kidnapping on your own. Is there a retirement home for useless old criminals?" I act surprised, like I've experienced a sudden revelation. "Of course there is. It's called prison."

Reginald smacks me again. "We want your money, ya mongrel. All of it."

"Sorry, I sank all my disposable income into building a house." It's my turn to look smug. "That would be the one you burnt to the ground."

Nigel rushes forward to grab Reginald's arm and yank it, forcing the Aussie plonker to turn toward him. "You did what? You can't keep changing the plan because it's not your plan. We told you to hold him until we got to America." Nigel's lip curls, and his tone becomes nastier. "But no, you had to do things your way. Burning down the house? What are we going to get out of this now?"

"He's got more money. He must."

I do, but I'm not going to admit to that. Luckily, Nigel doesn't trust his new mate.

"You stupid gorilla," Nigel says. "You bollocksed up the plan so you could have your revenge. And we've got nothing."

Reginald glances at Catriona. "She's from a big family. Some of them must have money."

Nigel narrows his eyes and speaks through his gritted teeth. "You're not in charge anymore. Julia and I will handle this. Get your blooming arse out of here."

"This was my idea. You can't run me off."

"Yes, I can."

Nigel is as tall as Reginald, and once upon a time he had a formidable physical presence. But today he looks old and worn out, more so than his years would suggest. Being a nasty piece of work clearly makes a person not age well.

"They think you're a moron, Reggie," I say. "I'd wager they never had any intention of cutting you in on the score."

Julia is loitering behind the other two, biting her lip, shifting her weight from one foot to the other.

"You festy little fucker," Reggie growls at Nigel. "I knew I should've done this on my own."

He pulls his fist back, about to wallop dear old Daddy.

Julia grabs something—I can't see exactly what—and whacks Reggie in the head with it.

Doubled over, he shouts in pain and whirls on her.

She whacks him again, harder by the sound of it.

Reginald crumples to the ground. His eyes close.

I can see Julia is holding a piece of metal, something that looks like the rubbish leftover from metalworking.

Nigel hops over the unconscious Aussie and hugs his wife.

Bollocks. I don't want them lovey-dovey. I want them at each other's throats, so they won't notice what Cat's doing. She'll have her cuffs off anytime now. At least Reginald is out of commission, but that leaves my erstwhile parents.

An idea pops into my head, and I stifle the urge to smile with smug satisfaction. Oh yes, I've got just the right bombshell to blast these two apart.

"Mummy darling," I say with syrupy and completely false affection, "I'm so sorry to have caused you strife. But I'm sure you and Daddy can work things out, like you did after that time when you left him so you could go shag that other bloke. What was his name? Oh yes. Selwyn, wasn't it?"

Nigel's expression goes blank. He stares at Julia for several seconds, like he's never seen her before, then he steps away from her. He wipes his hands on his trousers as if he's cleansing himself of her filth. "She wouldn't do that."

"Oh yes, she would. And she did." I cock my head at him. "Did she at least share the spoils with you after she conned that man out of his life savings?"

His eyes go wide, and his mouth crimps. He aims his glower at her this time. "Tell me that's a sodding lie."

"Of course it is. I would never betray you."

Nigel studies her with a look I remember so well. It's the way he looks when he's holding in his anger. "But you had posh new clothes when you came home. And new shoes, new jewelry, new everything. Where did the money for all that come from?"

"She stole it from Selwyn," I say. "And she didn't share it with you. I suppose she deserved to keep all the money since she's the one who had to fuck the man for months and months."

"You bitch," he snarls at his wife.

Julia races up to him, laying her hands on his chest. "I love you, Nigel. You know that. Whatever I did while we were apart has nothing to do with us. You're my true love."

I chuckle. "Is that right, Mummy? He's your true love. How sweet. So you shagged a man you didn't care about and bore his child strictly for the sake of the con."

Nigel grips Julia's arms. "You had his child?"

"Well—Nigel, you need to understand—"

"You filthy, lying slag!"

"It's a lie," she says, but she sounds panicked and not the least convincing. "I would never betray you that way."

"But she did," I tell Nigel. "She gave the baby to her lover. He raised the boy. I have a half-brother, and he's not yours."

I know my father won't hit her. Violence has never been his forte. Though he normally prefers subtler means of expressing his disappointment, right now he's shouting at his wife. She's shouting right back. They call each other every vulgar insult imaginable, and a few I've never heard before.

Distraction complete.

Maybe I'm not the grifter I used to be, but I can still manipulate these bastards.

Cat has freed her hands. She unties her feet, then kneels beside my chair to pick my handcuffs. She accomplishes the task faster this time, and I'm free by the time Nigel and Julia catch on to the con I've run on them.

The pair of them gape at us.

"You grab her," I whisper to Cat, "and I'll get him. Use the cuffs."

I snag one pair while she takes the other, and we rush at Nigel and Julia. We're younger and stronger and haven't just been in a rollicking row, so we have the upper hand. I collar one of Nigel's wrists before he realizes what I'm about, drag him over to the chair I'd been bound to, and handcuff him to it. Cat does the same with Julia. I can't resist tying the ropes around their ankles. The blighters deserve it.

We don't have anything to restrain Reginald with, so we decide to lock him in an old closet. I have no idea where the key is for that, but I'm sure Cat will pick that lock when the time comes. It takes both of us to move him, each grasping him under his arms. We've just dragged his worthless arse to the closet doorway when Reggie rouses.

He grabs Cat's ankle and yanks it.

She's ripped off her feet, smacking down on her bum, a cry bursting out of her.

Reggie reaches for my leg.

I kick him in the face. "Sod off, Reggie!"

He snarls like a rabid dog, jumps up, and spins around to make another attempt to seize Catriona.

Like hell he will.

I charge Reginald and tackle him from behind. We tumble to the floor together, with him underneath me, but he struggles like mad. Though I'm trying to punch him, I can't do it with his body face-down. Reggie flails until he flips us over, and suddenly I'm crushed under his body.

He hoists himself up on his straight arms and bares his teeth at me. "About time I smashed that pretty face, ya mongrel."

Christ, how I wish he'd stop calling me that. It's bloody irritating. I know it's an Australian insult, but I am not a ruddy dog.

"Sorry," I tell him. "You'll have to be disappointed again."

Then I do something I never imagined I'd ever do to another man. I grab his balls and twist as hard as I can.

Reginald screams.

I shove him off me and punch him in the face three times until he stops struggling and his eyes close. My hands are shaking and spattered with blood, the same blood that trickles from his mouth. I'm breathing hard too and feel...strange. I've rarely assaulted anyone, and only ever bastards who deserved it, but he started this.

Cat kneels beside me, touching my arm. "Are you all right?"

"Yes. Fine." I squeeze my eyes shut for a moment. "Well, not completely all right. But I'm doing better than he is." I press a finger to his throat, at the pulse point. It throbs under my finger. "At least I haven't killed him."

"Let's get him into the closet."

I nod.

Once we've got him locked away, we stand in front of my erstwhile parents. Cat wraps her arms around my waist, nestling her head in the hollow of my shoulder. I put my arms around her too.

Julia is gawping at me. "Alexis…"

"Don't call me that," I say. "My name is Alex Thorne."

She claps her mouth shut and stares down at the floor.

"How do we ring the police?" Catriona asks. "I don't have my mobile."

"Neither do I, but it doesn't matter. Logan will find us soon enough."

"But how?"

I pat the back of my shoulder, right where Logan had patted me with a touch more enthusiasm than necessary earlier today. "He planted a tracking beacon on me. He must've done. I'm sure he knew I'd notice he did it, but that's probably his way of expressing his fondness for us."

"We're all right, then?"

"Yes, we are."

Cat blows out a breath, and her shoulders sag.

I tug her closer, wrapping my arms around her. "You are wonderful, Catriona. If I'd been here alone, I never would've gotten out of those handcuffs."

She rests her chin on my chest and smiles up at me. "We work well together, don't we?"

"Perfectly."

The crunching of gravel outside the open doorway makes us turn to look in that direction. Logan walks through the door, followed closely by Lachlan and Rory.

Logan surveys the situation, then looks at me. "I missed the party, didn't I?"

"Don't feel bad. It wasn't much of a do." I tip my head toward Nigel and Julia. "These two are the most inept kidnappers in history. Really, I thought they would've learned that lesson years ago when they tried to abduct me, three times, and failed."

"I rang the police. They ought to be here soon."

"Good." I hug Cat tighter, grateful for the warmth of her body and the strength of her spirit. "I'm knackered. Hope you saved that enormous bed inside that enormous castle for us."

"We did," Rory says.

I want to go home, but I don't have one of those anymore. Then again, I have Cat in my arms. Sounds like home to me.

Chapter Forty-Two

Catriona

The sun beams through the windows into our room at Dùndubhan, muted slightly by the sheer curtains, and spills over Alex's face and bare chest. He's sleeping on his back, his mouth curved into a faint smile, like he's dreaming of something wonderful. I want to wake him, but I also don't want to do it. He looks more relaxed than I've ever seen him, asleep or awake.

So I lie on my side next to him, hands tucked under my cheek, and watch him sleep.

A few minutes later, his eyes open. He yawns and glances my way. "Good morning, Catnip."

"I love it when you tease me, but I still don't like that nickname."

"All right. I'll stick with Cat."

"Thank you. Should I call you Alexis?"

He winces. "Please don't. That's what Julia always called me."

"You mean your mother."

"No. My mother is Imogen Bennett." He rolls onto his side, lying so close to me that our noses almost touch. "What should we do today? It will be hard to top yesterday."

"Why don't we just relax? Lie in bed for a long time and then have a huge late breakfast."

He kisses me softly. "That sounds perfect."

I run my finger along his jaw, loving the rough texture of his morning stubble. "What were you dreaming about? Something good, by the look on your face."

"You, of course. I always dream of you." He slides a hand up and down my arm. "I heard a rumor your brother Rory once got his kit off in the Loch Fairbairn town square."

Why are we talking about that? It seems like a strange shift in the conversation.

"He only got his shirt off," I say. "Emery stopped him before he could unbutton his trousers."

"Jack told me Rory was trying to impress his wife with an outlandish public display, to convince Emery of how much he loves her."

"That's true. He sang an old Frank Sinatra song too."

"Did he? Hmm." Alex gets that look, the one I know means he's plotting something. After a few seconds, he sits up. "Let's commandeer the ground-floor bathroom like we did before. We can have lots of fun in there."

He's giving me his naughty look, and I never can resist that.

We rush downstairs completely naked. No one else seems to be awake yet, so no one sees us, but I still feel decadently wicked racing down the steps to the vestibule and down the main hallway to the large bathroom. We have a shower and a bath, splashing water everywhere. Luckily, the tile floor has a drain in it, so we aren't causing a flood. I don't even try not to make noise while Alex and I enjoy poke after poke after poke.

My brothers and cousins go home after breakfast. That leaves only me and Alex in the castle, though the Brodys are in their cottage beside the garden.

In the afternoon, Alex and I relax in the sitting room, on the sofa that faces the big windows. I decide it's time to bring up the subject he's been ignoring since Rory broke the news to him yesterday.

"Are you going to contact your brother?" I ask.

He bows his head. "I don't know."

"It's been a shock to find out you have a brother. But don't you want to meet him?"

"What if he's like my parents? Or me?"

"Oh Alex." I twist around to sit sideways to him and lay a hand on his cheek. "Grey Dixon would be lucky to be like you. From what Rory said about him, he's not a criminal."

"If he's really a good man, he won't feel lucky to have me as a brother."

"You *are* a good man."

He lets his head fall back against the sofa. "I realized yesterday that I'm not the grifter I used to be. Reginald conned me for almost three years, and I never suspected a thing."

"Why do you think that is?"

"I suppose I was...lonely. Reginald seemed like a kindred spirit, but I imagine that was all an act. He was running a very long con on me." He raises his head, smirking at me. "It's all your fault."

"My fault?"

"Yes. Those two years with you convinced me life can be all sunshine and kittens." His smirk fades away, and he brushes his fingers through my hair. "After you left me, I didn't know what to do with myself. I got a different job in a different town, but it didn't help. So I got another job in another town. By the time I met Reginald, I'd fully committed to being a cynical bastard with a 'who gives a toss' attitude toward life. I suppose Reggie realized I was damaged in some way and exploited that weakness."

"No one is immune to being tricked. Reginald Hewitt must've been very good at it."

"Oh, he was." Alex sighs, shaking his head. "I can't believe I fell for his act for so long. He embezzled from me, but I think I mentioned that before. He emptied the household account, which was only used for buying groceries and whatnot."

"What you need is family, Alex. People who support you and love you no matter what."

"I have you—and Henry and Imogen. That's all I need."

"You have more family than that. You have mine."

His lips quirk into a sly smile. "I suppose threatening to beat me to death is how your brothers show their affection."

"Aye, it is." I pat his cheek. "But you have more family than that. You have a brother and cousins of your own."

He puckers his lips, then the expression softens into a small smile. "Very clever, Cat. You worked your way back round to that like an expert grifter."

"Are you going to contact your brother?" When he makes an annoyed face, I climb onto his lap, straddling him, and loop my arms around his neck. "Do it for me, Alex. Please."

"Just because you have a family that's as tightly woven as a Persian rug doesn't mean my relatives will want me in their lives."

"You won't know unless you try." I lean into him, my breasts mounding against his chest, our lips millimeters apart. "Please, Alex, I'll do anything you want if you do this for me."

I push my hand between our bodies to cup his cock. It's already stiffening.

"Sex isn't the way to convince me," he says. "But your sweetly stubborn determination has done it."

"You'll ring your brother?"

He grasps my bottom. "Yes, Cat, I will."

"Thank you."

Alex kisses me slowly, deepening it until I'm moaning and plastering my body to every inch of his, feeling his shaft hardening against my sex. Then he pulls his head away.

"Let's go out on the green," he says.

"Why?"

"Don't you trust me? It's a surprise." He squeezes my bottom. "I've got something very special in mind for you."

"Cannae wait."

He kisses me again, but this time he doesn't stop with my mouth. He strips my clothes off and kisses me everywhere. Alex keeps his clothes on, but he uses his very talented mouth and tongue to give me the sort of kisses that make me writhe and cry out his name.

After that, I get dressed, and we go out on the green.

"Where's the surprise?" I ask, glancing around at the empty lawn.

"Right here."

Alex backs away from me several steps. "Afraid I can't sing, though I can outdo Rory in another way. We're doing this on the green because I don't care to be arrested. But I do want your entire family to know how much I love you."

"My family? What—"

He nods at something behind me.

I turn around.

My whole family is descending on the green. I see my brothers and sisters and their spouses, along with my cousins and their wives. Evan and Keely are here too, and so is Serena. They must have all flown in via Mac-Taggart family jets to get here so quickly. Everyone gathers behind me, and I wonder if they know what Alex plans to do.

Logan winks at me. He must know. Logan probably helped Alex plan this.

"Catriona," Alex says. "Look this way, please."

I do, but I'm still confused. "Are you going to throw more cabers?"

The cabers are still lying in a pile on the other side of the green.

Alex chuckles. "No, love, I have something more creative in mind."

He whips his shirt off over his head and tosses it away.

The shirt lands near my feet.

"Alex?" I say. "What are you doing?"

His lips curve into a self-satisfied smile as he kicks off his shoes and unbuttons his trousers.

From behind me, Logan shouts, "Cover your wives' eyes!"

I want to glance back and see if Logan is actually covering Serena's eyes, but I can't tear my gaze away from Alex. Logan's sarcastic tone suggests he's not doing anything of the sort.

Alex lets his trousers fall to his ankles, then he kicks them off and sheds his socks too. One hundred percent naked, he stands there with his arms spread wide. "I love Catriona MacTaggart!"

His voice booms across the green, echoing off the castle wall and the trees.

Someone whistles, and I suspect it's Emery. More whistles follow, probably from other members of the American Wives Club.

I gawp at Alex, still having no idea what he's about. He's gone off his head, for sure. Stripping in front of my family? I can't believe he's done this. Well, all right, I can believe it. The man is shameless. But getting his kit off in front of my family? I never knew until this moment exactly how shameless Alex Thorne is—and I love it.

Alex saunters up to me and drops to one knee.

My heart stutters. Every hair on my body goes stiff as a wave of excitement shivers over my skin.

He clasps my hand. "Catriona Sorcha MacTaggart, will you marry me?"

"Yes, Alex, yes." I fall to my knees in front of him and throw my arms around the man I love. "Of course I'll marry you. I've only waited fourteen bloody years for you to ask."

"Sorry. I can be rather slow to figure things out. I've wanted to marry you since the day we met, but yes, it took me fourteen bloody years to get round to it."

"Don't apologize. It was worth the wait." I bend closer to whisper in his ear, "We've been forgetting to use condoms."

"Have we? Are you…"

"Too soon to know. But I wanted to prepare you for the possibility."

"Let's make sure you are."

I grin and kiss him.

And the crowd cheers.

Chapter Forty-Three

Alex

Catriona lets me avoid dealing with the issue of my brother and my original parents for one full day, but on the next day she gets more insistent. I did promise her I would contact my brother, so I can't refuse to do it much longer. Rory gave me the phone number for Grey Dixon, which means I have no excuses left. But something else distracts me this morning.

Julia has asked to see me.

My first reaction is to say no, absolutely not. Cat doesn't try to influence my decision at all, and I love her even more for that. After deliberating on the issue for an hour, I decide to do it. Julia and Nigel are both on remand at the Inverness prison, so Cat and I make the three-hour drive to get there. Cat stays in the car while I go inside to find out what my original mother wants to say to me.

I'm slightly nauseous by the time I sit down at a table in the visit room. Normally, a visit requires twenty-four hours' notice, but I suspect Julia put on a good show of crying and pleading for the chance to see her son so she could get me here sooner.

Yes, dear Mummy excels at getting what she wants.

Julia Charnley-Ainsworth walks into the visit room and sits down across the table from me. She has dark circles under her eyes, which are red like she's been crying. Her posture is slumped. The wrinkles on her face seem deeper today, or maybe that's just the lighting. She looks tired, old, and defeated.

I want to feel triumphant about that, because this woman deserves to be miserable after everything she's done to me. But I can't muster any hatred for her. I feel numb and still slightly nauseous, and I'm even wringing my hands. It's ridiculous. I can't be nervous about speaking to this woman who's become a virtual stranger to me. Until the other day, I hadn't seen her in almost two decades.

But my palms are clammy.

"Hello, Alexis," she says. "Thank you for seeing me."

"Why am I here? I have nothing to say to you."

"I want to apologize. For everything." She reaches out like she intends to grab my hand but changes her mind and sets her hands on her lap. "I'm sorry for what we did to you when you were a boy. I know words can't make up for it, and I won't ask for your forgiveness because I don't deserve it. But I want you to know I've always loved you, in my own way. I didn't deserve to be your mother. I'm glad the Bennetts found you and fought for you, even when Nigel wanted to get you back. Those other two times we tried to steal you away, that was Nigel's idea too. Which doesn't excuse me for going along with it. I'm as guilty as he is."

My original father instigated those attempts to get me back legally? When I look into Julia's eyes, I discover I believe her. Something in her eyes and her voice convinces me she's telling the whole truth, possibly for the first time in her life.

"I hope you've had a good life," she says.

Have I? Two weeks ago, my answer might've been very different and much less optimistic.

"Yes," I tell her, "I've had a good life. Henry and Imogen saw to that."

"And now you have a girl. I'm happy for you, Alexis."

I don't know how to respond to that. To say "thank you" seems odd. This woman made my life hell for so many years that I know I can't ever forgive her. But I can stop letting those memories rule my life. I can stop living in fear of anyone finding out who I used to be and what I'd done because my parents told me to do it. I realize now that I've stayed alone all my life, except for those two years with Cat, because I was afraid to face up to my past, afraid to trust anyone completely.

All that has changed. I have everything I want and need, and I won't let anyone or anything take it away from me.

"We were never going to bother you again," Julia says, "Nigel and me. We've been living a normal life for a long time, no more cons. Then Reginald Hewitt rang us and convinced Nigel that you have a fortune in the bank and that we deserved some of that. He told us how you're as depraved as Caligula, you lie and cheat and bribe your way into jobs at universities, and you're secretly an antiquities thief. Nigel was easily convinced. He stopped taking his medication a few weeks ago, so he's been paranoid."

Yes, my original father has psychological issues that necessitate medication and weekly visits to a court-mandated psychiatrist. Rory had found that out, thanks to his investigator mate. And yes, I worried I might turn out like Nigel. Cat told me I wouldn't, but I didn't quite believe it until Jack assured me I'm not on the path to madness. After I moved to America, Nigel became a drug addict. Years of abuse have damaged his brain, causing paranoia, depression, and other issues even after he'd stopped using drugs.

I feel sorry for Nigel. He threw his life away, and for what? Brief moments of euphoria that have sentenced him to a lifetime of suffering. Maybe I should say he deserves what he's got, but I can't manage any cruel feelings toward him either. Loving my original parents is out of the question. But I can feel pity for them, or maybe it's empathy.

Tears glisten in Julia's eyes. "I shouldn't have gone along with the plan Nigel and Reginald came up with. I should have stopped them." She shrugs. "I was afraid, so I didn't."

"That's what you wanted me to hear? You let your husband bully you into kidnapping me and Cat. I'm not trying to be cruel, but you've had a lifetime to divorce that bastard."

She nods while tears start to trickle down her cheeks. "I know. I'm not making excuses, only explanations. I'm sorry, Alexis, and I hope you have a full and happy life. That's what I wanted to say to you, face to face. I'm sorry."

I sit there for a moment staring at her, trying to figure out how to respond. I don't feel anger or resentment or disgust. I feel sorry for her, and that's all.

"Thank you," I say. "I appreciate that you are genuinely sorry, but I don't think we have anything else to say to each other."

"You're right. I said what I needed to say." She stands up. "Goodbye, Alexis."

She walks away from me.

And I go home with Cat.

What else is there to do but get on with life? Hearing my mother's apology has no effect on me. The opinions of the people I love and who love me matter far more than what the woman I knew for eight years as a boy says to me today. When we arrive back at Dùndubhan, Rory informs us that Reginald will be extradited to the US and tried there. The Scots wanted him for the kidnapping, but the Americans won the argument since they had him for escaping from prison, two counts of arson, and two counts of breaking and entering. There's also the matter of the crime he'd been imprisoned for when he decided to escape. I think dear Reggie will be out of commission for a long, long time.

Julia and Nigel will get lighter sentences, I'm sure.

I'm allowed to rest until the next afternoon, when I find out what Cat's family has done. The MacTaggarts have arranged a party to celebrate the good news that the wanker who burnt down my house is on his way back to prison. I've invited my brother to visit today, so the clan has given me until this evening before they drag me into the great hall for the revelry they claim I need.

"You need whisky, for certain," Logan says, slapping me on the shoulder. "That and Catriona."

He winks at me.

Jack smiles. "Aye, Alex needs a bit of tender loving care."

"A bloody great poke, you mean," Logan says with a smirk. "The louder, the better."

"How many times have I told you," I say. "Talking about sex with you lot is not on my list of things to do before I die."

Jack turns more serious when tells me, "If you need me, just give a shout. I'm here for moral support, not official therapy."

"Thank you, but I'll be fine."

I leave Logan and Jack in the office, the one that used to belong to Rory, and make my way to the sitting room. Cat is waiting outside the door, which hangs open. I can see four people inside the sitting room. Four men. Four strangers.

Cat claims my hand.

We walk into the sitting room, and our four visitors turn toward us.

"Hello," I say, because it's the only word I can produce. My brain seems to have shut down. It's ludicrous. Why should I feel anxious about meeting these men? I don't care what they think of me.

Yes, I'm full of rubbish today.

One of the strangers, a blond man who seems older than the rest, approaches me and offers his hand. "I'm Chance Dixon, your cousin. It's a pleasure to meet you, Alex."

"Ah, yes, it's…nice to meet you too." I shake his hand. "This is my fiancée, Catriona MacTaggart."

"We know. She introduced herself before you got here."

"I had to greet them," she says when I raise my brows at her. "It would've been unfriendly to lock them in the sitting room without saying hello."

Another man steps up to shake my hand. "Reese Dixon, also your cousin. I'm the youngest one here, and the most fun." He grins, then points toward one of the other two men. "That's my brother Dane. He used to be no fun at all, but Rika loosened him up. She's his wife."

"I see."

Dane comes up to shake my hand too, which leaves only one person who hasn't spoken to me yet.

My brother approaches slowly, shuffling his feet. When he holds out his hand, he can't look me in the eye. "I'm Grey Dixon. Your, uh, brother. Half-brother. Julia's son. I never met her, but my father told me her name."

I shake his hand, but he still won't look me in the eye. "Have you heard anything about me?"

"Just that you're an archaeologist." He hunches his shoulders and finally meets my gaze. "I googled you."

"Have you?" I chuckle. "I imagine you saw that video of my last lecture, then. A student posted it online."

"Yes, I saw it." Grey's lips twitch, but he doesn't quite smile. "I never knew archaeology was so…interesting."

"Only when it's done right." I clap a hand on his shoulder. "Why don't you and I go for a walk and get to know each other?"

He smiles. "I'd like that."

Grey and I stay close to the house, wandering around the outside of the walled compound. It's a lovely, sunny day. My brother tries to explain to me what a business intelligence analyst does, but I don't quite understand it. Something to do with computers. And analysis of data.

"Sounds like you're a real dogsbody," I say. "I doubt many people want to analyze whatever it is you're staring at all day long."

"It's not a boring job that nobody else wants to do. It's challenging and fascinating."

"Hmm, I'll have to take your word for that." I decide to change the subject to something more interesting to me. "Do you have a girlfriend or a wife?"

"No."

"A boyfriend, then?"

He flashes me an irritated look. "No, I'm not gay. There is a girl, an American, but…it hasn't worked out the way I'd hoped."

"Have you shagged her?"

Grey scratches the back of his neck, pinching his whole face into a pained expression. "We did, yes. Once. It was bloody awful."

"Your fault or hers?" I realize I might be acting like a nosy arse, so I add, "Not trying to blame you. I am your brother, though, so it's my job to poke my nose into your business. Isn't it? That's what the MacTaggarts think siblings are for, but I'm not sure I can believe everything they say."

"I think that's what brothers do. It's how my cousins are, anyway." Grey twists his mouth into a sardonic smile. "I cocked it up. Now the girl says we're better off as friends and nothing more. We've been best friends since university."

"But you're in love with her, aren't you?"

He winces and nods. "I don't have a good record with women. They all think I'm rubbish in bed. And that girl, Jessica, she's been with a Scot for two years. They just broke off their engagement, but I think she's still in love with him." My brother huffs out a sigh. "Jess treats me like I'm a eunuch. She even tells me how incredible that Scot is at sex, like I want to know that."

At last, a topic on which I am an expert. I mean sex, of course.

I hook my arm around his shoulders and whisper, "Aren't you the luckiest bloke on earth to have me for a brother? I'm going to help you win your girl."

"How? She's not attracted to me anymore."

"Ah, but she will be." I pat his arm. "Don't worry. I have a plan."

Grey turns his head to look at me but pulls it back a touch. His brows wrinkle. "After watching that video of your lecture, I'm not sure I want advice from you about how to make Jess want me."

Well, we have just met. I can't blame him for that.

"Point taken," I say. "Let's revisit that idea after we've gotten better acquainted."

"That sounds like a better plan."

Grey and I spend another hour doing exactly that, getting acquainted, and then we invite our cousins to join us in the sitting room for lunch and a chat. They're not bad blokes, really. Reese and I get on well since we share the same wicked sense of humor. He saw my lecture video too, and he loved it. Chance says my lecture is "entertaining" but not his cup of tea. Dane hasn't watched it yet.

After spending time with my new family, I reach a conclusion about them. They're not criminals. They haven't polluted our gene pool with their depravity. I haven't told them about my past. Soon I will tell Grey, but our cousins can wait.

I don't see Cat again until the party.

She meets me at the entrance to the great hall. Behind her, strobe lights flash across the people gathered inside, most of whom are dancing. Cat leads me into the great hall, but she doesn't let me say hello to anyone or eat any of the food laid out on a buffet table. Instead, she drags me into a dark corner behind a screen that conceals the door to the office. She takes me in there, leaving the door open.

Catriona seizes my shirt and backs up to the desk, hauling me with her. "I want you, Alex. Right now."

"Here? On Rory's desk? Your entire family is on the other side of that screen, and the door is open."

"I know." She sets her arse on the desk and locks her legs around me. "It'll be like the lecture hall, only better. My brothers might hear us and decide to murder you."

"Why do you sound pleased about that prospect?"

"The risk makes it more exciting." She grabs my shirt again. "Fuck me, Alex. Or have you lost your naughty streak?"

"Never. But—" I scrub a hand over my mouth. "Maybe we should close the door."

She catches her lip with her teeth, releasing it little by little while she shakes her head. "Don't you want to have me on this desk? Rory's desk. In Rory's castle. While all my brothers and sisters and cousins are only meters away."

I do want that. My cock is already hard, and we haven't had sex in far too long. Which means more than six hours.

Her skirt has ridden up so I can see she's not wearing any knickers.

"Let's make noise," I say, "and find out if anyone can hear us over the music."

I unzip my trousers, grasp her hips, and plunge into her. Cat is so hot and wet, ready for anything I want to do to her, even if all those MacTaggarts in the other room, just meters away from us, hear her scream when I make her come. The thought makes me thrust harder, faster, while I lay her down on the desk with my hands planted on the cool, smooth surface. She gasps and grips my arms, her gaze locked on mine. She's so beautiful, so sensual, and so much naughtier than I'd ever realized until recently. I love this woman.

"Alex," she cries out, arching her back.

The music outside switches to a soft, romantic song. The lower volume means it's more likely someone might hear us.

I fuck her harder, making the desk bounce and thump on the rug beneath it. The scent of her lust surrounds us, intoxicating me. "Come for me, Cat. Hurry, I can't—"

She clutches me with her arms and legs, screaming my name while her body grips me in pulsating waves.

And I jump off that cliff with her, shouting her name.

We lie there for a few minutes, Cat spread across the desk with me on top of her, luxuriating in the pleasure we've given each other. Eventually, we straighten our clothes and go out to join the party. Logan smirks at me, and I wonder if he heard us in the office. I don't care if he did.

Jack finds us while we're shoveling hors d'oeuvres into each other's mouths like heathens. Sex always makes me hungry, especially bloody fantastic sex with Catriona.

"You two aren't shy," Jack says, "are you? Everyone heard that."

I shrug one shoulder. "Am I meant to be embarrassed?"

"No, not at all." He tips his head to the side, like he'd done during our so-called therapy session. "I'm glad to know you two don't have any sexual problems."

"I have never had that sort of problem." A thought occurs to me, and I ask Jack, "But I might know someone who could use your help in that area."

But yes, I'll ask Grey before I tell Jack all about him and his American girl.

"Happy to help," Jack says. "You know where to find me."

While he wanders off into the crowd, I pull Cat into my arms. "Let's try that again. But behind the screen this time, not in the office."

She grabs my shirt and drags me off.

Once I've got her backed up to the wall behind the screen, I tell her something I never imagined I would say. "I love you, and I love our life. Whatever that turns out to be. Everything will work out brilliantly, I know."

Cat leans forward, her lips grazing my ear. "You should write a book based on that lecture. Call it *Dirty-Sexy Archaeology*."

"My cousin Chance did mention he knows a bloke who owns a publishing company."

"And Iain offered me a job at the university where he works."

"He offered me one too." I shove her skirt up and sink my cock into her warm, soft body. "Let's do it. All of it. Let's buy a cottage too."

"Aye, let's do it."

I do love my life. It's bloody perfect.

Epilogue

Jack
Two months later

I told you from the start that every love story has a beginning, a middle, and an end, but sometimes the cycle repeats. At least Cat and Alex came to their senses after the second go-round. I don't think I could've stayed sane if I had to counsel Alex through another cycle. They have their happy ending, but it's not the end of their journey together. What will come next? Even I don't know the answer. But I do know they'll travel that road together.

Today, I'm lying on my back on a rattan sofa on the patio of the house where Alex and Catriona now live, enjoying the sunshine on my face and the company of the people around me. The others occupy rattan chairs around a glass-topped table. With my eyes closed, I can't see them anymore, but I can hear their conversation.

Logan is telling some story from his past as an MI6 agent, but I think he's exaggerating it a wee bit. Alex's brother, Grey, loves all of Logan's stories and keeps asking him to tell more of them. I'm glad to see Alex and Grey have gotten on well and spend a lot of time together. Grey lives and works in London, but he comes to Loch Fairbairn as often as he can to visit Cat and Alex at their cottage. Alex and Cat go to London sometimes too. Today, we're all relaxing on the large lawn behind their home.

Did my advice help Alex become the happy, settled man he is today? I'd like to think so, but I have a feeling Catriona played a more important role in his transformation. Of course, he hasn't completely overhauled his personality. He still likes to say "what if" and "maybe" when anyone other than Cat asks him a question.

Ever since they announced Cat is pregnant a few days ago, Alex is even happier.

"Jack, are you awake?" Alex asks.

"Aye." Opening my eyes, I yawn. "Sunshine makes me drowsy, though."

"I'm about to make an announcement that I'm sure you'll want to hear."

"Another one? I hope you're not up the duff too."

"Your humor needs work, Jack."

I yawn again, sitting up. "Go on with your announcement. I'm awake."

"My book has been accepted by the publisher I submitted it to, based on the outline and sample chapters I provided. It's the publishing company owned by Chance's mate." His smile widens into a wicked grin. "Before long, the whole world will get to experience *Dirty-Sexy Archaeology.*"

Can the world handle that? I haven't read Alex's book yet, but I'm sure he holds nothing back when he's writing about sex.

Alex tips his head toward Chance. "And I have my cousin to thank for the contract."

"You didn't get it because of me, or because I know the publisher," Chance says. He and his two brothers have joined us today, while everyone's wives convene inside the cottage. "Your book is excellent. But I'm glad I could introduce you to someone who appreciates your style of teaching history."

I lean back against the sofa, stretching my legs out. "When are you and Cat getting married? You proposed two months ago."

"We're making plans," Alex says, in the tone that tells me he's plotting something. "It will be an unusual wedding. We're tying the knot in America, but that's all I'm going to say right now. The wedding will be in six weeks."

"A mystery wedding. Do we at least get directions to the venue? Or will we be blindfolded for the whole trip to your secret American destination?"

"You'll get directions. When the time is right." Alex lifts his brows. "Don't you have a date this afternoon?"

"That's right. A blind date set up by you. Not sure it's safe to let Alex Thorne pick a girlfriend for me, but I'm giving it a go." I glance at my watch. "Bollocks. I'll be late."

Dane Dixon tosses me a set of keys. "Take my Jaguar. It's faster than your car."

I accept his offer, racing to the Jaguar and backing out of the driveway so fast that gravel sprays up around the car. I get to the cafe in Loch Fairbairn thirty-eight minutes past the time when I'd agreed to meet this girl. I glance around the outdoor section of the cafe but don't see a woman on her own, so I rush inside to check there.

The lad behind the counter waves for me to come over there.

When I do, he says, "Are you the one who was supposed to meet an American girl here for a blind date?"

"Aye. Have you seen her?"

The boy, who can't be more than sixteen, nods. "She left this note for you."

He hands me a folded piece of paper. *Mhac na galla*, I've missed her. I can't blame the lass for leaving when I've made her wait half an hour. I thank the lad and open the note.

You get one more chance. Loch Fairbairn Arms, Room 110.

She's inviting me to her hotel room? That's never happened to me before. I don't even know this woman's name. Alex wouldn't tell me because he thought it would be more fun to leave her identity a mystery. I know only that she's American.

I walk the two blocks to the Loch Fairbairn Arms, the only hotel in this village. The desk clerk barely glances at me when I cross the lobby and head down the hall to Room 110.

Maybe I shouldn't do this. Meet a stranger in a hotel room? If she wants to have sex and then leave... Why do I assume that's what she has on her mind? This woman is a stranger. She probably wants to tell me what a *bod ceann* I am for making her wait.

The door to Room 110 is in front of me.

Do I look all right? I straighten my clothes, as if they need it, run my fingers through my hair to smooth it out, and hold a hand to my face so I can puff a breath into it and make sure it doesn't stink of...anything. I've had a few dates since my divorce, but I never got past the first date with any of those women.

I raise my hand, hesitate, and finally knock on the door.

After a few seconds, the door swings open.

The woman standing in front of me gasps. Her ice-blue hair falls over one of her eyes, and she brushes it away.

I stare at her, frozen in place, my pulse racing and my skin going cold. "Autumn? What are you doing here?"

She shakes her head, eyes wide. "No, this can't be—You can't be—No, no, no."

"I, ah..." Pushing a hand into my hair, I shake my head too. "It's been a long time. You look...bonnie. I've never seen hair that color before."

Hers used to be blonde. Now it's blue?

"That's all you can say? You set me up for this, didn't you? Humiliating me doesn't seem like your style, but—"

"I didn't set this up. My friend Alex did." The sodding ersehole. He knew exactly what he was doing, I'm sure of that. "I'm sorry. This was not my idea, and believe me, you are the last person I expected to see."

Autumn shuts her eyes, squeezing her lips together. "Ugh. This is a mess. I flew all the way to Scotland for a vacation because my friend Rika suggested it. A blind date was supposed to be fun."

Rika. That would be Dane Dixon's wife.

What twist of fate resulted in my ex-wife being friends with the wife of Alex's cousin? This is too much. Whether Alex connived to introduce my ex-wife to Rika or it's rubbish luck to blame doesn't matter. I'm standing in front of my ex-wife, and I have no idea what to say to her.

"I'll go," I tell her. "Again, I'm sorry for this mix-up."

When I turn to leave, she grabs my arm. "You don't have to leave. Since we're both here, maybe we should have lunch and try to bury the hatchet."

The hatchet belongs to her, not me. She used it to cut me out of her life.

But the therapist part of me knows I need closure, so I say, "Lunch sounds good. How long are you in Scotland?"

"Two weeks." She steps out of her room and shuts the door. "Who knows? Maybe we'll become friends."

"Last time we saw each other, you told me I'm a shameless huckster."

"Are you going to hold that against me forever? Time to get over yourself, Jack. I might think your job is dumb, but you think the same thing about mine."

I sputter, like an eejit. "You quit medical school so you could become a blackjack dealer in Atlantic City. How is my profession a sham but yours is noble? And you didn't even discuss it with me. You announced you were moving to New Jersey, with or without me."

"You could have come with me. If you really loved me, you would have." She waves a hand, dismissing...everything, apparently. "Doesn't matter. Let's have a nice lunch and go from there. You're paying, right? I mean, you did stand me up."

"I was late. I didn't stand you up."

"Whatever. You're paying."

As I follow my ex-wife down the hallway, I make one very important decision. Alex Thorne is going to pay for this.

Jack MacTaggart returns in *Devastating in a Kilt*.

Love the

Hot Scots

series?

Visit
AnnaDurand.com

to subscribe to her newsletter
for updates on forthcoming books in this series

&

to receive a free gift for signing up!

*A*nna Durand is a bestselling, multi-award-winning author of contemporary and paranormal romance. Her books have earned bestseller status on every major retailer and wonderful reviews from readers around the world. But that's the boring spiel. Here are some really cool things you want to know about Anna!

Born on Lackland Air Force Base in Texas, Anna grew up moving here, there, and everywhere thanks to her dad's job as an instructor pilot. She's lived in Texas (twice), Mississippi, California (twice), Michigan (twice), and Alaska—and now Ohio.

As for her writing, Anna has always made up stories in her head, but she didn't write them down until her teen years. Those first awful books went into the trash can a few years later, though she learned a lot from those stories. Eventually, she would pen her first romance novel, the paranormal romance *Willpower*, and she's never looked back since.

Want even more details about Anna? Get access to her extended bio when you subscribe to her newsletter and download the free bonus ebook, *Hot Scots Confidential*. You'll also get hot deleted scenes, character interviews, fun facts, and more! You also get the short story *Tempted by a Kiss* and a bonus audio chapter narrated for you by Shane East. Visit AnnaDurand.com to sign up!

9 781949 406252